12/10
Replacement

Those
Who Hunt
The
Night

By Barbara Hambly
Published by Ballantine Books:

DRAGONSBANE

THE LADIES OF MANDRIGYN
THE WITCHES OF WENSHAR

THE SILENT TOWER
THE SILICON MAGE

The Darwath Trilogy
THE TIME OF THE DARK
THE WALLS OF AIR
THE ARMIES OF DAYLIGHT

THOSE WHO HUNT THE NIGHT

SEARCH THE SEVEN HILLS

Those Who Hunt The Night

—

Barbara Hambly

DEL
REY

A Del Rey Book

Ballantine Books · New York

A Del Rey Book
Published by Ballantine Books

Copyright © 1988 by Barbara Hambly

Library of Congress Cataloging-in-Publication Data

Hambly, Barbara.
  Those who hunt the night.

  "A Del Rey book"
  I. Title.
PS3558.A4215T45   1988   813'.54   88-47803
ISBN 0-345-34380-8

Text design by Holly Johnson

Manufactured in the United States of America

First Edition: December 1988

10 9 8 7 6 5 4 3 2 1

For
Adrian and Victoria

Those
Who Hunt
The
Night

One

___

Lydia?"

But even before the shadows of the stairwell swallowed the last echoes of his wife's name, James Asher knew something was desperately wrong.

The house was silent, but it was not empty.

He stopped dead in the darkened front hall, listening. No sound came down the shadowy curve of the stairs from above. No plump Ellen hurried through the baize-covered door at the back of the hall to take her master's Oxford uniform of dark academic robe and mortarboard, and, by the seeping chill of the autumn night that permeated the place, he could tell that no fires burned anywhere. He was usually not conscious of the muted clatter of Mrs. Grimes in the kitchen, but its absence was as loud to his ears as the clanging of a bell.

Six years ago, Asher's response would have been absolutely unhesitating—two steps back and out the door, with a silent, deadly readiness that few of the other dons at New College would have associated with their unassuming colleague. But Asher had for years been a secret player in what was euphemistically termed the Great Game, innocuously collecting philological notes in British-occupied Pretoria or among the Boers on the veldt, in the Kaiser's court in Berlin or the snowbound streets of St. Petersburg. And though he'd turned his back on that Game, he knew from experience that it would never completely turn its back on him.

Still, for a moment, he hesitated. For beyond a doubt, Lydia was somewhere in that house.

Then with barely a whisper of his billowing robe, Asher glided back over the threshold and into the raw fog that shrouded even the front step. There was danger in the house, though he did not consciously feel fear—only an ice-burn of anger that, whatever was going on, Lydia and the servants had been dragged into it.

If they've hurt her . . .

He didn't even know who *they* were, but a seventeen-year term of secret servitude to Queen—now King—and Country had left him with an appalling plethora of possibilities.

Noiseless as the Isis mists that cloaked the town, he faded back across the cobbles of Holywell Street to the shadowy brown bulk of the College wall and waited, listening. They—whoever "they" were in the house—would have heard him. They would be waiting, too.

Lydia had once asked him—for she'd guessed, back in the days when she'd been a sixteen-year-old schoolgirl playing croquet with her uncle's junior scholastic colleague on her father's vast lawns—how he kept from being dropped upon in foreign parts: "I mean, when the balloon goes up and they find the Secret Plans are gone or whatever, there you are."

He'd laughed and said, "Well, for one thing, no plans are ever *gone*—merely accurately copied. And as for the rest, my best defense is always simply being the sort of person who wouldn't do that sort of thing."

"You do that here." Those enormous, pansy-brown eyes had studied him from behind her steel-rimmed spectacles. Her thin, almost aggressive bookishness was at that time just beginning to melt into fragile sensuality. With the young men who were even then beginning to take an interest in her, she didn't wear the spectacles—she was an expert at blind croquet and guessing what was on menus. But with him, it seemed, it was different. In her sensible cotton shirtwaist and blue-and-red school tie, the changeable wind tangling her long red hair, she'd looked like a leggy marsh-fey unsuccessfully trying to pass itself off as an English schoolgirl. "Is it difficult to go from being one to being the other?"

He'd thought about it for a moment, then shook his head. "It's a bit like wearing your Sunday best," he'd said, knowing even then that she'd understand what he meant. And she'd laughed, the sound bright with delight as the April sunlight. He'd kept that laugh—as he'd kept the damp lift of morning fog from the Cherwell meadows or the other-world sweetness of May morning voices drifting down from Magdalen Tower like the far-off singing of angels—in the corner of his heart where he stored precious things as if they were a boy's shoe-box hoard, to be taken out and looked at in China or the veldt when things were bad. It had been some years before he'd realized that her laugh and the still sunlight shining like carnelian on her hair were precious to him, not as symbols of the peaceful life of study and teaching, where one played croquet with one's Dean's innocent niece, but because he was desperately in love with this girl. The knowledge had nearly broken his heart.

Now the years of scholarship, of rest, and of happiness fell off him like a shed University gown, and he moved down the narrow street, circling the row of its flat-fronted brick houses toward the labyrinthine tangle of the back lanes.

If anything had happened to her . . .

From the lane behind the houses he could see the gas burning in the window of his study, though between the mists and the curtain lace he could distinguish nothing within. A carriage passed along Holywell Street behind him, the strike of hooves and jingle of harness brasses loud in that narrow corridor of cobbles and brick. From the weeping grayness of the garden, Asher could see the whole broad kitchen, lit like a stage set. Only the jet over the stove was burning—even after dusk was well settled, the wide windows let in a good deal of light. That put it no later than seven . . .

Put what? In spite of his chill and businesslike concentration, Asher grinned a little at the mental image of himself storming his own home, like Roberts relieving Mafeking, to find a note saying, "Father ill, gone to visit him, have given servants night off—Lydia."

Only, of course, his wife—and it still startled him to think that after everything, he had in fact succeeded in winning Lydia as his wife—had as great an abhorrence as he did of confusion. She would never have let Mrs. Grimes and the two maids, not to speak of Mick in the stables, leave for the night without making some provision for his supper. Nor would she have done that or anything else without dispatching a note to his study at the College, informing him of changed plans.

But Asher needed none of this train of logic, which flickered through his mind in fragments of a second, to know all was not well. The years had taught him the smell of peril, and the house stank of it.

Keeping to the tangle of vine that overgrew the garden wall, conscious of those darkened windows overlooking him from above, he edged toward the kitchen door.

Most of the young men whom Asher tutored in philology, etymology, and comparative folklore at New College—which had not, in fact, been new since the latter half of the fourteenth century—regarded their mentor with the affectionate respect they would have accorded a slightly eccentric uncle. Asher played to this image sheerly from force of habit—it had stood him in good stead abroad. He was a reasonably unobtrusive man, taller than he seemed at first glance and, as Lydia generally expressed it, brown: brown hair, brown eyes, brown mustache, brown clothes, and brown mien. Without his University gown, he looked, in fact, like a clerk, except for the sharpness of his eyes and the silence with which he moved. It would have been coincidence, the undergraduates would have said, that he found the deepest shadow in the dark and dew-soaked garden in which to stow his gown and mortarboard cap, the antique uniform of Oxford scholarship which covered his anonymous tweeds. Certainly they would not have said that he was the sort of man who could jemmy open a window with a knife, nor that he was the sort of man who would carry such a weapon concealed in his boot.

The kitchen was utterly deserted, chilly, and smelling of the old-fashioned stone floor and of ashes long grown cold. No steam floated above the hot-water reservoir of the stove—a new American thing of black rococo iron which had cost nearly twenty-five dollars from a catalogue. The bland brightness of the gaslight, winking on the stove's nickel-plated knobs, and the silver of toast racks, made the stillness in the kitchen seem all the more ominous, like a smiling maniac with an ax behind his back.

Few of the dons at Oxford were familiar with the kitchen quarters of their own homes—many of them had never penetrated past the swinging doors that separated the servants' portions of the house from those in which the owners lived. Asher had made it his business to know not only the precise layout of the place—he could have passed through it blindfolded without touching a single piece of furniture, as he could indeed have passed through any room in the house or in his College—but to know exactly where everything was kept. Knowing such things was hardly a conscious effort anymore, merely one of the things he had picked up over the years and had never quite dared to put down. He found the drawer in which Mrs. Grimes kept her carving knives—the hideout he kept in his boot was a small one, for emergencies—then moved on to the archway just past the stove which separated kitchen from pantry, all the while aware that someone, somewhere in the house, listened for his slightest footfall.

Mrs. Grimes, Ellen, and the girl Sylvie were all there. They sat around the table, a slumped tableau like something from the Chamber of Horrors at Mme. Tussaud's, somehow shocking in the even, vaguely flickering light from the steel fishtail burner by the stove. All they needed was a poison bottle on the table between them, Asher thought with wry grimness, and a placard:

THE MAD POISONER STRIKES.

Only there was no bottle, no used teacups, no evidence in fact of anything eaten or drunk. The only thing on the table at all was a bowl of half-shelled peas.

Studying the cook's thin form, the parlor maid's plump one, and the huddled shape of the tweeny, Asher felt again that chill sensation of being listened for and known. All three women were alive, but he didn't like the way they slept, like broken dolls, heedless of muscle cramp or balance.

He had been right, then.

The only other light on in the house was in his study, and that was where he kept his revolver, an American Navy Colt stowed in the drawer of his desk; if one were a lecturer in philology, of course, one couldn't keep a revolver in one's greatcoat pocket. The other dons would certainly talk.

He made his way up the back stairs from the kitchen. From its unobtrusive door at the far end of the hall he could see no one waiting for him at the top of the front stairs, but that meant nothing. The door of the upstairs parlor gaped like a dark mouth. From the study, a bar of dimmed gold light lay across the carpet like a dropped scarf.

Conscious of the weight of his body on the floor, he moved a few steps forward, close to the wall. By angling his head, he could see a wedge of the room beyond. The divan had been deliberately dragged around to a position in which it would be visible from the hall. Lydia lay on the worn green cushions, her hair unraveled in a great pottery-red coil to the floor. On her breast her long, capable hand was curled protectively around her spectacles, as if she'd taken them off to rest her eyes for a moment; without them, her face looked thin and unprotected in sleep. Only the faint movement of her small breasts beneath the smoky lace of a trailing tea gown showed him she lived at all.

The room was set up as a trap, he thought with the business portion of his mind. Someone waited inside for him to go rushing in at first sight of her, as indeed his every instinct cried out to him to do . . .

"Come in, Dr. Asher," a quiet voice said from within that glowing amber chamber of books. "I am alone—there is in fact no one else in the house. The young man who looks after your stables is asleep, as you have found your women servants to be. I am seated at your desk, which is in its usual place, and I have no intention of doing you harm tonight."

Spanish, the field agent in him noted—flawless and unaccented, but Spanish all the same—even as the philologist pricked his ears at some odd, almost backcountry inflection to the English, a trace of isolative *a* here and there, a barely aspirated *e* just flicking at the ends of some words . . .

He pushed open the door and stepped inside. The young man sitting at Asher's desk looked up from the dismantled pieces of the revolver and inclined his head in greeting.

"Good evening," he said politely. "For reasons which shall shortly become obvious, let us pass the formality of explanations and proceed to introductions."

It was only barely audible—the rounding of the *ou* in *obvious* and the stress shift in *explanations*—but it sent alarm bells of sheer scholarly curiosity clanging in some half-closed lumber room of his mind. *Can't you stop thinking like a philologist even at a time like this . . . ?*

The young man went on, "My name is Don Simon Xavier Christian Morado de la Cadena-Ysidro, and I am what you call a vampire."

Asher said nothing. An unformed thought aborted itself, leaving white stillness behind.

"Do you believe me?"

Asher realized he was holding his intaken breath, and let it out. His glance sheered to Lydia's throat; his folkloric studies of vampirism had included the cases of so-called "real" vampires, lunatics who had sought to prolong their own twisted lives by drinking or bathing in the blood of young girls. Through the tea gown's open collar he could see the white skin of her throat. No blood stained the fragile ecru of the lace around it. Then his eyes went back to Ysidro, in whose soft tones he had heard the absolute conviction of a madman. Yet, looking at that slender form behind his desk, he was conscious of a queer creeping sensation of the skin on the back of his neck, an uneasy sense of having thought he was descending a stair and, instead, stepping from the edge of a cliff . . .

The name was Spanish—the young man's bleached fairness might well hail from the northern provinces where the Moors had never gone calling. Around the thin, high-nosed hidalgo face, his colorless hair hung like spider silk, fine as cobweb and longer than men wore it these days. The eyes were scarcely darker, a pale, yellowish amber, flecked here and there with pleats of faded brown or gray—eyes which should have seemed catlike, but didn't. There was an odd luminosity to them, an unplaceable glittering quality, even in the gaslight, that troubled Asher. Their very paleness, contrasting with the moleskin-soft black velvet of the man's coat collar, pointed up the absolute pallor of the delicate features, far more like a corpse's than a living man's, save for their mobile softness.

From his own experiences in Germany and Russia, Asher knew how easy such a pallor was to fake, particularly by gaslight. And it might simply be madness or drugs that glittered at him from those grave yellow eyes. Yet there was an eerie quality to Don Simon Ysidro, an immobility so total it was as if he had been there behind the desk for hundreds of years, waiting . . .

As Asher knelt beside Lydia to feel her pulse, he kept his eyes on the Spaniard, sensing the danger in the man. And even as his mind at last identified the underlying inflections of speech, he realized, with an odd, sinking chill, whence that dreadful sense of stillness stemmed.

The tonal shift in a few of his word endings was characteristic of those areas which had been linguistically isolated since the end of the sixteenth century.

And except when he spoke, Don Simon Ysidro did not appear to be breathing.

The carving knife still in his left hand, Asher got to his feet and said, "Come here."

Ysidro did not move. His slender hands remained exactly as they had been, dead white against the blued steel of the dissected gun, but no more inert than the spider who awaits the slightest vibration of the blundering fly.

"You understand, it is not always easy to conceal what we are, particularly if we have not fed," he explained in his low, light voice. Heavy lids gave his eyes an almost sleepy expression, not quite concealing cynicism and mockery, not quite concealing that odd gleam. "Up until ninety years ago, it was a simple matter, for no one looks quite normal by candlelight. Now that they are lighting houses by electricity, I know not what we shall do."

Ysidro must have moved. The terrifying thing was that Asher did not see the man do it, was not—for a span of what must have been several seconds—conscious of anything, as if he had literally slipped into a trance on his feet. One second he was standing, knife in hand, between Lydia's sleeping form and the desk where the slim intruder sat; the next, it seemed, he came to himself with a start to find the iciness of Ysidro's fingers still chilling his hand, and the knife gone.

Shock and disorientation doused him like cold water. Don Simon tossed the knife onto the desk among the scattered pieces of the useless revolver and turned back, with an ironic smile, to offer his bared wrist to Asher.

Asher shook his head, his mouth dry. He'd faked his own death once, on a German archaeological expedition to the Congo, by means of a tourniquet, and he'd seen fakirs in India who didn't even need that. He backed away, absurdly turning over in his mind the eerie similarities of hundreds of legends he'd uncovered in the genuinely scholarly half of his career, and walked to Lydia's desk.

It stood on the opposite side of the study from his own—in actual fact a Regency secretaire Lydia's mother had once used for gilt-edged invitations and the delicately nuanced jugglings of seating arrangements at dinners. It was jammed now with Lydia's appallingly untidy collection of books, notes, and research on glands. Since she had taken her degree and begun research at the Radclyffe Infirmary, Asher had been promising to get her a proper desk. In one slim compartment her stethoscope was coiled, like an obscene snake of rubber and steel . . .

His hands were not quite steady as he replaced the stethoscope in its pigeonhole once more. He was suddenly extremely conscious of the beat of the blood in his veins.

His voice remained level. "What do you want?"

"Help," the vampire said.

"What?" Asher stared at the vampire, he realized—seeing the dark amusement in Ysidro's eyes—like a fool. His own mind still felt twisted out of true by what he had heard—or more properly by what he had absolutely *not* heard—through the stethoscope, but the fact that the shadowy predator that lurked in the legends of every culture he had ever studied did exist was in a way easier to believe than what that predator had just said.

The pale eyes held his. There was no shift in them, no expression; only a remote calm, centuries deep. Ysidro was silent for a few moments as if considering how much of what he should explain. Then he moved, a kind of weightless, leisurely drifting that, like Asher's habitual stride, was as noiseless as the passage of shadow. He perched on a corner of the desk, long white hands folded on one well-tailored gray knee, regarding Asher for a moment with his head a little on one side. There was something almost hypnotic in that stillness, without nervous gesture, almost completely without movement, as if that had all been rinsed from him by the passing moons of time.

Then Don Simon said, "You are Dr. James Claudius Asher, author of *Language and Concepts in Eastern and Central Europe*, Lecturer in Philology at New College, expert on languages and their permutations in the folklore of countries from the Balkans to Port Arthur to Pretoria . . ."

Asher did not for a moment believe it coincidence that Ysidro had named three of the trouble spots of which the Foreign Office had been most desirous of obtaining maps.

"Surely, in that context, you must be familiar with the vampire."

"I am." Asher settled his weight on one curved arm of the divan where Lydia still lay, unmoving in her unnatural sleep. He felt slightly unreal, but very calm now. Whatever was happening must be dealt with on its own bizarre terms, rather than panicked over. "I don't know why I should be surprised," he went on after a moment. "I've run across legends of vampires in every civilization from China to Mexico. They crop up again and again—blood-drinking ghosts that live as long as they prey on the living. You get them from ancient Greece, ancient Rome—though I remember the classical Roman ones were supposed to bite off their victims' noses rather than drink their blood. Did they?"

"I do not know," Ysidro replied gravely, "having only become vampire myself in the Year of Our Lord 1555. I came to England in the train of his Majesty King Philip, you understand, when he came to marry the English queen—I did not go home again. But personally, I cannot see why anyone would trouble to do such a thing." Though his expression did not change, Asher had the momentary impression of amusement glittering far back in those champagne-colored eyes.

"And as for the legends," the vampire went on, still oddly immobile, as if over the centuries he had eventually grown weary of any extraneous gesture, "one hears of fairies everywhere also, yet neither you nor I expect to encounter them at the bottom of the garden." Under the long, pale wisps of Ysidro's hair, Asher could see the earlobes had once been pierced for earrings, and there was a ring of antique gold on one of those long, white fingers. With his narrow lips closed, Ysidro's oversized canines—twice the length of his other teeth—were hidden, but they glinted in the gaslight when he spoke.

"I want you to come with me tonight," he said after a brief pause during which Asher had the impression of some final, inner debate which never touched the milky stillness of his calm. "It is now half past seven—there is a train which goes to London at eight, and the station but the walk of minutes. It is necessary that I speak with you, and it is probably safer that we do so in a moving vehicle away from the hostages that the living surrender to fortune."

Asher looked down at Lydia, her hair scattered like red smoke over the creamy lace of her gown, her fingers, where they rested over that light frame of wire and glass, stained with smears of ink. Even under the circumstances, the incongruity of the tea gown's languorous draperies and the spectacles made him smile. The combination was somehow very like Lydia, despite her

13

occasionally stated preference for the more strenuous forms of martyrdom over being seen wearing spectacles in public. She had never quite forgotten the sting of her ugly-duckling days. She was writing a paper on glands. He knew she'd probably spent most of the morning at the infirmary's dissecting rooms and had been hurriedly scribbling what she could after she'd come home and changed clothes while waiting for him to arrive. He wondered what she'd make of Don Simon Ysidro and reflected that she'd probably produce a dental mirror from somewhere about her person and demand that he open his mouth—wide.

He glanced back at Ysidro, oddly cheered by this mental image. "Safer for whom?"

"For me," the vampire replied smoothly. "For you. And for your lady. Do not mistake, James; it is truly death that you smell, clinging to my coat sleeves. But had I intended to kill your lady or you, I would already have done so. I have killed so many men. There is nothing you could do which could stop me."

Having once felt that disorienting moment of psychic blindness, Asher was ready for him, but still only barely saw him move. His hand had not dropped the twenty inches or so that separated his fingers from the hideout knife in his boot when he was flung backward across the head of the divan, in spite of his effort to roll aside. Somehow both arms were wrenched behind him, the wrists pinned in a single grip of steel and ice. The vampire's other hand was in his hair, cold against his scalp as it dragged his head back, arching his spine down toward the floor. Though he was conscious of very little weight in the bony limbs that forced his head back and still further back over nothing, he could get no leverage to struggle; and in any case, he knew it was far too late. Silky lips brushed his throat above the line of the collar—there was no sensation of breath.

Then the lips touched his skin in a mocking kiss, and the next instant he was free.

He was moving even as he sensed the pressure slack from his spine, not even thinking that Ysidro could kill him, but only aware of Lydia's danger. But by the time he was on his feet again, his knife in his hand, Ysidro was back behind the desk, unruffled and immobile, as if he had never moved. Asher blinked and shook his head, aware there'd been another of those moments of induced trance, but not sure where it had been.

The fine strands of Ysidro's hair snagged at his velvet collar as he tipped his head a little to one side. There was no mockery in his topaz eyes. "I could have had you both in the time it takes to prove to you that I choose otherwise," he said in his soft voice. "I—we—need your help, and it is best that I explain it to you on the way to London and away from this girl for whom you would undertake another fit of pointless chivalry. Believe me, James, I am the least dangerous thing with which you—or she—may have to contend. The train departs at eight, and it is many years since public transportation has awaited the convenience of persons of breeding. Will you come?"

Two

It was perhaps ten minutes' walk along Holywell Street to the train station. Alone in the clinging veils of the September fog, Asher was conscious of a wish that the distance were three or four times as great. He felt in need of time to think.

On his very doorstep, Ysidro had vanished, fading effortlessly away into the mists. Asher had fought to keep his concentration on the vampire during what he was virtually certain was a momentary blanking of his consciousness, but hadn't succeeded. Little wonder legend attributed to vampires the ability to dissolve into fog and moonbeams, to slither through keyholes or under doors. In a way, that would have been easier to understand.

It was the ultimate tool of the hunter—or the spy.

The night was cold, the fog wet and heavy in his lungs—not the black, killer fog of London, but the peculiarly moist, dripping, Oxford variety, which made the whole town seem slightly shaggy with moss and greenness and age. To his left as he emerged into Broad Street, the sculpted busts around the Sheldonian Theater seemed to watch him pass, a dim assemblage of ghosts; the dome of the theater itself was lost in the fog beyond. Was Ysidro moving among those ghosts somewhere, he wondered, leaving no footprint on the wet granite of the pavement?

Or was he somewhere behind Asher in the fog, trailing silently, watching to see whether his unwilling agent would double back and return home?

Asher knew it would do him no good if he did. His conscious mind might still revolt at the notion that he had spent the last half hour conversing with a live vampire—*an oxymoron if ever*

16

I heard one, he reflected wryly—but the difference, if one existed, was at this point academic.

He had been in deadly danger tonight. That he did not doubt. As for Lydia . . .

He had absolutely no reason to believe Don Simon's claim to be alone. Asher had considered demanding to search the house before he left, but realized it would be a useless gesture. Even a mortal accomplice could have stood hidden in the fog in the garden, let alone one capable of willing mortal eyes to pass him by. He had contented himself with lighting the fires laid in the study fireplace and the kitchen stove, so that the servants would not wake in cold—as wake they would, Ysidro had assured him, within an hour of their departure.

And at all events, Ysidro knew where Asher lived. If the vampire were watching him, there was no chance of returning to the house and getting Lydia to safety before they were intercepted.

And—another academic point—what precisely constituted safety?

Asher shoved his gloved hands deeper into the pockets of the baggy brown ulster he had donned and mentally reviewed everything he had ever learned about vampires.

That they were the dead who infinitely prolonged their lives by drinking the blood of the living seemed to be the one point never in dispute, bitten-off noses in Rome notwithstanding. From Odysseus' first interview with the shades, there was so little divergence from that central theme that Asher was—intellectually, at least—mildly astounded at his own disbelief before he had pressed the stethoscope to that thin, hard ribcage under the dark silk of the vest, and had heard . . . nothing. His researches in folklore had taken him from China to Mexico to the Australian bush, and there was virtually no tongue which had not yielded some equivalent of that word, *vampire.*

Around that central truth, however, lay such a morass of legend about how to deal with vampires that he felt a momentary spasm of irritation at the scholars who had never troubled to codify such knowledge. He made a mental note to do so, provided Ysidro hadn't simply invited him to London for dinner with a few friends. Naturally, he reflected wryly, there wasn't a greengrocer open at this hour, and he would look fairly foolish investigating back-garden vegetable patches for garlic en route to the station . . . totally aside from missing his train. And given the general standard of British cookery, searching for garlic would be a futile task at best.

His ironic smile faded as he paused on the Hythe Bridge, looking down at the water, like slate the color of glass and smudged with the lights of Fisher Row, whose wet gray walls seemed to rise straight out of the stream. Garlic was said to be a protection against the Undead, as were ash, whitethorn, wolfsbane, and a startling salad of other herbs, few of which Asher would have recognized had he found them by the road. But the Undead were also said to be unable to cross running water, which Ysidro had obviously done on his way from the station—or *had* he come up from London to Oxford by train?

A crucifix allegedly protected its wearer from the vampire's bite—some tales specified a silver crucifix, and Asher's practical mind inquired at once: *How high a silver content?* But like tales of the Catholic Limbo, that theory left vast numbers of ancient and modern Chinese, Aztecs, ancient Greeks, Australian bushmen, and Hawaiian Islanders, to name only a few, at an unfair disadvantage. Or did ancient Greek vampires fear other sacred things? And how, in that case, had unconverted pagan vampires in the first century A.D. reacted to Christians frantically waving the symbols of their faith at them to protect themselves from having their blood drunk or their noses bitten off? *Not much* vincere in hoc signo, he mused ironically, turning his steps past the Crystal Palace absurdity of the old London and Northwestern station and along the Botley Road to the more prosaic soot-stained brick of the Great Western station a hundred yards beyond.

He was now not alone in the fog-shrouded roadbed between the nameless brick pits and sheds that railway stations seemed to litter spontaneously about themselves. Other dark forms were hastening from the lights of the one station to the lights of the other, struggling with heavy valises or striding blithely along in front of brass-buttoned porters whose breath swirled away to mingle with the dark vapors around them. From the direction of the London and Northwestern station, a train whistle groaned dismally, followed by the lugubrious hissing of steam; Asher glanced back toward the vast, arched greenhouse of the station and saw Don Simon walking, with oddly weightless stride, at his elbow.

The vampire held out a train ticket in his black-gloved hand. "It is only right that I provide your expenses," he said in his soft voice, "if you are to be in my service."

Asher pushed aside the ends of his scarf—a woolly gray thing knitted for him by the mother of one of his wilder pupils—and tucked the little slip of pasteboard into his waistcoat pocket. "Is that what it is?" They climbed the shallow ramp to the platform. In the harsh glare of the gaslights, Ysidro's face looked white and queer, the delicate swoop of the eyebrows standing out against pale hair and paler skin, the eyes like sulfur and honey. A woman sitting on a bench with two sleepy little girls glanced up curiously, as if she sensed something amiss. Don Simon smiled into her eyes, and she quickly looked away.

The vampire's smile vanished as swiftly as it had been put on; in any case, it had never reached his eyes. Like every other gesture or expression about him, his smile had an odd, minimal air, almost like a caricaturist's line, though Asher had from it a sudden impression of an antique sweetness, the faded-out shape of what it once had been. For a moment more Ysidro studied the averted profile and the silvery-fair heads of the two children pressed against the woman's shabby serge shoulders. Then his glance returned to Asher's.

"From the time Francis Walsingham started running his agents in Geneva and Amsterdam to find out about King Philip's invasion of England, your secret service has had its links with the scholars," he said quietly. The antique inflection to his speech, like its faint Castilian lisp, was barely discernible. "Scholarship, religion, philosophy—they were killing matters in those days, and at that time I was still close enough to my human habits of thought to be concerned about the outcome of the invasion. And too, it was still respectable among scholars to be a warrior, and among warriors to be a scholar, which it is no longer, as I'm sure you know."

Asher's old colleague, the Warden of Brasenose, sprang to mind, tutting disapprovingly over some minor Balkan flare-up in the course of which Asher had nearly lost his life, while Asher, cozily consuming scones on the other side of the hearth, had nodded agreement that no, *h'rm*, England had no business meddling in European politics, damned ungentlemanly, *hrmph, mphf.* He suppressed his smile, unwilling to give this slender young man anything, and kept silent. He leaned his shoulders against the sooty brick of the station wall, folded his arms, and waited.

After a moment Ysidro went on, "My solicitor—a young man, and agreeable to meet with his clients at late hours if they so desire—did mention that, when he worked in the Foreign Office, there was talk of at least one don at Oxford and several at Cambridge who 'did good work,' as the euphemism goes. This was years ago, but I remembered it, out of habit, and of interest in things secret. When I had need of an—agent—it was no great matter to track you down by the simple expedient of comparing the areas about which papers were published and their probable research dates with times and places of diplomatic unease. It still left the field rather wide, but the only Fellow younger than yourself who might possibly have fit the criteria of time and place would have difficulty passing himself off as anything other than an obese and myopic rabbit . . ."

"Singletary of Queens," sighed Asher. "Yes, he was researching in Pretoria at the same time I was, trying to prove the degeneracy of the African brain by comparative anatomy. The silly bleater still doesn't know how close he came to getting us both killed."

That slight, ironic line flicked into existence at the corner of Ysidro's thin mouth, then vanished at once. The train came puffing in, steam roiling out to blend with the fog, while vague forms hurried onto the platform to meet it. A girl with a face like a pound of dough sprang from a third-class carriage as it slowed, into the arms of a podgy young man in a shop clerk's worn old coat, and they embraced with the delighted fervor of a knight welcoming his princess bride. A mob of undergraduates came boiling out of the waiting room, noisily bidding good-by to a furiously embarrassed old don whom Asher recognized as the Classics lecturer of St. John's. Linking their arms, they began to carol "Till We Meet Again" in chorus, holding their boaters over their hearts. Asher did not like the way his companion turned his head, studying them with expressionless yellow eyes as if memorizing every lineament of each rosy face. Too like a cook, he thought, watching lambs play at a spring fair.

"The war was my last job," Asher went on after a moment, drawing Ysidro's glance once more to him as they crossed the platform. "I became—unsuitably friendly with some people in Pretoria, including a boy I later had to kill. They call it the Great Game, but it's neither. I came back here, got married, and incorporated the results into a paper on linguistic borrowings from aboriginal tongues." He shrugged, his face now as expressionless as the vampire's. "A lecturer's salary isn't a great deal, but at least I can drink with my friends without wondering if what they're telling me is the truth."

"You are fortunate," the vampire said softly. He paused, then continued, "I have taken a first-class compartment for us—at this time of night, we should have it to ourselves. I will join you there after the train leaves the station."

Oh, will you? Asher thought, his right eyebrow quirking up and his every instinct and curiosity coming suddenly alert as the vampire moved off down the platform with a lithe, disquieting stride, his dark Inverness cloak flaring behind him. Thoughtfully, Asher sought out their compartment, divested himself of bowler and scarf, and watched the comings and goings on the platform with great interest until the train moved away.

The cloudy halo of the platform lights dropped behind them; a scattering of brick buildings and signal gantries flipped past in the foggy dark. He saw the gleam of lights, like an ironic omen, on the ancient markers of the old graveyard, then on the brown sheet-silk of the river as they passed over the bridge. The darkness of the countryside took them.

Asher settled back against the worn red plush as the compartment door slid open and Ysidro entered, slim and strange as some Egyptian cat-god, his fair, cobweb-fine hair all sprinkled with points of dampness in the jolting flicker of the gas jet overhead. With a graceful movement, he shrugged out of his slate-gray Inverness; but, in spite of his flawless Bond Street tailoring, Asher was coming to wonder how anyone ever mistook him for anything human.

Folding his hands on his knee, Asher inquired casually, "Just whom are you afraid of?"

The long, gloved hands froze momentarily in their motion; the saffron eyes slid sharply to him, then away.

"In this day and age I'd be surprised to learn it's a mob with a crucifix and torches, but a man doesn't jump on a train at the last moment unless he's making damned sure who gets on ahead of him, and that no one's coming behind."

Ysidro's gaze rested on him for a moment longer, calm as ever, though his whole body seemed poised for movement; then he seemed infinitesimally to relax. He set his coat aside and sat down. "No," he said presently. "That is our strength—that no one believes, and, not believing, lets us be. It is a superstition that is one of the many things 'not done' in this country. We learned long ago that it is good policy to cover our traces, to hide our kills or to make them look like something else. Generally it is only the greedy, the careless, the arrogant, or those with poor judgment who are traced and killed, and even they not immediately. At least so it has been."

"So there are more of you."

"Of course," the vampire said simply. He folded his gloved hands, sitting very straight, as if, centuries after he had ceased to wear the boned and padded doublets of the Spanish court, the habit of their armoring persisted. Long used to judging men by the tiny details of their appearance, Asher marked down the medium-gray suit he wore at fifty guineas or better, the shoes as made to order in the Burlington Arcade, the gloves of kid fine as silk. Even minimal investments, he thought dryly, must accrue an incredible amount of interest in three hundred years . . .

"There were some—two or three, a master vampire and her fledglings—at one time in Edinburgh, but Edinburgh is a small town; late in the seventeenth century the witch-hunters found the places where they hid their coffins. There are some in Liverpool now, and in that packed, crass, and stinking cesspit of factories and slums that has spread like cancer across the north." He shook his head. "But it is a young town, and does not offer the hiding places that London does."

"Who's after you?" Asher asked.

The champagne-colored eyes avoided his own. "We don't know."

"I should think that with your powers . . ."

"So should I." The eyes returned to his, again level and cool as the soft voice. "But that does not seem to be the case. Someone has been killing the vampires of London."

Asher raised one thick brow. "Why does that surprise you?"

"Because we do not know who it is."

"The people you kill don't know who you are," Asher pointed out.

"Not invariably," the vampire agreed. "But when they do, or when a friend, or a lover, or a member of their family guesses what has happened to them, as occasionally chances, we usually have warning of their suspicions. We see them poking about the places where their loved ones were wont to meet their killers—for it is a frequent practice of vampires to befriend their victims, sometimes for months before the kill—or the churchyards where they were buried. Most of us have good memories for faces, for names, and for details—we have much leisure, you understand, in which to study the human race. These would-be vampire hunters in general take several weeks to bring themselves to believe what has happened, to harden their resolve, and in that time we often see them."

"And dispose of them," Asher asked caustically, "as you disposed of their friends?"

"*Dios,* no." That flexible smile touched his face again, for one instant; this time Asher saw the flicker of genuine amusement in the pale, ironic eyes. "You see, time is always on our side. We have only to melt into the shadows, to change our haunts and the places where we sleep for five years, or ten, or twenty. It is astounding how quickly the living forget. But this time . . ." He shook his head. "Four of us have died. Their coffins were opened, the light of the sun permitted to stream in and reduce their flesh to ashes. The murders were done by daylight—there was nothing any vampire could have done to prevent them, or to catch the one who did them. It was this that decided me to hire help."

"To hire help," Asher said slowly. "Why should *I* . . ." He stopped, remembering the still gaslight of the library shining on Lydia's unbound red hair.

"Precisely," Ysidro said. "And don't pretend you did not know that you were hired to kill by other killers in the days when you took the Queen's Coin. Wherein lies the difference between the Empire, which holds its immortality in many men's consciousness, and the vampire, who holds it in one?"

It could have been a rhetorical question, but there was not that inflection in the vampire's voice, and he waited afterward for an answer.

"Perhaps in the fact that the Empire never blackmailed me into serving it?"

"Did it not?" There was the faintest movement of one of those curving brows—like the smile, the bleached echo of what had once been a human mannerism. "Did you not serve it out of that peculiarly English brand of sentimentalism that cherishes sodden lawns and the skyline of Oxford and even the yammering dialects of your peasants? Did you not risk your own life and take those of others, so that 'England would remain England'—as if, without Maxim guns and submarines, it would somehow attach itself to the fabric of Germany or Spain? And when this ceased to be a consideration for you, did you not

24

turn your back in disgust upon what you had done like a man falling out of love?

"We need a man who can move about in the daylight as well as in the hours of darkness, who is acquainted with the techniques of research and the nuances of legend, as well as with the skills of a killer and a spy. We merely agree with your late Queen as to the choice of the man."

Asher studied him for a long moment under the jumpy glare of the gas jet in its pierced metal sheath. The face was smooth and unwrinkled and hard, the slender body poised and balanced like a young man's in its well-tailored gray suit. But the jeweled eyes held in them an expression beyond defining, the knowledge of one who has seen three and a half centuries of human folly and human sin reel gigglingly by; they were the eyes of one who was once human, but is no longer.

"You're not telling me everything," he said.

"Did your Foreign Office?" Ysidro inquired. "And I am telling you this, James. We will hire you, we will pay you, but if you betray us, in word or in deed, there will be no place on this earth where you or your lady Lydia will be safe from us, ever. I hope you believe that, for both your sakes."

Asher folded his hands, settled his shoulders back into the worn plush. "You hope I believe it for your own sake as well. In the night you're powerful, but by daylight you seem to be curiously easy to kill."

"So," the vampire murmured. For an instant his delicate mouth tightened; then the expression, if expression it was, smoothed away, and the pale eyes lost some of their focus, as if that ancient soul sank momentarily into its dreams. Though the whole car vibrated with the rush of the dark rails beneath their feet, Asher had a sense of terrible silence, like a monster waiting in absolute stillness for its prey.

Then he heard a hesitant step in the corridor, a woman's, though traffic up and down the narrow passage had long ceased. The compartment door slid open without a knock. Framed in the slot of brown oak and gaslight stood the woman who had watched over her two sleeping children on the platform, staring before her like a sleepwalker.

Ysidro said nothing; but, as if he had invited her in, the woman closed the door behind her. Stepping carefully with the swaying of the train, she came to sit on the edge of the seat at the vampire's side.

"I—I'm here," she stammered in a tiny voice, her eyes glassy under straight, thin lashes. "Who—why . . . ?"

"It is nothing you need trouble about, *bellisima*," Ysidro whispered, putting out one slim hand in its black glove to touch her face. "Nothing at all."

"No," she whispered mechanically. "Nothing at all." Her dress was of shabby red cloth, clean but very old, the fabric several times turned; she wore a flat black straw hat, and a purple scarf round her neck against the cold. She couldn't have been more than twenty-five—Lydia's age—and had once been pretty, Asher thought, before ceaseless worry had graven those petty lines around her mouth and eyes.

Tersely he said, "All right, you've made your point . . ."

"Have I?" The delicate black fingers drew forth the wooden pin that held the hat to the tight screw of fair hair; caressingly, like a lover's, they began to work loose the pins from the hair itself. "In all the rather silly legends about us, no one ever seems to have pinpointed the true nature of the vampire's power—a kind of mesmerism, as they used to call it, an influence over the minds of humans and, to some extent, beasts. Though I am not sure into which category this creature would fall . . ."

"Send her away." Asher found his own voice was thick, his own mind seeming clogged, as if he, too, were half dreaming. He made as if to rise, but it was like contemplating getting out of bed too early on a foggy morning—far easier to remain where he was. He was aware of Ysidro's glance on him, sidelong under long, straight eyelashes nearly white.

"She was only along in one of the third-class carriages, she and her daughters." With slow care the vampire unwound the purple scarf, letting it slither heedless to the carriage floor; unfastened the cheap celluloid buttons of the woman's collar. "I could have summoned her from anywhere on the train, or, had she not been on it, I could have stood on the platform at Paddington and called her; and believe me, James, she would have gotten the money somehow and come. Do you believe that?"

Like dark spiders, his fingers parted her collar, down to the sad little ruffle of her mended muslin chemise; the milky throat rose like a column from the white slope of her breast. "Do you remember your wife and her servants, asleep because I willed that they should sleep? We can do that, I and my—friends. I know your people now. At my calling, believe me, they would come—that big mare of a chambermaid, your skinny little Mrs. Grimes, your stupid scullion, or the lout who looks after your gardens and stables—do you believe that? And all without knowing any more about it than this woman here." His black leather fingers stroked the untouched skin. The woman's open eyes never moved. As if he were deep in the sleep of exhaustion, Asher's mind kept screaming at him, *Get up! Get up!* But he only regarded himself with a kind of bemusement, as if separated from his body by an incredible distance. The noises of the train seemed dulled, its shaking almost lulling, and it seemed as if this scene, this woman who was about to die, and indeed everything that had happened since that afternoon, which he'd spent explaining the Sanskrit roots of Romany to an undergraduate named Pettifer, were all a dream. In a way it made more sense when viewed so.

"A poor specimen, but then we feed upon the poor, mostly— they're far less likely to be avenged than the rich." A fang gleamed in the trembling gaslight. "Do you believe I can do this to whomever I will? To you or to anyone whose eyes I meet?"

No, thought Asher dully, struggling toward the surface of what seemed to be an endless depth of dark waters. *No.*

"No." He forced himself to his feet, staggering a little, as if he had truly been asleep. For a moment he felt the vampire's naked mind on his, like a steel hand, and quite deliberately he walled his mind against it. In his years of working for the Foreign Office there were things he had willed himself not to know,

27

the consequences of actions he had taken. The night he had shot poor Jan van der Platz in Pretoria he had forced himself to feel nothing, as he did now. The fact that he had succeeded in it then was what had turned him, finally, from the Great Game.

As deliberately as he had pressed the trigger then, he walked over to the woman and pulled her to her feet. Ysidro's pale eyes followed him, but he did not meet them; he pushed the woman out of the compartment ahead of him and into the corridor. She moved easily, still sleepwalking. On the little platform between the cars the wind was raw and icy; with the cold air, his mind seemed to clear. He leaned in the doorframe, feeling oddly shaken, letting the cold smite his face.

Beside him the woman shuddered. Her hands—ungloved, red, chapped, and callused, in contrast to that white throat—fumbled at her open collar as her eyes flared with alarm and she stared, shaken and disoriented, up into his face. "What—who—?" She pushed away from him, to the very rail of the narrow space, as if she would back off it entirely into the flying night.

Asher dropped at once into his most harmless, donnish stance and manner, an exaggeration of the most gentle facet of his own personality that he generally used when abroad. "I saw you just standing in the corridor, madam," he said. "Please forgive my liberty, but my wife sleepwalks like that, and something about the way you looked made me think that might be the case. I did speak to you and, when you didn't answer, I was sure of it."

"I . . ." She clutched at her unbuttoned collar, confusion, suspicion, terror in her rabbity eyes. He wondered how much she recalled as a dream, and became at once even more consciously the Oxford don, the Fellow of New College, the philologist who had never even *heard* of machine guns, let alone wadded up plans of them into hollowed-out books to ship out of Berlin.

"Fresh air will wake her up—my wife, I mean. Her sister sleepwalks, too. May I escort you back to your compartment?"

She shook her head quickly and mumbled, "No—thank

28

you, sir—I—you're very kind . . ." Her accent Asher automatically identified as originating in Cornwall. Then she hurried over the small gap between the cars and into the one beyond, huddled with cold and embarrassment.

Asher remained where he was for some minutes, the cold wind lashing at his hair.

When he returned to the compartment, Ysidro was gone. The only thing that remained to tell him that all which had passed was not, in fact, a dream was the woman's purple scarf, collapsed like a discarded grave band on the floor between the two seats. Asher felt the anger surge in him, guessing where the vampire was and what he would be doing, but knowing there was nothing he could do. He could, he supposed, run up and down the train shouting to beware of vampires. But he had seen Ysidro move and knew there was very little chance of even glimpsing him before he found another victim. In a crowded third-class carriage or an isolated sleeping car, a dead man or woman would pass unnoticed until the end of the journey, always provided the body were not simply tipped out. Mangled under the train wheels, there would be no questions about the cause of death or the amount of blood in the veins.

But of course, if he issued a warning, nothing at all would happen, save that he would be locked up as a bedlamite.

Filled with impotent rage, Asher flung himself back in the red cushioned seat to await Don Simon Ysidro's reappearance, knowing that he would do as the vampire asked.

Three

———

Her name was Lotta." Don Simon's soft voice echoed queerly in the damp vaults of the tomb. "She was one of . . ." He hesitated fractionally, then amended, "A hatmaker, when she was alive." Asher wondered what Ysidro's original description of her would have been. "In life she was a rather poor specimen of a human—cocky, disrespectful of her betters, a thief, and a whore." He paused, and again Asher had the impression that the Spaniard was picking through a jewel box of facts for the few carats' worth of information with which he was willing to part. "But she made a good vampire."

Asher's left eyebrow quirked upward, and he flashed the beam of Ysidro's dark lantern around the low stone vaults above their heads. Shadowed niches held coffins; here and there, on a keystone arch, a blurred coat of arms had been incised, though why, if Death had not been impressed by the owner's station, the family expected Resurrection to be, he was at a loss to decide. Highgate was not a particularly old cemetery, but it was intensely fashionable—vaults in this part started at well over a hundred guineas—and the tomb, with its narrow stair leading down from a tree-lined avenue of similar pseudo-Egyptian mausoleums, was guarded by its well-paid-for isolation and was, at the same time, far easier to enter than the crypt of some City church would have been.

"And what makes a good vampire?"

For a moment he thought Ysidro would evade the question. The Spaniard stood for a moment, nearly invisible in the shadows of a dark niche, his aquiline face inscrutable in its long frame of colorless hair. Then he said slowly, "An attitude of mind, I suppose. You must understand, James, that the core of a vampire's being is the hunger to live, to devour life—the will not to die. Those who have not that hunger, that will, that burning inside them, would not survive the—process—by which the living become Undead and, even if they did, would not long continue this Unlife we lead. But it can be done well or poorly. To be a good vampire is to be careful, to be alert, to use all the psychic as well as the physical faculties of the vampire, and to have that flame that feeds upon the joy of living.

"Lotta, for all her vulgarity—and she was amazingly vulgar—was a truly attractive woman, and that flame of life in her was part of the attraction. Even I felt it. She truly reveled in being a vampire."

The yellow lance of the lantern beam passed over the short flight of granite steps leading down from the level of the avenue outside—the avenue that, even in daylight, would have been dim with subaqueous green shade—and gleamed faintly on the metal that sheathed the vault doors. Even entering the place, Asher could see that the dust and occasional blown leaves lay far less thickly on those steps and on the sort of trodden path that led to this niche to the right of the vault. It marked Lotta's nightly comings and goings and obviated any specific track of the one who had found her sleeping here.

"I take it you knew her when she was alive?"

"No." The vampire folded his arms, a gesture which barely stirred the black folds of his Inverness.

In the glaring gaslights of Paddington Station Asher had seen that Ysidro had lost some of his terrible pallor, looking almost human, except for his eyes—presumably, Asher thought with a sort of dark humor, he had dined on the train. It was more than could be said for himself. While Ysidro summoned a cab from the rank of horse-drawn hansoms before the station, he'd bought a meat pasty from an old man selling them from a cart, and the taste of it lingering in his mouth was as bizarre an incongruity in this macabre gloom as had been the act of eating it in the cab with the vampire sitting ramrod-straight at his side. Ysidro had offered to pay the halfpenny it had cost—Asher had simply told him to put it on account.

"Then you didn't make her a vampire?"

Either he was growing more used to the minimal flickers that passed for the vampire's expressions or Ysidro had held the woman in especial contempt. "No."

"Who did, then?"

"One of the other vampires in London."

"You're going to have to give me some information sometime, you know," Asher remarked, coming back to Don Simon's side.

"I see no reason for you to know who we are and where to find us. The less you know, the less danger there will be for all of us, yourself included."

Asher studied that cool, ageless face by the amber kerosene glow and thought, *They plan to kill me when this is over.* It was only logical if, as Ysidro had said, the first defense of the Undead was the disbelief of the living. He wondered if they thought he was a fool or merely believed him to be controllable in spite of this knowledge. Anger stirred in him, like a snake shifting its coils.

And more than anger, he was aware of the obscure sense that he had picked up in his years of working for the Department, an impression of looking at two pieces of a puzzle whose edges did not quite match.

He walked back to the niche, with its thick stench of fresh ashes, and raised the lantern high.

The coffin that lay on the hip-high stone shelf was reasonably new, but had lost its virgin gloss. Its lid had been pulled forward and lay propped longways against the wall beneath the niche itself; there were multiple scratches on the stonework, where the coffin had been pulled forward and back, of various degrees of freshness, difficult to determine in the tin lantern's shadows.

He held the light low, illuminating the interior, the hot metal throwing warmth against his wrist between shirt cuff and glove, the smell of burning kerosene acrid in his nostrils. His first thought was how intense the heat must have been; it had eaten at the bones themselves, save for the skull and the pelvis. The long bones of arms and legs were attenuated to bulb-ended rods, the vertebrae little more than pebbles, the ribs charred to crumbling sticks. Metal glinted, mixed with the ash—corset stays, buttons, a cut-steel comb, the jeweled glitter of rings.

"So this is what happens to vampires when the sun strikes them?"

"Yes." Ysidro's noncommittal features could have been carved of alabaster for all the expression they showed, but Asher sensed the thoughts behind them, racing like a riptide.

He moved the lantern, flashing its beam around the crypt close to the coffin's base—mold, dirt, dampness. "Yet she made no effort to get out of the coffin."

"I am not sure that burning would have waked her." The vampire drifted over to stand at his side, looking down over his shoulder into the casket. "Exhaustion comes upon us at dawn; once we sleep, there is no waking us until darkness once more covers the land."

From the mess in the coffin, Asher picked the stump of a half-decomposed bone, blew sharply on it to clear away the ashes, and held it close to the light. "Not even if you burst into flames?"

"It is not 'bursting into flames,'" Ysidro corrected in his soft, absolutely level voice. "It is a burning, a corrosion, a searing away of the flesh . . ."

Asher dropped back the first bone he had found, fished about for another. Given the number of murders Lotta had committed over the years, he thought, her remains didn't rate much in the way of respect. "How long does it take, first to last?"

"I have no idea, having never, you understand, been able to witness the process. But I know from my own experience that its onset is instantaneous upon contact with the sun's light."

Glancing up swiftly, for an instant Asher found himself looking into the crystalline labyrinth that stretched into endless distance behind the colorless eyes.

Ysidro went on, without change in the timbre of his voice, "I was, as you see, able to reach shelter within a second or so— I do not know how long it would have taken me to die. My hands and face were blistered for months, and the scars lasted for years." After a moment he added, "The pain was like nothing I had ever experienced as a living man."

Asher studied the vampire for a moment, that slender young man who had danced with Henry VIII's remarkable daughters. "When was this?"

The heavy eyelids lowered infinitesimally. "A long time ago."

There was a silence, broken only by the faint hiss of the hot metal lantern slide, and by Asher's solitary breath. Then Asher turned back, to pick again through the charred ruin of bones. "So merely the opening of her coffin wouldn't have wakened her, in spite of a vampire's powers. I'm still a bit surprised; by the way the coffin lining is undamaged all around the top, she didn't even try to sit up, didn't even move . . ."

Ysidro's thin, black-gloved hand rested on the edge of the coffin near Asher's down-turned face. "The vampire sleep is not human sleep," he said softly. "A friend of mine says she thinks it is because the mental powers that waken with the transition to the vampire state weary the mind. I myself sometimes wonder whether it is not because we, even more so than the living, exist day to day by the sheer effort of our own wills. Perhaps it amounts to the same thing."

"Or perhaps," Asher said, lifting another small stump of bone from the charred mess, "it was because Lotta was already dead when her flesh ignited."

The vampire smiled ironically. "When her flesh ignited," he remarked, "Lotta had already been dead for approximately a hundred and sixty years."

Asher held the fragment of bone up in the beam of the lamp. "There's not much left, but the bone's scratched. This is one of the cervical vertebrae—her head was severed. Her mouth may have been stuffed with garlic . . ."

"That is customary in such cases."

"Not in 1907, it isn't." He set the lantern on the corner of the coffin and pulled a handkerchief from his pocket to wrap the charred scraps of bone. "It indicates, among other things, that the killer entered the tomb, closed the door, opened the coffin, severed the head, and only then reopened the door to allow daylight to destroy the flesh. So he knew what to expect. I take it Lotta was not the first victim?"

"No," Ysidro said, looking expressionlessly down over Asher's shoulder as he began once more to sift the ash, gems, and decomposing bones. The saffron light picked splinters of brightness from the facets of jewels and the edges of charred metal. Asher's probing fingers dug, searched, and tossed aside, seeking for what he knew had to be there.

"Were the other victims beheaded also? Or staked through the heart?"

"I have no idea. The bodies, you understand, were nearly as badly decomposed as hers. Is it important?"

"It would tell us—particularly the condition of the first body you found—whether the killer knew initially that he was going after vampires. Real vampires, physiological vampires, and not just lunatics who enjoy sleeping in coffins."

"I see."

Asher wondered what it was he *did* see, veiled behind those lowered eyelids. Certainly something. "What are your theories on this?"

"I'm paying you for yours."

Asher's mouth quirked with irritation. "There are things you aren't telling me."

"Many of them," the vampire agreed evenly, and Asher sighed and abandoned that tack.

"Did she play with her victims?"

"Yes." Disdain glinted along the edge of his tone. A vulgar Cockney, Asher thought, amused; scarcely to the taste of this fastidious hidalgo from the court of Philip II. "She liked rich young men. She would play them along for weeks, sometimes, meeting them places, letting them take her to supper—since one seldom actually watches one's dinner partner eat, it is a simple enough illusion to maintain—or to the theater or the opera, not that she had the slightest interest in music, you understand. She could not make of them a steady diet—like the rest of us, she subsisted chiefly upon the city's poor. But she enjoyed the knowledge that these silly youths were entertaining their own killer, falling in love with her. It pleased her to make them do so. She savored the terror in their eyes when they finally saw the fangs. Many vampires do."

"Do you?"

Don Simon turned away, a flicker of tired distaste in his eyes. "There was a time when I did. Are we finished here?"

"For now." Asher straightened up. "I may come back in the daylight, when there's more chance of seeing something. Where were her rooms?" When Ysidro hesitated, he insisted, "She can't have strung her suitors along for centuries wearing just the one dress." He held up the latchkey he had taken from the ashes.

"No." The vampire drifted ahead of him across the narrow vault and mounted the steps while Asher thrust closed the iron-sheeted vault door behind them. The areaway around it was thick with leaves, though they had been swept away time and again by the opening of the door: it had been thirty years since the Branhame family had died out, leaving their tomb to those who slept and the one who, up until the night before last, had not. The air outside was foggy and still. The vampire's caped greatcoat hung about his slender form in folds, like the sculpted cloak of a statue. His head was bare; his eyes were hooded pits of gleaming shadow. "No, and Lotta was one of those women who saw immortality in terms of an unlimited wardrobe.

"I went there last night, after I discovered . . . this." He gestured behind them, as Asher slid shut the lantern slide and trod cautiously along the utter darkness of the wet, fog-drowned slot of the avenue of tombs. After a moment the light, steel-strong touch of the vampire's hand closed on Asher's arm, guiding him along in the total darkness. Intellectually he understood that he was perfectly safe, so long as Ysidro needed his help, but still, he made a mental note to be careful how often he found himself in this particular situation.

"How did you happen to discover it?" he inquired as they emerged from the end of the avenue under a massive gateway carved by the cemetery's developers to resemble some regal necropolis of the Pharaohs. "If, as you say, you never got along with Lotta, what would you be doing visiting her tomb?"

"I wondered how long it would take me to fall under suspicion." Asher caught the glint of genuine humor in Simon's ironic glance. "I plead innocence, my lords of the jury—I had, as they say in the novels, retired to my room and was sound asleep at the time."

In spite of himself Asher grinned. "Can you bring a witness?"

"Alas, no. In truth," he went on, "I had been—unquiet—for some weeks before any evidence of trouble arose. There was a vampire named Valentin Calvaire, a Frenchman, who had not been seen for two, three weeks. I was beginning to suspect ill had befallen him—he was only recently come to London, by our standards, and might have been unfamiliar yet with the hiding places and the patterns of this city's life. It is easy in those circumstances for a vampire to come to grief, which is one of the reasons we do not often travel."

Asher had the momentary impression that Ysidro had more to say on the subject of Valentin Calvaire; but, after the briefest of inner debates, he seemed to think better of it and simply went on, "I think now that he was the first victim, though no body, no burned coffin, was ever found. But then, none of us knew all of his sleeping places.

"But eighteen days ago some—a friend of mine—came to me saying that one of the other vampires, a friend to us both, had been killed on the previous day, his coffin left open to the sun. She was distraught, though it is the kind of thing which can happen accidentally—for instance, many of our secret hiding places, the ancient cellars where we had hidden our coffins for years, were broken open and destroyed when they cut for the Underground. This vampire—his name was Danny King—had indeed slept in such a cellar. The window shutters were wide open, as was the coffin's lid."

Enough thin moonlight filtered through the fog so that Asher could see his companion's face, calm and detached, like the faces of the cold stone children they had passed in the rustling murk of the cemetery around them. The curving wall of tombs that surrounded them like a canyon opened out into a stair, over-hung with trees that shadowed again the vampire's white face, and Asher was left with that disembodied voice like pale amber, and the steely strength of the long fingers on his arm.

"Perhaps ten days after that, Lotta and a friend of hers came to me saying they had gone up to the rooms of another vampire, an Edward Hammersmith, who lived in an old mansion in Half Moon Street that his father had owned when he was a man. They had found all the shutters pried off the windows and the coffin open, filled with bones and ash. And then I knew."

"And neither King nor Hammersmith appeared to have awakened or tried to get out of their coffins?"

"No," Ysidro said. "But with Calvaire's death the killer would have known what it was that he hunted."

"The question is," Asher said, "whether he knew it before."

"We asked that of ourselves. Whether anyone had been seen dogging our steps, lingering about, as humans do when they are working up their resolve even to believe that one they loved was indeed the victim of a vampire. In Mr. Stoker's interesting novel, it is only the coincidence that the heroine's dear friend and also her husband were victims of the same vampire and that the husband had seen other vampires at their hunt that leads her and her friends to put all the rest of the details together and come up with the correct answer. Most people never reach that stage. Even when the vampire is careless, and the evidence stares them in the face, they are always far more eager to believe a 'logical explanation.'

"I find it typical," he added, as they passed through the softly echoing gloom of an enclosed terrace, a catacomb of brick vaults and marble plaques that marked the modest tombs of its sleepers, "that vampirism is portrayed as an evil *only just* entering England—from the outside, naturally, as if no true-born Englishman would stoop to become a vampire. It had obviously never occurred to Mr. Stoker that vampires might have dwelt in London all along."

They left the cemetery as they had entered it, over the wall near St. Michael's Church, Ysidro boosting Asher with unnerving strength, then scrambling lightly up after him. The fog seemed less thick here as they strolled beside the cemetery wall and down Highgate Hill. The woolly yellow blur of the lantern, now that it would no longer bring the watchmen down on them, picked pearled strands of weed and web from the darkness of the roadside ditch, as it had picked the jewels from the coffin ash. Asher's breath drifted away as steam to mingle with the cloudy brume all around them, and he was interested to see that, even when he spoke, Don Simon's did not.

"How long *have* there been vampires in London?" he asked, and the shadowed eyes flicked sidelong to him again.

"For a long time." The shutting once again of that invisible door was almost audible, and the rest of the walk was made in silence. Behind them in the fog, Asher heard the clock on St. Michael's chime the three-quarters—while passing through the cemetery itself he had heard it speak eleven. Highgate Hill and the suburban streets below it were utterly deserted, the shops and houses little more than dark bulks in the drifting fog through which the gaslights made weak yellow blobs.

"Thought you toffs was never comin' back," their cabby began indignantly, struggling up out of the tangle of his lap robes in the cab, and Ysidro inclined his head graciously and held out a ten-shilling note.

"My apologies. I hope it caused you no inconvenience?"

The man looked at the money, touched his hat brim quickly, and said, "Not at all, guv'—not at all." His breath was redolent of gin, as was the inside of the cab. It was, Asher reflected philosophically as he climbed in, a cold night.

"Albemarle Crescent, Kensington," Ysidro said through the trap, and the cab jolted away. "Insolent villain," he added softly. "Yet I have found it seldom pays to engage in quarrels with menials. Regrettably, the days are past when I could have ordered him thrashed." And he turned his cool profile to gaze—not quite tranquilly, Asher thought—into the night.

Albemarle Crescent was a line of houses that had seen better days, though a kind of faded elegance clung to them still, like a duchess' gown bought third-hand at a rag fair. At that hour, the neighborhood was deathly silent. Standing on the flagway, wrapped in a fog that was thicker now, here closer to the river, Asher could hear no sound of passers-by. In Oxford at this hour, the dons would still be up, wrangling metaphysics or textual criticism, undergraduates carousing or scurrying through the streets, gowns billowing behind them, in the course of some rag or other; in other parts of London, the very rich, like the very poor, would be drinking by lamplight. Here the stockbrokers' clerks, the junior partners of shopkeepers, the "improved" working class, kept themselves to themselves, worked hard, retired early, and did not question overmuch the comings and goings of those around them.

Ysidro, who had stood for some moments gazing into the fog at the barely visible bulk of the terraced row, murmured, "Now we can enter. I have deepened their sleep against the sound of my own footfalls, but I have never before had call so to mask a living man's. Tread soft."

Lotta's rooms were on the second floor; the ground floor smelled of greasy cooking, the first of stale smoke and beer. They left the lantern unobtrusively cached in the entryway. No lights were on anywhere, save over the entry, but Ysidro guided him unerringly as he had before. The old-fashioned, long-barreled key Asher had found with the latchkey proved, as he'd suspected, to open Lotta's door, and it was only when they had closed it again and locked it behind them that he took a lucifer from his pocket and lit the gas.

Color smote his eyes, magnified and made luminous by the soft shimmer of the gaslight; the room was an incredible jumble of clothes, shoes, peignoirs, trinkets, shawls, laces, opera programs, invitations, and cards, all heaped at random over the cheap boarding house furniture, like an actress' dressing room between scenes. There were evening gowns, scarlet, olive, and a shade of gold which only a certain shade of blonde could wear with effect, kid opera gloves spotted with old blood, and fans of painted silk or swan's-down. A set of sapphires—necklace, earrings, double bracelets, and combs—had been carelessly dumped on a tangle of black satin on the mahogany of the table, glinting with a feral sparkle as Asher's shadow passed across them.

The clutter in the bedroom was worse. Three giant armoires loomed over a bed that had obviously never been used for sleep; their doors sagged open under the press of gowns. Other dresses were heaped on the bed, a shining tangle of ruffles in which pearls gleamed like maggots in meat—yards of flounced organdy three generations out of date and narrow, high-waisted silks, older still and falling apart under the weight of their own beading as he gently lifted them from the shadowy disarray. Cosmetics and wigs, mostly of a particular shade of blonde, cluttered the dressing table, whose mirror frame bulged with cards, notes, bibelots, and bills; jewels trailed among the mess in prodigal clusters, like swollen and glittering fruit. Near the foot of the bed, Asher saw an old shoe, broad-toed, square-heeled, with paste gems gleaming on its huge buckle and ribbons faded to grayish ghosts of some former indigo beauty. Gold sovereigns strewed a corner of the dressing table under a layer of dust and powder. Picking one up, Asher saw that they bore the head of the unfortunate Farmer George.

"Did her beaux give her money?" he asked quietly. "Or was she in the habit of robbing them after they were dead?"

"Both, I expect," Ysidro replied. "She never saved much. Hence her need to live in rooms—or in any case to rent them to store her things. But, of course, she could not risk sleeping here, with the possibility of her landlady entering to ask questions. And more questions would be asked, of course, if she shuttered the windows tightly enough to cut out all sunlight."

"Hence Highgate," Asher murmured, removing a dress-maker's bill from the table and turning it over in his hands.

"The propensity of the vampires for sleeping among the dead," Ysidro said, standing, arms folded, just within the connecting door, "stems not so much from our fondness for corpses—though I have been told many vampires in the so-called Gothic ages considered it no more than proper—but from the fact that the tombs would be undisturbed by day. And by night, of course, interference would not matter."

41

"On the contrary, in fact," Asher remarked. "Must have played hob with the Resurrection trade." He was systematically removing all the cards, all the notes, and all the invitations that he could find from the mirror frame and dressing table, shoving them into an old-fashioned beaded reticule for examination later at leisure. "And I presume *your* money comes from investments?"

"That is not something which concerns you."

He flipped open a drawer. The reek of old powder and decaying paper rose to his nostrils like the choke of dust. The drawer was crammed with a chowchow of bills, most of them yellow and cracking with age, letters still shoved into embossed envelopes which bore illegible handwritten franks instead of postage marks or stamps, and little wads of notes issued by banks long collapsed. "It concerns me how I'll get money to pursue my investigations."

Ysidro regarded him for a moment from beneath lowered eyelids, as if guessing that reimbursement was, in fact, the least of Asher's concerns. Then he turned away and began picking up and discarding the dozens of reticules of various ages, styles, and states of decomposition that lay among the anarchy of the bed or drooped from drawers of kerchiefs and underclothes. He opened them, plucking forth small wads of bank notes or emptying glittering streams of gold or silver onto the dressing table carelessly, as if the very touch of the money disgusted him.

A true hidalgo of the Reconquista, Asher thought, amused again and interested to see that three and a half centuries among a nation of shopkeepers hadn't changed him.

"Will that suffice?"

Asher sorted through the money, discarding anything more than twenty years old, except for one George III gold piece he pocketed as a souvenir. "For now," he said. "Since Lotta was the fourth victim, it isn't tremendously likely the killer started his investigations with her, but there might be something in all this paper—the name of a recent victim, an address, something. I'll want to see the rooms of the others—Calvaire, King, and

Hammersmith—and I'll want to talk to these 'friends' of King's you spoke of . . ."

"No."

"As you wish," Asher said tartly, straightening up and flipping shut the drawer. "Then don't expect me to find your killer."

"You will find the killer," Ysidro retorted, his voice now deadly soft, "and you will find him quickly, ere he kills again. Else it will be the worse for you and for your lady. What you seek to know has nothing to do with your investigation."

"Neither you nor I has any idea what has to do with my investigation until we see it." Anger stirred in Asher again, not, as before, anger with the vampires, but the frustration he had known when dealing with those bland and faceless superiors in the Foreign Office who could not and would not understand field conditions, but demanded results nevertheless. For a moment he wanted to take Ysidro by his skinny neck and shake him, not solely from his fear of what might happen to Lydia, but from sheer annoyance at being ordered to make bricks without straw. "If I'm going to do as you ask, you're going to have to give me something . . ."

"I will give you what I choose." The vampire did not move, but Asher sensed in him a readiness to strike and knew the blow, when it came, would be irresistible as lightning and potentially as fatal. Nothing altered in the voice, cold and inert as poison. "I warn you again—you are playing with death here. What bounds I set are as much for your own protection as for mine. Take care you do not cross them.

"Understand me, James, for I understand you. I understand that you intend to work for me only so long as it will take you to find a way to destroy me and those like me with impunity. So. I could have found a man who is venal and unintelligent, who would not even have been told who and what I am, to whom I would simply have said: Find me this; find me that; meet me with the results tonight. There are men who are too unimaginative even to ask. But it would not have answered. One does not select cottonwood to fashion a weapon to preserve, perhaps, one's life; one selects the hardest of teak. But with that hardness comes other things."

They faced each other in silence, in the silken chaos of that cluttered chamber with its stinks of ancient perfume. "I won't have you coming to Oxford again."

"No," Ysidro agreed. "I, too, understand. Whoever is behind these murders, I will not lead him to your lady. Take rooms here in this city—I will find you. For those of us who hunt the nights, that will be no great task. You might remember that, also, should it cross your mind to ally yourself with our murderer."

"I'll remember," Asher promised quietly. "But you remember this: if you and your fellow-vampires kill me, you'll still have a problem. And if you play me false, or try to take hostages, or so much as go *near* my wife again, you'll have an even bigger problem. Because then you'll have to kill me and you'll still need to find someone else to do your day work for you. I'll play straight with you, but, in a sense, you've put yourself in my hands, as I am in yours. I believe in your existence now . . ."

"And whom would you tell who would believe you?"

"It's enough that I believe," said Asher. "And I think you know that."

Four

——

How does one go about investigating the personal life of a woman who's done murder on a regular basis for the last hundred and fifty years?"

Lydia Asher paused, the handkerchief-wrapped fragments of bone in hand, and tilted her head consideringly at her husband's question. With her long red hair hanging down over nightgowned shoulders and her spectacles glinting faintly in the misty gray of the window light, she looked more like a fragile and gawky schoolgirl than a doctor. Asher stretched out his long legs to rest slippered feet on the end of the bed. "She must have hundreds of potential enemies."

"Thousands, I should say," Lydia guessed, after a moment's mental calculation. "Over fifty thousand, counting one per night times three hundred and sixty-five times a hundred and fifty . . ."

"Taking off a few here and there when she went on a reducing diet?" Asher's mustache quirked in his fleet grin; only his eyes, Lydia thought, were not the same as they had been. Below them in the house, Ellen's footsteps tapped a half-heard pulse as she went from room to room, laying fires; further off, on the edge of awareness, Lydia could detect the regular clatter and tread of breakfast being prepared.

Ellen had insisted on remaining awake long enough to fix a scratch dinner, after they had all wakened mysteriously in the chilled depths of the night. Lydia had sent them all to bed as soon as possible. The last thing she'd needed was the parlor maid's unbridled imagination, the cook's self-dramatization, and the tweeny's morbid credulity to add to what she herself had found a deeply disturbing experience. That James had been home she'd deduced from the fact that the fires were built up,

45

though why he should have taken apart his revolver and left the knife he didn't think she knew he carried in his boot among the pieces on his desk had left her somewhat at a loss. Characteristically, she had spent the remainder of the night searching through her medical journals—which she kept in boxes under the bed, as they'd overflowed the library—for references to similar occurrences, alternately outlining an article on the pathological basis for the legend of Sleeping Beauty and dozing in the tangle of lace-trimmed counterpane and issues of the *Lancet*. But her dreams had been disturbing, and she had kept waking, expecting to find some slender stranger standing silently in the room.

"I don't think so," she said now, shaking back the clouds of her sleeve-lace and pushing up her specs. "*Could* a vampire go on a reducing diet? There isn't any fat in blood."

Her mind scouted the thought while Asher hid his grin behind a cup of coffee.

She unwrapped the two vertebrae from James' handkerchief, and held them to the slowly brightening light of the window. Third and fourth cervical, badly charred and oddly decomposed, but, as James had described, the scratch on the bone was clearly visible. "There must be tissue repair of some kind, you know," she went on, wetting her finger to rub some of the soot away, "if Don Simon's burns 'took years to heal.' I wonder what causes the combustion? Though there are stories of spontaneous human combustion happening in very rare instances to quite ordinary people—if they *were* ordinary, of course. Did you get a look at the coffin lining? Was it burned away, too?"

Asher's thick brows pulled together as he narrowed his eyes, trying to call back the details of that silent charnel house. He hadn't had medical training, but, Lydia had found, he had the best eye for detail she had ever encountered in a world that ignored so much. He would be that way, she thought, even if his life hadn't depended on it for so many years.

"Not burned away, no," he said after a moment. "The lining at the bottom was corroded and stained, almost down to the wood; charred and stained to a few inches above where the body

46

would come on the sides. The clothes, flesh, and hair had been entirely destroyed."

"Color of the stains?"

He shook his head. "I couldn't see by lantern light."

"Hmn." She paused in thought, then began patting and shaking the pillows, comforter, and beribboned froth of shams around her, looking for her magnifying glass—she was sure she'd been using it to peruse some dissecting-room drawings the other night in bed.

"Night stand?" Asher suggested helpfully. She fished it out to look more closely at the third cervical.

"This was done with one stroke." She held it out—he leaned across to take it and the glass and studied it in his turn. "Something very sharp, with a drawing stroke: a cleaver or a surgical knife. Something made for cutting bone. Whoever used it knew what he was doing."

"And wasn't about to lose his nerve over severing a woman's head," Asher added thoughtfully, setting aside the bone. "He'd already killed three other vampires, of course. Presumably whatever started him on his hunt for vampires was enough to overcome his revulsion, if he felt any, the first time—and after that, he'd have proof that they do in fact exist and must be destroyed." As he spoke, he tugged gently on the faded silk ribbons of the old reticule, coaxing it open in a dry whisper of cracking silk.

"Surely the mere circumstances of their loved one's death would have proved that." When James didn't answer, she looked up from examining the oddly dissolved-looking bone. What she saw in his face—in his eyes, like a burned-on reflection of things he had seen—caused the same odd little tightening within her that she'd felt when she was four and had awakened in the night to realize there was a huge rat in her room and that it was between her and the door.

Slowly he said, "If that's the reason behind the killings, yes. But I think there's more to it than that—and I don't know what. If Ysidro's telling the truth, vampires can generally see ordinary mortals coming."

"*If* he was telling the truth. It might have been a lie to make you keep your distance, you know." She shook one long, delicate finger at him and mimicked, " 'Don't you try nuthin' wi' me, bucko, 'cos we'll see you comin'.' "

"You haven't seen him in action." The somberness fled from his eyes as he grinned at himself. "That's the whole point, I suppose: *nobody* sees them in action. But no. I believe him. His senses are preternaturally sharp—he can count the people in a train coach by the sound of their breathing, see in the dark . . . Yet the whole time I was with him, I could feel him listening to the wind. I've seen men do that when they think they're being followed, but can't be sure. He hides it well, but he's afraid."

"Well, it does serve him right," Lydia observed. She hesitated, turning the vertebra over and over in her fingers, not looking at it now any more than she looked at the grass stems she plucked when she was nervous. She swallowed hard, trying to sound casual and not succeeding. "How much danger am I in?"

"Quite a lot, I think." He got up and came around to sit on the pillows beside her; his arm in its white shirt sleeve was sinewy and strong around her shoulders. Her mother's anxious coddling—not to mention the overwhelming chivalry of a number of young men who seemed to believe that, because they found her pretty, she would automatically think them fascinating—had given Lydia a horror of clinginess. But it was good to lean into James' strength, to feel the warmth of his flesh through the shirt sleeve, the muscle and rib beneath that nondescript tweed waistcoat, and to smell ink and book dust and Macassar oil. Though she knew objectively that he was no more able to defend either of them against this supernatural danger than she was, she cherished the momentary illusion that he would not let her come to harm.

His lips brushed her hair. "I'm going to have to go down to London again," he said after a few minutes, "to search for the murderer and to pursue investigations as to the whereabouts of the other vampires in London. If I can locate where they sleep, where they store their things, where they hunt, it should give me a weapon to use against them. It's probably best that you leave Oxford as well . . ."

"Well, of course!" She turned abruptly in the circle of his arm, the fragile suspension of disbelief dissolving like a cigarette genie with the opening of a door. "I'll come down to London with you. Not to stay with you," she added hastily, as his mouth opened in a protest he was momentarily too shocked to voice. "I know that would put me in danger, if they saw us together. But to take rooms near yours, to be close enough to help you, if you need it . . ."

"Lydia . . . !"

Their eyes met. She fought to keep hers from saying *Don't leave me,* fought even to keep herself from thinking it or from admitting to a fear that would only make things harder for him. She squared her pointed little chin. "And you will need it," she said reasonably. "If you're going to be investigating the vampire murders, you won't have time to go hunting through the public records for evidence of where the vampires themselves might be living, not if Don Simon wants to see results quickly. And we could meet in the daytime, when—when *they* can't see us. If what you say about them is true, I'd be in no more danger in London than I would be in Oxford—or anywhere else, really. And in London you would be closer, in case of . . ." She shied away from saying it. "Just in case."

He looked away from her, saying nothing for a time, just running the dry ribbons of the vampire's reticule through the fingers of his free hand. "Maybe," he said after a time. "And it's true I'll need a researcher who believes . . . You *do* believe they're really vampires, don't you?" His eyes came back to hers.

She thought about it, turning that odd, anomalous chunk of bone over and over in her lap. James was one of the few men to whom she knew she could say anything without fear of either shock, uncertain laughter, or—worse—that blankly incomprehending stare that young men gave her when she made some straight-faced joke.

"Probably as much as you do," she said at last. "That is,

there's a lot of me that says, 'This is silly, there's no such thing.'
But up until a year or so ago, nobody believed there was such
a thing as viruses, you know. We still don't know what they
are, but we do know now they exist, and more and more are
being discovered . . . A hundred years ago, they would have
said it was silly to believe that diseases were caused by little
animals too small to see, instead of either evil spirits or an im-
balance of bodily humors—which really are more logical explanations, when you think of it. And there's something definitely odd about this bone."

She took a deep breath and relaxed as her worst fear—the
fear of being left alone while her fate was decided elsewhere
and by others—receded into darkness. James, evidently re-
signed to his fate, took his arm from around her shoulders and
began picking out the reticule's contents, laying them on the
lace of the counterpane—yellowing bills, old theater pro-
grammes folded small, appointment cards, invitations—in his
neat, scholarly way.

"Are you going to get in touch with the killer?"

"I certainly intend to try." He held up an extremely faded
calling card to the light. "But I'll have to go very carefully. The
vampires will know it's a logical alliance to make . . . What is
it?"

Against his side, through the bed, he had felt her start.

Lydia dropped the card she had been looking at, her hand
shaking a little with an odd sort of shock, as if she'd seen someone she knew . . . Which, she reflected, was in a way exactly
what had happened. She didn't know what to say, how to define
that sense of helpless hurt, as if she'd just seen a very brainless
cat walk straight into the savaging jaws of a dog.

He had already picked up the card and was reading the as-
signation on the back. Then he flipped it over to see the front,
where the name of the Honorable Albert Westmoreland was
printed in meticulous copperplate.

"I knew him," Lydia explained, a little shakily. "Not well—
he was one of Uncle Ambrose's students when I was still in
school. His father was a friend of Papa's in the City."

"One of your suitors?" The teasing note he sometimes had when speaking of her suitors was absent. She had had flocks of them, due in part to the Willoughby fortune, which had paid for this house and everything in it, and in part to her waiflike charm. After being told for years that she was ugly, she enjoyed their attentions and enjoyed flirting with them—though not as much as she enjoyed a good, solid analysis of nervous lesions—and charming people had become second nature to her. A just girl, she didn't hold it against those earnest young men that they'd frequently bored her to death, but the distinction was something her father had never been able to grasp. With Baptista-like faith in man's ability to change a woman's personality, he had encouraged them all, never, until the last, losing his touching hope that he'd see his wayward daughter marry her way into the peerage.

She smiled a little, mostly at the recollection of her father's face when she'd announced her intention to marry a middle-aged Lecturer in Philology without an "Honorable" to his name, and shook her head. "He was already engaged to Lord Carringford's daughter. But he was in their set. So I saw him a good deal. I knew—well, nobody spoke of it before me, of course, and Nanna would have killed them if they had, but I guessed that when they went larking about in town it wasn't with girls like me. I remember Dennis Blaydon coming round and telling me Bertie had died."

She shivered, and he drew her close again, his hand warm and strong on her shoulder. Oddly enough, the news hadn't upset her much at the time, though she'd felt shocked and sad, for Bertie had been the first contemporary, the first of her set, who had died. Even then, she had been familiar with death—old Horace Blaydon, chief Lecturer in Pathology at Radclyffe, had said it was positively indecent to watch her carve up cadavers—but it was different, it seemed, when it was someone you knew. Dennis, she recalled, had done his best to comfort her, with disappointing results.

"Did he say how?"

She shook her head. "But it was very sudden. I remember

thinking I'd seen him only a few weeks before, when all their set went down to watch Dennis play in the rugger match against Kings. Poor Bertie." The memory made her smile again wanly. "The Honorable Bertie—he made straight for the shadiest seat and spent the whole time being terrified the bench would leave spots on his trousers, lemonade would drip onto his sleeve, or his buttonhole would wilt. His brother, the Equally Honorable Evelyn, was on the Gloucester side and nearly died of embarrassment."

What a thing to be remembered for, she thought. She wondered if he had cried out, if he had known what was happening to him, or if this vampire woman had taken him in his sleep, as Ysidro could so easily have done to them all. Her hand closed tighter around James'.

After a very long silence, she asked, "Can we meet in the daytime?"

"I don't know," he said quietly. "Not safely, I don't think. The killer can be about by day, even if the vampires can't. Until I can contact him—talk to him—see how and why he's doing this—I don't want anyone knowing where to get at you." His arm tightened a little around her, his fingers feeling hers, gently, as if treasuring even the bones within her thin flesh. She felt the tension in his body and turned to look up into his face.

"And it isn't only that," he said. "There's something Ysidro isn't telling me, Lydia, something critical. Whatever he says, he'd be a fool to hire a human; and whatever else he is, Don Simon Ysidro isn't a fool. He had a reason beyond what he's telling me. And whatever that reason is—whatever it is that he knows—it's the first thing I'm going to have to find out if either of us is going to make it to Guy Fawkes' Day alive."

Before noon Asher was on his way back to London. Over breakfast he had informed Ellen and Mrs. Grimes that the night's events had left Lydia in such a state of nervous prostration that he thought it better to arrange for her to see a specialist in London, a story which disgusted the phlegmatic Lydia and puzzled Ellen. "She was fine, Mr. Asher, sir, indeed she was, when she woke up me and Cook. And she's never been one to take on."

"Well, I've just spent the morning with her, and, believe me, she needs to see a specialist," Asher said firmly. Twenty-four hours without sleep on top of the events and exertions of the night had left him in no mood for invention.

Ellen had regarded his pallor and his dark-circled eyes with deep disapproval. "It isn't my place to say so, sir, but if anyone needs a nerve doctor . . ."

"No, it isn't your place to say so," Asher retorted, draining his coffee. "So just assist Mrs. Asher to pack her things, and I'll be back to fetch her this evening." It would probably take that long, he reflected bemusedly, for Lydia to assemble everything she considered essential for a few weeks in London.

The mere thought of another train trip before nightfall made his bones ache, but no husband as worried about the state of his wife's health as he currently purported to be would entrust her on the journey with no other escort than her maid. Besides, once in London it would be difficult to get rid of Ellen, who, in addition to being more intelligent than she sometimes seemed, was incurably inquisitive.

Why was it, Asher wondered, crossing the Magdalen Bridge on his way out of Oxford a short time later, that qualities deemed laudable in anyone else were nothing but a damned nuisance in servants? Past the bridge's gray stone balustrade, he had a flying glimpse of the tops of the willows and a distant fragment of brown-green waters; he recalled Ysidro's words about teak and cottonwood and smiled in spite of himself. Coming off the bridge, he veered onto St. Clement's Street, which led through wooded byways toward the green rise of the downs.

In preference to another two hours on the Great Western, he had elected to take his motorcycle down to London, a five horsepower American V-twin Indian that had always been a bone of contention between himself and the other dons. There were Lecturers of All Souls and Fellows of Christ Church who might possess motorcars, but, it was implied, such things were thought to be far more typical of Cambridge men. To own a motorcycle, much less ride it through the countryside, was generally looked upon as scarcely above the level of an undergraduate. Out of deference for his colleagues' sensibilities, as well as for his own reputation of mild harmlessness—to say nothing of what such behavior would do to his academic gown—Asher did not generally ride within the Town itself.

At the moment, however, time was of the essence. There were things which needed to be arranged while the sun was yet in the sky and Ysidro and the other vampires safely asleep in their coffins, and the quickest way to London was over the downs and through High Wycombe. The road was execrable, potholed and unpaved in places and awash in yellowish mud which liberally splattered his boots, leather jacket, goggles, and hair. But their silence enfolded him. For the first time he was alone, in that vast stillness of rolling chalk hills and hair-fine, dull-olive turf, to think and to plan, and the stillness seeped imperceptibly into thought and muscle and soul, like salve on a burn.

On the high backbone of the downs, he stopped and turned to look back on the green valley, the far-off glitter where half a dozen streams met amid a lingering suggestion of damp mists and dark clouds of trees. He could pick out the towers of the colleges, not as the crystal company of dreaming spires that dawn or sunset made them, but gray, lichen-stained, familiar— the ogee cupola of Tom, Magdalen seeming to float above its trees, Merton's spires and the square proportions of his own New College Tower, like the faces of friends lined up on a railway platform to see him off—the place that had been his home, on and off, for the better part of twenty-seven years.

Abroad, he remembered, he had lived in constant danger, to the point where he could almost forget about it; there had been times when he could have been killed as easily as a candle being snuffed out. But through it he had always had this place, the memory of this gentle haven, at his back. He had always thought: *If I can make it back to Oxford . . .* And latterly had been the knowledge that Oxford had included Lydia.

Half the women he knew, he thought with an inward grin, would have swooned at the story he'd told her this morning or else gone into feverish speculation on how Asher had been hoaxed. Beneath her occasional and wholly illusory façade of scatter-witted loveliness, Lydia had a doctor's cool practicality and a willingness to deal with facts—however bizarre—as they stood. He was reminded of himself, with his own life and hers at stake, concerning himself with the archaic pronunciation of the vampire's speech.

Perhaps that was one reason why, out of all the men—mostly younger than he, and all a good deal wealthier than he—who had been captivated by her waiflike charm, it was he who lived with her now, and would, he hoped, for the next forty years.

Ysidro would be sorry, he thought grimly, that he had dragged Lydia into this.

He squeezed the throttle lever, startling a dozen larks into swift, slanting flight; turning the 'bike, he began to make his way down the long slopes toward Beaconsfield and Wycombe and, eventually, toward the distant smear of gray-yellow smoke that was London.

His journeys through the back blocks of Europe in quest of Latin roots or stranger things had given Asher a good deal of practice in finding lodgings quickly. He settled on two lodging houses in Bloomsbury, not far from the Museum, facing onto different streets, but backing on the same alley; the rear window of the small suite of rooms he engaged for Lydia at 109 Bruton Place could be seen from his own solitary chamber at 6 Prince of Wales Colonnade. They weren't as close as he would have liked, and there would be a good deal of shinning up and down drain pipes and climbing fences in the event of a real emergency, but it was as good as he could get in the time. Even so, it was getting perilously close to dark when he stumbled once more onto the Oxford train.

He slept all the way up. As he had feared, his dreams were troubled by the image of the coffin full of ashes in Highgate Cemetery and by the dim sense of dread that, if he went there and listened, those ashes might whisper to him in a voice that he could understand.

Lydia was waiting for him, simply but beautifully dressed and carefully veiled to hide the fact that she was far less wan and pale than he. On the train down, fortified by yet more of the black coffee that had latterly kept his body and soul together, Asher explained the message-drop system he'd worked out at the cloakroom of the Museum's reading room, and the signals between Bruton Place and Prince of Wales Colonnade: one curtain open, one shut, if a meeting was necessary, and a telegram to follow; a lamp in the window in case of an emergency.

"I'd suggest you start at Somerset House," he said as the leaden dusk flashed by the windows. Coming over the hills that afternoon had been pleasant; but, as the cold of the night closed in, he admitted there was a great deal to be said for the cozy stuffiness of a train after all. "You can match information from the Wills Office and Registry with the old Property Rolls in the Public Records Office—it's my guess that at least some of the vampires own property. I can't see Ysidro entrusting his Bond Street suits, let alone his coffin, to the care of a ten-bob-a-month landlady. Get me records of places where the leasehold hasn't changed ownership for—oh, seventy years or longer. Reader's Passes are easy enough to get. All the records of the original estate ground-landlords should be available. You might also see what you can get me on death certificates for which there was no body. We're eventually going to have to check back issues of newspapers as well for deaths which could be attributed to vampires, but, from the sound of it, those may be concealed. God knows how many cases of malnutrition or typhus were really Ysidro and his friends. I suspect that, during epidemics of jail fever at Newgate and Fleet, a vampire could feed for weeks without anyone being the wiser or caring. Poor devils," he added and studied in silence that clear-cut white profile against the compartment's sepia gloom.

More quietly, he asked, "Will you mind learning what you can about Albert Westmoreland's death? I'll look into that, if you'd rather not."

She shook her head, a tiny gesture, understanding that she was affected, not because she had particularly cared about the man, but simply because it brought the reality of her own danger closer. Without her spectacles, her brown eyes seemed softer, more dreamy. "No. You're going to need your time to follow the main trail. Besides, I knew him and his friends. I don't suppose I could look up Dennis Blaydon again without him pouting and fretting because I married you instead of him, but I could talk to Frank Ellis—Viscount Haverford he is now—or to the Equally Honorable Evelyn—Bertie's brother. He was a freshman, I think, the year Bertie . . . died."

"I don't like it," Asher said slowly. "Having you do research in London is one thing; when I send a letter to my leftover Foreign Office connections on the *Daily Mail*, it won't introduce you under your own name. Ysidro spoke of vampires knowing when a human—a friend or relative of a recent victim—is on their trail; they go about interviewing people or loitering in churchyards, and the vampires eventually see them at it. I don't want them to see you, Lydia. That would surely be the death of us both."

Her back stiffened. "I don't see how . . ."

"Nor do I," he cut her off. "But for the moment, I'm going to have to assume that it's true. They have powers we do not; until we know more about them, I'm not disposed to take chances."

"Maybe," she said. "But they also have weaknesses, and the more we learn about them—the more we can talk to people who have actually dealt with a vampire—the more we may be able to put together a means of dealing with them if . . . if worse comes to worst. As long ago as Bertie's death was, it isn't likely there's a connection, but at least we'll have another view of them."

"I still don't like it," he said again, knowing she was probably right. "I'd rather you didn't, but if you do, *please* be careful. Take every precaution, no matter how foolish it seems. As for what you may learn . . . Have you ever tried to piece together an account of an accident from witnesses, even ten minutes after it happened? And Bertie's death was . . . when?"

"Nineteen hundred." Her mouth twitched in an ironic smile. "Turn of the new century."

"That was seven years ago." He'd been in Africa then, riding across tawny velvet distances by the light of the swollen and honey-colored moon. He sometimes found it difficult to believe it was any longer ago than seven weeks. He leaned across and kissed her, her hat veils tickling the bridge of his nose; it was odd to remind himself once again that she was, in fact, his wife. He went on, "Even had Lotta been the first victim instead of the fourth, that's a long time between. But we need any background, any leads we can get. Can you look up all that?"

"Certainly, Professor Asher." She folded her gloved hands primly in her rose twill lap and widened her eyes at him sweetly. "And what would you like me to look up in the afternoon?"

He laughed ruefully. "Gas company records for private residences that show abnormally high consumption? I'd like to get at banking records, but that means pulling F.O. or Yard credentials, and that might get back to Ysidro. Leave whatever notes you make in the message-drop at the Museum—I'll keep them in a locker at Euston rather than at my rooms overnight. At the moment, I'd rather Ysidro and his friends have no idea the way my research is tending. And, Lydia—let me know if you run across any evidence that someone else is following the same trails."

"The killer, you mean." By her voice she'd already thought of it; he nodded. "Will you kill them, then?"

Something in her tone brought his eyes back to her face; its look of regret surprised him. She shook her head, dismissing her reservations. "It's just that I'd like the chance to examine one of them medically."

The concern was so typical of Lydia that Asher nearly laughed. "Yes," he said, and then the lightness faded from his face and his soul. "I'll have to for a number of reasons, not the least of which is that if I *don't* catch the killer, sooner or later they're going to suspect me of killing them anyway, and using the original murders to mask whatever I may do. They have to be destroyed, Lydia," he went on quietly. "But if—and when—it comes to that, I'd better get them all, because God help both of us if even one survives."

Asher got off the train at Reading, taking a slow local to Ealing and then the Underground the long way round, through Victoria and the City, and thence back to Euston Station, to avoid being anywhere near Paddington when Lydia debarked. It was now fully dark. Staring through the rattling windows at the high brick walls and the occasional flickering reflection of gaslight where the Underground ran through cuts rather than tunnels, he wondered whether the vampires ever took the Underground, ever hunted its third-class carriages. Could they use its passages as boltholes, emergency hiding places safe from the sun? How much sun *was* fatal to that white, fragile flesh?

Not a great deal, he thought, crossing the platform and ascending the steps that led upward to the open square of night outside. Even with its door open, the crypt in Highgate wouldn't be brightly lighted, looking as it did into the gloom of the narrow avenue of tombs.

As he reached the flagway, he felt a pang of uneasiness for Lydia, disembarking by herself at Paddington. Not that she wasn't perfectly capable of looking out for herself in the crowd of a railway station, where she would undoubtedly have six or seven handsome young men fighting to carry her luggage, but his brush with Ysidro had frightened him.

How much *were* the vampires capable of knowing or guessing about those who began to piece together their trails? Perhaps Lydia was right—perhaps the warning was only intended to keep him away. There must be very few relatives and friends of victims who looked past the comfort of the "logical explanation," particularly, as Ysidro had pointed out, if there was no second set of suspicious circumstances to link it with. And yet . . .

He reminded himself firmly, as he joined the crowding throng on Euston Road, that Ysidro would have no way of

59

knowing that he had gone up to Oxford and returned twice that day, instead of once. *He might have guessed . . .*

Asher shook his head firmly. He was exhausted past the point, he was beginning to suspect, of rational thought. He'd been without unbroken sleep for over thirty-six hours; he was starting at shadows. That queer prickling on the back of his neck was nerves, he told himself, not the instincts of years of the secret life whispering to him. His uneasiness was simply the result of knowing he might be watched, rather than a certainty that he was.

He slowed his steps. Casually, he scanned the hurrying line of traffic, the crowds jostling along in the glare of the gas-lights—clerks and shopgirls bustling toward the Underground to catch the next train to whatever dreary suburb they called home, laborers eager for a cheap dinner of bubble and squeak and a few beers at the local pub. The gaslight was deceptive, making all faces queer, but he could see no sign of any whiter and more still than the rest.

Why, then, he wondered, did he have the growing conviction of missing something, the sensation of a blind spot somewhere in his mind?

At the corner, he crossed Gower Street, walking down its western side, casually scanning the stream of traffic passing before the long line of Georgian shops. There were a number of motorbuses and lorries, an omnibus and motorized cabs, and horse trams with gaudy advertising posters on their sides, but for the most part it was a crowding mêlée of horses and high wheels—delivery vans drawn by hairy-footed nags, open Victoria carriages, the closed broughams favored by doctors, and high-topped hansom cabs. He was very tired and his vision blurred; the glare of streetlight and shadow made it all the worse, but it would have to be risked. The traffic was thick and therefore not moving fast, except where an occasional cabby lashed his horse into a dash for a momentary hole. Well, there was always that chance . . .

Without warning, as he came opposite the turning of Little Museum Street that led to Prince of Wales Colonnade, Asher stepped sideways off the curb and plunged into the thick of the mêlée. With a shrill neigh, a cab horse pulled sideways nearly on top of him. Hooters and curses in exotic dialect—*What was a Yorkshireman doing driving a cab in London?* he wondered—pursued him across the road. The macadam was wet and slippery with horse dung; he ducked and wove between shifting masses of flesh, wood, and iron, and on the opposite side turned suddenly, looking back at the way he had come.

A costermonger's horse in the midst of the road flung up its head and swerved; a motorcab's brakes screeched. Asher wasn't sure, but he thought he saw a shadow flit through the glare of the electric headlamps.

Good, he thought, and turned down Little Museum Street, still panting from his exertions. *Pit your immortality against that one, my haemophagic friend.*

At Prince of Wales Colonnade he turned up the gas, leaving the window curtains open. He shed coat, bowler, scarf, and cravat and opened the valise he'd brought down from Oxford strapped to the narrow carrier of the motorcycle, now safely bestowed in a shed in the yard—half a dozen clean shirts, a change of clothing, clean collars, shaving tackle, and books. Whatever else he would need of the arcane paraphernalia of vampire-hunters, he supposed, could be purchased in London, and his ill-regulated imagination momentarily conjured a small shop in some dark street specializing in silver bullets, hawthorn stakes, and garlic. He grinned. With HARKER AND VAN HELSING painted above the door, presumably. Keeping himself in the line of sight of the window, he turned toward the dresser, frowned, and looked around as if something he had meant to bring were missing from its chipped marble top, then strode impatiently from the room.

He descended two flights of curving stairs at a silent run, and another to the basement. His landlady looked up, startled, as he passed the kitchen door, but he was already out in the tiny, sunken well of the areaway, standing on the narrow twist of moss-flecked stone steps to raise his eye level just above that of the pavement of the alley behind the house.

Evidently taken in by his feigned exit, the dark shape in the alley was still watching his lighted window. It stood motionless, nearly invisible in the dense gloom between the tall rows of houses; even so, he could make out the almost luminous whiteness of an unhuman face raised toward the light above. For a moment he kept his eyes on that dark form, scarcely daring to breathe, remembering the quickness of vampire hearing. Then, as if he had blinked, the figure was gone.

Thirty minutes later he had unpacked and put away the last of his things, changed clothes, and shaved. Though this refreshed him slightly, he still ached for sleep, feeling half-tempted to leave Ysidro to wait in his damp alley, if that was what he wanted to do, while he went to bed. But in that case, he was certain, the vampire would simply break in, Don Simon having apparently never heard that vampires could not enter any new place save at the bidding of one of its inhabitants.

On the other hand, Asher thought as he stepped from the lighted doorway of Number Six and strolled slowly up the pavement through the foggy darkness, what place in London could be called new? Six Prince of Wales Colonnade had obviously been standing since the latter days of George IV's reign; his own house in Oxford since Anne's. Don Simon Ysidro had been quietly killing in the streets of London since long before either place was built.

It crossed his mind to wonder about that ancient London— a thick gaggle of half-timbered houses, tiny churches, old stone monasteries near the river, and a dozen conflicting legal jurisdictions whose officers could not cross the street to apprehend criminals—a London whose jammed houses spilled across the bridge onto Southwark, with its cheap theaters where Shakespeare was learning his trade as an actor and cobbler-up of plays, and taverns where men who sailed with Francis Drake could be found drinking to the health of the red-haired queen . . .

"We cannot continue to meet this way," purred a soft, familiar voice beside him. "People will begin to talk."

Asher swung quickly around, cursing his momentary abstraction of mind. He was tired, true, but ordinarily he was more aware of someone that close to him.

Ysidro had fed; his face, though still pale, had lost the cold gleam that had caught Asher's attention in the gloom of the alley. His black cloak half concealed sable evening dress; his stiff white shirt front was of silk, and several shades paler, now, than the skin tailored so delicately over his cheekbones. As always, he was bare-headed, the high horns of his forehead gleaming faintly as they passed beneath the lamps of the houses round the square. Pearl-gray gloves clasped the crystal head of a slender ebony stick.

"I had a good mind to let you wait in that alley," Asher retorted. "You should know for yourself I'll have nothing to report except that, as you've seen, I've taken rooms here." He nodded back toward Number Six, indistinguishable from the other houses of the terrace, its glowing windows casting soft spangles of light on the trees of the narrow square across the street. "Now that we've spoken, I have every intention of going back to them and getting some sleep."

"Alley?" The vampire tilted his head a little, a gesture somehow reminiscent of a mantis.

"You didn't follow me as soon as it grew dark? Watch me from the alley while I was unpacking?"

Ysidro hesitated for a long moment, sifting through possible replies, picking and choosing what it was best to admit. Exasperated, Asher stopped upon the pavement and turned to face him. "Look. You don't trust me, I know, and I'd certainly be a fool to trust you. But it's you who's in danger, not me, and unless you give me more information—unless you stop this endless game of 'Animal, Vegetable, Mineral' with anything I want to know—I won't be able to help you."

"Is helping us your object?" The vampire tipped his head to one side, looking up the handspan of difference in their heights. There was no hint of sarcasm in his tone—he asked as if truly interested in the answer.

"No," said Asher bluntly. "But neither is killing you—not at the moment. You've made the stake pretty high for me. So be it. I've taken what precautions I can to keep Lydia safe, as you've probably guessed, and, believe me, it wasn't easy to come up with answers to her questions about why she had to leave Oxford. But I can't do anything until you're willing to answer some questions so I'll have something to work on."

"Very well." The vampire studied him for the count of several breaths, leisurely as if this quiet Bloomsbury square were a private room and entirely at his convenience. "I will meet you here tomorrow at this time, and we shall visit, as you say, the scene of the crime. As for what you saw in the alley . . ." His small silence lay in the conversation like a floating spot of light upon water, too deliberate to be called a hesitation; nothing in his face changed to indicate the flow of his thoughts. "That was not me."

Five

————

"Oh, Lord, yes," said the woman whom the shop sign identified as Minette as clearly as her accent indicated that the name had probably originally been Minnie. "That hair! A truer blonde could never have worn that vivid a gold—turn her yellow as cheese, it would. But it just picked up the green in her eyes. My gran used to tell me folk with that dark rim 'round the iris had the second sight."

She regarded Asher with eyes that were enormous, the most delicate shade of clear crystal blue and, though without any evidence of second sight whatsoever, clearly sharp with business acumen. Though he had shut the shop door behind him, Asher could still hear the din of traffic in Great Marlborough Street—the clatter of hooves, the rattle of iron tires on granite paving blocks, and the yelling of a costermonger on the corner—striving against the rhythmic clatter of sewing machines from upstairs.

He tugged down the very slightly tinted spectacles he wore balanced on the end of his nose—spectacles whose glass was virtually plain but which he kept as a prop to indicate harmless ineffectuality—and looked at her over their tops. "And did she tell you she was an actress?"

Minette, perched on a stool behind the white-painted counter, cocked her head a little, black curls falling in a tempting bunch, like grapes, on the ruffled ecru of her collar lace. "Wasn't she, then?" There was no surprise in her voice—rather, the curiosity of one whose suspicions are about to be confirmed.

Asher made his mouth smaller under his thick brown mustache and sighed audibly. But he held off committing himself until the dressmaker added, "You know, I thought there was something a bit rum about it. I know actresses at the Empire

65

don't get up and about 'til evening and are on 'til all hours, but they do get days off, you know. I always figured she spent them with one of her fancy men, and that was why she always insisted on coming in the evenings—between houses, she said. I will say for her she always did make it worth my while, which comes in handy in the off season when all the nobs are out of town."

"Fancy men," Asher reiterated, with another small sigh, and produced a notebook in which he made a brief entry. The blue eyes followed the movement, then flicked back to his face.

"You a 'tec?"

"Certainly not," he replied primly. "I am, in fact, a solicitor for a Mr. Gobey, whose son was—or is—a—er—friend of Miss Harshaw's—or Miss Branhame's, as she called herself to you. Did Mr. Gobey—Mr. Thomas Gobey—at any time buy Miss Lotta Harshaw anything here? Or pay her bills for her?"

Thomas Gobey's had been among the freshest-looking of the cards of invitation found in Lotta's reticule; it was better than even odds that, even if he were dead by now, the dressmaker hadn't heard of it. As it transpired, Gobey had, two years ago, paid seventy-five pounds to Minette La Tour for a gown of russet silk mull with a fur-trimmed jacket to match, ordered and fitted, like everything else Lotta had purchased there, in the evening.

Discreetly peering down over Mlle. Minette's shoulder as she turned the ledger pages, Asher noted the names of other men who had paid Lotta's bills, on those frequent occasions on which she did not pay them herself. Most were familiar, names found on cards and stationery in her rooms; poor Bertie Westmoreland had disbursed, at a quick estimate, several hundred pounds to buy his murderess frocks and hats and an opera cloak of amber cut velvet beaded with jet.

Six months ago, he was interested to note, Lotta had purchased an Alice-blue "sailor hat"—Lydia had one, and it was nothing Asher had ever seen any sailor wear in his life—with ostrich plumes, which had been paid for by Valentin Calvaire, at an address in the Bayswater Road.

He shut his notebook with a snap. "The problem, my dear Mademoiselle La Tour, is this. Young Mr. Gobey has been missing since the beginning of the week. Upon making inquiries, his family learned that Miss Harshaw—who is not, in fact, an actress—has also disappeared. At the moment we are simply making routine inquiries to get in touch with them—searching out possible friends or people who might know where they have gone. Did Miss Harshaw ever come here with female friends?"

"Oh, Lor' bless you, sir, they all do, don't they? It's half the fun of fittings. She came in once or twice with Mrs. Wren— the lady who introduced her to us, and a customer of long standing, poor woman. In fact it was because I *am* willing to oblige and do fittings at night by gaslight—for a bit extra, which she was always willing to pay up, like the true lady she is . . ."

"Do you have an address for Mrs. Wren?" Asher inquired, flipping open his notebook again.

The dressmaker shook her head, her black curls bouncing. She was a young woman—just under thirty, Asher guessed— and still building her clientele. The shop, though narrow and in a not quite fashionable street, was brightly painted in white and primrose, which went a long way toward relieving the dinginess of its solitary window. It took a wealthy and established modiste indeed to live comfortably and pay seamstresses and beaders during the off season when fashionable society deserted the West End for Brighton or the country—by August, Minette would probably have agreed to do fittings at midnight just to stay working.

"Now, that I don't, for she'll pay up in cash. In any case, I doubt they're really friends. Goodness knows how they met in the first place, for a blind man could see Mrs. Wren wasn't her sort of woman at all—not that it's Mrs. Wren's real name, I'll wager, either. She has a drunkard of a husband, who won't let her out of the house—she has to slip out when he's gone to his club to buy herself so much as a new petticoat. I suggest you look up her other friend, Miss Celestine du Bois, though if you was to ask me . . ." She gave him a saucy wink. ". . . Miss du Bois is about as French as I am."

Though thoroughly tickled and amused, Asher managed to look frostily disapproving of the whole sordid business as he stalked out of Mlle. La Tour's.

The address given by Celestine du Bois on those occasions when bills were sent to her and not to gentlemen admirers— one of whom, Asher had been interested to note, was also Valentin Calvaire—was an accommodation address, a tobacconist's near Victoria Station and reachable from any corner of London by Underground. Calvaire's address in the Bayswater Road was also an accommodation address, a pub—both vampires had picked up their letters personally.

"Does Miss du Bois pick up letters here for anyone else?" Asher inquired, casually sliding a half-crown piece across the polished mahogany of the counter. The young clerk cast a nervous glance toward the back of the shop, where his master was mixing packets of Gentlemen's Special Sort.

"For a Miss Chloé Watermeade, and a Miss Chloé Winterdon," the young man replied in a hushed voice and wiped his pointy nose. "She comes in—oh, once, twice a week sometimes, usually just before we puts the shutters up."

"Pretty?" Asher hazarded.

"Right stunner. Short little thing—your pocket Venus. Blond as a Swede, brown eyes I think—always dressed to the nines. Not a loafer'll speak to her, though, with the big toff what comes in with her half the time— Cor, there's a hard boy for you, and never mind the boiled shirt!"

"Name?" Asher slid another half crown across the counter.

The boy threw another quick look at the back shop as the owner's bulky form darkened the door; he whispered, "Never heard it," and shoved the half crown back.

"Keep it," Asher whispered, picked up the packet of Russian cigarettes which had been his ostensible errand, and stepped back into the street to the accompaniment of the tinkling shop bell.

Further investigation of Lotta's grave in Highgate yielded

little. It was a discouragingly easy matter to enter the cemetery by daylight—the narrow avenue of tombs behind the Egyptian gate and the dark groves and buildings around it were absolutely deserted, silent in the dripping gloom. Anyone could have entered and completely dismembered every corpse in the place uninterrupted, not just planted a stake through the heart and cut off the head.

With the door left wide, a thin greenish light suffused the crypt, but Asher still had to have recourse to the uncertain light of a dry-cell electric torch, whose bulky length he'd smuggled in under his ulster, as he examined every inch of the coffin and its niche. He found what might have been remains of a stake among the charred bones, though it was difficult to distinguish it from the fragments of rib or tell whether it was wood or bone—he wrapped it in tissue and pocketed it for later investigation. It told him nothing he did not already know. In a far corner of the tomb, he found a nasty huddle of bones, hair, and corset stays rolled in a rotting purple dress: the former occupant, he guessed, of the coffin Lotta had commandeered.

What remained of the afternoon he spent in a back office at the *Daily Mail*, studying obituaries, police reports, and the Society page, matching names with those on the list he'd assembled from the debris in Lotta's rooms and from Mlle. La Tour's daybooks. Poor Thomas Gobey, he saw, had in fact succumbed to a "wasting sickness" only months after the purchase of the russet silk dress. Asher noted the address—the Albany, which told him everything he needed to know about that unfortunate young man—and the names of surviving brothers, sister, parents, fiancée.

It had been disconcerting to recognize names on those cards of invitation which dated from a certain period seven or eight years ago. Poor Bertie Westmoreland had not been the only member of that gay circle of friends who had sent her invitations or bought her trinkets, though he was evidently the only one who had paid the ultimate price.

The others were lucky, he thought. Though Albert Westmoreland had died in 1900, the Honorable Frank Ellis—another of Lydia's suitors, though Asher had never met the boy—had bought the vampire a loden-green crepe tea gown as late as 1904. Who knew how many others had also kept up the connection?

He shivered, thinking how close Lydia had passed to that unseen plague then, and thanked all the strait-corseted deities of Society for the strict lines drawn between young girls of good family and the type of women with whom young men of good family amused themselves between bouts of "doing the pretty."

Lydia had been very young then. Eighteen, still living in her father's Oxford house and attending lectures with the tiny clump of Somerville undergraduates interested in medicine. The other girls had dealt as best they could with the comments, jokes, and sniggers of male undergraduates and deans alike— apologetic, frustrated, or defiant. For the most part Lydia had been blithely oblivious. She had been genuinely puzzled over her father's blustering rage when she'd chosen studying for Responsions over a Season on the London matrimonial mart; had she had brothers or sisters, he might well have threatened to disinherit her from the considerable family estates. Even her uncle, the Dean of New College, though her supporter, had been scandalized by the direction of her studies. Education for women was all very well, but he had been thinking in terms of literature and the Classics, not the slicing up of cadavers and learning how the human reproductive organs operated.

Asher smiled a little, remembering how even the most anti-woman of the dons, old Horace Blaydon, had come around to her support in the end, though he'd never have admitted it. "Even a damn freshman can follow what I'm doing!" he'd bellowed at a group of embarrassed male students during his lectures on blood pathology . . . he'd called Lydia a damned schoolgirl everywhere but in the classes. And the old man would have acted the same, Asher thought, even had his son not been head over heels in love with her.

Staring at the obituaries spread out on the grimy and ink-stained table top before him, Asher glanced at his list of Lotta's admirers since the early '80s and thought about Dennis Blaydon.

Lydia was probably the last person anyone would have expected to capture Dennis Blaydon's fancy, let alone his passionate and possessive love. Bluff, golden, and perfect, Dennis had been used to the idea that any woman he chose to honor with his regard would automatically accept his proposal; the fact that Lydia did not had only added to her fascination. Since the first time he'd seen her without her spectacles and decided that she was possessed of a fragile prettiness as well as great wealth, he had wanted her and had put forth all his multitude of charm and grace into winning her, to Asher's silent despair. Everyone in Oxford, from the Deans of the Schools to the lowliest clerk at Blackwell's, had accepted his eventual triumph in the Willoughby matrimonial lists as a matter of course. Her father, who considered one intellectual more than enough in the family, had been all in favor of it. To Horace Blaydon's query as to what his son would want with a woman who spent half her time in the pathology laboratories, Dennis had replied, with his customary shining earnestness, "Oh, she isn't really like that, Father." Presumably he knew better than she did what Lydia *was* like, Asher had thought bitterly at the time. Pushed into the background, a middle-aged, brown, nondescript colleague of her uncle, he could only watch them together and wonder how soon it would be that all hope of making her a part of his life would disappear forever.

Later he'd mentioned to Lydia how astonished he'd been that she hadn't married such a dazzling suitor. She'd been deeply insulted and demanded indignantly why he thought she'd have been taken in by a strutting oaf in a Life Guards uniform.

He grinned to himself and pushed the memories away. However it had transpired, Dennis and his other friends—Frank Ellis, the mournful Nigel Taverstock, the Honorable Bertie's Equally Honorable brother Evelyn—had had a close escape. Lotta had known them all. They were all the type of young men she liked—rich, good-looking, and susceptible. How long would it have been before she had chosen another of them as her next victim, when enough years had passed for them to forget poor Bertie's death?

What old score was Lotta paying off, he wondered, folding up his jotted lists, in the persons of those wealthy young men? He donned his scarf and bowler and slowly descended the narrow stairway past the purposeful riot of the day rooms, stopping briefly to thank his reporter friend with a discreet reference to "King and Country."

Had it been some ancient rape or heartbreak, he wondered as he descended the long hill of Fleet Street, its crush of cabs and trams and horse-drawn buses dwarfed by the looming shadow of St. Paul's dome against the chilly sky. Or merely the furious resentment of a cocky and strong-willed girl who hated the poverty in which she had grown up and hated still more the satin-coated young men whose servants had pushed her from the flagways and whose carriage wheels had thrown mud on her as they passed?

Judging by Mlle. La Tour's books, Celestine—or Chloé— seemed to be far more apt to pay for her own dresses than Lotta was, and the men who did buy her things were not the men of Lotta's circle. Their names were always different; evidently few men lived long enough to supply her with two hats. She was either more businesslike about her kills than Lotta, or simply less patient.

Was she, he wondered, also a "good vampire"? Like Lotta, did she savor those kisses flavored with blood and innocence? Did she make love to her victims?

Were vampires capable of the physical act of love?

The women would be, of course, he guessed—capable of faking it, anyway. As he descended to the Underground at the Temple a woman spoke to him in the shadows where the stair gave onto the platform, her red dress like dry blood in the gloom and her glottal vowels scrawling *Whitechapel* almost visibly across her painted mouth. Asher tipped his hat, shook his head politely, and continued down the steps, thinking: *They would have to feed somewhere else before undressing, to warm the death-chill from their flesh.*

Back at Prince of Wales Colonnade he returned to the now-neat catalogue of Lotta's finances. Seated tailor-fashion on the bed in his shirt sleeves, he sorted through the bills, letters, and cards, arranged by probable date. Mlle. La Tour had only served her vampire clientele for a few years, of course—the earliest entry for Mrs. Anthea Wren was in 1899. Lotta's pile of yellowing bills dated back through the nineteenth century and into the eighteenth, paid by men long dead to modistes whose shops were closed, sold, or incorporated with others'—a woman cannot keep the same dressmaker for seventy-five years if she herself doesn't age.

There were only four names on the recent invitations not accounted for either in the obituaries or last week's Society pages.

There was a Ludwig von Essel who had bought Lotta things between April and December of 1905 and was then heard of no more. There was Valentin Calvaire, who had first bought Lotta a yoked waist of *peau de soie,* embroidered and finished with silk nailheads, whatever those were, in March of this year; and a Chrétien Sanglot, who had sent her a card of invitation to meet him at the ballet and who not only picked up his mail at the same pub as Calvaire did but, to Asher's semitrained eye, at least, wrote in the same execrable French hand. And lastly, there was someone whose name appeared on bills dating from the Napoleonic Wars and on notes of Eaton's finest creamy pressed paper, less than two years old: someone who signed himself *Grippen* in black, jagged writing of a style not seen since the reign of James I.

He made an abstracted supper of bread and cold tongue while writing up a précis of his findings, lighting the gas somewhere in the midst of his work without really being aware of it. He doubted that the families of any of Lotta's victims were responsible for the killings, but if Lotta and Calvaire had hunted together, her victims' friends might be able to offer leads. Lydia would undoubtedly know where he could reach the Honorable Evelyn and Westmoreland's fiancée, whatever her name was, but again, he'd have to be careful—careful of the vampires, who must, he knew, be suspecting his every move, careful, too, of the killer, and careful of whatever it was that Ysidro wasn't telling him.

His Foreign Office habits prompted him to add a shorter list, just for the sake of off-chances: Anthea Wren; Chloé/Celestine Watermeade/Winterdon/du Bois; Valentin Calvaire/Chrétien Sanglot; Grippen. And looking up, he discovered to his utter surprise that it was quite dark outside.

He hadn't strolled for very long along the crowded flagways of Gower Street when he was suddenly aware of Ysidro beside him. The vampire's arrival was not sudden—indeed, once Asher glanced to his left and saw the slender form in its black opera cape at his elbow, he knew he had been there for some time. He had concentrated on watching for his appearance, but it seemed to him that something had distracted him—he could no longer remember what.

Annoyed, he snapped, "Would you stop doing that and just come up to me like a human being?"

Ysidro thought about it for a moment, then countered quietly, "Would you stop identifying all the exits from a house before you go into it? I have a cab waiting."

The houses in Half Moon Street were Georgian, red brick mellowed by time and somewhat blackened by the veiling soot of the city's atmosphere, but retaining the graciousness of moderate wealth. Most of them showed lights in their windows; in the gaslight, Asher could make out the minuscule front gardens—little more than a few shrubs clustered around the high porches—groomed like carriage horses. An indefinable air of neglect clung to Number Ten, three-quarters of the way down the pavement. Asher identified it as the result of a jobbing gardener who had not been kept up to his work, and front steps that went weeks or months without being scrubbed—fatal, in London.

"Housekeeping presents its own problems for the Undead, doesn't it?" he remarked quietly as they ascended the tall steps to the front door. "Either you keep servants or scrub your doorstep yourself—the windows here haven't been washed, either. Every doorstep on the street is brickbatted daily but this one."

"There are ways of getting around that." Ysidro's face, in profile against the reflection of the street lamps as he turned the key, retained its calmly neutral expression.

"I'm sure there are. But even the stupidest servant is going to notice something amiss when nobody orders any food or uses the chamber pots."

The vampire paused, the tarnished brass door handle in his gloved hand. He regarded Asher enigmatically, but in the back of his brimstone-colored eyes, for an instant, Asher half thought he glimpsed the flicker of amused appreciation. Then the black cloak whispered against the doorframe, and Ysidro led the way into the house.

"Edward Hammersmith was the youngest son of a nabob of the India trade, almost exactly one hundred years ago," he said, his light, uninflected voice echoing softly in the darkness. "The house was one of three owned by the family; Hammersmith asked for and got it from his father after he became vampire, thereafter gaining a reputation as the family's reclusive eccentric. He was in his way a reclusive eccentric even as a vampire— he seldom went out, save to hunt."

There was a faint scratch, the whiff of sulphur overriding for a moment the general foetor of must and dampness that filled what, by the sound of the echoes, must be a large and lofty front hall. The sharp sliver of matchlight confirmed this an instant later, racing in threads along tarnished gilt panel moldings and the graceful medallions of a high Adam ceiling, almost invisible overhead in the gloom. For that first moment, Ysidro's face, etched in those hard-cut shadows, seemed, too, something wrought of unbelievably delicate plaster. Then he touched the flame to the wick of an oil lamp that stood with several others on a Sheraton sideboard. The light leaped and slithered over the square mirror set in the sideboard, the web-shrouded lusters of the chandelier, the rounded glass of the smutted chimney which gray-gloved fingers, seeming so disembodied in the warm glow, fitted over the flame.

"Did he hunt with Lotta?"

"Upon occasion." Sprawling shadows followed them up the stairs, flowing over carved wall panels warped with damp. "They were both . . ." Again that pause, that sense of veering, like a small boat before gusty wind, into potentially less dangerous seas. "Edward liked a change now and then. Usually he hunted alone."

"Was he a 'good vampire'?"

"Not very." At the top of the first flight of stairs, Ysidro turned right and pushed open the double doors to what had once been the large drawing room. He held his lamp aloft as he did so, and the light scattered across books—literally thousands of books, crammed into makeshift shelves which not only lined every inch of wall nearly to the curve of the ceiling, but stacked the floor hip-deep in places. Little paths threaded between the stacks, like the beaten hoof lines or dassie tunnels that stitched unseen through the deep grass of the veldt. Towers of books ascended drunkenly from the two sideboards that loomed up out of the gloomy maze, and more were visible through the sideboards' half-opened caned doors; they piled the seats of every chair but one in untidy heaps. Bundles of papers were scattered over them or lay loose like leaves blown in an autumn wind. Bending down, Asher picked up one that lay nearest the door—brown and brittle as Lotta's oldest petticoats, it was sheet music of some obscure aria by Salieri.

Like a little island, there was an open place in the middle of the room, where grimy gray patches of lichenous carpet could be seen; it contained a chair, a small table supporting an oil lamp, a mahogany piano, and a harpsichord whose faded paint had nearly all flaked away. Sheet music heaped the floor under both instruments.

Beside him, Ysidro's calm voice continued, "There is a regrettable tendency among vampires to become like the little desert mice, which hoard shining things in holes."

"If passion for life is the core of your nature," Asher remarked, "that isn't surprising, but it must make for awkward domestic arrangements. Do all vampires do it?"

He looked away from the gloomy cavern, with its smells of mildew and damp, and found the vampire's strange eyes on him, a flicker of inscrutable interest in their depths. Ysidro looked away. "No." He turned from the door and moved toward the stairs at the far end of the hall, Asher following in his wake. "But I find the ones who do not rather boring."

It was on the tip of Asher's tongue to ask Ysidro what his hobby was, what passion filled the dark hours of his wakefulness when he was not actively hunting his prey, but he decided to take advantage of the Spaniard's relatively communicative mood with matters less frivolous. "Did Calvaire hunt with Lotta?"

"Yes. They became quite good friends."

"Were they lovers?"

Ysidro paused at the top of the second flight of stairs, the lamp held low in his hand, its light streaming up onto the narrow, fragile-boned face and haloing the webby stringiness of his hair, casting a blot of shadow on the low ceiling above. Carefully, he replied, "As such *vampires* understand the concept, yes. But it has nothing to do with either love or sexual union. Vampires have no sex—the organs are present, but nonfunctional. And neither Lotta nor Calvaire would even have considered the happiness of the other, which is what I understand to be one of the tenets of mortal love."

"Then what was between them?"

"A shared ecstasy in the kill." He turned to open the small door to the left of the stairs, then paused and turned back. "There is, you understand, an ecstasy, a surge of—I don't know what. A 'kick,' I think they call such things now—in the drinking of the life as it pours from the veins of another. It is not only in the taste of the blood, which I am told not all of us find pleasant, though I do. We are as much creatures of the psychic as the physical. We perceive things differently from human perceptions. We can taste—feel—the texture of the minds of others, and at no time more intensely than when the human mind is crying out in death. That is what we drink, as well as the blood—the psychic force, which answers to and feeds our own psychic abilities to control the minds of others."

He leaned in the doorway, cocking his head a little, so that the strands of his pale hair fell in attenuated crescents on his shoulders. The lamp in his hands touched face and hair, warming them, alike colorless, into the illusion of goldenness, like honey-stained ivory. Asher was conscious, suddenly, of the empty darkness of the house all around.

His voice continued, light and disinterested and absolutely without inflection, committing nothing of the enigma of his eyes. "As a vampire, I am conscious at all times of the aura, the scent, of the human psyches near me, as much as I am conscious of the smell of live blood. Some vampires find this almost unbearably exciting, which is why they play with their victims. There is never a time—I am told—when they are not thinking, *Shall it be now or later?* It is that which feeds us, more than the physical blood—it is that which we hunt. And that psychic hunger, that lust for the draining of the soul, is as far beyond the knife-edge instant before the cresting of sexual orgasm as that instant is beyond—oh—after you have had two pieces of marzipan, and you are wondering whether you might like a third one, or a bit of honey cake instead."

After a long while Asher said quietly, "I see."

"You don't," Ysidro replied, his voice whispering away in soft echoes against the darkness of the empty house, "and you can't. But you would do well to remember it, if ever you find yourself in the company of other vampires than I."

There were candles in all the wall sconces of the room where Edward Hammersmith had kept his coffin. Ysidro thrust one of them down into the lamp chimney to touch the flame, then went around the room, lighting the others, until the whole place blazed with a quivering roseate glow unlike the soft steadiness of gaslight. Asher noted boxes of candles stacked carelessly in every corner and puddles of wax, raised to lumpy stalagmites four and five inches high, on the Turkey carpets beneath each wax-clotted sconce. In the center of the room, the print of the coffin lay clear and dark upon the dusty rug, though the coffin itself was gone. There were no traces of ash or burning around the edge of that sharp, dust-free oblong—only a scuffed path leading there from the door, worn by Hammersmith's feet, and a few smudgy tracks in the dust, leading beyond it to the room's two tall windows. The heavy shutters that had covered these had been stripped of the three or four layers of black fabric that curtained them and ripped from their nails.

Skirting the tracks, Asher walked to the windows, holding the lamp to the wooden frames, then to the shutters themselves.

"My height or better," he remarked. "Strong as an ox—look at the depths of these crowbar gouges." Going back, he fished his measuring tape from his pocket—a miniature one of Lydia's in an ivory case—and noted the length and width of the track, and the length of the stride.

"The coffin was fitted with interior latches," Ysidro said, remaining where he had been in the restive halo of the candelabrum's light. "They were crude, of course—Danny King installed them for Neddy—and the lid had been simply levered off, tearing the screws from the wood."

"Where is it now?" Asher held the lamp high, to examine the plaster of the low ceiling above.

"We buried it. In the crypt of St. Albert Piccadilly to be precise—there being no danger of infection or smell."

"Who is 'we'?"

Ysidro replied blandly, "My friends and I." He half shut his eyes, and one by one the candles around the room began to go out.

He had spoken of a vampire's psychic powers—Asher had seen both Western mediums and Indian fakirs who could do much the same thing. Still, he picked up his lamp hastily and joined Ysidro by the door before the last of those firefly lights snuffed to extinction, leaving only darkness and the lingering fragrance of beeswax and smoke.

"Tell me about Danny King," he said, as they descended the stairs to the drawing room once again. "He was obviously a friend of Neddy's, if he fixed up his coffin for him. Was he a friend of Lotta and Calvaire's as well?"

"He was a friend to most of us," Ysidro said. "He had an unusually easygoing and amiable temperament for a vampire. He was an uneducated man—he had been a carriage groom, a 'tiger' they were called, to . . . during George IV's Regency for his father."

Asher found candles, and began lighting lamps and wall sconces in the vast drawing room as they had done upstairs. With the increased illumination, the clutter only appeared worse, mounds of music, of books, and of bundled journals scattered everywhere. Strewn among them were small bits of personal jewelry, stickpins and rings such as a man might wear, and literally scores of snuffboxes, most of them covered with dust and filled with snuff dried to brown powder, whose smell stung Asher's nose.

"Where did he keep his things?" He turned back to the tambour desk in one corner, its top, like everything else in the room, a foot and a half thick in books, in this case the collected works of Bulwer-Lytton—by its appearance, well-thumbed, too. Asher shuddered. The solitary vampire's evenings must have hung heavy indeed.

"He did not have many."

"He couldn't have carried them round London in a carpet-bag." Asher opened a drawer.

It was empty.

He brought the lamp down, ran his hand along the drawer's upper rim. There was dust on the first few inches, as if the drawer had been left ajar for years, but there was no dust in the bottom. He hunkered down to open the drawer below.

That, too, was empty. All the other drawers in the desk were.

"Had this been done when you and your friends found Hammersmith's body?"

Ysidro drifted over to the desk, contemplated the empty drawers for a moment, then let his disinterested gaze float back over the clutter of music pieces, books, and journals that bulged from every other available receptacle in the room. He reached into a corner of a bottom drawer, drew out a fragment of what had clearly been a bill for a servants' agency, paid in full in 1837. "I don't know."

Asher remained where he was for a moment, then stood, picked up the lamp, and threaded his way between stacks of books to the fireplace. It was clear that it had once contained books, too—they were now heaped at random all around it. He knelt and ran his fingers over their covers. The dust that lay thinly over everything else was absent. The fireplace was heaped with ashes—fresh.

He glanced up at the vampire, who, though Asher had not seen him do so, had joined him by the cold hearth.

"Burned," he said quietly, looking up into that narrow, haughty face. "Not taken away and sorted through to trace other vampires or possible contacts. Burned." He got to his feet, feeling again the stir of frustrated anger in him, the annoyance with Ysidro and his invisible cronies. For a moment he had thought he'd seen puzzlement on that thin-boned face and in the pucker of the slanting brows, but if he had it was gone now.

"Was this done at King's place also?"

"No."

"How do you know?"

"Because King did not keep such things," Ysidro replied smoothly.

Asher started to retort, *Then who kept them for him?* and stopped himself. The dark eyes were fixed on his face now, watching, and he tried to keep the sudden cascade of inferences out of his expression.

More calmly he said, "It all comes back to Calvaire. It started with him, and he seems to have been a linchpin of some kind in this; I'm going to have to see his rooms."

"No." As Asher opened his mouth to protest, Ysidro added, "That is as much for your protection as for ours, James. And in any case, he was not found in his rooms—in fact his body was not found at all."

"That doesn't mean he couldn't have been followed to them, taken away in his sleep, and killed."

81

Ysidro's eyes glinted angrily, but his voice remained absolutely level. "No one follows a vampire."

"Then why do you keep looking over your shoulder?" Disgusted, Asher picked up the lamp and strode through the mazes of books toward the door, the stairs, and the outer, saner world of the cold London night.

Six

At the British Museum Asher had his cab set him down and stood before the shut iron palings, listening to the rattle of wheels retreat away down Great Russell Street in the darkness. He knew this area of Bloomsbury the way a jack hare knew its burrows—alleys, mews, quiet squares, and pubs that had inconspicuous doors into back lanes and owners who didn't much mind who used them. It was one reason he'd chosen it.

The streets were relatively deserted, save for an occasional cab clattering its way to Euston or back from the theaters on Shaftesbury Avenue. He made his way swiftly down small turnings, across a mews behind Bedford Place and through a deep-shadowed lane between high houses whose sunken areaways formed an unbroken line of pits, like a protective moat, between pavement and rose-brick walls. He crossed Bruton Place and found the black slot of the alley that backed both it and Prince of Wales Colonnade. There in the moist and potholed darkness he halted, the stenches of a hundred garbage bins floating in the wet night air about him, and looked down the alley, letting his eyes grow accustomed to the dark.

The vampire was watching his window.

It took some moments for Asher to distinguish the dark angular shape against the blackness of the alley wall—had it possessed Ysidro's weird quality of stillness, he doubted he'd have ever been able to. But the vampire must have moved slightly, resolving what at first seemed to be paler patches on the bricks into an angular white face and big white hands, hands that picked uncomfortably at the ill-setting collar of a black coat. For a moment, Ysidro's words floated into Asher's mind: *I am conscious of the smell of live blood . . . You would do well to remember it, if ever you find yourself in the company of other vampires than I . . .*

To hell with it, he thought irritably, angry that they'd be following him, watching him. *With Ysidro as my only source of information, I'm certainly never going to get anywhere. If I'm working for them, they jolly well can't kill me.*

Yet, his mind added, as he began to walk down the alley.

The vampire swung around at his footstep. For a heart-shaking second, the creature's eyes caught the dim light, reflective as a cat's; Asher saw the gleam of the long teeth. A split instant before it would have charged to take him, he said, "Come here," in the tone that had always gotten the best results from Prussian farm hands, and it worked. The vampire checked, baffled, and then seemed to realize who he was.

He came shamblingly, without Ysidro's invisibility and without Ysidro's deadly grace, and Asher breathed again.

"And you are . . . ?"

The vampire stopped a few feet from him, staring at him with glinting eyes under a narrow, craggy brow. "Bully Joe Davies is me name," he said, in an accent which Asher placed within half a mile of New Lambeth Cut. He licked his lips, showing his fangs disquietingly, a nervous gesture which, after Ysidro's poise, made him seem incredibly gauche. Truculently he added, "You cry out or make a noise and I'll suck you dry afore the cat can lick her ear."

Asher studied him for a moment with deliberate contempt. He was a man in his twenties, long-armed, raw-boned, and awkward-looking in a black suit that did not fit well—that hard little nut of a face would have looked more at home above the corduroy work pants and frieze jacket of a mill hand or docker. Black hair was slicked back under a five-shilling derby; there was blood under the uncut nails.

"If you didn't have some reason to speak to me, I assume you would have done that already," Asher retorted. "Days ago, in fact . . . Why have you been following me?"

Davies took a step closer. The smell of old blood in his clothes was repulsive. When he spoke his whisper was rank as a charnel house. "That toff Ysidro—he gone?"

Asher's every sense of danger came alert. "I haven't the faintest idea," he said coldly. "He could have followed me back here. We parted rather abruptly. I haven't seen or heard him, but then, one doesn't."

Bully Joe threw a swift glance around him, and Asher saw fear gleam in his bloodshot blue eyes. He edged closer still, his long-nailed fingers picking at Asher's sleeve, his voice lowered to a hoarse breath. "Has he spoke of me?" he whispered. "Does he know of me?"

With an effort Asher kept the surge of overwhelming curiosity out of his voice. "Shouldn't he?"

The hand closed around his arm, reminding Asher of that other tenet of vampire lore—that they had the strength of ten men. Ysidro certainly had. "If you speak of me, if you say aught of me, I'll kill you," Davies breathed. "They'd kill me, they would—Grippen, and that chilly Papist bastard Ysidro—if they knew about me, knew Calvaire had made me. First, I thought it was Grippen and the others what done for Calvaire. Then I heard them others had been killed—Neddy Hammersmith and Lottie. Christ, they was Grippen's own get! Sodding bastard'd never kill his own! And now I'm being followed, being watched . . ."

"By whom?" Asher demanded sharply. "How do you know?"

"Dammit, you think I'd be askin' a mortal man if I knowed that?" Bully Joe swung around, twisting his hands, his hard face contorting with rage rooted in fear, and Asher fought not to step away from him, not to show his own fear. "Summat's after me, I tell you! And I hear the others talking— Coo, ain't that a tickler? I can stand acrost the street in the shadows and hear every word they says! And they say there's some bloke killin' us wi' a stake in the heart, just like in them old books, and lettin' the sun in! You gotta protect me, same as you're helpin' the others . . ."

His hands closed around Asher's sleeve again, and Asher

thought fast. "I will protect you," he said, "if you'll help me, answer my questions. Who are you? Why do the others want to kill you?"

The calm authority in his voice seemed to quieten Davies, but the vampire's reply was still sulky and impatient. "I told you, I'm Calvaire's get. Grippen's the Master of London. None of the others'll dare get a fledgling wi'out his say-so. Grippen don't want none in London but his own get, his own slaves . . ."

"But Calvaire wasn't Grippen's get."

Davies shook his head, goaded, weary, confused. "Narh. He come in from Paris, he said, though he talked English like a regular man. He made me, said I'd live forever, have all the gelt I wanted, never die! He never said it'd be like this!" Desperation crept into his tone. "For a month now I been livin' from pillar to post, never sleepin' the same place twicet! Hidin' from Grippen, hidin' from Ysidro . . . Calvaire said he'd take care of me, show me what I got to know! But it's all gone wrong now! Everything's all dinnin' and burnin' in my ears, smellin' the blood of every livin' soul . . ."

He broke off, licking his lips, his burning eyes fixing on Asher's throat, like a drunkard forgetting his thought in mid-sentence. Slowly, thickly, he whispered, "I killed a girl last night—Chink girl, down by the Limehouse—and I don't dare hunt another for a couple o' days at least. But my brain's burnin' for it! I dunno how the others do it, kill and not get the flatties down on 'em . . ."

Asher felt the hand tighten again around his arm, begin to draw him inexorably closer to that twisted, fanged face. With deliberate calm, he asked, "And now you're being followed?"

Davies flinched, as if he'd been shaken from sleep; he loosed his grip and stepped back, wiping his lips with a hand that shook. "I dunno," he whispered. "Sometimes it's like I can feel summat in the night, watchin' me, and I'll turn around and there's nuthin'! Other times . . . I dunno." He shook his head, his lip lifting back from stained yellow fangs.

"I don't want to die! I died once already. I went through it with Calvaire! I wouldn't of let him do this to me, 'cept that I didn't want to die! Christ Jesus, I didn't know it'd be like this!"

There was a noise at the end of the alley. Davies swung around, his hand tightening with bone-crushing force on Asher's elbow. Through the pain, Asher was still interested to note that no sweat stood out on the vampire's white face. A man and a teen-age boy stood momentarily framed in the lighter slot of the alley's mouth, the boy looking coyly away as the man bent his head down. Then, as if they heard Asher's involuntary gasp of pain, they paused, peering sightlessly into the darkness. After an uneasy moment they moved away.

Davies let go of his arm, wiped his lips again. "I got to go," he said, his voice thick.

It was Asher's turn to catch at his sleeve. "Can you take me to Calvaire's lodgings?"

"Not tonight." The vampire glanced nervously around and flexed his big hands. "I ain't killed yet tonight and I need it bad. Just bein' this close to you turns my brain wi' the wantin' of it. Like me dad, when he gets the cravin' for the gin." He shot a quick, sullen glance at Asher, daring him to disapprove or to show fear.

Asher had dealt with enough drunkards and addicts to know that, if he did either, Bully Joe might very well kill him from sheer pique. He was uncomfortably aware, too, of Ysidro's warning, and of how long the interview had lasted already. What effect would that psychic pungence have on a mind not oriented, not taught how to handle the influx of new sensation?

"Tomorrow night, then?"

"Late," Davies said, his eyes turning once again to the alley mouth. "I'll come here and wait for you, after I been and killed. Seems like, until I do, I can't properly think. I'll keep away from the coppers somehow. It keeps hurtin' at me and hurtin' at me. Christ, I saw my sister last night—Madge, the youngest, sixteen she is. She'll still come and see me, look for me—she don't know what happened to me, nor why I left me old lodgings, nor nuthin'. I hadn't killed yet, and by God it was all I could do to keep from sinkin' my fangs into her!

"You seen the others," he went on, with a gesture of helpless rage which seemed to abort itself midsweep into a kind of futile wave. "You talked to other vamps, now, you must have. Are they all like this? Killin' the ones they love, just because they're handy-like? Calvaire said he'd teach me, tell me, help me to get on, but he's dead now. And the one that done for him is comin' after me . . ."

He swung wildly around at another sound, but it was only a girl, sixteen or so and plain as an old boot, stepping, candle in hand, out into an areaway from the tradesmen's door of one of the houses that backed onto the alley. Asher heard the flap of a shaken rag and the spattering of crumbs on the cement and, beside him, the soft hiss of the vampire's murmured, "Ahhh . . ." In the faint reflection of the light, Asher saw the young man's eyes, blue and shallow in life, blaze with the strange inner fire of the Undead.

Bully Joe muttered thickly again, "I got to go."

Asher's hand clinched down on the vampire's arm, holding him back. The vampire whirled, enraged, his other hand lifted to strike, and Asher met the hungry devil-eyes coldly, daring him to go through with it. After a moment Bully Joe's arm came down slowly. Beyond his craggy silhouette, Asher saw the smudge of candle flame disappear into the house from which it had come.

An evil anger twisted at the fanged mouth. "So it's bargainin' now," Bully Joe whispered. "You know, and because of it I got to do what you say. Yeah, Calvaire played that game, too. I'll tell you this and I'll tell you that, if you do as you're bid . . . faugh!" His arm twisted free as if Asher's hand had been the weak grip of a child. They faced each other in silence, but Asher felt nothing of the terrible dreamy coercion of the vampire mind—only a kind of inchoate buzzing in his head, as if Bully Joe were groping to do that which he had no notion of how to accomplish. Then this, too, faded, and Bully Joe passed his hand across his mouth again in a gesture of frustration and defeat.

"You hadn't any choice with Calvaire," Asher said quietly,

"and you haven't any now, if I'm to find this killer before he—or she—finds you. Be here tomorrow night after midnight. I'll let you know anything I've found."

"Right," Davies muttered, backing a few paces away, a dark bulk against the paler darkness of the alley mouth. "I'll be here. But I tell you this right now, Professor: You tell Ysidro or any of them others about me or about where you're goin', and I'll break your back."

It was meant to be his exit line, so Asher spoiled it by saying coolly, "You're a vampire, Bully Joe. Do you think I, as a mortal man, can keep Ysidro from following me if he wants to? Don't be ridiculous."

The vampire snarled, his long fangs glinting in the dark, trying, Asher guessed, to collect a fitting rejoinder.

He wasn't up to it, however. After a long pause, he turned and strode off up the alley toward the gaslights of Bruton Place. Asher felt, as clearly as if the vampire had pointed and said, *Look over there,* the momentary urge to turn his head, to check for danger in the dark pit of the areaway closest to him. He forced his eyes to remain on Bully Joe and so saw him silhouetted briefly against the street lamps at the alley's narrow mouth. Then he was gone.

Asher threw a quick glance down the areaway to reassure himself that the urge of danger had been, in fact, only a clumsy effort at the psychic glamour which Ysidro wielded so adeptly. Then he pulled his brown ulster more closely about him and walked up the alley and around the corner, to the dim lights and freer air of Prince of Wales Colonnade.

From the doorway of Number 109, Lydia watched the vampire emerge into Bruton Place. She'd seen Asher crossing that street fifteen minutes earlier when she'd come to the front parlor to buy a stamp from her landlady—she was wearing her specs, as she did when working—but had meticulously taken no notice. When she'd seen the tall, brown, rather melancholy-looking figure turn into the alley which she knew led through to his own lodgings, she'd merely assumed he was playing at spies, something he sometimes did in Oxford sheerly out of habit. Nevertheless, a glimpse of him was a glimpse of him. *Schoolgirlish,* she thought, swiftly climbing the narrow oval of stairs and hurrying down the hall to her little bedroom at the back of the house, *but there you have it.* After living with him for six years, she was surprised at the depth of her need to see him, if only for a second.

And then she had seen the vampire.

The only light in the alley was what leaked down from the windows of the houses on both sides, but with no light on in her own room—that was another thing she'd learned from James—Lydia could see fairly well. They were talking when she came to the window, moving the lace curtain only barely; James' back was to her, and in the gloom she could see the cold, inhuman white of the other man's face, and realized with a shiver that he must have been waiting down there.

A vampire. The Undead.

They were real.

She had not doubted James' story—not consciously, she reflected, at any rate. But the quickening of her heart, the coldness of her hands, told her now that there had been a part of her that had not really believed. Not *really.*

Until now.

Even at this distance, her trained eye picked out the coloring of a corpse, the different way he held himself and moved. This man did not fit the description of Don Simon Ysidro—another vampire, then. After the first shock her whole soul swelled into one vast itch to get a closer look at the tongue and mucous membranes of the eyes, at the hair follicles and nails which grow after death, and at the teeth. She'd spent the last thirty-six hours, more or less, in reading, and between the drier tomes of leasehold and quitclaim at the Public Records Office, she'd come home to peruse the trunkful of medical journals she'd brought along—articles on porphyria, pernicious anemia, and the various nervous disorders which constituted the "logical explanations" so dear to the heart of modern man. She realized that she, too, had wanted them to be true.

Now . . .

Keeping an eye on the window, she pulled her medical bag to her from its place near the bed. By touch in the dark, she found her two largest amputation knives and slipped their cased lengths into her coat pocket as she put the garment on. They were polished steel, not the supernaturally recommended silver; she cast her mind about for possibilities for a moment, then dug in the bag again for her little bottle of silver nitrate and slipped that in her pocket as well. If worse came to worst, she could always throw it and hope the legends were right.

There was no time for anything more. Already James and the vampire were parting, the vampire pulling free of James' grip and stepping back; Lydia fancied she saw the glint of eyes in the shadows. For a moment, despite the fact that she knew the vampires had hired him and would not harm him under the circumstances, she felt afraid for him, for there was murder latent in every line of that half-crouching dark form. Then, with an angry gesture, the vampire moved away.

With swift silence, Lydia was down three flights of stairs, coiling up her hair and pinning on a hat on the run; people who knew her to take three hours assembling herself for a party would not have credited her speed in an emergency. She was waiting in the dark of the entryway when the shambling, raw-boned shape of the young man emerged from the alley. She had no intention of getting anywhere near him, nor of coming close enough to let herself be seen; even from half a block's distance, it would be possible to observe how he moved, how those closer to him would be affected by the aura—if there was one—that James had described. It was the best she could do for now.

They were close to Shaftesbury Avenue. Lydia followed the vampire southeast, her high heels tapping like a deer's tiny hooves on the pavement. There were still plenty of people about, crowding the sidewalks under the glare of the gaslights in throngs that had not the purposeful hurry of the day. Women in bright clothes strolled on the arms of gentlemen, laughing and leaning their shining curls close to dark shoulders; jehus, bundled in coats and scarves against the bite of the October night, read newspapers on the high boxes of their cabs in the street-side ranks, their horses breathing steam like dragons. Groups of young swells, of impecunious medical students, and of home-going shop clerks jostled along the pavement. Lydia found it hard to keep the vampire in sight.

And yet, she saw, the vampire was having his own problems. Part of this was because people simply did not look at him, or apparently did not see him when they did, with the result that they did not move aside, as people did for her. The irony of that entertained her a good deal as she moved along, hands in pockets—she'd mislaid her gloves and had no time to hunt for them—in his wake. She herself had no trouble following him when the ever-growing crowds permitted, but, then, she knew what to look for. He was tall. The cheap black bowler floated over the general crowd like a roach in a cesspool.

He turned one corner and another. The crowds thinned out, and Lydia had to fall back again, glad that her coat was of a nondescript color—unusual for her, and in this case deliberate—and wishing her hair were, too, where it showed beneath the brim of her hat. The vampire was moving slower now, and Lydia observed that people now moved aside from him, and treated him as if he were there.

So it was something that came and went, she thought.

And there was something else.

They were near Covent Garden, a tangle of little streets and alleys, the cramped, cheap lodgings of servants and seam-stresses, costermongers hawking at half price from carts what they couldn't get rid of earlier in the day, and the smell of rotting vegetables piled with the dung in the gutters. A couple of loun-gers outside a pub whistled admiringly and called out to her. She ignored them and hoped the vampire did, too. Though she vastly preferred the quieter life of Oxford for her work, at her father's insistence she'd spent a certain amount of time in Lon-don, but the graceful houses of Mayfair, the green spaciousness of Hyde Park and St. James, and the quiet opulence of the Savoy and Simpson's might have been in another city. This tangle of wet cobblestones, loud voices, and harsh lights was alien to her experience; though she wasn't particularly frightened—after all, she knew she had only to summon a cab and return to Bruton Place—she knew she would have to go carefully.

She saw the vampire turn into a little court whose broken cobbles leaked black water into the wider street; she ducked her head and passed its entrance swiftly, not daring even to look. In this part of London, circling a block was always a chancy business, but she took the next turning and hurried her steps down the insalubrious and deserted court until she found a dirty alley that seemed to lead through.

She hesitated for a long time—nearly a minute, which, given her quarry and the danger she knew she would be in, was long. The alley, what she could see of it, was dark and crooked. Though the houses of the little court at her back gave evidence of life in the form of lights burning in the windows and shadows crossing back and forth over the cheap curtains or baldly un-curtained glass, all the ground-floor shops had been locked up, and the wet, narrow pavement lay deserted under the chill drift of evening mist. She shivered and huddled deeper into her coat, for the first time conscious of why so many people disliked being alone. The vampire was in the next court. She had a strong suspicion that he had gone there to seek his prey.

Her hand closed tighter on the sheath of the amputation knife in her pocket. A six-inch blade seemed like a broadsword in the dissecting room; she wondered if, put to it, she could bring herself to use it against living flesh.

Or even, she added with involuntary humor, *Undead. One way of getting a blood sample, but risky.* If the other vampires didn't know of her connection with James, they would have no reason for sparing her life.

And James would be furious.

Like the whisper of a breath, of a footfall, or of the half consciousness of the smell of blood, she knew there was some-one behind her.

She swung around, her heart hammering, galvanized into terror such as she had never felt before, the knife whipping out of her pocket, naked in her slim hand. For a moment she stood, flattened to the brick of the corner of the alley wall, the scalpel held before her, facing . . . nothing.

The court behind her was deserted.

But, she thought, only just.

Her glance dropped instantly to the wet pavement behind her. No footprint but her own little smudges marred its moist shine. Her hand was shaking—it, her mouth, and her feet all felt like ice as all the blood in her body retreated from her extremities in reaction to the shock. She noted the effect with a clinical detachment, at the same time conscious of the heat of her breath, and how it smoked as it mingled with the mists that had begun to drift through this dark and tangled part of the city. *Had it been this misty before?*

There had been something there. She knew it.

A smell, she thought, her mind taking refuge in analysis while her eyes swept here and there, to the shadows which suddenly clotted blacker, more twisted, beneath the doorways and shutters of the locked and empty shops—a smell of blood, of rot, of something she had never smelled before and never wanted to smell again . . . A smell of something wrong.

And close to her. So terrifyingly close.

It was perhaps forty seconds before she gained the courage to move from the protection of the wall at her back.

She kept as close to the wall as she could, making her way back swiftly to the populated noises of Monmouth Street; she felt every doorway and every projection of the shop fronts concealing invisible threats. As she passed the entrance to the next court, movement caught her eye. She turned her head to see a girl, fourteen or fifteen and dressed in secondhand finery from the slop shops of the East Side, an exuberantly trimmed orange and blue frock standing out in the darkness. She heard the nasal voice say, "Well, Mister, wot yer doin' 'ere, all by yourself?" It was young and coaxing and already with a professional's edge.

She stood for a long moment, sickened, the knife still in her lowered hand, wondering if she should call out. Beyond the girl's form, in the black darkness of the court, she could see nothing, but half felt the gleam of eyes.

She quickened her steps, cold and shaking, and hailed the first cab she saw to take her back to Bloomsbury.

What little sleep she achieved that night was with the lamp burning beside her bed.

The morning post brought Asher an envelope without return address, containing a blank sheet of paper in which was folded a cloakroom ticket from the British Museum. He packed up the précis of yesterday's findings, the list of relatives of Lotta Harshaw's victims, and the measurements of tracks and footprints taken at Half Moon Street and put them in a brown satchel, which he took with him to the Museum and checked in to the cloakroom. After half an hour's quiet perusal of court records of the brief reign of Queen Mary I in the vast hush of that immense rotunda, he slipped an envelope from his pocket, addressed it to Miss Priscilla Merridew, sealed his own cloakroom ticket in it, affixed a penny stamp, and left, presenting the ticket he'd received by post and receiving another brown satchel whose contents, opened in his own rooms after posting his missive to Lydia, proved to be several folded sheets covered with his wife's sprawling handwriting.

Even a preliminary list of houses in London which had not changed hands, either by sale or by testamentary deposition, in the last hundred years was dauntingly long. Given the vagaries of the Public Records Office, there were, of course, dozens of reasons why a piece of property would have no records attached to it—everything from bequests by persons living outside Britain to purchase by corporations—but Asher was gratified to note that 10 Half Moon Street was on the list. And it was a start, he thought, a preliminary list against which to check . . .

A name caught his eye.

Ernchester House.

For a moment he wondered why it was familiar, then he remembered. One of the names Lotta had used on old dressmaker's bills was Carlotta Ernchester.

Lydia was not at the Public Records Office in Chancery Lane when Asher got there, a circumstance which he thought just as well. Though by daylight he knew he had nothing to fear from the vampires of London, he was uneasily conscious that the man he was stalking was not of the Undead and, like himself, was able to operate both in the daytime and the nighttime worlds.

He established himself at a desk in the most inconspicuous corner of the reading room and sent in his requests with the clerk, aware that the killer could, in fact, be any of the nondescript men at the various desks and counters around the long room, turning over leaves of laborious copperplate in the old record books, searching the files of corporation and parish records for houses which had never been sold, or bodies which had never been buried. The chap at the far side of the room with the graying side whiskers looked both tall enough and strong enough to have wrenched loose the shutters from Edward Hammersmith's window. Asher leaned idly around the edge of his desk and studied the man's square-toed boots with their military gloss. Far too broad for the single clear track he'd been able to measure.

A tall man and a strong one, he thought, staring abstractedly through the long windows down at the courtyard and at the frilly Gothic fantasies of the roof line beyond. A man capable of tracking a vampire? Even an inexperienced fledgling like Bully Joe Davies? Or was Bully Joe, disoriented and maddened by the flood of new sensations and now further confused by his master Calvaire's death, merely prey to a chronic case of what Asher himself had occasionally experienced abroad—the conviction of perpetual pursuit. God knows, Asher thought, if even Ysidro had picked up the trick of glancing continually over his shoulder, what shape would Davies be in after—a month, had he said, since Calvaire's death?

And he made a mental note of the fact that Bully Joe seemed in no doubt that Calvaire had, in fact, been "done for," and had not merely disappeared, as Ysidro had once hypothesized.

It was likelier that the killer, like himself, was a man of education, able to track by paper what he could not track in the flesh.

Arguably, he was a man of patience, Asher thought, running his fingers along the dusty leaves of the St. Bride's parish roll book; a man willing to go through the maddening process of sifting records, names, deeds, and wills, checking them against whatever clues he might have found in the vampires' rooms before he—or someone else—burned it all.

Certainly a man of resolution and strength, to slice off the head of the blonde woman in Highgate Cemetery with a single blow.

And—perhaps most odd—a man who had sufficiently believed in vampires in the first place to make his initial stalking, his initial kill, which would conclusively prove to him that his prey, in fact, existed at all.

That in itself Asher found quite curious.

For that matter, he thought uneasily, turning back to his work, it might be Ysidro or the mysterious Grippen whom Bully Joe sensed on his heels. If that were the case, Asher knew he stood in double danger, for if Bully Joe realized it was Ysidro on his trail, he would never believe Asher had not betrayed him.

After a tedious examination of ward records and parish rolls, he ascertained that Ernchester House had been sold in the early 1700s by the Earls of Ernchester, whose town house it had once been, to a Robert Wanthope. The house itself stood in Savoy Walk, a name only vaguely familiar to Asher as one of the innumerable tiny courts and passageways that laced the oldest part of London in the vicinity of the Temple. Oddly enough, there was no record of any Robert Wanthope having ever purchased any other property in London, in St. Bride's parish or any other.

Ten minutes' walk to Somerset House and a certain amount of search in the Wills Office sufficed to tell Asher that Mr. Wanthope had never made a will—an unusual circumstance in a man who had sufficient funds to buy a town house. A brief visit to the Registry in another wing of the vast building informed him, not much to his surprise, that no record existed of Wanthope's death or, for that matter, his birth.

In the words of Professor Dodgson, Asher thought, *curiouser and curiouser*. Almost certainly an alias. Ernchester House had not surfaced in any record whatsoever since.

It was nearly five when he left Somerset House. The raw wind was blowing tatters of cloud in over the Thames as he crossed the wide, cobbled court, emerging on the Strand opposite the new Gaiety Theatre. For a few minutes he considered seeking out Savoy Walk, but reasoned that there would be no one stirring in Ernchester House until dark—and in any case there was something he very much wanted to buy first.

So he turned his steps westward, dodging across the tangles of traffic in Piccadilly and Leicester Square. Lights were beginning to go up, soft and primrose around the wrought-iron palisade of the public lavatories in Piccadilly Circus, brighter and more garish from the doors of the Empire and Alhambra. He quickened his pace, huddling in the voluminous folds of his ulster and scarf as the day faded. He had no idea how soon after sunset the vampires began to move, and above all, he did not want Ysidro to spot him now.

The fashionable shops were still open in Bond Street. At Lambert's he purchased a silver chain, thick links of the purest metal available; he stopped in a doorway in Vigo Street to put it on. The metal was cold against his throat as it slid down under his collar. As he wrapped his scarf back over it, he was torn between a vague sensation of embarrassment and wondering whether he shouldn't have invested in a crucifix as well.

But silver was spoken of again and again as a guard against the Undead, who far transcended the geographical and chronological limits of Christianity. Perhaps the crucifix was merely a way of placing a greater concentration of the metal near the big vessels of the throat. He only hoped the folklore was right.

If it wasn't, he thought, he might very well be dead before morning.

Or, at least according to some folklore, worse.

Now that was curious, he mused, jostling his way back

through the thickening press of young swells and gaily dressed Cyprians around the Empire's wide, carved doors. The folklore all agreed that the victims of vampires often became vampires themselves, but at no time had Ysidro spoken of his own victims, or those of the other mysterious hunters of the dark streets, as joining the ranks of their killers. Bully Joe Davies had spoken of a vampire "getting" fledglings, as Calvaire had "gotten" him—evidently against the commands of the master vampire Grippen.

So it wasn't automatic—not that Asher had ever believed that it was, of course. Even without Lydia's projection of the number of victims a single vampire might kill in the course of a century and a half, logic forbade that simple geometrical principle; the vampires kept on killing, but the world was not innundated with fledgling vampires.

There was something else involved, some deliberate process . . . a process jealously guarded by the Master of London.

Grippen.

A big toff, the tobacconist's clerk had said. A hard boy, and never mind the boiled shirt.

Grippen's get, Bully Joe Davies had said. Grippen's slaves.

Was Ysidro? It was hard to picture that poised, pale head bending to anyone.

Yet there was so much that was being hidden: an iceberg beneath dark waters; wheels within invisible wheels; and the power struggles among the Undead.

He left the streaming traffic of Drury Lane, the jumbled brightness of Covent Garden behind him. Crossing the Strand again, he got a glimpse of the vast brooding dome of St. Paul's against the darkening bruise of the sky. The lanes were narrow here, lacing off in all directions, canyons of high brown buildings with pubs flaring like spilled jewel boxes at their corners. Somewhere he heard the insouciant clatter of buskers, and a woman's throaty laugh.

He passed Savoy Walk twice before identifying it—a cobbled passage, like so many in the Temple district, between two rows of buildings, not quite the width of his outstretched arms. It curved a dozen feet along, cutting out the lights from Salisbury Place. His own footsteps pierced the gloom in a moist whisper, for fog was rising from the nearby river.

The tiny passage widened to a little court, where the signs of small shops jutted out over the wet, bumpy stones—a pawnbroker's, a second-hand bookshop, a manufacturer of glass eyes. All were empty and dark, crouching beneath the tall gambreled silhouette of the house at the rear of the court, a jewel of interlaced brickwork and leaded glass, nearly black with soot. The lights of the populous districts to the north and east caught in the drifting fog to form a mephitic, dimly luminous backdrop behind a baroque jungle of slanting roofs and chimneys. The house, too, was dark; but as Asher walked toward it, a light went up in its long windows.

The steps were tall, soot-stained, and decorated with decaying lions in ochre stone. There was long stillness after the echoes of the door knocker died. Even listening closely, Asher heard no tread upon the floor.

But one leaf of the carved double door opened suddenly, framing against the dark honey of oil light the shape of a tall woman in ivory faille, her reddish-dark hair coiled thick above a face dry, smooth, and cold as white silk. By the glow of the many-paned lamps behind her, he could see the Undead glitter of her brown eyes.

"Mrs. Farren?" he said, using the family name of the Earls of Ernchester, and it surprised her into replying.

"Yes." Then something changed in her eyes.

"Lady Ernchester?"

She didn't answer. He felt the touch of that sleepiness, that mental laziness of not paying attention, and forced it away; he saw in those glittering eyes that she felt that, too.

"My name is Dr. James Asher. I'd like to talk to you about Danny King."

Seven

———

C ome in." She stepped back from the door, gestured him to a salon whose pilastered archway opened to the right of the hall. Her voice was low and very sweet, without seductiveness or artifice of any kind. As he followed her, Asher was acutely conscious of the thudding of his own heart. He wondered if she was, too.

The salon was large, perfectly orderly, but had a chilled air of long neglect. One dim oil lamp on the corner of a curlicued Baroque mantelpiece picked out the edges of the furnishings nearest it—graceful Hepplewhite chairs, the curve of a bow-front cabinet, and the claret-red gleam of carved mahogany in a thick archaic style. Asher wondered who would dust the place and brickbat that dingy front step, now that Danny King was dead.

Mrs. Farren said, "I've heard of you, Dr. Asher." As in Ysidro's, there was neither commitment nor emotion in her voice. Standing before her in the small pool of lamplight, he could see the gleam of her protruding fangs, and the fact that, except when she spoke, the creamy thickness of her breasts did not rise or fall.

"My apologies for intruding," he said, with a slight bow. "If you've heard of me you know I'm seeking information— and if you know Don Simon Ysidro, you probably know I'm not getting much. Was Daniel King your servant?"

"Yes." She nodded once. Unlike Ysidro, though her voice was absolutely neutral, there was a world of brightness, of watchfulness, of feeling in her large, golden-brown eyes. "He was my husband's," she added after a moment, and inwardly Asher sighed with relief—he'd been afraid for a moment that all vampires were as utterly uncommunicative as Don Simon.

"His carriage-groom—a tiger, they used to call them. That was during our last . . ." She hunted for the word for a moment, dark brows flinching slightly together, and suddenly seemed infinitely more human. "Our last period of being of the world, I suppose you could say. We had a number of servants. In those days such extravagant eccentricities as barring a whole wing of the house and leading an utterly nocturnal existence were more accepted by servants than they are now. But Danny guessed."

She stood with her back to the mantelpiece, her hands clasped lightly before her slender waist, in an attitude regal and slightly archaic, like a stiffly painted Restoration portrait. In life, Asher guessed, she had been a little plump, but that was all smoothed away now, like any trace of archaism in her speech. Her gown with its flared tulip skirt was modern, but the baroque pearls she wore in her ears could only have been so extravagantly set in the days of the last of the Stuart kings.

When she moved, it had the same unexpectedness Ysidro's movements did, that momentary inattention, and then finding her at his side. But she only said, "I suppose now that he's gone, it's I who must take your coat . . ."

"Did you make him a vampire?"

"No." She hesitated a moment in the act of laying ulster, hat, and scarf on a nearby sideboard, her eyes moving from his, then back. "Grippen did that, at our request—and Danny's. Danny was very devoted to Charles—my husband."

"Could you have?"

"Is that question pertinent?" she inquired levelly. "Or just curiosity?"

"The answer is that we would not have," a voice spoke from the shadows, and Asher turned swiftly, having heard no creak from the floorboards that had murmured beneath his own weight. The man who stood there, face white as chalk in the gloom, seemed more like a ghost than a human being—thinnish, medium height, and with an indefinable air about him of shabbiness, of age, as if one would expect to see cobwebs caught in his short-cropped light-brown hair. "Not without Lionel's permission."

"Lionel?"

"Grippen." The vampire shook his head, as if the name tasted flat and old upon his tongue. There was a weariness to his movements, a slowness, like age that had not yet reached his face. Glancing swiftly back at Mrs. Farren, Asher saw her eyes on this newcomer filled with concern.

"He never would have stood for it," the vampire explained. "He would have driven poor Danny out of every hole and corner within a year. He's very jealous that way." He held out one thin hand, said, "I'm Ernchester," in a voice that echoed the resonance of that vanished title.

Asher, who had gained a certain amount of familiarity with the Earls of Ernchester from his afternoon's researches, guessed: "Lord Charles Farren, third Earl of Ernchester?"

A faint smile brushed that white, square-jawed face, and for a moment there was a flicker of animation in the dead eyes. He inclined his head. "I fear I don't look much like the portrait," he said. Any number of portraits of ancient gentlemen lurked on the gloomy salon walls, too obscured with time and shadow to be even remotely recognizable. But Asher reasoned that, since the third Earl of Ernchester had died in 1682, and any portrait would have been two-thirds devoted to an elaborate periwig, it scarcely mattered.

And, in fact, the third Earl of Ernchester had not died.

Asher frowned, trying to recall the name of the Countess, and with the curious perspicacity of vampires Mrs. Farren said, "Anthea." She stepped over beside her husband and guided him to a chair near the cold hearth; in her brown eyes was still that wariness, that concern when she looked at him and that watchful enmity when she regarded Asher. Asher saw the way Ernchester moved when he took his seat—with the same economy of movement he had seen in Ysidro, and indeed in Lady Anthea, but without life.

"Did Danny sleep here?" he asked, and it was Anthea who replied.

"Only very occasionally." She straightened up and walked

back to the hearth; it was a relief to Asher not to have to fight to see them move, as he did with Ysidro.

"And I take it it wasn't here that you found his body?"

From the corner of his eye Asher was conscious of Ernchester looking away, resting his brow on his hand in a gesture that hid his face. It came as a shock to him that the Earl felt grief, and he saw anger for that, too—a protective anger—in Anthea Farren's brown eyes.

"If it had been," she replied coolly, "you may be sure that the killer would have dispatched the both of us as well."

He bit his lip. Then, answering her anger and not her words, "I'm sorry."

Some of the tension seemed to slack in her strong frame, and the anger left her eyes. She, too, answered not his words. "It was foolish of you to come here," she said. "Ysidro can be maddening, but, believe me, if he has kept things from you, it is because there is ground that it is perilous for a living man to tread."

"That may be," Asher said. "But as long as he has a pistol to my head—as long as someone I love will suffer for it if I don't find this killer—he's not going to be able to have it both ways. I want to be shut of this business quickly—before he finds where I've hidden away the woman whose life is in hostage to him, before the killer realizes he has a day hunter on his trail, learns who I am, and tracks down this woman also—before I get any deeper entangled into the side of this affair that isn't my business. But I can't do that unless I have more information than Ysidro's willing to give."

She considered him for a long moment, her head a little tilted, as if with the glossy weight of her dark hair. "He is—a very old vampire," she said after a time. "He is cautious, like an old snake in a hole; he errs on the side of caution, maybe. Maybe it's because he doesn't really care much about anything."

It was odd to hear her speak of Ysidro as "old," for the Spaniard had the queerly graceful air of a young man, almost a boy. It was Ernchester, thought Asher, with his oddly dead motions and his weary eyes, who seemed old. Asher glanced back at the chair where the Earl had sat, but the vampire was no longer there. Asher could not recall just when he had vanished. It was early evening, he remembered, and neither of his hosts had fed. But somehow, speaking to this quiet and beautiful woman who had been dead long before he was born, he could not fear her.

He wondered if that were because she meant him no harm, or because she was using some subtle variation of the mental glamour of the vampire on him, as Ysidro had tried to do on the train. Ysidro's words about "other vampires than I" lingered unnervingly in his thoughts.

After a long pause, Anthea went on, "I'm not sure whether he or Grippen is the elder—they were both made about the same time, by the same master. Rhys the White, that was. A minstrel, who was master vampire of London—oh, years, years.

"You understand that it was never usual for a commoner to survive as a vampire until cities began to get large enough for deaths to be invisible," she added after a moment. "Only the landed had money and a place to be secure during the days when we sleep. Simon tells me that even in his time, London was like a small market town." She smiled a little, her teeth white against a lip full but pale as wax. "And I suppose you'd think the London I grew up in paltry—we used to pick catkins in the marshes where Liverpool Station now stands.

"It was the nobles who could sustain their security, who could hunt far enough afield—who could live on the blood of cattle and deer, if need be, to prevent suspicion from falling on themselves. But one cannot live for too long on the blood of animals. One cannot go too long without the kill. One grows— dull. Stupid. Weary. All things begin to seem very pointless. And out of that dullness, it is very easy to be trapped and killed."

She raised her eyes to his, folding her hands—soft and large and strong enough, he knew, to break his neck—over one another, her rings gleaming coldly. "That sounds vile, doesn't it? But that blunting of mind—that laxing of the concentration—

is death to a vampire, whom the rising sun will reduce to ashes. Do you think us vile?"

"I think that what you are is vile," Asher said evenly. "Does that matter to you?"

Her eyes left his again, to consider the pearls and moonstones of her ring. "If it mattered all that greatly I suppose I would have died years ago." Another woman might have shrugged—he only sensed her setting the thought aside with some attenuated shift of musculature he did not quite see, before her eyes returned to his. "Of course Rhys was gone by the time Charles and I became what we are. He lived in the crypts below the old Church of St. Giles, haunting the waterfronts for sailors at night. He made his money playing in taverns, in Eastcheap and the Steelyard—the German Hansa merchants loved him. Simon tells me his touch upon the lute could bring tears to your eyes. That's where Simon met him, a thin, little, white-haired man, Simon says, so fragile to look at, like a little spider in strange garb two centuries out of date. There was a great frenzy of witch-killing in the days of old King James, and those in London who survived it perished in the Fire, all save Grippen and Simon. God knows where they found to sleep, in the days the fire burned."

"But you weren't made until after the fire?" It was ancient history to him, like the Fall of Rome; the woodcuts of that monster conflagration that had devoured London in 1666.

"Years after," she said. "I remember, as a little girl, standing on Harrow Hill in the dark, looking down on the city like a carpet of flame, and feeling the heat blowing off it onto my face on the wind. It had been windy all that week, hot and dry . . . I remember the crackle of the air in my hair, and being afraid the fire would cover all the earth." She shook her head, as if wondering at that child's naïveté. "They said there were buildings whose stones exploded like bombs in the heat, and little streams of molten lead from the church roofs were seen running like water down the gutters. Even after I became—what I am—it was years before I saw Ysidro; after the turn of

106

the new century. His face was still covered with scars from the Fire, his hands like the scabby-barked branches of a tree."

"And Grippen?"

Her mouth tightened a little. "Lionel got a lot of fledglings in the years after the Fire," she said. "Charles was far from the first. He needed money, needed protection . . ."

"Protection?"

Her voice was deliberately colorless. "There are always feuds. All his fledglings had perished in the Fire. For years I thought Charles was dead." She gave a little shake of her head, as if putting aside some old letter she had been reading, and glanced up at him again, the oil light glowing amber in her eyes. "But that isn't what you came here to hear."

"I came here to hear about vampires," Asher said quietly. "About who you are and what you are; what you do and what you want. You're a hunter, Lady Farren. You know that you must see the pattern first, before you can see where it breaks."

"It's dangerous," she began, and a thread of anger seeped into Asher's voice.

"Ysidro didn't give me any choice."

He was still standing in front of her, in the small pool of light that surrounded the vast marble edifice of the carved mantel, close enough now that he could have reached out and touched her face. Her face did not change its expression, but he saw her eyes alter their focus, flick past his shoulder to the dark cavern of the room behind him; her hand shot out, dragging at his arm even as he whirled to see the massive shadow looming only feet behind him and the terrible glint of red eyes.

Anthea cried, "Grippen, no . . . !" at the same instant Asher swung with his forearm to strike away the huge hand that clutched at his throat. It was like striking a tree, but he managed to twist aside. Hairy and powerful, the vampire Grippen's hand shut around the shoulder of his coat instead of his neck.

Asher twisted, slithering out of the garment. Grippen was massive, as tall as Asher and broad as a door, with greasy black hair falling in his eyes, his face pocked with old scars and ruddy with ingested blood. For all his size, he was blindingly fast. His massive arm locked around Asher's chest, trapping him with his own arms tangled still in his half-discarded coat; he felt the vampire's mind smothering his, cloudy and strong as steel, and fought it as he had fought Ysidro's in the train. The arm around his chest crushed tighter, and he twisted with both his hands at the fingers buried in his coat—he might just as well have tried to break the fingers of a statue.

Anthea, too, was tearing at Grippen's wrists, trying to force them loose. He heard her cry, "Don't . . . !" as he felt the man's huge, square hand tear his shirt collar free, and thought, with bizarre abstraction, *And now for a little experiment in applied folklore . . .*

"God's death!" Grippen's hand jerked back from the silver chain, the reek of blood on his breath nauseating. Asher dropped his weight against the slackened hold, slipping free for an instant before the enraged vampire struck him a blow on the side of the head that knocked him spinning into the opposite wall. He hit it like a rag doll—the strike had been blindingly fast, coming out of nowhere with an impact like that of a speeding motorcar. As he sank, stunned, to the floor the philologist in him picked out the sixteenth-century rounded vowels—far more pronounced than Ysidro's—as the vampire bellowed, "Poxy whoreson, I'll give you silver!"

His vision graying out, he saw two shapes melt and whirl together, black and ivory in the lamplight. Anthea had hold of both of Grippen's wrists, trying to drag him back, her storm-colored hair falling loose from its pins around her shoulders. Though his mind was swimming, Asher staggered to his feet and stumbled the length of the room to the pillared archway. An inglorious enough exit, he thought dizzily. Properly speaking, a gentleman should remain and not let a lady take the brunt of a fracas, but the fact was that she was far more qualified than he for the task. It was also very unlikely Grippen could or would kill her, and virtually certain that, if Asher remained, he was a dead man.

Savoy Walk was silent, empty, wreathed thickly now in fog.

If he could make it to the end of the street, up Salisbury Court to the lights of Fleet Street, he'd be safe . . .

He stumbled down the tall stone steps, scarcely feeling the raw cold of the river mist that lanced through his shirt sleeves and froze his throat through his torn collar. *Dangerous ground for a mortal to tread indeed,* he thought, as his feet splashed in the shallow puddles of the uneven cobbles. Heedless of appearances, he began to run.

He made it no farther than the black slot where the court narrowed into the crevice of the lane.

In that shadowy opening a form materialized, seeming to take shape, as they were said to, out of the mist itself—a diminutive girl, a pocket Venus, primrose curls heaped high on her head and dark eyes gleaming feral in the diffuse glow from the lights of the house. He turned, seeking some other escape, and saw behind him in the fog the pale face of a world-weary ghost that belonged to the third Earl of Ernchester.

Their hands were like ice as they closed around his arms.

"I'm sorry," Ernchester said softly, "but you have to come with us."

Eight

———

"S" even years is a long time." The Honorable Evelyn Westmoreland stirred at his coffee with a tiny spoon, looking
down into its midnight depths. Across the table from
him, Lydia hoped that seven years was long enough.

"I know," she said softly and rested her hand on the table,
close enough to his to let him know that, had she not been
married, he could have covered it with his. The plumes on her
hat, like pink-tinged sunset clouds, moved as she leaned forward; from the lace of her cuffs, her kid-gloved hands emerged
like the slim stamens of a rose. Her brown eyes were wide and
gentle—she could see him as a soft-edged pattern of dark and
light, but had decided that in this case it was better to look well
than to see well. Besides, she had learned how to interpret the
most subtle of signs. "Believe me, I wish I could let the matter
rest."

"You should." There was an edge of bitter distaste in his
voice. "It's not the sort of thing you should be asking about
. . . Mrs. Asher." The soft lips, fleshy as those of some decadent
Roman bust, pinched up. Past him, the red-and-black shape of
one of Gatti's well-trained waiters glided by and, though it was
well past the hour when teas ceased being served, fetched a little
more hot water, which he soundlessly added to the teapot at
Lydia's elbow, and removed the ruins of the little cake-and-
sandwich plate. The restaurant was beginning to smell of dinner
now rather than tea. The quality of the voices of the few diners
coming in was different; the women's indistinct forms were
colored differently than for daytime and flashed with jewels.
Beyond the square leads of the windowpanes, a misty dusk had
fallen on the Strand.

Those seven years, Lydia reflected privately, had not been

particularly kind to the Equally Honorable Evelyn. He was still as big and burly as he'd been in those halcyon days of rugger matches against Kings; but, even without her specs, she could tell that under his immaculate tailoring he'd put on flesh. When he'd taken her arm to lead her to their little table, Lydia had been close enough to see that, though not yet thirty, he bore the crumpled pouchiness of dissipation beneath his blue-gray eyes, the bitter weariness of one who does not quite know what has gone wrong; his flesh smelled faintly of expensive pomade. He was not the young man who had so assiduously offered her his arm at croquet matches and concerts of Oriental music, no longer Dennis Blaydon's puppylike brother-in-arms against all comers on the field. Even back when she'd been most impressed with his considerable good looks, Lydia had found his conversation stilted and boring, and it was worse now. It had taken nearly an hour of patient chitchat over tea to relax him to the point of, she hoped, confidences.

She looked down at her teacup, fingering the fragile curlicues of its handle, aware that, with her eyes downcast, he was studying her face. "How *did* he die, Evelyn?"

"It was a carriage accident." The voice turned crisp, defensive.

"Oh," she said softly. "I thought . . . I'd heard . . ."

"Whatever you heard," Evelyn said, "and whomever you heard it from, it was a carriage accident. I'd rather not . . ."

"Please . . ." She raised her eyes to his once more. "I need to talk to you, Evelyn. I didn't know who else I could ask. I sent you that note asking to meet me here because . . . I've heard there was a woman."

Anger flicked at the edges of his tone. "She had nothing to do with it. He died in a . . ."

"I think a friend of mine has gotten involved with her."

"Who?" He moved his head, his eyes narrowing, the wary inflection reminding her of her father when he was getting ready to say things like "station in life" and "not done."

"No one you know," Lydia stammered.

111

He paused a moment, thinking about that, turning things over in his mind with the slow deliberation she had remembered. The Honorable Bertie, dimwitted though he had been, had always been the brighter brother. Then he said slowly, "Don't worry about it, Lydia . . . Mrs. Asher. Truly," he added more gently, seeing the pucker of worry between her copper-dark brows. "I . . . You see, I heard recently that . . . that someone I know had been seeing her. Of course, you were barely out of school when Bertie was found . . . when Bertie died, and there was a lot we couldn't tell you. But she was a pernicious woman, Lydia, truly evil. And a week or so ago I . . . er . . . I met her and warned her off . . . paid her off . . . gave her money and told her to leave the country. She's gone." He didn't look at her as he spoke.

Embarrassment? she wondered. *Or something else?*

"Truly?" She leaned forward a little, her eyes on his face, trying to detect shifts of expression without being obvious about it.

She heard the weary distaste, the revulsion in his voice as he said, "Truly."

She let another long pause rest on the scented air between them, then asked, "What was she like? I have a reason for asking," she added, as the Equally Honorable Evelyn puffed himself up preparatory to expostulation on the subject of curiosity unseemly for a woman of her class and position. "You know I've become a doctor."

"I do," he said, with a trace of indignation, as if he'd had the right to forbid it, and she'd flouted his authority anyway. "Though I really can't see how Professor Asher, or any husband, could let his wife . . ."

"Well," she continued, cutting off a too-familiar tirade with an artless appearance of eagerness, "in my studies I've come across two or three cases of a kind of nervous disorder that reminded me of things J—my friend—told me about this—this woman Carlotta. I suspect that she may be insane."

That got his interest, as she'd found it got nine people's out of ten, even those who considered her authority for the accusation an affront to their manhood. He leaned forward, his watery eyes intent, and she reached across the small table with its starched white cloth and took his chubby hand in both of hers. "But I haven't met her, or seen her, and you have . . . if you'd be willing to talk about it. Evelyn, please. I do need your help."

In the cab on her way back to Bruton Place she jotted down the main points of the subsequent discussion—it would have looked bad, she had decided, to be taking notes while Evelyn was talking, and would have put him off his stride. The waiters at Gatti's, well-trained, had observed the intentness of the discussion between the wealthy-looking gentleman and the delicate, red-haired girl, and had tactfully let them alone—something they probably would not have done had she been scribbling notes.

The interview had been frustrating, because Evelyn was as much wrapped up in sports—and now in the stock market—as his brother Bertie had been in clothes and fashion and was grossly inobservant of anything else, but with patient questioning she'd been able to piece certain things together.

First, Lotta had been seen as early as an hour after sunset, when the sky was still fairly light—Evelyn had thought that was in spring, but wasn't sure.

Second, sometimes she had been paler, and sometimes rosier—though it was difficult to tell by gaslight—indicating that sometimes she had fed before joining the Honorable Bertie and his friends. Evelyn did not remember whether she had ever been rosy on those occasions upon which she had met them early, which would indicate that she had risen *just* after sunset to hunt.

Third, she often wore heavy perfume. James had said nothing about vampires smelling different from humans, but presumably, with a different diet, they might have a different odor, though a very faint one—she tried not to think about the smell of blood and strangeness that had touched her nostrils in the dark of the Covent Garden court.

Other than that, he'd thought there was something odd about her fingernails, he couldn't say what. And her eyes, but he couldn't say what either, so had fallen back on "an expression of evil," which was no help toward clinical analysis.

About the circumstances of his brother's death he would not speak at all, but Lydia guessed, from things James had told her about the techniques of spying, that when Lotta finally killed her victim, she had arranged for the body to be found in circumstances that were either disgraceful or compromising, such as dressed in women's clothing, or in an alley behind an opium den, or something equally damning.

And lastly, Evelyn had told her that Bertie had once had a charm made, a lover's knot, out of Lotta's red-gold hair. It was still among Bertie's things. He would send it to her by the morning post, to the accommodation address where she picked up her mail.

She sat back in the cab as it jolted along the crowded pavement of Gower Street, staring abstractedly out at the blurred yellow halos of the street lamps where they shone through the mists against the monochrome cutouts of the house fronts behind. The rising fog seemed to damp noises, making all things slightly unreal; omnibuses like moving towers loomed out of it, their knife-board advertisements for Pond's Arthriticus or Clincher Tires—Still Unequaled for Quality and Durability— transformed into strange portents by the surrounding gloom.

When the cab reached Number 109 Bruton Place, Lydia paid the driver off quickly and hurried inside, displeased to find her heart racing with a swift, nervous fear. She found she was becoming uncomfortable at the thought of being outside, even for a few moments, after dark.

The room to which the vampires took Asher was a cellar, not of Ernchester House but of a deserted shop whose narrow door opened into the blackness of the lane. Ernchester produced the keys to its two padlocks from a waistcoat pocket and led the way into a tiny back room, piled high with dusty boxes and crates and boasting an old soapstone sink in one corner, whose rusty pump, silhouetted against the dim yellowish reflection of the window, had the appearance of some wry-necked monster brooding in the darkness. An oil lamp stood on the side of the sink; Ernchester lighted it and led the way to another door nearly hidden behind the crates, whose padlock and hasp had been ripped off with a crowbar—recently, by the look of the gouges in the wood. The smell of mildew and dampness rose chokingly to engulf them as they descended the hairpin spiral of stairs to a cellar, certainly much wider, Asher guessed, than the building above; probably deeper, he thought, glancing at its far end, nearly obscured in shadows, and beyond a doubt older. Rough-hewn arched beams supported a ceiling of smoke-stained stone; just below them, at the other end of the room, two pairs of locked shutters indicated windows either at street level or set into a light well just below it.

"They're barred behind those shutters," the Earl remarked, taking an old-fashioned, long-barreled key from a nail beside the door. "So even if you could get the padlocks on them open, it wouldn't do you much good. Chloé, my dear, would you be so good as to fetch Dr. Asher's coat? And mine as well?"

The fair-haired vampire girl shot him a look that was both sullen and annoyed, childish on that angelic face. "Don't trust me to stay with 'im while you get 'em yourself, ducks?" she mocked in accents that put her origins within half a dozen streets of the Church of St. Mary-Le-Bow. She threw a glance back at Asher in the flickering light of the oil lamp they'd collected when they'd passed through the room above. "And don't go givin' yourself airs over that bit o' tin you got hung round your gullet, Professor—we can drink from the veins in your wrists, you know."

She raised Asher's wrist to her mouth, pressed her cold lips to the thin skin there in a smiling kiss. Then she turned and with barely a rustle of her silk petticoats was gone in the darkness.

Asher became aware that he was shivering. Though the cellar was dry, it was intensely cold. Beside him Ernchester, lamp still in hand, was frowning at the narrow black slot of the door through which Asher knew the girl must have gone, though

115

he had not seen her do so. She, like Ysidro, moved largely unseen.

"An impertinent child." Ernchester frowned, his sparse brows bristling queerly in the shaky light. "It isn't just a question of breeding—though of course I understand that things do change. It just seems that no one knows how to behave anymore." He set the lamp down on the floor beside him and held thin hands in the column of heat that rose from its chimney.

"Anthea has gone to look for Ysidro," he went on after a moment. "Neither of us approved of Don Simon's plan for hunting the killer—for reasons which are obvious by your mere presence here. But now that he has hired you, I agree with her that it would be most unfair simply to kill you out of hand, leaving aside the fact that you are, in a sense, a guest beneath my roof." Those dulled, weary blue eyes rested on him for a moment, as if seeking reasons other than an old habit of *noblesse oblige* for sparing his life.

Dryly, Asher said, "I take it Grippen voted against it, also?"

"Oh, there was never a question of a *vote*." By his tone the elderly vampire had entirely missed the sarcasm. "Don Simon is and always has been a law unto himself. He was the only one of us to think it necessary to hire a human. But he has always been most high in the instep and will carry his humors against all opposition."

Asher rubbed his shoulder, which ached where Grippen had flung him into the wall. "He might have mentioned that."

Beneath their feet, the stone floor vibrated; the glass of the lamp chimney sang faintly in its metal socket. "The Underground Railroad runs very close to this cellar," Ernchester explained, as the rumble died away. "Indeed, when they were cutting for it, we feared they might break through, as in fact they did in another house we own a few streets away. That cellar was deeper than this one, without windows—it had been the wine room of an old tavern, paved over and forgotten after the Fire. There are a great number of such places in the old City, some of them dating back to Roman times. It was desperately damp and uncomfortable, which was why no one was sleeping there when the workmen broke in."

Asher stroked his mustache thoughtfully and wandered across the uneven slab floor to the coffin against the wall. Opening it, he saw the lining burned entirely away at the bottom, only clinging in charred shreds around the upper rim. Nothing but a faint film of scraped-at ash lay over the charred wood of the coffin's floor.

He wondered in what church's crypt they had buried the remains. St. Bride's, beyond a doubt. Odd, that after so many years that should still be a concern to them . . . or perhaps not so odd.

He replaced the lid and turned back. "Were the padlocks on the windows open, then, when you found Danny's body?"

Ernchester glanced quickly at the barred shutters of the windows, then back at the empty coffin. For a moment he seemed to be trying to figure out how much he should tell a human; then, with a tired gesture, he gave it up. "Yes. The key was on the sill."

Asher walked over to the window, stretched his long arm up to touch the tips of his fingers to the lock. He looked back at the vampire. "But the bars were undisturbed?"

"Yes. Had someone—a tramp, or a vagabond—entered this cellar and been looking about, it would be natural for him to open the shutters to obtain light, you see."

"Was there any sign of a tramp elsewhere in the building? Cupboards open, drawers ajar? Or in the rest of the house? Any sign that the place had been searched?"

"No," Ernchester admitted. "That is—I don't think so. I really don't know. Anthea would." Another man—a living man—might have sighed and shaken his head, but, as with Anthea and Ysidro, such gestures seemed to have been drained from him by the passing weariness of centuries. There was only a slight relaxing of that straight, stocky body, a loosening of the tired lines of the face. "Anthea—does such things these days. I know it's the portion of the man to manage affairs, but . . . it seems as if all the world is changing. I used to keep up better than I do now. I dare say it's only the effect of the factory soot in the air or the noise in the streets . . . it usen't to be like this, you know. I sometimes think the living suffer from it as much as we. Folk are different now from what they were."

Keyed and alert for the silent approach of some new peril, Asher saw the girl Chloé enter the cellar again, his own jacket and greatcoat and Ernchester's seedy velvet coat over her arm. She was dressed, he saw now, in an expensive and beautiful gown of dark green velvet, beaded thickly with jet; her soft white hands and pale face seemed like flowers against the opulent fabric. Here was one, he thought, who would have no trouble winning kisses from strangers in alleyways. As he took the coat from her arm he said, "Thank you," and the brown eyes flicked up to his, startled at being thanked. "Did you hunt with Lotta Harshaw?"

She smiled again, but this time the mockery did not quite hide the frightened flinch of her lips. "Still the nosy-parker, then? You saw what it'll buy you." She reached up to touch his throat, then drew back as the silver of his neck chain caught the lamplight. "You know what they said curiosity did to the cat."

"Then it's a good thing cats have nine lives," he replied quietly. "Did you hunt with Lotta?"

She shrugged, an elaborately coquettish gesture with her bare white shoulders, and looked away.

"I know you went for dress fittings with her. Probably other shopping as well. I imagine the pair of you looked very fetching together. Personally I find it a bore to have dinner alone—do you?"

The conversational tone of his voice brought her eyes back to his, flirtatious and amused. "Sometimes. But y'see, we don't ever have dinner quite alone." She smiled, showing the glint of teeth against a lip like ruby silk.

"Did you like Lotta?"

The long lashes veiled her brown eyes once more. "She showed me the ropes, like," she said, after a long moment, and he remembered Bully Joe Davies' frantic cry: *I dunno how the*

118

others do it . . . To achieve the vampire state, the vampire powers, was evidently far from enough. "And we—birds, I mean—hunt differently from gents. And that . . ." She stopped her next words on her lips and threw a quick, wary glance at Ernchester, silent beside the lamp. After a long pause for rewording, she continued, "Lotta and me, we got along. There's some things a lady needs from another lady, see."

And that . . . That what? How would this beautiful, over-dressed porcelain doll of a girl see the quiet antique lady Anthea? *As a stiff-necked and uncongenial bitch,* Asher thought, *beyond a doubt.* Mlle. La Tour had known at a glance that Lotta and Chloé were two of a kind and that Anthea—for undoubtedly it was she who went by the name of Mrs. Wren—was far other than they.

"Did you know her rich young men?" he asked. "Albert Westmoreland? Tom Gobey? Paul Farrington?"

She smiled again, playing hard to get. "Oh, I met most of 'em," she said, toying with one of her thick blonde curls. "Lambs, they were—even Bertie Westmoreland, so stiff and proper, like it killed him to admit he wanted her, but following her wherever she went with his eyes. We'd go to theatre parties together—Bertie's brother, me and Lotta, and some girls Bertie's friends might have along . . . It was all I could do sometimes not to drink one of 'em right there in the shadow of the back of the box. Like smelling sausages frying when you're hungry . . . It would have been so easy . . ."

"It's a trick you could only have done once," Asher remarked, and got a sullen glance from under those long lashes.

"That's what Lionel said. Not when others are around, no matter how bad I want it—not where anyone will know." She moved closer to him, her head no higher than the top button of his waistcoat; he could smell the patchouli of her perfume, and the faint reek of blood on her words as she spoke. "But no others are around now—and no one will know."

Her tongue slipped out, to touch the protruding tips of her teeth; her fingers slid around his hand, warm with the evening's earlier kill. He could see her eyes on his throat and on the heavy silver links of the chain. Though he dared not look away from her to check, he had no impression of Ernchester being in the room. Perhaps it was only that the vampire Earl would not have cared whether she killed him or not.

"Ysidro will know," he reminded her.

She dropped his hand and looked away. A shiver went through her. "Cold dago bugger."

"Are you afraid of him?"

"Aren't you?" Her glance slid back to his, brown eyes that should have been angelic, but had never been so, he thought, even in life. Her red mouth twisted. "You think he'll protect you from Lionel? That'll last just as long as he needs you. You'd better not be so quick about findin' the answers to your questions."

"And I have already told him he had best not be slow," the soft, drawling voice of Ysidro murmured. Turning, Asher saw the Spanish vampire at his elbow, as Grippen had appeared earlier that evening; his glance cut quickly back in time to see Chloé start. She hadn't seen him either.

"So perhaps," Don Simon continued, "we had best stick simply to things as they are and not attempt to mold them to what we think they ought to be. You should not have come here, James."

"On the contrary," Asher said, "I've learned a great deal."

"That is what I meant. But as the horses are well and truly gone, permit me to open the barn door for you. Calvaire's rooms are upstairs—or one set of Calvaire's rooms. I know of at least two others that he had. There may have been more."

"Hence all the secrecy," Asher said, as he preceded the vampire into the dark stair outside. "Any in Lambeth?"

"Lambeth? Not that I knew of." He was aware of those cold yellow eyes piercing his back.

They ascended the neck-breaking twist of steps to the stuffy back room again; though he listened closely, Asher could hear no footfall behind him from either Ysidro or Chloé and only the faintest of rustles from the girl's petticoats. He thought Ernchester must have left at the same time Ysidro had entered, for the Earl had been nowhere in the cellar as they departed. And, in fact, Charles and Anthea were both waiting for them in the parlor of a small flat which had been fitted up on the second floor, with its Tiffany-glass lamps all lighted, giving their strange, white faces the rosy illusion of humanity, save for their gleaming eyes.

"I trust you're not still sleeping in the building, Chloé?" Ysidro inquired, as they entered and the girl set her lamp on the table.

"No," she said sullenly. She retreated to a corner of the room and perched there on one of the patterned chintz chairs; the place was furbished up in several styles, fat overstuffed chairs alternating with pieces of Sheraton and Hepplewhite, and here and there a lacquered cabinet of chinoiserie filled with knickknacks and books. The parlor was tidily kept, with none of the decades-deep clutter of other vampire rooms Asher had seen. Through an open door beyond Lady Anthea's chair, he could see a neat bedroom, its windows heavily shrouded and, no doubt, shuttered beneath those layers of curtain. There was no coffin in sight—Asher guessed it would be in the dressing room beyond.

"Lionel's gone," Lady Ernchester said softly. Her tea-brown eyes went to Asher. She had put up her hair again and bore no evidence of her struggle with Grippen beyond the fact that she had changed her dress for a dark gown of purple-black taffeta. Asher wondered if Minette had made it for her.

"You've made a dangerous enemy; his hand's welted up where he touched the silver of your chain."

Asher privately thought it served the master vampire right, but refrained from saying so. His whole body was stiff and aching from the impact with the wall. He was still, he reminded himself, quite probably in desperate and immediate danger, but, nevertheless, Grippen's absence comforted him. He prowled over to the small cabinet that stood under the gas jet and opened its drawers. They were empty.

"Lionel did that," Anthea's voice came from behind him. "He tells me he did the same at Neddy's house."

"*He's* the one who seems to be locking the barn door after

the horse has escaped." Asher turned back, roving cautiously about the room, examining the French books in the bookshelves, the cushions on the camel-backed divan. He glanced across at Ysidro, who had gone to stand next to Anthea's chair. "If silver affects you that badly, how do you purchase what you need?"

"As any gentleman of fashion can tell you," Anthea said with a faint smile, "one can go for years—centuries, even—without actually touching cash. In earlier years we used gold. Flimsies— bank notes, and later treasury notes—were a godsend, but one must always tip. I've found that in general there is enough of a chill at night to warrant the wearing of gloves."

"But they've got to be leather," Chloé put in ungraciously. "And I mean good leather, none of your kid; it'll burn right through silk."

Anthea frowned. "Does it? I never found it so."

Ysidro held up one long, white hand. "I suspect it toughens a little with time. I know if you had touched silver as Grippen did, Chloé, your arm would have been swollen to the shoulder for weeks, and you would have been ill into the bargain. So it was with me, up almost to the time of the Fire. It is curiously fragile stuff, this pseudoflesh of ours."

"I remember," Anthea said slowly. "The first time I touched silver—it was bullion lace on the sleeve of one of my old gowns, I think—it not only hurt me at the time, but it made me very ill. I remember being desperately thirsty and unable to hunt. Charles had to hunt for me—bring me . . ." She broke off suddenly and looked away, her beautiful face impassive. Thinking about it, Asher realized that the logical prey to capture and bring back alive to Ernchester House had to be something human—since it was the death of the human psyche as much as the physical blood that the vampires seemed to crave—but small enough to be easily transportable.

"Kiddies?" Chloé laughed, cold and tingling, like shaken silver bells. "God, you could have had the lot of my brothers and sisters—puking little vermin. Dear God, and the youngest of 'em has brats of her own now . . ." She paused and turned her face away suddenly, her mouth pressing tight; a delicate, beautiful face that would never grow old. She took a deep breath, a conscious gesture, to steady herself, then went on evenly. "Funny—I see girls who was in the Opera ballet with me back then, years too old to dance now—years too old to get anythin' on the streets but maybe a real nearsighted sailor. I could go into the Opera right now and get my old job back in the ballet, you know? Old Harry the stage man would even recognize me, from bein' the prop boy then."

She fell silent again, staring before her with her great dark eyes, as if seeing into that other time—like Anthea, Asher thought, standing on Harrow Hill and feeling the furnace heat of burning London washing over her mortal flesh. After a moment, Chloé said in a strange voice, "It's queer, that's all." Asher felt the pressure of her mind on his, as she made her swift, sudden exit from the room.

Anthea glanced quickly at her husband; Ernchester, much more quietly, almost invisibly, followed the girl out.

"It becomes easier," the Countess said softly, turning back to Asher, "once those we knew in life are all—gone. One is not—reminded. One can—pretend." Her dark brows drew down again, that small gesture making her calm face human again. "Even when one is for all practical purposes immortal, age is unsettling." And getting to her feet, she followed her husband in a whisper of dark taffeta from the room.

For a long time Asher stood where he had been by the fireplace, his arms folded, regarding Ysidro by the pink and amber glow of the shaded lights. The vampire remained standing by the vacated chair, his gaze still resting thoughtfully on the door, and Asher had the impression he listened to the lady's retreating footfalls blending away into the other sounds of London, the rattle of traffic in Salisbury Place and the nocturnal roar of Fleet Street beyond, the deep vibration of the Underground, the sough of the river below the Embankment, and the voices of those who crowded its flagways in the night.

At length Ysidro said, "It is a dangerous time in Chloé's life." The enigmatic gaze returned to him, still remote, without giv-

123

ing anything away. "It happens to vampires. There are stages—
I have seen them myself, passed through them myself, some of
them . . . When a vampire has existed thirty, forty years, and
sees all his friends dying, growing senile, or changing unre-
cognizably from what they were in the sweetness of a shared
youth. Or at a hundred or so, when the whole world mutates
into something other than what he grew up with; when all the
small things that were so precious to him are no longer even
remembered. When there is no one left who recalls the voices
of the singers which so inextricably formed the warp and weft
of his days. Then it is easy to grow careless, and the sun will
always rise."

He glanced over at Asher, and that odd ghost of what had
once been a half-rueful, bittersweet smile flicked back onto the
thin lines of his face. "Sometimes I think Charles and Anthea
are becoming—friable—that way. They change with the times,
as we all must, but it becomes more and more difficult. I still
become enraged when shopkeepers are impertinent to me, when
these grubby hackney cabs dart out in front of me in the street,
or when I see the filth of factory soot fouling the sky. We are,
like Dr. Swift's Struldbruggs, old people, and we tend to the
unreasonable conservatism of the old. Very little is left of the
world as it was in King Charles' day, and nothing, I fear, remains of the world I knew. Except Grippen, of course." The
smile turned sardonic. "What a companion for one's immortality."

He strolled over to the fireplace where Asher stood and prod-
ded with one well-shod toe at the cold debris within, a *mille-
feuille* of white paper ash, like that which had decorated Neddy
Hammersmith's long-cold hearth. "That is, provided, of
course," he added ironically, "one survives the first few years,
the terrible dangers of simply learning how to be a vampire."

"Did Rhys the Minstrel teach you?"

"Yes." It was the first softening Asher had seen in those
gleaming eyes. "He was a good master—a good teacher. It was,
you understand, more dangerous in those days, for in those
days folk believed in us."

It was on the tip of Asher's tongue to ask about that, but instead he asked, "Did you know Calvaire created a fledgling?"

The cold eyes seemed to widen and harden, the long, thin nostrils flared. "He *what?*"

"He created a fledgling," Asher said.

"How do you know this?"

"I've spoken to him," Asher said. "A man named Bully Joe Davies, from Lambeth or thereabouts—he said he'd break my neck if I told anyone of it, particularly yourself. You seem," he added dryly, "to enjoy a certain reputation among your peers."

"Do you refer," the vampire asked coldly, "to that rabble of stevedores, sluts, and tradesmen as my peers? The Farrens come close, but, when all's said, his grandfather was no more than a jumped-up baron . . ."

"Your fellows, then," Asher amended. "And in any case, I trust you'll protect me. He says he's being followed—stalked. I'm supposed to meet him later tonight, to go to another of Calvaire's safe houses."

Ysidro nodded; Asher could see the thought moving in the pale labyrinth of his eyes.

He walked over to the cabinet again, ran a finger, idly questing, through its emptied pigeonholes, every scrap of evidence of contacts burned by the cautious Grippen lest any should do what Asher had done—trace a name, a shop, an address, that would lead him to another cellar where a vampire might sleep. He glanced back at the vampire, standing quietly in the molten halo of the lamplight.

"I hadn't intended on telling you that," he went on after a moment. "But I've been finding out some things tonight about Calvaire, a little, and about vampires. I understand now why you've been lying to me all along. In a way, Grippen is right. You'd be an absolute fool to hire a human to track down your killer, much less tell him who and what you are—if your killer is human. But you don't think he is.

"In fact, you think the killer is another vampire." ·

125

Nine

I don't see how that could be." As she walked, Lydia folded her arms across her chest against the chill that dampened even the changeable sunlight of the autumn forenoon. Beside the dull purple-brown of her coat, her red hair, pinned under the only unobtrusive hat in her vast collection, seemed blazingly bright; her spectacles winked like a heliograph when she turned her head. In spite of them, she looked absurdly young, with a delicate prettiness which would have seemed touchingly vulnerable to anyone who had never seen her in the dissection rooms.

Asher, at her side, kept a weather eye out across the sepia vistas of lawn and copse to both sides of the walk, but saw few other strollers. It had rained late in the night, and Hyde Park bore a slightly dispirited air; scudding clouds were collecting again overhead. A few black-clothed nannies hustled their charges at double time through a rapid constitutional before the rain should commence again; that was all.

"Neither does Ysidro," Asher said. "But he suspected all along that the killer wasn't human. It's why he had to hire a human and, moreover, find one who could or would believe in vampires, who could operate to some degree independently—why he had to tell me what he was, in spite of the opposition from the other vampires. I think the others might have suspected they were dealing with a vampire, too. No human could stalk a vampire unseen—a human would be lucky to see one in the first place, let alone either recognize it for what it is or keep it in sight."

"You did," she pointed out.

Asher shook his head. "A fledgling, and an untrained one, at that." His glance skimmed the borders of the trees that half

126

hid the steely gleam of the Serpentine, off to their left. Like Bully Joe Davies, he found himself wondering all the time now about shadows, noises, bent blades of grass . . .

"Did Bully Joe Davies ever turn up?"

"No. Ysidro and I waited until almost dawn. He just might have seen Ysidro and sheered off, but I doubt it. However, I think we'll be able to locate Calvaire's rooms in Lambeth—if he has them, and I'm virtually certain he does—by tracking property purchases since February, which was when Calvaire came here from Paris. If Calvaire was attempting to establish a power base in London—which he seems to have been doing, since he made a fledgling—he'd have bought property. Since Grippen didn't know about it, either, we may find something there."

They walked in silence for a time, the wind tugging now and then at the ends of Asher's scarf and at Lydia's skirts and coat.

Lydia nodded. "I'm wondering whether *all* vampires fall asleep at the same time—into the deep sleep. For, of course, just because the windows were opened to let in the sunlight doesn't mean that it was done while the sun was in the sky."

"I suppose, if the killer were a vampire, he might have—oh, a half-hour or so—to get to safety," Asher said. "More than enough, in London. And it would certainly solve the question of why he believed in vampires in the first place, let alone knew where to look."

"In all the books, the vampire hunter drives a stake through the vampire's heart," Lydia remarked thoughtfully. "If this one did, everything's been too charred to tell, but Lotta's head was certainly severed. If the sun weren't yet in the sky, I wonder if that would wake a sleeping vampire?—for that matter, if the mere opening of the coffin would do so? Are you sure I can't put my hand in your pocket?"

"Quite sure," Asher said, fighting his own inclination to walk closer to her, to hold out his arm to hers, or to have some kind of physical contact with this woman. "In spite of the evidence that the killer is a vampire, I still don't feel safe meeting you, even by daylight . . ."

She widened her brown eyes at him behind the schoolgirl specs. "Perhaps I could disguise myself as a pickpocket? Or if I tripped and stumbled, and you caught me? Or fainted?" She put a gloved hand dramatically to her brow. "I feel an attack of the vapors coming on now . . ."

"No," Asher said firmly, grinning.

She frowned and tucked her hands primly into her muff. "Very well, but the next time Uncle Ambrose goes on about Plato and Platonic friendship, I'll have a few words to say to him. No wonder Don Simon didn't seem to worry too much about your allying yourself with the killer, as you'd originally thought you might. Do you still plan to do that, by the way?"

"I don't know," Asher said. "It isn't out of court entirely, but I'd have to know a good deal more than I do now. The fact that he's destroying them for reasons of his—or her—own doesn't mean he wouldn't destroy me with just as much alacrity." *Or you,* he added to himself, looking at that slim figure beside him, like a heroine of legend lying beside the hero, separated by a drawn sword.

Lydia nodded, accepting the change in a situation upon which her life depended with her usual calm trust. They walked along for a time, Lydia apparently sunk in her own trains of thought; Asher was content—almost—only to be with her, the dun gravel of the damp path scrunching faintly under their feet. Off across the gray lawns, a dog barked, the sound carrying fantastically in the cold air.

"Have you any idea how much light it takes to destroy their flesh?"

Asher shook his head. "I asked Ysidro last night. I've been trying to work that out, too—that half-hour or so of leeway. That's what's puzzling me. Ysidro was caught at dawn on the second morning of the Great Fire of 1666. He says the thinnest gray light before sunrise burned his face and hands as if he'd stuck them into a furnace—more than that, his arms, chest, and parts of his legs and back beneath his clothes were scarred and blistered as well. According to Lady Ernchester, it was nearly fifty years before the scars went away."

"But they did go away," Lydia murmured thoughtfully. "So vampire flesh *does* regenerate . . ." Her dark brows pulled even deeper, an edge of thought hardening her brown eyes, as if she looked past the piled whites and grays of the late-morning sky to some arcane laboratory of the mind beyond.

"Pseudoflesh, he called it," Asher said.

"Interesting." She reached up to unsnag a long strand of hair from the braided trim of her collar—Asher had to keep his hands firmly in his pockets to avoid helping her. "Because I got that lover's knot from Evelyn this morning. I've had a look at it and those vertebrae under my microscope, and they look—I'm not sure how to put it and I wish it were capable of greater magnification. The bone was pretty damaged, but the hair . . . I'd like to be able to examine it at a subcellular level—and their flesh and blood, for that matter."

Of course, Asher thought. He himself saw the vampires linguistically and historically, when he wasn't simply trying to think of ways to avoid having his throat cut by them; Lydia would see vampirism as a medical puzzle.

"Do you know how petrified wood comes about?" she asked, as they neared Marble Arch with its scattered trees and loafers and turned back the way they came, two solitary and anonymous figures in the wide, cleared spaces of the Park's brown lawns. "Or how fish and ferns and dinosaur bones are fossilized in the Cambrian sandstones? It's a process of replacement, cell by cell, of the organic by the inorganic. There's been a lot of research done lately on viruses, germs that are smaller than bacteria, so small we can't see them with a microscope—yet. Small enough to operate at a subcellular level. I've been reading Horace Blaydon's articles on viruses in the blood; he did a lot of work on it while I was studying with him. I'm wondering whether a vampire's immortality comes from some kind of cellular replacement or mutation—whether vampirism is in fact a virus or an interlocking syndrome of viruses that alter the very fabric of the cells. That would account for the extreme photosensitivity, the severe allergic reactions to things like silver and garlic and certain woods—why you'd have to fill the mouth with garlic to deaden the brain and stake the heart with one of those allergic woods to paralyze the cardiovascular system— why you'd have to separate the central nervous system . . ."

"And transmitted by blood contact." Again he wondered tangentially why, in the face of such an overwhelming body of corresponding evidence, there was such paucity of belief. "All the legends speak of vampires' victims becoming vampires. The vampires themselves speak of 'getting' fledglings, but that's apparently a matter of choice. Ernchester said that Grippen would not have stood for anyone but himself making a new vampire, but Calvaire evidently had no trouble initiating Bully Joe Davies."

"Initiating, but not training," Lydia said thoughtfully. "Or—*was* it just a lack of training that made him clumsy enough for you to spot him? Do the psychic abilities that seem to be part of this viral syndrome only develop with time? How old were the vampires who were murdered?"

"Another interesting point," Asher said. "Lotta had been a vampire since the mid-1700s; Hammersmith and King were younger, almost exactly one hundred years. Ysidro saw all of them made. I don't know about Calvaire. One of the many things," he added dryly, "that we don't know about Calvaire."

"Valentin Calvaire," Ysidro murmured, settling back against the worn leather squabs of the hansom cab and tenting his long fingers like a stack of ivory spindles, reminding Asher somehow of a marmalade tomcat so old that its fur has gone nearly white. "Curious, how many trails seem to lead back to Valentin Calvaire."

"He was the first victim—presumably," Asher said. "At least the first victim killed in London; the only victim not *from* London; the only victim whose body we have never found. What do you know about him?"

"Less than I should like," the vampire replied, his voice soft beneath the rattling clamor of the theater-going crowds in

Drury Lane all about them. "He was, as I said, one of the Paris vampires—he came here to London eight months ago."

"Why?"

"That was a topic which he never permitted to arise."

The vampire's tone was absolutely neutral, but Asher's mustache twitched as he detected the distaste in that chilly statement. Ysidro, he surmised with a hidden grin, had probably had very little use for M. Calvaire.

"I take it he was not of the nobility."

"What passes for nobility in France these days," Ysidro stated, with soft viciousness, "would not have been permitted to clear away the tables of those whose birth and style of breeding they so pitifully attempt to emulate. Anything resembling decent blood in that country was flushed down the gutters of the Place Louis-Quinze—excuse me, the Place de la Concorde—a hundred and seventeen years ago. What is left is the seed of those who fled or those who made themselves useful to that *condottiere* Napoleon. Scarcely what one would call honorable antecedents."

After a moment's silence, he went on, "Yes, Calvaire claimed noble birth. It was precisely the sort of thing he would do."

"How long had he been a vampire?"

Ysidro's dark eyes narrowed with thought. "My guess would be less than forty years."

Asher raised his eyebrows in surprise. He had, he realized, subconsciously equated age with power among the vampires— it was to the two oldest vampires, Ysidro and Grippen, that the others bowed in fear. The younger ones—Bully Joe Davies and the Opera dancer Chloé—seemed weak, almost pathetic.

"Consider it," Ysidro urged levelly. "Paris has been in a state of intermittent chaos since the fall of the Bourbon kings. Thirty-five years ago it underwent siege by the Prussians, shelling, riots, and government—if such it can be termed—by a rabble of rioters who formed a Commune and gave short shrift to anyone whom they suspected of treason—for which read, disagreement with their ideals. Vampires as a group rely largely upon a tranquil society to protect them. Wolves do not hunt in a burning forest."

Just as well, Asher thought dourly. During the riots in the Shantung Province, he'd had enough to worry about without a red-eyed kuei creeping up on him in the burned ruins of the Lutheran mission where he'd been hiding. After a moment, he asked, "And how did Grippen react to Calvaire's coming here?"

Ysidro was silent for a time, while the cab jolted its way through the increasing crowds of traffic toward the Waterloo Bridge. Rain made a faint, brittle whispering sound on the hardened leather roof of the cab. It had begun again late in the afternoon, while Asher was in the Public Records Office in quest of property bought in the last eight months in Lambeth by either Valentin Calvaire, Chrétien Sanglot, or, just possibly, Joseph Davies. Now the whole city smelled of moisture, ozone, the exhaust of motorcars, the dung of horses, and the salt-and-sewage pungence of the river.

"Not well," he said at length. "You understand, we—vampires—find travel unnerving in the extreme. We are conservatives at heart; hence the myth that a vampire must rest within his native soil. Rather, he must always have a secure resting place, and such things are difficult to come by on the road. Calvaire had naturally heard of both Grippen and myself. When he arrived he—promenaded himself, I suppose you would say—and did not drink of human blood until he had been contacted by the master vampire of the city."

"Grippen," Asher said. "Not yourself."

For the first time, he saw the flash of irritation, of anger, in the Spaniard's yellow eyes. But Ysidro only said mildly, "Even so."

"Why?" he pressed.

Ysidro merely turned his head a little, haughtily contemplating the throngs on the crowded flagways from beneath the lowered lids of his eyes.

"I've heard of Grippen's cadre, Grippen's get," Asher persisted. "Lord Ernchester, Anthea, Lotta, Chloé, Ned Hammersmith . . . Even though Danny King was the Farrens' servant, even though it was to them that he owed loyalty, it was Grippen who made him, 'at Charles' request and his own.' According to Anthea Farren, you were both made by the same master vampire at about the same time. Why is he the Master of London, and not yourself?"

The memory of Anthea's face returned to him, framed in the dark hair with its red streaks like henna. She had warned him, had pulled him out of Grippen's hold; she had held the enraged vampire back from killing him while he escaped. Yet she and her husband were also Grippen's get—as Bully Joe Davies had said, Grippen's slaves.

Why slaves?

For a moment he thought Ysidro would maintain that disdainful alabaster silence. But without turning his head back, the vampire replied, "Perhaps because I do not care to trouble myself." The familiar supercilious note was absent from his voice as he said it; he sounded, if anything, a little weary. Asher had the momentary sense of dealing, not with a vampire, but with the man whose occasional, oddly sweet smile flickered across those narrow features.

But like the smile, that evanescent glimmer of resignation, of a vanished humanness, was gone—like the things one thinks one sees by starlight. Ysidro's voice became again as neutral as his coloring, as if even the holding of opinions had become meaningless to him over the years. "And it would be a trouble, as well as a certain amount of peril, to challenge Grippen's authority. I personally do not care to disrupt my existence by stooping to fight with a *peon* such as he. Calvaire was evidently not so fastidious. He swore allegiance to Grippen, but it is clear that he never intended to submit himself to our medical friend's authority . . ."

"Medical?" Asher's voice was sharp, and Ysidro looked at him once more with all his old chilly disinterest.

"Lionel Grippen was a Doctor of Medicine and accounted very learned in his time, though, considering the practices of the day, this was not praising him to the skies. For a few decades past his initiation to the vampire state, he kept up with medical practice. Now he reads the journals, curses, and hurls them across the room, enraged that they no longer speak of anything with which he is familiar. Though I understand," he added, "that it has been nearly two centuries since he has done even that."

"Has he, indeed?" Asher stroked his mustache thoughtfully. "You wouldn't know if he still has any of his old kit?"

"I doubt the originals still exist, though he would know where and how to obtain more." The vampire regarded him now with interest, his head tipped a little to one side, his long, colorless hair blowing against the fragile cheekbones with the movement of the night.

"Interesting," Asher said. "Here, cabby! Pull up!"

The man drew rein, cursing as he edged his horse out of the stream of traffic pouring off the Waterloo Bridge. Foot traffic was heavy here as well. Ysidro slipped from the cab and vanished at once into the jostling shapes beneath the blaze of the bridge's lights. At Asher's command, the cabby started forward again, grumbling at care-for-nothing toff fares, and proceeded to the chaos of cabs, carts, omnibuses, and pedestrians surrounding the half-constructed sprawl of Waterloo Station, a Dantesque vision of brick, gaslight, scaffolding, and smoke. As the cab jostled through the porridge of vehicles, Asher pulled off his gloves and drew from his ulster pocket a thick package. LAMBERT'S, said the modest label, with a discreet crest.

With chilled fingers, he drew out two silver chains like the one he wore around his neck beneath his starched and respectable collar. It was tricky fastening the small clips around his wrists; but, for obvious reasons, it had been impossible to solicit Ysidro's help. He tugged his shirt cuffs down over them and pulled his gloves back on, for the night was cold as well as wet; there was another shape in the tissue wrappings, narrow, like a child's arm bone. He freed it and held it to the rain-streaming light—a sterling silver letter opener in the shape of an ornamental dagger. Having only bought it that afternoon, he had had no time to whet it and doubted in any case that the blade would hold much of an edge, but the point was certainly sharp enough to pierce flesh. Like a Scotsman's *skean dhu* it had no guard. It fit neatly into his boot.

He paid off the cab in front of the station. The man grunted, cracked his whip over his jaded old screw of a horse, and vanished as surely as the vampire had into the teeming mob.

For a time, Asher stood in the open space of light and noise before the station, hearing the screeches of the trains, the hiss of steam, and the voices of thousands of travelers shouting, and feeling the rumble of the engines through the ground under his feet. Weariness made him feel slightly disoriented, for he had waited for Bully Joe Davies in the alley behind Prince of Wales Colonnade for hours after his return from Ernchester House, and had risen to meet Lydia at the Park after only a few hours' sleep. He had meant to nap during the day; but, between Chancery Lane and Lambert's in Bond Street, the rainy afternoon had slipped too quickly away.

Now he felt chilled and weary, trying to recall when he had last slept through the night. A woman jostled past him, unseeing; as he watched her too-bright plaid dress retreat across the square to the platform, he remembered the blonde woman with the two children on the train from Oxford and shivered.

In the field—"abroad," as he and his colleagues politely termed those places where they were licensed to steal and kill— the train station was God's own gift to agents, particularly one as vast as Waterloo, even with half its platforms still under construction: a thousand ways to bolt and so absolutely impersonal that you might brush shoulders with your own brother on the platform and never raise your eyes. Beyond question it was one of the hunting grounds of the vampire.

Pulling his bowler down over his eyes and hunching his shoulders against the rain, he crossed the puddled darkness of the pavement toward the blazing maw of the Lambeth Cut.

As he traversed that squalid and tawdry boulevard, his feeling of oppression grew. The crowds around the theatres and gin palaces there were scarcely less thick than those around the station, and far noisier. Music drifted from open doors; men in evening clothes crowded the entryways with women whose rain cloaks fell open to show brightly colored dresses beneath; jewels flashed in the lamplight, some real, some as fake as the women's smiles. Now and then, a woman alone would call to him or crowd through the people on the flagway to stride a few steps with him, with a few jolly words in the characteristic slur he'd recognized in Bully Joe Davies' voice. As he smiled politely, tipped his hat, and shook his head, he wondered if one of them was Davies' sister Madge.

This, too, was an ideal hunting ground.

It depressed him, this consciousness of those silent killers who drank human life, Ysidro had told him, one night in perhaps four or five. It was, he supposed, like the consciousness he had developed in all those years with the Department, the automatic identification of exits and the habitual checking of a man's shoes, sleeves, or hands.

Horace Blaydon's bellowing voice echoed in his mind, in the big carbolic-smelling theatre at Radclyffe: "I'll tell you one thing that'll happen to you, if any of you manages to stay the course and become a doctor, which, looking at your pasty little faces, I sincerely take leave to doubt—you'll be spoiled forever for the beauty of life. You'll never see a girl's rosy blush again without wondering if it's phthisis, never hear your fat old uncle's jolly laugh without thinkin': 'The old boy's ridin' for a stroke.' You'll never read Dickens again without pickin' it apart for genetic blood factors and unhealthy drains."

"A rather unfortunate choice of examples," Lydia had remarked, when she'd joined Asher by the door where he'd been waiting to escort her to tea at her uncle's college, "since, with a complexion like his and that prematurely white hair, it's obvious the man's heading for an apoplexy himself. I wonder if the godlike Dennis will turn into that in twenty years' time?"

And Asher, suffering under the sting of being brown and unobtrusive and skirting the shadowy borders of middle age, had felt insensibly cheered.

But, he thought, recalling Lydia's clinical reaction to being surrounded by vampires, old Blaydon had, of course, been absolutely right.

He turned from the Cut to Lower Ditch Street, a dingy thoroughfare whose few gaslights did little to dispel the rainy gloom. It was a neighborhood of crumbling brick terraces and shuttered shops, grimy, cramped, and sordid. Down the street, yellowish light shone on the pavement outside a gin shop; other than that, the street was dark. Asher's own footfalls sounded loud, as did the thin, steady patter of the rain. Halfway down the unbroken frontage was the door he sought: Number 216. Its windows were dark; looking up, he saw them all heavily shuttered. The door was barred with a padlock and hasp.

Asher stood for a long time before it, listening, as if, like the vampires, he could scent peril at a distance. In spite of his weariness, the ache in his bones as if he had fallen down a flight of stairs, and the hurt of his flesh for sleep, he forced all his senses alert. Bully Joe Davies had said that he was being stalked. The killer, a vampire who moved so silently that he could, in fact, stalk other vampires, might be watching him from the shadows of those dark buildings, waiting for him to leave the lights of the street.

For that matter, Asher thought ironically as he crossed back to the mouth of the alley that ran behind Lower Ditch Street, Davies himself might be waiting for him. The fledgling vampire had moved so clumsily he doubted Davies' ability to detect Ysidro, either last night or now, if Ysidro was, in fact, watching over him. However, if he was wrong . . .

Uneasily, Asher scanned what little he could see of the smelly cleft of the alley and the street behind him for sign of the vampire. There was none, of course. He was reminded of the picture an old Indian fighter in Arizona had once drawn for him—a white page with a horizon line bisecting it, two pebbles, and a minuscule cactus. It was titled "Arizona Landscape with Apaches."

He drew the silver knife from his boot, holding it concealed against his arm. 216 Lower Ditch Street had been purchased three months ago by Chrétien Sanglot, shortly after, Asher guessed, Bully Joe Davies had met the Frenchman.

Cautiously, he advanced down the back lane, rain trickling

from his hat brim and into his collar. There was a sharp crash from the brimming dustbins, and tiny red eyes glinted at him in irritation from the darkness. The alley was filthy beyond description, garbage and refuse of all kinds mingling into a kind of primordial slop under the steady patter of the rain.

Counting the cramped little slots of yards, Asher found Number 216 easily and slipped through the broken boards of its back fence without trouble. The ground oozed with reddish mud; at the back of the yard, barely visible in the gloom, a broken-down outhouse simmered in a pool of nameless slime. "The Houses of Parliament," he recalled abstractly, such buildings were christened in some areas of London . . .

The rain had eased to a whisper. He strained his ears as he crossed the yard, trying to catch some sound, some signal of danger.

In the yard he might be safe, at least from Bully Joe. He doubted the fledgling could come at him through that much water and mud without a sound. But once he was in the house, if Davies had seen Ysidro waiting for him, he was a dead man.

The wet wood of the back steps creaked sharply beneath his weight. The door was only a vague outline in shadow, but he could see no padlock. Cautiously he turned the knob. The door creaked inward.

"Come no further until I have lighted the gas," Ysidro's voice said softly from the darkness, startling Asher nearly out of his skin. "I think you should see this."

Ten

A pin-burst explosion of gold came in the darkness, bright to Asher's straining eyes, and there was a sting of sulphur. Already his mind was taking in the smell that filled his nostrils; the ashy, fetid choke of burned meat overpowering the mustiness of mildew and dust.

Slow and gold, the light swelled around the steel fishtail of the burner, widening out to fill the whole of the square and dingy room.

A coffin lay five feet from where Asher stood in the doorway, filled with ash and bone. From here, it looked like a lot of bone, the whole skeleton intact and black, but for the moment he didn't go to check. He looked instead at the stone floor around the coffin, then sideways, past where Ysidro stood near the stove, to the dripping puddle beneath the vampire's shed Inverness, which lay over the warped wooden counter top. There was no trace of dripped water anywhere else in the room, save where Ysidro himself had walked from the outer door to where he stood, just beside the stove.

"So much," he said quietly, "for a vampire who remains awake a little longer than his brethren. The rain didn't stop until nearly dawn. The ground wouldn't have been even spongy-dry until well into daylight."

He walked past the coffin to the cellar door, an open black throat on the other side of the room, taking his magnifying glass from his pocket. Fresh scratches and faint shuffling tracks marked the dusty linoleum of the floor, and here and there was a dim footprint, outlined in crusts of dried mud. After a moment's study he put the glass away and replaced it with the measuring tape.

"Two of them," he said, kneeling to mark the length of one

pale smudge. "One nearly my height, the other three or four inches taller, by the length of the stride. Together they carried the coffin up from the cellar to here, where there was daylight." He sat back on his haunches, studying the shuffled and over-lapped spoor.

"Your friend Mr. Davies," Ysidro murmured softly. Asher knew the vampire was going to cross to the coffin then and concentrated on watching him. Through a haze of what felt like almost unbearable sleepiness, he saw Ysidro take two long, quick strides; when it passed he was standing above the black-ened remains, a colorless specter in his pale gray suit and webby hair. "The bones are intact."

He folded himself like an ivory marionette down beside the coffin and picked with fastidious fingers at what was inside. There was no expression on his thin face. Pocketing the mea-suring tape, Asher joined him in time to see him slide from between the ribs something that crumbled even in the inhuman lightness of Ysidro's touch—something about a foot and a half long that was too straight to be a bone.

Ysidro dropped it almost at once, pulled a silk handkerchief from some inner pocket, and wiped his fingers, still without expression. "Whitethorn," he said. "Burned nearly to ash, but still it stings."

Asher caught the long, narrow hand in his and turned it palm-up to the light. Faint red welts could already be seen on the white flesh. The fingers felt utterly cold to his touch, fragile as the sticks of an antique fan. After a moment, Ysidro drew his hand away.

"They were taking no chances."

"They knew what to use, obviously."

"Any clown with access to a lending library would," the vampire returned.

Asher nodded and turned his attention to what was left of the corpse. There were, as he'd hoped, a number of keys in the vicinity of the blackened pelvis—*trouser pocket,* he thought ab-sently, *the carryall of a man who isn't used to wearing a jacket when he works.* Don Simon had been right about vampires' combustibility: the bones were intact, not seared to crumbling and unrecognizable fragments as Lotta's had been. The place where the spine had been severed to separate head and body was horribly clear.

"Why is that?" he inquired softly. "*Is* vampirism a type of petrification that slowly alters first the flesh, then the bone, into something other than mortal substance? Is that why the younger vampires go up like flashpaper, while the older ones burn more slowly, more completely?"

"I don't think it can be so simple as that," Simon replied, at the end of a long hesitation. "There are—interlocking effects, psychic as well as physical. But yes—I have often believed it to be as you say. Grippen was burned once by the sun, fifty, seventy years ago. It was nowhere near as bad as my own experience during the Fire, and now the scars are almost gone. We toughen a little, as I said, even to daylight. But not to this extent."

There was silence as they looked at each other, then, across the coffin contents of ash and heat-split buttons, brown mortal eyes looking into immortal gold.

"How old," Asher asked at last, "is the oldest vampire in Europe?"

"Three hundred and fifty-two years," Ysidro responded softly, "give or take a few."

"You?"

A slight inclination of that strange, demon head. "To the best of my knowledge."

Asher got to his feet and hunted the cupboards until he found a brass lamp, which he lit from the gas, mildly cursing the inconvenience in Ciceronian Latin and wishing that electric torches were either small enough to carry easily about his person or reliable enough to warrant the nuisance of lugging them. A brief examination showed him no locks or hasps, though five of the keys he'd picked from the ashes were of the cheap padlock type. Perhaps Davies, like Calvaire, had several different safe houses. Ysidro followed him without a word as he crossed to the cellar steps. The stink of mold and wet earth rose about them like chokedamp as they descended.

"I thought the killer might be Grippen, you know," he said, and Ysidro nodded, absolutely unsurprised by the theory. "I suspect you did, too."

"The thought crossed my mind. It was why I sought out a mortal agent. This was not sheerly because I consider him a lout and a brute: he had good reason to wish Calvaire dead. Calvaire was a challenge to his authority. It was clear that Calvaire was trying to establish his own power here in London, even when none of us knew he was purchasing property, let alone creating a fledgling who would do his bidding. And Grippen is of the height to have made the marks upon Neddy Hammersmith's windows."

They paused at the foot of the steps, Asher lifting the lamp nearly to the low ceiling beams to illuminate the cellar around them. Its glare smudged the dusty boards of a nearly empty coalbin in light and caught the fraying edges of translucent curtains of cobweb, thick with dust.

"Would he have harmed his own fledglings? Davies didn't think he would."

"Davies did not know Grippen." Ysidro paused for a long moment, a faint line flexing briefly between his ash-colored brows. "You must understand that the bond between a master vampire and the fledgling he creates is an incredibly strong one. It is not merely that, without the teaching of the master, the fledgling cannot hope to survive in a world where the veriest touch of sunlight will ignite every cell in his body—cannot hope even to make sense of the new world dinning and crying and burning into senses that suddenly gape like an open wound."

He spoke hesitantly now, not picking over what he would and would not tell, but struggling with things that in 350 years he had not told anyone. "In the making of the new vampire, their minds lock. The dying man's or woman's clings to that of one who has already passed through the experience of physical death. In a sense," he went on, not awkwardly but very slowly, like a demon trying to explain to the living what it is like to exist surrounded by the damned, "the fledgling must give his soul to the master, to hold for him while he—crosses over. I cannot explain it more nearly than that."

"A man must love his life very desperately," Asher said, after long silence, "to do that."

"It is easier to do than you think," Simon replied, "when you are feeling your own heart falter to a stop." Then he smiled, wry in the dim glow of the lamp but with that faint echo of an old charm, like a faded portrait of someone he had once been. "A drowning man seldom pushes a plank away, no matter who holds the other end. But you understand how absolute is the dominance established."

Queer and sharp to Asher's mind, like the image in a dream, rose the vision of a slim, fair hidalgo in the pearl-sewn black velvets of the Spanish court, his head lying back over the white hand of the thin little man who knelt beside him. Like a fragile spider, Anthea had said . . .

"Is that why you've never made a fledgling?"

Ysidro did not look at him. *"Sí,"* he whispered, lapsing for an instant into the antique Spanish of his past. His eyes flicked back to Asher's, and the wry, sweet smile returned. "That, and other reasons. Master vampires distrust their fledglings, of course, for the resentment engendered by that dominance, that iron intimacy, is enormous. They distrust still more those who are not their fledglings, over whom they have no control. In any event to be vampire is to have an almost fanatic desire to command absolutely one's environment and everyone about one. For we are, as you have observed, oddly fragile creatures in our way, besides being necessarily selfish and strong-willed to begin with in order to survive the transition to the vampire state at all.

"So yes," he added, segueing abruptly back to the original topic of conversation, "I believe Grippen would kill his own fledglings, did he think they might be leaguing with another vampire to dispute his mastery, either from fondness for his rival, like Lotta, or weakness, like Neddy, or resentment; though Danny King might accept Grippen's dominance over himself, he hated Grippen for holding it over Charles and An-thea. Many things pointed to a vampire killing his own, and the logical candidate was Grippen. But there are two of them, as you said, and Grippen, like us all, is a creature of the night."

He paused for a moment, considering Asher sidelong from cold, pale eyes. Then he continued, "I believe this is what you seek?" His cold fingers took the lamp from Asher's hand, lifting it high as he stepped a short way into the cellar.

What Asher had taken for a shadow denser than the rest he now saw was a doorway, its lintel barely five feet in height, its thick oak door hanging open to reveal a throat of blackness beyond. The light picked out the shapes of old stonework, a medieval ceiling groin and the top of a worn spiral of stone steps.

"A merchant's house once stood on this ground," the vam-pire said, crossing the cellar with that odd, drifting walk, Asher at his heels. "Later it was an inn—the Goat and Compasses; originally, of course, it was 'God Encompasseth Us,' a pious motto painted above the door which did not save it from being burned by Cromwell's troops." He led the way carefully down the foot-hollowed twist of steps to the cellar that lay below— small, bare, and circular, containing nothing but the ruin of mildewed sacking, rats' nests, and four bricks, set in a coffin-shaped rectangle in the middle of the floor to keep whatever had once rested upon them up off the damp.

"London is full of such places," Ysidro continued, his voice the whisper of a bleached ghost in the muffling darkness. "Places where old priories, inns, or houses were burned, their foundations later built upon by men who knew nothing of the cellars beneath."

Asher walked to the bricks, studied their layout thoughtfully, then returned to hold the lantern close to the framing of the stair's narrow arch. Without a word, he ascended again, study-ing the walls carefully as he went. The door at the top, examined more thoroughly, had once been padlocked from the inside. The padlock remained closed—it was the hasp that had been ripped free of the wood.

"Why not a hasp on the outside as well, for when he was gone?"

"If he was gone," Ysidro said, "what purpose would it serve beyond telling an intruder that there might be some thing of value hidden there? An empty coffin is not a thing one steals easily."

Behind him in the stair, the vampire's soft-toned words continued to echo weirdly against the old stonework. "I have no doubt that this is one of the places where Calvaire slept, utterly beyond the reach of sunlight. Davies would have known of it and come here when he needed shelter."

"Didn't help him much." Asher scratched a corner of his mustache, fished from his pocket the padlock keys he had taken from Bully Joe's ashes, and tried them in the lock. "It just made more work for his murderers, carrying his coffin up to the kitchen to ignite the body in the sunlight." The second key sprang the lock open—Asher noted it, returned it to his pocket, and moved a pace or two down the steps to reexamine the ancient stone wall at the turn of the stairs. "Calvaire was his master; it's clear he used Bully Joe's knowledge of the neighborhood to purchase the ground lease on the building, so, of course, Bully Joe would have keys." He frowned—even with the magnifying lens he took from his pocket, he did not find the thing he sought. "He said Calvaire was dead—he seemed pretty sure of it."

"Perhaps he buried him, as Anthea and I buried Danny and poor Ned Hammersmith. The poor . . . " Ysidro paused, looking about him at the narrow confines of the stair and the hairpin turn of the enclosing wall. A slight frown tugged at his sparse brows. "But if the coffin were carried up from the subcellar . . ."

"They'd have had to carry it upright to get it around the corner, yes. I'm not certain, but I don't think a single man could have done so with a body in it—carried it so firmly and lightly that it left no scratches on the walls or the doorjambs. Even two men carrying it at a steep angle would have conceivably left some mark. There's enough light in the cellar above to have

145

begun burning the body there, so they couldn't have carried it separately. And then there's the door itself."

Simon followed him up the stairs and regarded the twisted hasp with its bent screws, the wood still clinging to their threads. In the ochre glow of the lamp, his eyes were somber—he was beginning to understand.

"There is no mark of a crow on the doorjambs," he said, and Asher recognized the Elizabethan word for spanner.

"No," Asher said. "Nor is there anything that could have been used for a fulcrum to get a lever under the door handle. It was jerked out with a straight pull. Again, it's *just* within the realm of possibility that a human could have done it, but it isn't very probable."

There was long silence, in which, faintly, Asher could hear the patter of renewed rain from above. Then Ysidro said, "But it cannot have been a vampire. Even had he worn a glove to protect his hand from the stake, the daylight would have destroyed him."

"Would it?" Asher led the way up the cellar steps to the gaslighted kitchen above. The coffin gaped on the floor before them, like some monstrous fish platter displaying a horrid *chef d'oeuvre* on the worn and ugly linoleum. In a kindling drawer near the stove, Asher found a piece of candle, angled it down the lamp chimney to get a flame, and bore it through the door that gave into the front part of the house.

"Did Calvaire ever speak of Paris? Of what caused him to leave?"

"No." Ysidro drifted beside him, a soundless ghost in his gray suit. With the gas turned up full, it was obvious no one had crossed the dust-choked parlor or the hall from the front door. "He was not a man who dwelt upon the past, even so recent a past as that. Perhaps he had a reason, but many of us are that way. It is better so."

"You said when he came here that he 'promenaded himself'—waited to make his kill until Grippen had contacted him, and swore fealty to Grippen, in exchange for Grippen's permission to hunt. But it's obvious that even an inexperienced fledgling, if he's careful, can conceal himself from the two oldest known vampires in Europe, at least for a time."

Again Ysidro was silent, turning the implications of that over in his mind.

"Was there ever any talk of vampires older than yourself? Much older, say, a hundred years older? Two hundred years?"

An odd expression flickered in the back of Don Simon's pale eyes. He paused on the stairs to the first floor, his pale hair haloed in the parlor gaslight behind him. "Of what are you thinking, James?"

"Of vampirism," Asher said quietly. "Of the slow change of the body, cell by cell, into something other than mortal flesh and mortal bone—of the growth of the vampire's powers. My wife's a pathologist. I know that diseases change, like syphilis, the Plague, or chicken pox, even sometimes producing new symptoms, if they continue long enough without killing the patient."

"And you think the vampire state a disease?"

"It's a blood-borne contagion, isn't it?"

"That is not all that it is."

"Alcoholism alters the brain, driving its victims to madness," Asher said. "High fevers can destroy the mind or parts of the mind; the mind itself can bring on physical ailments—nervousness, declines, what women call 'vapors,' brain fever. Any family practitioner could have told you that, even before Freud started doing his work on nervous hysteria. Emotional shock can cause anything from a stroke to a miscarriage. If you've traveled in India, seen the things the fakirs do, you'll know the mind can perform stranger feats upon the body than that.

"What I'm getting at is this: Does vampirism have symptoms, developments, which only manifest themselves after a certain span of years? A long span, longer than most vampires live or can remember? Would one eventually, in the span of years, toughen even against daylight? And you didn't answer my original question."

Instead of replying at once, Ysidro resumed his climb to the floor above, Asher following at his heels, the burning candle still in his hand. He lit the gas in the upper hall and opened the two doors there. One room was a parlor, the other a bedroom, both obviously long out of use.

"It is an odd thing," Ysidro said slowly, "but there are not many vampires in Europe—or in America, which has had its own troubles—much over two hundred and fifty years old. These days vampirism is a phenomenon of the cities, where the poor are uncounted and deaths are relatively invisible. But cities tend to trap vampires in their own cataclysms."

He opened the door at the end of the hall, leading to the attic stair. Asher paused briefly to study the two heavy hasps screwed into the wood of its inner side. Neither had been torn out; the padlocks, neatly open, were hooked through the steel staples on the doorframe.

He tried Bully's remaining keys out of sheer routine—two of them fitted. Unlike the cellar, the attic door had a single hasp on the outside, but it was clear from the locks that no one had forced his way in or out.

They traded a glance, and Asher shrugged. "We might as well see what's up there anyway—there may be papers."

"Dr. Grippen and I were the only two who survived the Fire of London," Ysidro went on, as they ascended the stair. "I only lived by lucky chance. As far as I know, no Munich vampire survived the troubles of the forties, and no Russian vampire Napoleon's invasion, occupation, and incineration of Moscow. Rome has always been a perilous city for the Undead, certainly since the founding of the Inquisition."

At the top of the attic stairs, the door stood open. A square of grimy yellowish light indicated a window and a street light somewhere below.

"*Qué va?*" Ysidro whispered behind Asher in the dark. "Did he sleep here, the windows would be muffled . . ."

It took Asher a moment, in the almost total darkness beyond the feeble circle of the candle's light, to see what lay on the floor halfway between the door and the left-hand wall.

"Calvaire?" he asked softly, as Ysidro brushed past him and strode to that grisly heap of bones, ash, and seared metal odd-

148

ments. Buttons, brace buckles, the lacing tips of shoes, and the charred metal barrel of a stylographic pen all glinted briefly in the fluttering yellow glow as he came to stand behind the kneeling vampire. Then he looked on past them, to the farther wall. A hinged panel gaped open, showing a coffin within a small closet which would have been totally indistinguishable from the wall itself when shut. Thick draperies and shutters had been torn from the attic's single window. In the silence, the rain on the low roof was like the ominous tattoo of Prussian drums.

"At least a man," he added, lowering his candle again to shed its weak radiance on the remains, "since there are no corset stays." He was interested to note that, judging by the relative wholeness of the bones, Ysidro seemed to be correct about the French vampire's age.

The vampire lifted a gold ring clear of the mess and blew the thin coating of ash and dust from it. A chance draft made the candle flame waver; the diamond of its setting winked like a bright and baleful eye. "Calvaire," he affirmed softly. "So he must indeed have wakened, with the searing of the light, to stagger already dying from his coffin . . ."

"Which is a curious thing," Asher remarked, "if our killer, being a vampire himself, knew from the first that the head had to be cut off to prevent such a thing from happening. Almost as curious as the fact that the door downstairs wasn't locked." He stooped beside Ysidro to pick a couple of keys from the ghastly debris. He matched the wards and found them duplicates of Bully Joe's keys. "There's no mark of charring on the floor between the coffin's place of concealment and the body, either. If, as you say, the flesh begins to burn at once . . ."

"He could not have admitted the killer himself," Ysidro said. "Whatever the capabilities of the killer, Calvaire at least could not have gone anywhere near the door at the bottom of the steps during the hours of daylight."

"And yet the killer entered that way."

Ysidro lifted an inquiring brow.

"Had he not, he could simply have left the way he came, without unlocking the door at the bottom of the step at all.

What it looks like is that Calvaire knew his killer, and admitted him himself, by night . . . Is it usual for a vampire to have two coffins in the same building?"

"It is not unusual," Ysidro said calmly. "Fledglings frequently take refuge with their masters. And then, there are few houses which are safe for vampires, and those which are, ofttimes become veritable rookeries of the Undead, as you yourself found in Savoy Walk. That was one of my reasons for keeping from you as many details as possible. Not for their protection, you understand, but for yours."

"I'm touched by your concern," Asher said dryly. "Could the killer have killed or incapacitated Calvaire in some other way, leaving the body to be destroyed when daylight came?"

The vampire did not answer for a moment, sitting hunkered beside the burned skeleton, his arms extended out over his knees. "I do not know," he said at length. "But if he had broken Calvaire's neck or back—and the skull seems to be lying at a strange angle, though that, of course, might simply be the way it rolled when the muscles were consumed—it would have incapacitated him, so that he lay here on the floor, conscious but unable to move, while the light slowly brightened in the window. If our killer is himself immune to daylight," he added neutrally, "it is possible that he remained to watch."

"Another argument," Asher said, "for the fact that Calvaire knew him, it being less entertaining to watch the sufferings of those to whom we are unknown and indifferent."

"Interesting." Ysidro turned the ring he held this way and that, the candlelight shattering through its delicate facets to salt that alabaster face with a thousand points of colored fire. "The odd thing is that among vampires, there *is* a legend of an ancient vampire, so old and powerful that no one ever sees him anymore—so old that even other vampires cannot sense his passage. Even a hundred and fifty years ago, other vampires were avoiding his haunts. To them he was semifabulous, like a ghost. Traditions among them said that he had been a vampire since before the days of the Black Death."

"And what were his haunts?" Asher asked, knowing already what the Spaniard would say.

The expressionless eyes raised from the glitter of the gem before them. "He slept—or was said to sleep—in the crypts below the charnels of the churchyard of the Holy Innocents, in Paris."

Eleven

———

It is not the city that it was."

If there were nuances to that soft, light voice of bitterness, anger, or regret, it would have taken a vampire's hyperacute perceptions to read them—Asher himself heard none. Around him the closed cab jostled and swayed. When his elbow, raised where his hand, linked through the hanging strap, came in contact with the window, he felt through his coat sleeve the chill of the glass. The noises of the street came to him dimly: the clatter of wheels, on pavement of wood and asphalt, rebounding from the high brown walls of the *immeubles*; the occasional hoots of motorcars; the pungent cursing of the sidewalk vendors; and the gay, drifting frenzy of violin and accordion that spoke of some *caf' conc'* in progress.

Blindfolded, he could see nothing, but the sounds of Paris were distinctive and as bright a kaleidoscope as its sights. No one, he thought, who had ever been here ever questioned how it was in this place that Impressionism came to be.

Ysidro's voice went on, "I have no sense of being at home here—this sterile, inorganic town where everything is thrice washed before and after anyone touches it. It is the same everywhere, of course, but in Paris it seems particularly ironic. They seem to have taken this man Pasteur very seriously."

The noises changed; the crowd of vehicles around them seemed more dense, but the echoes of buildings were gone. Asher smelled the sewery stink of the river. A bridge, then— and judging by the length and the din of a small square and buildings halfway along, it could only be the Pont Neuf, a name which, like that of New College, Oxford, had not been accurate for a number of centuries. In a short time, they turned right, and continued in that direction. Asher calculated they were headed for the old Marais district, the one-time aristocratic neighborhoods that had not been badly damaged by either the Prussians, the Communards, or Baron Haussmann, but said nothing. If Ysidro chose to believe that blindfolding him would keep him in absolute ignorance of the whereabouts of the Paris vampires, he—and they—were welcome to do so.

He was uncomfortably aware that the Paris vampires had not even the threat of the day killer to reconcile them to the presence of a human in their midst.

"My most vivid memories of Paris are of its mud, of course," the vampire went on quietly. "Everyone's were, who knew it then. It was astounding stuff, *la boue de Paris*—black and vile, like a species of oil. You could never eradicate either its stain or its smell. It clung to everything, and you could nose Paris six miles away in open country. In the days when every gentleman wore white silk stockings, it was pure hell." The faintest hint of self-mockery crept into his voice, and Asher pictured that still and haughty face framed in the white of a court wig.

"The beggars all smelled of it, too," Ysidro added. "Hunting in the poor quarters was always a nightmare. Now . . ." He paused, and there was a curious flex in that supple voice.

"It would take me a long time to relearn Paris. Everything has changed. It is strange territory to me now. I do not know its boltholes or hiding places; I no longer even speak the language properly. Every time I say *ci* instead of *ce, je ne l'aime point* instead of *je ne l'aime pas*, every time I say *je fît quelquechose* instead of *je l'ai fait*, I mark myself as a stranger."

"You only mark yourself as a foreigner who has learned French from a very old book," Asher replied easily. "Have you ever talked to a Brahman in London for the first time? Or heard an American southerner speak of 'redding up a room'?" The cab stopped; under the silk scarf bound over his eyes, Asher could detect very little light and knew that the street itself was quite dark, particularly for a city as brightly illuminated as Paris. The place was quiet, too, save for the far-off noises of traffic in some nearby square—the Place de la Bastille at a guess—but the smell was the smell of poverty, of too many families sharing too few privies, of cheap cooking, and of dirt. The Marais, Asher knew, had declined drastically from the days when Louis XV had courted Jeanne Poisson through its candlelit salons.

There was a slight jogging as the vampire got out of the cab and the muted exchange of voices and, presumably, francs. Then a light, firm hand touched his arm, guiding him, and he heard the cab rattle away down the cobbles. "Do you speak Spanish any more at all?"

There was level pavement, then a step down, and a sense of close walls and cold shade—the doorway vestibule whose gates would open into the central court of one of the big old *hôtels particuliers*. Beside him, very quiet, came Ysidro's voice: "I doubt I could even make myself understood in Madrid."

"Have you never gone back there, then?"

In the ensuing moment of silence, Asher could almost see Ysidro's eyes resting on him with their calm, noncommittal gaze while the vampire sifted through all possible responses for the one which would give the least. "What would be the point?" he asked at last. "My people are, and have been since the Reconquista, suspicious and intolerant." Asher realized with a small start that by *my people* he meant Spaniards, not vampires. "With the Inquisition probing every cellar for heretics and Jews, what chance would a vampire stand? It is possible in most circumstances to avoid the touch of silver, but such avoidance is, in civilized countries, not marked. Were it noticed in Spain in those days, it would have been fatal."

Asher heard then a faint scratching, like the furtive scuffle of a mouse behind a wainscot, as the vampire scraped at the panels of the door with his nail, a sound which only other vampires would hear.

But other vampires, of course, would have detected their voices in the street.

He heard nothing within, but sensed feet floating weightlessly down the stair; his heart, it seemed, was thumping uncomfortably fast. "Do they know about me?" he asked.

They had taken the night mail by way of Calais. The porters had grumbled at the size and awkwardness of the huge leather-

and-iron trunk that was ticketed as part of Asher's luggage, but had been surprised at its comparative lightness. "Wot you got in there, mate, bleedin' feathers?"

"I trust that all travel arrangements will go as we have made them," Ysidro had commented, leaning on the *Lord Warden*'s aft rail and watching the few twinkling lights on the Admiralty Pier fade into the thin soup of iron-colored mist. "But it never pays to take chances."

He glanced beside him at Asher, whose mind had already recorded the slight flush of color in the white cheeks, the warmth in those cool fingers. Standing beside him, gloved hands on the rail and collar turned up against the raw cold of the night, Asher had been conscious of a vague disgust and alarm, not at the vampire, but at himself, for noting these signs as a mere deductive detail and not the certain evidence of some poor wretch's murder in a London slum. He had felt angry at himself and frustrated, as he had often been in his latter dealings with the Foreign Office, burdened with a sense of performing what was only marginally the lesser of two colossal wrongs.

The vampire's gaze had turned, as if he could still descry the dark shape of Dover's cliffs, invisible now in the west. "At the risk of sounding crude," he had gone on carefully, "I would like to point out to you that at present I am the only one protecting you from Grippen and his cadre. Were you to destroy me, you might perhaps ensure your lady's safety for a season, for I am the only one who knows the terms of our agreement . . ."

Asher had started, relief loosening a knot of apprehension in his chest that had been with him, it seemed, so long that he had almost forgotten its origin.

With the possibility of a daylight-hunting vampire looming uneasily in his mind, he had not dared another meeting with Lydia, but it had been one of the hardest things he had ever done simply to take his leave of her by anonymous telegram. Ysidro, he presumed, would be able to protect him in Paris— if protecting him was in fact his intention—but he turned cold with dread at the thought of Lydia staying in London alone.

Only the knowledge that she was enormously sensible and would wait, as ordered, to hear from him before undertaking anything remotely dangerous—the knowledge that she understood the situation—made it bearable and, then, bearable only in relative terms.

He felt a surge of gratitude toward the vampire of which he was almost ashamed—gratitude and surprise that Ysidro would have told him this.

"But you would never be able to go near her again," the vampire went on. "The others would track you and destroy you, as one who knows too much. In so doing, they would undoubtedly find her as well."

Asher glanced sourly at his companion. "And how do I know that won't be the case in any event, when this affair is over?"

The vampire's gaze had been unfathomable in the dim glow of the steamer's deck lights, but Asher thought he heard a trace of unhuman amusement in his voice. "From that, too, I shall protect you. Do you not trust me, as I perforce trust you?"

As usual, he could not tell whether Ysidro was being ironic or not.

Long before the train had reached the Gare du Nord, Ysidro had left their compartment; Asher had not seen him anywhere in the station during the nuisance of customs in the Salle des Bagages, nor in the square or the streets outside. He was becoming used to this. The sky was already paling; he'd wired ahead to the Chambord, a small hotel in the Rue de la Harpe where he often stayed when in Paris in his Oxford persona, and they had rooms waiting for him. Entering the tiny lobby, with its fusty smells of cooking and its moldering Empire furnishings, it had troubled him that in all the years that he had known Paris, the city had been the abode of vampires. That was true of London as well, and he wondered if he would ever be able to return to the way in which he had once looked on the world.

Of course, early on in his career, he had lost the innocence of looking on the world as the bright surface of a beautiful pond. His tamperings with the Foreign Office, with the shadow life of information, and the murky dramas into which the cursed

Department had pitchforked him had taken care of that. But beneath his continual awareness of secrets, boltholes, and dangers, there was a new awareness, as if he had suddenly become cognizant, not only of the fish that swam beneath the surface of the pond, but of things utterly unimaginable that moved through the black mud at its bottom.

He had slept until late in the day in his small room up under the high bulge of the roof slates, then bathed and dressed in a thoughtful frame of mind. He had written to Lydia, assuring her of his safe arrival, and mailed the letter enclosed in another to one of his students who had agreed to forward anything for Miss Merridew. It would reach her a day late, but better that, he reasoned, than risk the vampires tracing her. After a light dinner in a café, he sought out the Place des Innocents, the square near the vast central markets of the city, where once the Church of the Holy Innocents and its notorious cemetery had stood.

There was nothing there now—a tree-lined *place* with a Renaissance fountain, hemmed in by the gray bulk of the *Halles* on one side and high, brown-fronted *immeubles* on three others. The vampire of the Holy Innocents had slept in the crypt, Ysidro had said—like Rhys the Minstrel, haunting the crypts of the old Church of St. Giles near the river until the town grew large enough around him so that its inhabitants became strangers to one another and did not notice one more white-faced stranger walking the night in their midst.

Standing now at Ysidro's side, straining his ears to catch even the whisper of descending feet crossing the cobbled court beyond the door, he wondered if that crypt was still there, buried beneath the soil like the subcellar of Calvaire's house in Lambeth, forgotten to all save those who were interested in places proof against the light of day.

The vampires might know. That and other things. He had turned from the Place des Innocents, followed the Rue St. Denis toward the gray sheet of the river, shining between the dove-colored buildings of its banks. To them, this startlingly clean city, with its immaculate streets, its chestnut trees rusty with autumn, was only a topcoat of varnish on a dark swamp of memories, another city entirely.

He had stood for some time on the bank above the quays of the Seine, staring at the gray tangle of bridges upstream and down, the gothic forest of pinnacles that clustered on the Île de la Cité and the square, dreaming towers of Notre Dame. And just beneath them, on the embankment, he had gazed consideringly at the massive iron grillworks that barred passers-by from the subterranean mazes of the Paris sewers.

"The sewers?" Elysée de Montadour wrinkled her long nose in a deliberate gesture of distaste, her diamonds winking in the blaze of the gaslight. "What vampire in his right mind would haunt them? Brrr!" She shivered affectedly. All her gestures, Asher observed, were theatrical, a conscious imitation of human mannerism rather than a reminiscence of its actual spontaneity, as if she had studied something not native to her. He found himself preferring Don Simon's uncanny stillness—the Spanish vampire stood, gray-gloved hands resting like hunting cats on the curving Empire back of the lady's divan, seeming by comparison more than ever immobile—petrified long ago, as Lydia had said, in ectoplasmic ivory.

"Do you ever hunt in them?" Though none of the other vampires in the long, gold-papered salon came near them, he was conscious of the light run of their voices behind him, as they played cards with spectral speed and deftness or chatted with the half-murmuring whisper of the wind. Seated in a spindly Louis XVI chair opposite Elysée, he knew they were watching him and listening as only vampires could listen, like so many suave and mocking sharks lying just beneath the surface of water, whose shore he could never hope to reach in time. In one corner of the salon, a tall girl whose dark shoulders rose like bronze above a gown of oyster-colored satin played the piano—Tchaikovsky, but with a queer, dark curl to it, a sensuousness and syncopation, like music trickling from behind a mirror that looked into Hell.

"*Foi*, and subject myself to the rheumatism?" Elysée laughed, a cold and tinkling sound without mirth, and made a great play with her swan's-down fan.

"And for what, *enfin?*" One of the graceful young men who made up her coterie of fledglings lounged over to the end of her divan. This one was brown-haired, his blue eyes bright against rounded and beautiful features; Asher wondered if Elysée had made them all vampires for their looks. Like all of the half dozen or so of Elysée's cadre, he was dressed in the height of fashion, his jet black evening clothes meticulously tailored, contrasting sharply with the white of his shirt and of the flesh above. "A sewer sweeper, whom one must kill without conversation and hide, like a dog burying carrion? Where is the fun in that?" His fangs gleamed as he grinned down at Asher.

Elysée shrugged alabaster shoulders above a dark green gown. "In any case, their superintendents count the sweepers very carefully when they go down, and when they come up. And they are *canaille*, as Serge says, and no fun in the hunt." She smiled briefly, dreamy delight in her green eyes with their terrible vampire glitter, like a greedy girl savoring the taste of forbidden liqueur. "*Alors*, there are eight hundred miles of sewers down there. He would wither up like a prune, this Great, Terrible, Ancient Vampire of Paris whom no one has ever seen . . ."

"What about the catacombs?" Simon asked softly, disregarding the mockery in her voice. A curious silence lifted into the room like an indrawn breath. The piano stilled.

"We all been there, sure." The dark girl rose from the instrument's bench, moved across the room with a deliberate, lounging slowness that somehow partook of the same eerie weightlessness that comprised the other vampires' speed. Instinctively Asher forced himself to concentrate on watching her, sensing that if he did not, she would be all but invisible in the movement of his eye. They had been speaking French—Ysidro's, as he had said, not only old-fashioned but with an occasional queer childish singsong quality to its pronunciation—but this girl spoke English, with a liquid American drawl. In spite of the almost unbearable lentitudinousness of her movements, she was behind him before he was ready for it, her tiny hand molding its way idly across his shoulders, as if memorizing the contours of them through the cloth of his coat. "They keep count there, too, of workers and visitors. You hid there, didn't you, Elysée, during the siege?"

There was just a touch of malice in her voice, like the artfully accidental stab of a pin, and Elysée's green eyes flickered at the reminder of what must have been an undignified flight from the rioting Communards. "And who would not have?" she demanded after a moment. "I took refuge there during the Terror as well, with Henriette du Caens. They weren't ossuaries then, you know—just old quarries in the feet of Montrouge, stretching away into darkness. *Bien sûr*, Henriette used to say she thought there might be—something else—there. But I never saw nor heard anything." There was a touch of defiance in her voice.

"But you were a fledgling then," Simon replied in his soft voice, "were you not?"

"Fledgling or not, I was not blind." She tapped half-irritably, half-playfully at his knuckles with her fan—when the ivory sticks came down Simon's gloved fingers were no longer beneath them, though Asher did not see the hand move. She turned back to Asher, a handsome woman if not pretty, with the face and body of a woman in her prime and eyes that had long since ceased to be human. She shrugged.

"*Eh bien*, that was long ago. And toward the end Henriette feared everything. François and I had to hunt for her, among the mobs that roamed the city by night; we brought them to her there. Aye, and risked our lives, when wearing the wrong color of kerchief could set them all baying '*à la lanterne*' like the pack of scurvy hounds they were! François de Montadour was the original owner of this *hôtel*, you understand." Her wave, wrist properly leading, was airy and formal, like a painting by David; the white plumes nodded in her hair. There were a dozen huge candelabra burning as well as the gas jets along walls and ceiling—the light caught in the glittering festoons of crystal lusters, in the long mirrors that ranged one wall, and in the black glass of the twelve-foot windows along the other, all thrown back in an unholy halo around her.

"He, Henriette, and I were the only ones to escape the Terror, and even François did not, in the end, escape. After it was over . . ." She shrugged again, a gesture designed to show off the whiteness of her shoulders. Behind him, Asher could feel the dark American girl move closer to his chair, her body touching his back, her hands resting on his shoulders, the cold of them seeming to radiate against his flesh.

"Henriette never recovered, though she lived near a life span after that. *Eh bien*, she was after all a lady of Versailles. She used to say, nights when we had brought her some drunkard whose blood filled her with wine in turn, that no one who had not experienced the sweetness of those days could ever understand just what it was which had been lost. Perhaps she could not get used to the fact that it was gone."

"She was an old lady," the dark girl's voice said, syrupy and languorous from behind Asher's head. "She didn't need no drunkard's blood to loosen her tongue about the old days, about the kings and about Versailles." Her nails idled at the ends of his hair, as if she toyed with a pet dog. "Just an old lady whinin' for yesterday."

"When one day you return to Charleston, Hyacinthe," Ysidro said quietly in the English in which Hyacinthe spoke, "and see where the American army shelled the streets where you grew up, when you find that men themselves have changed there, I hope you will remember."

"Men never change." She shifted her body again, her hip touching Asher's shoulder, a disturbing shiver passing into his body as if communicated by electricity. "They only die . . . and there are always more men."

"Even so."

Asher found himself sitting very still, aware that Simon, behind Elysée's divan, was poised on the verge of lightning speed; aware, too, of the touch of a quarter-inch of Hyacinthe's fingertip against the skin of his throat. At Ysidro's request, he had left his silver chains behind at the hotel. They would never have let him in, the vampire had said, if they'd suspected, and such a show of bad faith would have damaged Ysidro's own somewhat questionable standing among them. Though Asher could not see it, he was aware of the quadroon girl's glance, teasing and defiant, daring Simon to stop her if she decided to kill this human protégé of his, challenging him to try his speed against hers.

Ysidro went on softly, his eyes never leaving hers, "As for Henriette, she was a lady of Versailles, speaking even the language of 'this country,' as they used to call it: that enchanted Cythera that floated like an almond blossom balanced on a zephyr's breath above a cesspit. I understand her comparing the world after Napoleon marched through it to what it was before and finding it wanting. I think she simply grew tired of watching for danger, tired of struggling—tired of life. I saw her the last time I visited Paris, before the Prussians came, and I was not surprised to hear that she did not survive the siege. Did she ever speak, Elysée, of the Vampire of the Innocents?"

"No." Elysée fanned herself, a nervous gesture, since Asher had observed that the other vampires seemed to feel neither heat nor cold. The others were slowly gathering around his chair in a semicircle behind Hyacinthe, facing Elysée on the divan and Simon at her back. "Yes. Only that there was one." She made a scornful gesture which did not quite disguise her discomfort at the topic.

"The Innocents was a foul place, the ground mucky with the bodies rotting a few inches beneath the feet, skulls and bones lying everywhere on the ground. It stank, too. In the booksellers' and lingerie vendors' stands that were built in the arches, you could look up and see through the chinks in the rafters the bones stacked in the lofts above. The Great Flesh-Eater of Paris, we called it. François and the others—Henriette, Jean de Valois, old Louis-Charles d'Auvergne—sometimes talked about the stories of a vampire who lived there, a vampire no one ever saw. After I became vampire I went there to look for him, but the place . . . I didn't like it." An old fear flickered briefly in those hard emerald eyes.

162

"Nobody blames you for that, honey, I'm sure," Hyacinthe purred with malicious sympathy. "I'm thinking if he ever bided there at all, he's got to have been crazy as a loon."

"Did Calvaire ever go there?" Asher inquired, turning his head to look up into her face, and she smiled down at him, beautiful as a long-contemplated sin.

"It was all gone 'fore Calvaire was even bit, honey."

"Did he go to the catacombs, then? Did he ever speak of this—this spectral vampire?"

"Calvaire," sniffed one of the other vampires, a dark-haired boy whom Asher had guessed had barely begun to grow a beard when Elysée had claimed him. "The Great Vampire of Paris. He might just."

Asher glanced over at him curiously in the shimmering refulgence of light. "Why?"

Behind him, Hyacinthe replied with silky scorn, "Because it was the kind of thing the Great Vampire of Paris would do."

"He was very taken with being—one of us," explained Elysée slowly.

The brown-haired young man, Serge, seated himself gracefully on the divan at Elysée's feet. "We all have a little fun, when we can," he explained with a grin that would have been disarming, but for the fangs. "Calvaire was just a little grandiose about it."

"I don't understand."

Hyacinthe's fingers touched his hair. "You wouldn't, under the circumstances."

"Calvaire was a braggart, a boaster," Elysée said, closing her swan's-down fan, stroking the soft white fluff between fingers as hard and as pale as the ivory of the sticks. "Like some others." Her glance touched Hyacinthe for a malignant instant. "To sit with your victim in an opera box, a café, or a carriage—to feel the blood with your lips through the skin, spinning it out as long as you can, waiting . . . then to go drink elsewhere, only to quench the thirst, and go back the next night to him again, to that personal, innocent death . . ." She smiled dreamily once more, and Asher was conscious of a slight movement among the vampires behind him and of the swift flick of Ysidro's eyes.

"But Valentin carried it a step further, a dangerous step. Perhaps it was partly that he wanted power, that he wanted fledglings of his own, though he dared not make them here in Paris, where I rule, where I dominated him through that which he gave me in passing from life to . . . everlife. But I think he did it for the—the 'kick,' as you say in English—alone. He would sometimes let his victim know, especially the victims who found it *piquant* to know how near they flirted with death.

"He would lead them into it, seduce them . . . he had a fine grace and would play death like an instrument, drinking it, in all its perverse sweetness. *Bien sûr*, he could not be permitted to continue . . ."

"It is a dangerous thing," the boy vampire to Asher's right said, "to let anyone know just who we are and what we are, no matter what the reason."

"He was furious when I forbade it him," Elysée remembered. "Furious when I forbade him to make fledglings of his own, his own coterie . . . for that was the reason he gave. But I think that it was just that he enjoyed it."

"But then," Hyacinthe murmured, "the ones he told always expected to win."

Something in her voice made Asher look up; her hand caught him very lightly under the jaw, forcing his head back so that his eyes met hers. Under her fingers, he could feel the movement of his own pulse; she was looking down into his eyes and smiling. For a moment it did not seem to him that he breathed, sensing Simon's readiness to spring and knowing there was no way—even if Elysée's fledglings did not try to stop him—that he could cross the distance in the time it would take Hyacinthe to strike.

Elysée's voice was soft, as if she feared to tip some fragile balance. "Let him alone." He saw Hyacinthe's mocking smile widen and felt the slight tensing of her fingertips against his throat.

Quite deliberately, he put up his hand and grasped the cold

wrist. For an instant it was like pulling at the limb of a tree; then it yielded, mockingly fluid in his, and she stepped back as he stood up. But she still smiled into his eyes, lazily amused, as if he'd failed some test of nerve, and there was in the honey-dark eyes the savoring of what it was like to seduce a victim who knew what was happening. His eyes held hers; then, just as deliberately, he dismissed her and turned back to Elysée.

"So you don't believe Calvaire sought out this—this most ancient vampire in Paris."

The fan snapped open again, indignant. Elysée's eyes were on Hyacinthe, not on him. "*I* am the most ancient vampire in Paris, *Monsieur le Professeur*," she said decidedly. "There is no other, nor has there been for many years. And *en tout cas*, you—and others—" Her glance shot spitefully from Hyacinthe to Ysidro, who had somehow come around the divan to her side and within easy grasping range of Asher. "—would do well to remember that the single law among vampires, the single law that *all must obey*, is that no vampire will kill another vampire. And no vampire . . ." Her eyes narrowed, moved to Asher, and then back to the slender, delicate Spaniard standing at her side. ". . . will do that which endangers other vampires by giving away their haunts, their habits, or the very fact of their existence, to humankind."

Ysidro inclined his head, his pale hair falling forward over the gray velvet of his collar, like cobweb in the bonfire of gaslight and crystal. "Fear nothing, mistress. I do not forget." His gloved hand closed like a manacle around Asher's wrist, and he led him from the salon.

Twelve

———

She's afraid," Asher said, later. "Not that she didn't have plenty of company," he added, remembering the cold touch of Hyacinthe's fingers on his throat. "Are all master vampires that nervous of their own power?"

"Not all." Behind them, the rattle of the cab horse's retreating hooves faded along the wood and asphalt of the street, dying away into the late-night hush. Down at the corner, voices could still be heard in a workingmen's *estaminet*, but for the most part the district of Montrouge was silent. It was as different as possible from the crumbling elegance of Elysée's *hôtel* or the rather grubby slum in which it stood. Here the street was lined with the tall, sooty, dun stone buildings so common to Paris, the shabby shops on the ground floors shuttered tight, the windows of the flats above likewise closed, dark save for a chink of light here and there in attics where servants still labored. Simon's feet made no sound on the narrow asphalt footway. His voice might have been the night wind murmuring to itself in a dream.

"It varies from city to city, from person to person. Elysée has the disadvantage of being not that much older than her fledglings and of not having been vampire long herself when she became, in effect, Master of Paris. And she has not always been wise in her choice of fledglings."

"Do you think Calvaire contacted the Vampire of the Innocents as part of a power play against Elysée?"

"I suspect that he tried." Simon stopped in the midst of the row, before an anonymous door. The main entrance to the catacombs was on the Place Denfert-Rochereau, which would be uncomfortably full of traffic even at this hour—the rattle of carriages and fiacres on the boulevards was audible even on this silent street. The moon was gone. Above the cliff of buildings and chimneys behind them, the sky was the color of soot.

"Elysée is certainly convinced of it," the Spaniard went on. "She was, you observed, most anxious that her fledglings—and particularly Hyacinthe, whom I guess to be *not* of her getting—disabuse themselves of any notion of doing the same. Did he exist at all, this Vampire of the Innocents, he would be vastly more powerful than Elysée—vastly more powerful than any of us."

"A day stalker, in fact."

Simon did not reply. For a long time the vampire stood as if abstracted in thought, and Asher wondered what the night sounded like to the vampire, whether those quick ears could pick up the breath of sleepers in the house beside which they stood or that queer, preternatural mind could sense the moving color of their dreams. At length the vampire signed to him, and Asher, after a swift glance up and down the deserted street, produced his picklocks from an inner pocket and went to work.

"The watchman is in the office at the other entrance," the vampire murmured, the sound more in Asher's mind than his ears. "Doubtless asleep—we should remain undisturbed."

The door gave under Asher's cautious testing. He pocketed the picklocks and let Ysidro precede him into the cramped vestibule which was all there was above ground at this end of the catacombs. He heard the soft creak of a hinge, the muffled sounds of someone rifling a cupboard; then the scratch of a match. Ysidro had found a guard's lantern. Asher stepped inside and shut the door behind him.

With its boot-scarred desk in front of the iron grille that closed off one end of the room, the place was barely large enough for the two of them to move about. The lantern stood on a corner of the desk, shedding eerie illumination across Ysidro's long hands as he sorted through a ring of keys, skeletal and yet queerly beautiful in the isolation of the light. "So efficient, the French," the vampire murmured. "Here is a map of the passages, but I suggest that you stay close to me."

"I'll be able to see the light for some distance," Asher pointed out, taking the thumbed and grubby chart.

Ysidro paused in the act of unlocking the grille. "That isn't what I mean."

They descended the stair, narrow and spiraling endlessly down into the darkness.

"Do you believe he is really here, then?" Asher asked softly, his hands pressed to the stone of wall and centerpost to keep his balance on the perilous wedges of the steps. "That he is still here at all?"

"It is the logical place. As Elysée pointed out, the sewers are perpetually damp. Whereas we are not subject to the normal ills of the body, when a vampire begins to grow old—to give up—he does begin to suffer from joint ache. Some of the very old vampires I knew here in Paris, Louis du Bellière-Fontages and Marie-Thérèse de St. Arouac, did. Louis had been a courtier of Henri the Third, one of his lace-trimmed tigresses—I knew him for years. I don't think he ever got used to the way the Sun King tamed the nobility. *Les fruits de Limoges,* he called them—china fruit, gloss without juice. But the fact is that he was afraid, passing himself off at Versailles. He was growing old, old and tired, when I saw him last; his joints hurt him, and going outside his own *hôtel* frightened him. He was hunting less and less, living on beef blood and stolen chickens and the odd Black Mass baby. I was not surprised when I heard he had been found and killed."

"When was that?"

"During one of the witchcraft scandals of the Sun King's reign." Simon halted at the bottom of the stairs, listening to the darkness, turning his head this way and that.

"If the killer we're looking for exists," Asher murmured, and the echoes picked up his voice as if all the dead sleeping in the dark whispered back at him, "he'll be in London still."

Ysidro shook his head, a gesture so slight it was barely perceptible. "I think you are right." His voice was like the touch of wind among the ancient tunnels. "I feel no presence here," he breathed. "Nothing—human, vampire, ghost. Only a muted resonance from the bones themselves." He held the lantern aloft, and the gold light glistened on damp stone walls, wet pebbles, and mud underfoot, dying away in the intensity of the subterranean gloom. "Nevertheless, follow close. The galleries cross and branch—it is easy to lose one's way."

Like spectres in a nightmare, they moved on into the darkness.

For an endless time, they traversed the bare galleries of the ancient gypsum mines beneath Montrouge, black tunnels hewn of living rock whose walls seemed to press suffocatingly upon them, and whose ceiling, stained with the soot of tourists' candles, brushed the top of Asher's head as he followed Ysidro's fragile silhouette into the abyss.

Now and then they passed pillars, shoring up the vast weight of the earth to prevent subsidence of the streets above, and the sight of them caused Asher's too-quick imagination to flirt with what it would be like, should the ceiling collapse and trap him here. In other places, the lamplight glanced over the black squares of branching passageways, dark as no darkness above the ground could be, or flashed across the water of wells, mere inches beneath the level of their feet.

And in all that realm of the dead, Asher thought, he was the only living man. The man who walked beside him, who listened so intently to that darkness, had not been alive for three and a half centuries; the man whose lair they sought had been dead for nearly six.

If indeed he had ever existed at all.

Who was the ghost that the dead believed in?

"Apparently there have been no killings of the Paris vampires." The echoes traded the remark back and forth among themselves down the branching corridors; Asher was uncomfortably reminded of the peeping croak of the chorus of frogs said to guard the way to Hell. "Why would he have gone after Calvaire?"

"Perhaps Calvaire told him too much." Ysidro paused to make a chalk arrow on the wall, then walked on. "Calvaire wanted to become a master vampire. If he spoke to the Vampire of the Innocents at all, perhaps he offended him or roused in him a resolve to prevent Calvaire from gaining the power he sought; perhaps Calvaire had some other scheme afoot besides power alone. We do not know when Calvaire spoke to him. He might have fled Paris because of him, rather than because he had been thwarted by Elysée. And it may be something entirely different—the fact that Calvaire was a Protestant heretic, for instance. A hundred years ago, I would never have employed you myself, had I suspected you of adherence to that heresy, no matter how well qualified you were."

"Try applying for a government job in Ireland," Asher grunted. "It still doesn't explain why he'd have killed Calvaire's associates in London."

"If we find his lair," the vampire said softly, "such matters may become more clear."

Ahead of them, something white gleamed in the darkness— pillars? They drew closer, and the pale blurs resolved themselves into oblong patches whitewashed carefully onto the black-painted pillars of a gate. Surrounded by utter darkness, there was something terrifying about its stark simplicity—final, silent, twenty meters below street level, and carved of native rock. Above the lintel, black letters on a white ground spelled out the words:

STOP!
THIS IS THE EMPIRE OF THE DEAD.

Beyond the gate, the bones began.

The catacombs were the ossuary of Paris. All the ancient cemeteries within the confines of the city had been emptied into these rock-hewn galleries, the bones neatly ranged into horrible six-foot retaining walls built of tibias and skulls, with everything else dumped in a solid jumble behind, like firewood in a box. Brown and shiny, the bones stretched out of sight into the darkness of the branching galleries, the eye sockets of the courses of skulls seeming to turn with the lantern's gliding light, an occasional bony jaw seeming to smile. Nobles decapitated in the Terror, street sweepers, washerwomen, monks, Merovingian kings—they were all here somewhere, side by side in macabre democracy.

The Empire of the Dead indeed, Asher thought. They passed an altar, like the gates, painted simple black and white, a dim shape that seemed to shine out of the darkness. Before the bones were occasional placards, announcing from which cemetery these tumbled remains had been taken, or exhorting the viewer, in French or in Latin, to recall his own mortality and remember that all things were dust.

As an Englishman, Asher was conscious of a desire to pretend that this taste for the gruesome was a manifestation of some aspect of the French national character, but he knew full well that his own countrymen came here in droves. Following Simon as he wound farther and farther back through the narrow tunnels of the ossuary, pausing every now and then to mark the walls with numbered arrows to guide them back, he was conscious of the terrible fascination of the place, the morbid urge to muse, like Hamlet, on those anonymous relics of former ages.

But then, he wondered, to how many of those brown, weathered skulls *could* his companion have said, "I knew him well . . ."?

That train of thought led to others, and he asked, "Did you ever have your portrait painted?" The vampire's glance touched the ranks of bones that heaped the walls in a head-high wainscot all around him, and he nodded, unsurprised.

"Only once," he said, "shortly before I left Spain. I never sent for it because it was a stiff and rather ugly effort—the Renaissance did not reach Madrid until many years later. Afterward—it is a very difficult thing, you understand, to paint portraits by candlelight."

They moved on—one dark turning, two.

Then the lamplight flicked down a side tunnel and Asher stopped short. Simon, a step ahead of him, was back at his side before he was even conscious that the vampire had heard him; Ysidro was keeping, he realized, close watch upon him, as he had in the Hôtel Montadour.

Silently, Asher took the lantern and pointed its beam away into the darkness, not certain he had seen what he thought he'd seen.

He had.

Simon glanced sidelong at him, fine-arched brows swooping down in disbelief. Asher shook his head, as baffled as he. After a moment's uneasy pause, they moved on together into that narrow seam of rock and bone.

Everywhere in the ossuary, the bones had been formed into neat walls, with the remainder heaped behind. But here those walls had been torn down. The bones lay scattered in a deep drift, like mounds of brittle kindling; in places along the walls the floor was waist deep. Asher heard them crunch beneath his feet, and, listening, beneath Simon's as well—the first time he had ever been aware of the vampire making a sound when he walked. Then the floor was clear once more, and Asher blinked in astonishment at what lay beyond.

"A demented workman?"

Slowly Simon shook his head. "There is no soot on the ceiling," he said. "It is a place the tourists never come—the guards, either. You see for yourself that ours were the first feet to break those bones."

"I've seen something of the kind in that Capuchin monastery in Rome, but . . ."

The walls of the tunnel, from that point on, were lined entirely with pelvic bones. Lamplight and shadow glided over them as Asher and Ysidro moved on again, thousands of smooth, organic curves, like some perverted variety of orchid. They stacked the wall as high as the bones elsewhere, and over a yard deep on either side, pelvises and nothing but pelvises. In time they gave place to skulls, a mournful audience of empty sockets, vanishing away into the dawnless night. In side tunnels, Asher caught glimpses of sheaves of ribs, like frozen wheat in the wind, cracked and crumbling nearly beyond recognition; scapulas like flat brown plates; drifts of vertebrae; and, beyond them, like tide-separated sand and gravel, finer dunes of finger bones, meticulously sized, smaller and smaller, back into the eternity of night. At the end of that tunnel was another altar, the third Asher had seen since entering the ossuary, small and starkly painted, its white patches gleaming like skulls in the gloom.

Asher shook his head, and turned to Simon, baffled. "Why?"

"It is something difficult to explain," the vampire replied softly, "to a man of your century—or indeed, to any who lived after your so-called Age of Reason."

"Do you understand?"

"I did once."

Asher bent down, and took a finger bone from the nearest heap; they drifted the walls of the tunnel just here like piles of grain in a granary. He turned it over in his fingers, unconsciously imitating Lydia's examination of Lotta's severed vertebra—small, delicate, efficient in its thin shank and bulbous joints, stripped of the fragile miracle of muscle and nerve that had made it responsive to a lover's caress or the grip on the handle of a gun. He was turning to go, the bone still in his hand, when from the darkness he heard a whisper: *Restitute.*

He froze.

He could see nothing—only the shadows of the sheaved ribs behind and around him. He glanced at Simon, but the vampire's eyes were darting from shadow to shadow, wide and shocked and seeking, evidently able to see nothing; moreover, it was clear he could not even locate the speaker with his mind.

Return it, the voice had whispered in Latin, and in the same tongue Asher whispered, "Why?"

He had thought Simon's voice soft; he wasn't certain whether he heard these words at all, only a murmur of Latin half within his own skull.

"She will come looking for it."

"Who will?"

"She whose it was. They will all come looking for them— skulls, ribs, toes, the little ear bones like the jewels of rings. The Trumpet will blow—they will all scramble to assemble themselves, to find their own bones, wrap them up in cloaks of ashes. And when they find them, they will climb all those stairs, each with his own bones. All save we."

Something changed in the darkness; Asher felt the hair of his nape lift as he realized that what he had taken for a heap of bones and shadow less than a yard away was the shape of a man. He felt Simon flinch, too—even with his preternatural senses, the vampire had been unable to see.

The Latin voice whispered again, "All save we."

He wore what had probably been a monk's robe once, rotted and falling to pieces over limbs scarcely less emaciated than the bones that surrounded them on all sides. He seemed bent with age, huddled like a frozen crone desperate for warmth; in the sunken, waxen flesh, the strangely glittering vampire eyes seemed huge, green as polar ice. His fangs were long and sharp against the delicate, hairless jaw. Through the open throat of the robe, Asher could see a crucifix, black with age and filth.

Like the claw of a bird, one shaky hand pointed at Simon; the nails were long and broken. "We will hear the Trumpet far off," the vampire whispered, "but we will not be able to go, you and I. We will continue undead, unjudged, and alone, after all the others are gone—we will never know what lies upon the other side. They may speak for me—I hope they will understand why I have done this and speak for me . . ."

Simon looked puzzled, but Asher said, "Before the Throne of God?"

The old vampire turned those luminous green eyes on him, eager. "I have done what I can."

"What is your name?" Simon asked, falling into the heavily Spanish-accented Latin of his own early education.

"Anthony," the vampire whispered. "Brother Anthony of the Order of the Friars Minor. I stole this . . ." He touched his black habit—a chunk of it fell off in his hand. "Stole from the Benedictines in the Rue St. Jacques—stole and killed the man who wore it. I had to do it. It is damp here. Things rot quickly. I could not go abroad naked before the eyes of men and God. I had to kill him . . . You understand that I had to do it."

Then he was beside Asher, with no sense of time elapsed or

174

of broken consciousness at all; the touch of his fingers was like the light pricking of insect feet as he removed the tiny bone from Asher's grasp. Looking down into his face, Asher could see that Brother Anthony appeared no older than Simon or any of the other vampires did; it was only his posture and the whiteness of the long hair that straggled down over his bent shoulders that gave the queer, white, ageless face its look of senility.

"To save your own life?" he asked.

Brother Anthony's fingers continued to rove lightly over the back of his hand, as if feeling the armature of bone within flesh, or warming their coldness on the subcutaneous heat of blood. With his other hand he held Asher's little finger in a frail grip that Asher knew he could no more break than he could have pulled his hand from dried cement. "I had not fed—not truly fed—in months," the vampire whispered anxiously. "Rats—a horse—chickens. But I could feel my mind starting to go, my senses turn sluggish. I've tried—over and over I've tried. But each time I grow terrified. If I do not feed properly, drink of the deaths of men, I will grow stupid, grow slow. I cannot do that. After all these years, all these deaths, running from the Judgment . . . And each life I take in running is another to the tally that would fall upon me, did I die. So many—I used to keep count. But the hunger drove me to madness. And I will never be forgiven."

"It is one of the tenets of faith," Asher said slowly, "that there is no sin, *nothing*, that God will not forgive, if the sinner is truly repentant."

"I can't be truly repentant," Brother Anthony whispered, "can I? I feed and go on feeding. I am stronger than all those who have sought to kill me. The hunger drives me to madness. The terror of what awaits me beyond the wall of death—I cannot face it. Maybe if I help those who will go there, if I make it easy for them to find their bones . . . If I help them they will speak for me. I have done what I can for them. They must. They must . . ." He drew Asher close to him—his breath reeked of blood, and, close-to, Asher saw that his robe was stiff

175

with gore decades dried. He nodded toward Simon. "When he kills you," he whispered, "will you speak for me?"

"If you answer me three questions," Asher said, conscious of the framework of tales with which the ancient vampire would be familiar and trying desperately to frame mentally what he wanted to ask into three parts and good Latin. Thank God, he thought, they were speaking Church Latin, which was no more difficult than French. *If this were Classical, the whole conversation would come to a standstill while I arranged things in that damn inside-out order that Cicero used.*

The Franciscan did not reply, but seemed only to be waiting, his thin fingers icy on Asher's hand. Simon, standing silently by, watched them both. Asher felt that he was keyed up, ready to intervene between them, though he himself sensed no danger from the little monk.

After a moment he asked, "Can you hunt by daylight?"

"I would not so offend the face of God. The night is mine; here below, all night is mine. I would never take the day above the ground to myself."

"Not *would* you . . ." Asher began, exasperated, then realized that that might be counted as a second question and fell silent for a moment. Hundreds of questions leaped to mind and were discarded; he was aware that he had to go carefully, aware that the old vampire could vanish as silently, as easily, as he had appeared. He felt as he did when he watched Lydia feeding the sparrows in the New College quadrangle, coaxing them with infinite patience to take bread crumbs from her outstretched fingers. "Who were your contemporaries among the vampires?"

"Johannis Magnus," the old vampire whispered, "the Lady Elizabeth; Jehanne Croualt, the horse tamer; Anne La Flamande, the Welsh minstrel who sang in the crypts of London; Tulloch the Scot, who was buried in the Holy Innocents. They have destroyed the Innocents. They carted the bones away. His they burned. The flesh shriveled off them in the noonday sun. That was in the days of the Terror, the days when men slew one another as we the Undead never dared to do."

176

"Yet there are those who swear they saw the Scot fifty years ago in Amsterdam," Ysidro murmured in English. He seemed to understand without comment why Asher had chosen that question to ask. "As for the others . . ."

Asher turned back to the old vampire. "Have you ever killed another vampire?"

Brother Anthony shrank back from him, covering his white face with skeletal white hands. "It is forbidden," he whispered desperately. " 'Thou shalt not kill,' they say, and I have killed— killed over and over. I have tried to do good . . ."

"Have you ever killed another vampire?" Simon repeated softly, not moving, but Asher could feel the tension in him like overstretched wire.

The monk was backing away, his face still covered. Asher took a step after him, reaching out his hand to catch the rotting black sleeve. He understood then how the legends came about, that vampires can command the mists and dissolve into them at will. There was, as before, not even a sense of his mind blanking, and not one of the brittle bones that hemmed them all around so much as shifted. He was simply standing, a shred of crumbling black cloth in his hand, staring at the shadowed tangle of bones and the shadowy altar beyond.

In his mind he heard a whisper, like the breath of a dream. "Speak for me. Tell God I did what I could. Speak for me, when he kills you . . ."

Thirteen

Do you plan to kill me?" Asher closed the iron grille behind him, turned the heavy key, and followed Simon back into the deserted vestibule, where Ysidro was fastidiously poking among the papers of the desk. The vampire paused to regard him with dispassionate eyes, and, as so often with Ysidro, Asher found it impossible to divine whether he was contemplating the mortal state or simply wondering whether he felt peckish. In any case he did not answer.

Instead he asked, "What do you think of our Franciscan brother?"

"Other than that he's mad, you mean?" Asher removed a couple of wax tablets from his pocket, of the sort that he had habitually carried in his Foreign Office days, and methodically took impressions of all the keys on the ring. "I don't believe he's our culprit."

"Because he's here instead of in London? Never think it. He is silent as the fall of dust, James; he could have followed us back to Paris, and I would never have been the wiser; could have overheard any of our conversations and preceded us . . ."

"In Latin?"

"In English, if he was friend to Rhys and to Tulloch the Scot. Most of us learn one another's languages, even as we keep abreast of the changes in the tongues of the lands where we dwell—conspicuousness is our death. The fact that he lives hidden in the catacombs does not mean he has not walked the streets of men unseen. He understands at least some of the changes that have taken place since the Fall of the Kings . . . And he claims, incidentally, to have seen Tulloch the Scot's flesh shriveled from his bones by the light of the noonday sun . . ."

"Meaning he was up and around by day?" Asher used his fingernail to pry the last key gingerly from the wax, thinking to himself that, if that were the case, the Minorite's assumption that Ysidro intended to murder him might be far from a random guess. "But you say yourself that the Scot was seen years later . . ."

"I say that there are those who swear they saw him—as unreliable a contention as our religious friend's, if, like Anthony, Tulloch's abilities to pass unseen grew with time. There has been no reliable report of his presence since the days of the Terror—indeed, none for half a century before, but that means nothing."

Asher wiped the last telltale fragments of wax from the wards and replaced the key on its hook beside the grilled door. "And the others he named?"

"Two at least I know to be dead—three, if La Flamande is the same woman I knew during the wars over Picardy. I've never heard of Croualt . . ." He waited until Asher had opened the outer door, then turned down the lantern wick until its flame snuffed into darkness. Asher reflected with an inner grin that Ysidro's candle snuffing trick didn't seem to work too well with three-quarters of an inch of woven wick and a reservoir full of kerosene.

"So we have three—perhaps four, if you want to count Grippen and figure out some way he could have jiggered the daylight problem." He stepped through the outer door into the dark Rue Dareau.

"None of those he named has been seen or heard of for centuries."

"That doesn't mean they haven't been hiding somewhere, as Brother Anthony has been hiding," Asher replied quietly. "If one of them survived, he—or she—would be a day stalker, like Brother Anthony, toughened, as you said, against garlic and silver and other countermeasures."

"It also does not mean that Brother Anthony is not himself the killer."

"Do you believe he is?"

Ysidro's smile flickered briefly into existence. "No. But there are few other candidates for the role." Their footsteps echoed hollowly against the dingy walls of dark brick as they made their way north, through the crisscrossings of the empty back streets that led toward the wider boulevards. There was no way of telling how late it was, but leaden darkness now possessed even the most late-carousing of bistros, and the prostitutes seemed to have sought their beds for good. " 'I have killed over and over,' he said, and also, 'I have tried to do good.' The killing of other vampires could be interpreted as a major effort in that direction. Is it not what you yourself plan to do, if you get the chance?"

Asher glanced sharply across at him, but met only matter-of-fact inquiry in those cool, strange eyes. Instead of replying, he said, "If he wanted to slay his own kind, there are plenty to begin on here, without going to London for the purpose. And if the killer is his contemporary, with the same alterations of powers, Brother Anthony may be our only hope of tracking him."

"If he will." They crossed a street. Asher had a momentary sense of movement in the noisome blackness of an alley to their right and the mutter of voices as the local toughs wisely decided not to molest this particular pair of passers-by. "And if, given that you can coax him from the earth to which he has gone, he consents to assist us and not ally himself with the killer."

Asher shivered, remembering how the little monk had seemed to melt from the darkness, the cold tickle of those frail fingers on his hand, and their unbreakable strength. He knew what his own reaction would be to a mortal man who allied himself with vampires. Perhaps it was best after all to let sleeping dogs lie.

They passed through a darkened square whose fountain sounded unearthly loud in the stillness, turned into the Boulevard St. Michel. Even that great artery was virtually empty. The chestnut trees that lined it rustled overhead like a dim woods, their leaves lying in soggy drifts along the walls of the great hospitals which clustered in that neighborhood. The electric street lamps threw too-bright halos, making the gloom seem all the more dense. Now and then, a passing fiacre broke the eerie silence with the sharp tap of hooves, but that was all. The night was still and cold; Asher pulled his scarf more closely around his throat and huddled deep into the folds of his ulster.

Presently he asked, "If there is a strange vampire operating in London—be it Tulloch the Scot, even Rhys himself, or some other—might we not trace it through unexplained kills? Would a vampire that ancient have to kill as often?"

"Any city on earth," Don Simon replied austerely, "gives forth such spate of unexplained kills of its own, through disease, cold, filth, and uncaring, that it were difficult to trace a single vampire's poor efforts. As for needing blood less frequently— or needing, rather, the life, the death cry of the mind to feed the powers of the mind on which our very survival depends— that I do not know."

He paused for a moment on the pavement. A whisper of straying wind moved in his dark cloak and lifted the pale hair from his collar. For a moment, it seemed as if he himself would drift onto it like a vast gray leaf. Then he walked on.

"It is not merely that we are dependent on the nourishment of the blood, James, and the psychic feed of the passing of the soul. Many of us are addicted to them. Some suffer this to greater or lesser degree, and some, in fact, take great pleasure in the addiction. Lotta used to prolong her fasts from the ultimate kill as much as possible, to sweeten them when they came, but it is a dangerous practice. In some, the craving rises almost to madness. It can make us hasty or careless, and in all things concerning us, carelessness is death."

They were nearing the miniature maze of streets near the river where the Hotel Chambord stood; the cold smell of the Seine hung in the air, and already, down the cobbled side streets, the milk sellers were about. Asher studied sidelong the delicate profile, the white, hooked nose and loose thickness of colorless hair.

"You haven't relaxed in three hundred and fifty years," he said softly, "have you?"

"No."

"Do you relax when you sleep?"

The vampire did not look at him. "I do not know. We all learn too late that sleep is not the same as it was."

"Do you dream?"

Ysidro paused, and again Asher had the impression he was on the point of being lifted and whirled away by the faint stirring of the wind. A faint flex line of a bitter smile touched the white silk of the skin, then smoothed away. "Yes," Simon said expressionlessly. "I dream. But they are not like human dreams."

Asher wondered whether, when Simon sought whatever lair he had made for himself in Paris, he would dream of Brother Anthony, sorting bones in the dark.

Then suddenly he was alone. Somewhere in the back of his mind he had the sensation of having once dreamed, himself, about a slim, cloaked form walking away toward the whitish mists of the Seine, but that was all.

SAVAGE MURDERS IN LONDON
THE RIPPER STALKS AGAIN?

A series of shocking crimes rocked London last night when nine people—six women and three men—were brutally murdered in the Whitechapel and Limehouse districts of London between the hours of midnight and four in the morning. The first of the bodies, that of variety actress Sally Shore, was found by dustmen in the alley behind the Limehouse Road. She had been much bruised and cut about, so savagely that, when found, her body was almost completely drained of blood. The eight other victims, found in various places in the neighborhood, were in a similar condition. Police remarked upon the fact that in no instance were screams or cries for help heard and upon the fact that, though the bodies were nearly drained of blood, very little was found at the scenes, leading them to believe that the murders took place elsewhere

and the bodies were transported to the places where
they were found . . .

Asher set down the newspaper beside his midday breakfast
of croissant and coffee, feeling cold to his bones. *Nine!*

What had Simon said? After a long fast, the time always
comes when the craving sets in and will not be denied.

Nine.

He felt sick.

It wasn't the London vampires. That much he knew. They
had to live in London—Grippen, the Farrens, Chloé. But a
strange vampire, hiding from them in London, might indeed
be traceable through his kills, by those who knew what to look
for. He had lain hidden as long as he could, fasting and silently
murdering . . .

He glanced at the date. It was this morning's paper. Last
night, when he and Simon had been stalking Anthony in the
darkness of the catacombs, the murderer had struck again. This
time it was not vampires who were his victims, but humans.

Admittedly, he thought, glancing down the article, not particularly important humans—the women were all listed as "variety actresses," seamstresses, or simply, "young women."
Given the area in which they were found and given the hour
they were killed, there was no real doubt as to their true profes-
sions. But it made their murders no less atrocious; and it made
the lives of everyone else in London no more secure.

They had not cried out. Horribly, the thin, dreamy face of
the woman on the train returned to him, the way her hand had
fumbled willingly at her collar buttons, the glazed somnam-
bulance of her eyes. He remembered Lydia's red hair, gleaming
in the dim radiance of the gas lamps, and his palms grew cold.

No, he told himself firmly. *She knows the danger—she's sensible
enough to stay indoors, close to people, at night . . .*

That knowledge did not help.

He raised his head, staring sightlessly at the traffic jostling
past the café where he sat. The thin mist of early dawn had
burned away into a crisp, brittle sunlight, like crystal on the

sepia buildings across the street and the India-ink traceries of the bare trees. The boulevardiers were out for a stroll, reveling in the last fine weather of autumn—leisured gentlemen in well-tailored blazers, men of letters, self-proclaimed wits and *artistes*. Open-topped carriages rolled past on their way to the Bois de Boulogne, affording glimpses of the elegant matrons of the Paris *gratin* or of expensively dressed sin—the "eight-spring luxury models" of the demimonde.

Asher saw none of it. He wondered where Simon might be found. Elysée de Montadour's *hôtel* was, he was virtually certain, somewhere in the Marais; he supposed that given a day in which to search through the building records, he could locate the place. But there was no guarantee that Ysidro was sleeping there—somehow he doubted that slim, enigmatic hidalgo would put himself anywhere near the power of Elysée and her cicisbeos—and his visit to Ernchester House had taught him the folly of entering vampire nests alone. And in any case, what he wanted now most to know was something which could only be ascertained while the sun was in the sky.

He felt absently in his pocket for the wax tablets and wondered what time the guards at the catacombs had their dinner.

One of the advantages of working for the Foreign Office, Asher had found, had been a nodding acquaintance with the fringes of the underworld in a dozen cities across Europe. His Oxford colleagues would have been considerably startled had they realized how easily their unassuming Lecturer in Philology could have obtained any number of strange services, from burglary to murder to "nameless vices"—most of which had perfectly good names, in Latin, at least. In spite of the fact that England and France were the closest of allies, he had in the past had cause to need keys cut in a hurry in Paris with no questions asked and, on this occasion, he knew precisely where to go.

As it was neither the first nor the third Saturday of the month, he had little fear of meeting parties of tourists at the catacombs or the large numbers of guards that the Office of Directory and Treasury considered necessary to herd them through. The catacombs would be staffed by one or at most two old pensioners of the State, and, though the dinner hour was long over by the time Asher reached Montrouge, with the aid of luck and human nature, they might be together gossiping instead of keeping watch at both entrances.

And why should they watch? The doors were locked, and who in their right mind would wish to break into the Empire of the Dead?

Luck and human nature seemed to be in full operation that afternoon when Asher reached the inconspicuous back door of the catacombs through which they had entered last night. It was locked. Although a sign instructed him to apply for information in the Place Denfert-Rochereau several streets away, still he thumped for several seconds on the door.

Only silence greeted him, which was as he had hoped. The keys Jacques la Puce had made for him that afternoon worked perfectly—even on this quiet street, picking the lock would have been noticed by someone. He slipped inside, appropriated another tin lantern, and made his way down the stair, locking the grille again behind him. It was just past three in the afternoon; these days darkness was complete by about six. If nothing else, he thought, he might ascertain whether vampires past a certain age were free of the leaden trance of the daylight hours. Beyond that . . .

He didn't know. As a mortal it was laughable to think he could locate Brother Anthony in the haunted maze. But it was not beyond the bounds of possibility that his presence there, alone and unprotected, might pique the ancient friar's curiosity and draw him out of hiding, as it had done last night.

After a long inner debate he had left his silver chains back at his hotel, since in all probability they would afford him no protection should Brother Anthony turn against him, and might very well be construed as a gesture of bad faith. In last night's case it had been merely manners—like carrying a gun to a wedding reception, Ysidro had said; Asher hadn't mentioned that he'd done that upon occasion. But he was uncertain how much Brother Anthony would sense, and it was vital that he speak to the old man this afternoon.

Six hundred years, he thought, as the first of Ysidro's chalked arrows came into the wavery circle of the lantern's light. The last of the Capets had been on the throne when Anthony had first refused to die—when he had made the decision to accept immortality upon any terms. Asher wondered whether the monk had been hiding all that time, or whether he had been driven gradually to it and to madness, living among the corpses in the crypts of the Holy Innocents.

His breath puffed in faint smoke in the glow of the lamp; it was cold in the endless galleries. The only sounds were the soft scrunching of wet pebbles underfoot and the occasional creak of the lantern's handle. It had been unnerving to come here last night, with Ysidro as protection, even though at that time they had expected to encounter no one. It was terrifying now, absolutely alone with the darkness under the earth waiting just beyond the glow of the lamp. Oddly enough, Asher's fears turned less upon the vampire he sought and more upon the occasional, illogical fits of dread that the roof should cave in and bury him alive in the darkness.

He saw the dark gates with a kind of relief—for he had feared, too, lest he miss one of Ysidro's chalked arrows. The ranked walls of brown bones and staring skulls seemed less dreadful to him than those silent aisles of empty rock.

It took him longer than he had counted upon to find Brother Anthony's private haunts in the ossuary. He missed his way twice and wandered—he did not know how long—among the brown walls of bones, searching for the branching tunnel, the tiny altar. At last he thought to trace Ysidro's slender bootprints in the watery mud among the pebbles of the floor, and after that found the arrow fairly easily. It came to him then that the psychic miasma that the vampires were capable of throwing around themselves had extended itself to Anthony's entire territory. Simply, it was easy to miss the place, easy to be thinking of something else. No wonder none of the guards came near here. They were probably not even aware of avoiding the place at all. They merely did. It explained certain things about Ern-chester House as well.

He passed the chaos of the fallen bones, then the neat rows of pelvises, the decaying skulls assembled against the eventuality of final Judgment. With a kind of medieval morbidity, the ossuary had been established, like the ancient charnel houses, to turn the mind to man's mortality; in spite of himself, Asher found his reflections drawn to the men he had killed, and, disturbingly, the men who would undoubtedly die in any future war because of all those charts and plans and information he had smuggled out of Austria, China, and Germany, tucked away in his socks or his notes on consonantal shift.

From what he knew of some of them, he had the uncomfortable sensation that in terms of ultimate responsibility, his personal death toll might well end up rivaling poor Anthony's, who only killed to prolong his guilt-riddled Unlife.

Before the steps of the altar, scattered with drifts of bone fragments, Asher stopped, listening to the terrible silence all around him. Banked along the walls, decaying skulls watched him with mournful eyes.

His whisper ran like water along the bones, vanishing into the stony darkness. "*Frater Antonius . . .*"

The sibilance of it hissed back at him.

"*In nomine Patris, Antonius . . .*"

Perhaps he did not sleep near this place at all. Asher sat gingerly down on the bare stone of the step, setting the lantern beside him. He took out his watch and was both surprised and vexed at how much time it had taken him to reach this place—it would be difficult to tell, now, whether a sufficiently ancient vampire would be awake in the daylight hours. But it could not be helped. He pulled his coat more closely around him, rested his chin on his drawn-up knees, and settled down to wait.

The lantern's metal hissed softly in the absolute stillness. He listened intently, hearing nothing but now and then the far-off slither of a rat picking its way across the bones. The cold seemed to deepen and intensify with his inactivity—he rubbed his hands over the lantern's heat, wishing he had thought to bring gloves.

Once the red eyes of a rat glinted at him from the darkness beyond that tiny pool of light, then vanished. Ysidro had said vampires could summon certain beasts, as they could humans—how long, he wondered, had Brother Anthony depended upon that ability for his dinner?

That led to the unnerving reflection that he might be doing so now. How *did* the vampire glamour work, once the vampire's eyes had met those of his chosen victim? Was that why it had seemed to him such a good idea to come here, alone and in daylight? *I could have summoned her from anywhere on the train . . .* , Ysidro had said, unwinding the purple scarf from the poor woman's throat, drawing the pins gently from her hair. *Do you believe I can do this to whomever I will?*

True, he felt no sleepiness, none of the dreamy unreality of that episode on the train, but that might only mean that after centuries of practice, Brother Anthony was very, very good.

The craving becomes unbearable . . .

He remembered the newspaper headline and shivered.

Still Brother Anthony did not appear.

The kerosene in the lantern's reservoir was now almost gone. He realized he'd have to leave if he were to find his way back out of the dark; the thought that the light might fail him while he was yet in the tunnels was terrifying and made him curse himself for not searching the vestibule for the stubs of the tourists' candles while he was about it. He straightened his back and looked around him in the darkness. "Anthony?" he whispered in Latin. "I'm here to talk to you. I know you're there."

There was no response. Only the skulls, staring at him with blank eyeholes, a hundred generations of Parisians, their bones neatly sorted and awaiting the final collation of Judgment Day.

Feeling a little silly, Asher spoke again to the empty dark. At least, if what Ysidro and Bully Joe Davies had said was true, Anthony could hear him from a great distance away. "My name is James Asher; I am working with Don Simon Ysidro to find a renegade vampire in London. We think he can hunt by day as well as by night. He is a killer, brutal and indiscriminate, of

188

men and vampires, bound not even by the laws that your kind make among themselves. Will you help us?"

There was no movement in the darkness, only stillness, like the slow fall of dust.

"Anthony, we need your help, humans and vampires alike. He has to be one of your contemporaries, or older yet. Only you can track him, can find him for us. Will you help us?"

A rhyme singsonged its way around in his head, turning back on itself like a child's chant:

But the silence was unbroken,
  And the stillness gave no token,
And the only word there spoken
  Was the whispered word, "Lenore."
This I whispered, and an echo
  Murmured back the word, "Lenore."
Merely this and nothing more.

Poe, he thought, and totally appropriate for this waiting hush, this darkness that was not quite empty, and not quite dead.

Merely this and nothing more . . . merely this and nothing more.

On impulse, he took the newspaper from his pocket and laid it on the steps of the altar, folded open to the article about the murders. He lifted the almost-empty lantern, and the moving light twisted over the dead faces like a sudden shriek of mocking laughter, the laughter of those who have learned the secret of what lies on the other side of the invisible wall of death.

"I must go," he said to the darkness. "I'll be back tomorrow night, and the night after that, until you speak to me. Please help us, Anthony. Nine humans and four vampires have died already, and now we know there will be more. We need your help."

Like a curtain swinging to, the darkness closed behind him as he passed along the corridors; and whether any watched him out, he did not know.

Fourteen

―――

How did one destroy a vampire who had passed beyond vulnerability to daylight? he wondered. Or presumably to silver and garlic and all the rest of it? He wished he could talk to Lydia, to hear her speculations on the problem, and he tried to think what they might be.

If Anthony did not help him . . .

Did this mutation in the course of time open other vulnerabilities—to cold, for instance? Simon had mentioned an extreme sensitivity to cold in the very old vampires. But short of luring the killer into a giant refrigerator, he didn't see how that knowledge, even if it were true, would be of any assistance. He grinned wryly at the thought of himself and Ysidro, Eskimo-like in furs, grimly driving an icicle through the renegade's heart, cutting off his head, and stuffing the mouth with snowballs. And, of course, the monthly bill for ice would be prohibitive.

Perhaps, if Lydia was right and vampirism was simply a pathology of the blood, there might be a serum which could be devised to combat it. *More applied folklore,* he thought wryly. Maybe a concentration of whatever essence was in garlic, injected straight into the bloodstream . . .

By whom? You and Sexton Blake?

And in any case, vampirism was not simply a physical pathology. It had its psychic element, too, and that, like the physical abilities, seemed to increase with time. Could it perhaps be fought on psychic grounds?

As he walked down the empty back streets toward the lights of the boulevards, he shivered at the thought of those slow-ripening powers, vampire pawns advancing powerlessly across the chessboard of time, until they could become queens . . .

In the deserted darkness of the street ahead of him, a figure faded from the mists. A dusky face stood out above the white blur of a dress, framed in loose masses of thick, black hair. Small, soft hands reached toward him, and he felt himself go cold with dread. There was another reason, he remembered, for wanting to leave the catacombs while daylight lingered in the sky.

The white figure drifted toward him, with that same almost unbearable slowness he'd seen in Elysée's drawing room, as if propelled only now and then by a vagrant breeze. But if he took his eyes from her, she would be on him like lightning; that much he knew. The murmur of that soothing-syrup voice was so low it was impossible that he should hear it at this distance as clearly as he did: "Why, James, there's no need to run away. I just want to talk with you . . ."

She was already much closer than she should have been, drifting that slowly; he could see the smile in her sinful eyes. Feeling naked, he began to back slowly away, never taking his eyes from her . . .

Granite hands seized him from behind, pinning his arms, crushing suffocatingly over his mouth and twisting his head back. The foetor of old blood clogged his nostrils as other hands closed around him, dragging him into the darkness of an alley, cold and impossibly strong. His body twisted and fought like a salmon on a line, but he knew already that he was doomed.

They pressed closer around him, white faces swimming in the gloom; he kicked at them, but his feet met nothing, and their laughter was sweet and rippling in his ears. A hand tore his collar away; he tried to cry "No!" but the palm over his mouth was smothering him, the brutal grip that dragged his head back all but breaking his neck. Against the naked flesh of his throat, the night air was cold, cold as the bodies pressing closer and closer . . .

Slashing pain, then the long, swimming drop of weakness. He felt his knees give way, the massive grip on his arms holding him up. He thought he heard Hyacinthe's husky laugh. Small hands, a woman's, stripped back his shirt cuff and he felt her

191

rip open the vein and drink. Darkness seemed to flutter down over his mind, a dim consciousness of chill, bright candles seen far away, spinning over a terrifying abyss; for a moment, he had the impression that these people had been there with him when he had shot Jan van der Platz in Pretoria and played croquet with Lydia in her father's garden.

A woman's arms were around his body. Opening his eyes he saw Elysée's face near his, her auburn hair tickling his jaw as she bent to drink. Beyond her was Grippen, bloated and red, blood smudging his coarse, grinning lips. Others crowded up— Chloé, Serge, the dark-haired boy, and others still—clamoring in sweet, thin voices for their turn. He tried again to whisper, "No . . ." but his breath was gone.

Red darkness swallowed him and turned swiftly black.

"I'm sorry, dear." Mrs. Shelton came out of the narrow little dining-room door beneath the stairs, wiping her hands on her apron—she must have been watching, Lydia thought, looking quickly up from the little pile of the evening's post on the hall table. "Nothing for you, I'm afraid."

In the face of that kindly sympathy, Lydia could only smile back and, tucking her book bag awkwardly under her arm, start up the stairs, groping one-handed to unpin her hat from her hair. Mrs. Shelton followed her up a few steps and laid an anxious hand on her arm. "It's hard, dear," the landlady said gently. "Your young man?"

Lydia nodded. Disengaging herself, she went on up the stairs, thinking, *I'll strangle him.* And then, *He's got to come back soon.*

Reasons why he didn't—or couldn't—crowded unpleasantly to her mind. She pushed them away, letting herself think only, *I've got to get in touch with him somehow . . .*

I've got to let him know . . .

The note to the charwoman was still pinned to the door with a blue-headed drawing pin: RESEARCH IN PROGRESS. PLEASE DO NOT CLEAN. She had half expected to have to fight for unviolated space, as she had always had to fight with every woman with whom she'd lived from her nanny down to Ellen, but evidently

Dolly, the woman who did the cleaning for Mrs. Shelton, valued her own leisure far above "what was proper." Lydia was confident the woman hadn't so much as crossed the threshold.

She dumped her book bag on the floor beside the stacks of journals already there, removed her hat, and turned up the lamp. Though she knew James would have communicated to her in some fashion if he had come back to London at all, she walked through to the bedroom and looked out, down the grimy slit of the alley, to the window of 6 Prince of Wales Colonnade.

Both curtains were closed. No lamp burned behind them.

Drat you, Jamie, she thought, turning back to the sitting room with a queer, terrible tightness clenching inside her, *Drat you, drat you, drat you, WRITE to me! Come back. I have to tell you this.*

She leaned in the doorway between the two rooms, scarcely aware of the headache she'd had since two or three in the afternoon—scarcely aware, in fact, that she'd eaten nothing since breakfast—gazing at her desk with its heaps of journals, its notes, and its books: Peterkin's *Origins of Psychic Abilities*, Freiborg's *Brain Chemistry and the Seventh Sense*, Mason's *Pathological Mutation*. On top of it lay the hastily written note from James, telling her he was dreadfully sorry, but he and Ysidro were leaving for Paris; beside it was the letter he had written from Paris itself, telling her he had arrived safely and was going to visit the Paris vampires that night.

Her heart seemed to be jarring uncomfortably beneath her stays. She understood, with the possibility of a day-stalking vampire, that he could not have met her to say farewell; it was her safety he was trying to protect, and she had guessed that he felt the vampires' nets closer than ever about him. Anger at him was irrational, she told herself calmly; anger at the situation was irrational, because it was how it was and there were far worse things to happen to one; anger at him for not writing was irrational, because God only knew where he was, and he would write when he could. Screaming and kicking the walls would not help either him, her, or Mrs. Shelton's charlady.

But I know the answer, she thought, and the steel-spring coil of knowledge, fear, and dread twisted itself a notch tighter within her. *I know how we can find them. Jamie, come back and tell me I'm doing this right.*

Jamie, come back, please.

Mechanically she shed her coat and her hat and pulled the pins from her hair, which uncoiled in a dry silken whisper down her back. For a time, she stood over the mounds of papers, the articles on porphyria, that hideous and deforming malady of anemia and photosensitivity, on plague, on vampires—there were even two of James'—and on telepathy. She'd been working at Somerset House, at the newspaper offices, at Chancery Lane all day for days, then coming back to the lending libraries to get medical and folkloric journals, and returning every night to this.

From among the papers, she lifted something small and golden, like a flattened flower, soft and dry in her hands—the lover's knot, braided by a shop which specialized in such things, from Lotta's no-longer-human hair. As the tiny bud of knowledge had opened before her eyes like a rose, she had thought, *I have to check this with James.* It made perfect sense to her, but she didn't know whether it was, in fact, practicable, and now there was literally no one to whom she could go.

But it's the answer! she thought. *I know it is!*

She had promised James.

Frank Ellis' fancy motorcar came to mind; to impress her he'd run the throttle out full but wouldn't engage the engine; she, too, was fighting to go and knowing there was nothing to do but remain in this room and wait.

Wait for how long? She had to talk to him, had to tell him.

She walked to the window and drew the curtain—lately she had become uneasy about that, too. For the last two nights she had dreamed of lying half-asleep in bed, listening to a deep, muttering voice calling her name—calling her name from somewhere quite nearby. But something about that voice had terrified her, and she had buried herself in the covers, trying to hide, wanting to call for James and knowing she dare not make a sound . . .

And she had wakened, trying to get out of bed.

She had taken to buying extra kerosene and leaving a small lamp burning low all night. This childishness troubled her, but not, she had decided, as much as waking in the darkness did.

He had to come back.

She took her seat at the desk, picked up the top journal of the stack she had marked to scan, and opened it, though she knew it would do nothing but confirm what she already suspected. All she could do for the moment was work, until James came back from Paris.

With a sigh, she settled into her study, carefully avoiding, for one more night, the question of what she would do if he did not.

Asher woke up dying of thirst. Someone gave him something to drink—orange juice, of all things—and he slept again.

This happened three or four times. He never had the strength to open his eyes. He could smell water, the cold stink of filth, and the moldery reek of underground; it was utterly silent. Then he slept again.

When he finally could open his eyes, the light of the single candle, burning in an ornate gilt holder near the opposite wall, seemed unbearably bright. It took all the strength he had to turn his head, to see that he lay on a narrow bed in a small cell which still contained half a dozen stacked crates of wine bottles caked with plaster and dust. One open archway looked into a larger room beyond; the archway was barred all across, the narrow grilled door padlocked. On the other side of the bars stood Grippen, Elysée, Chloé, and Hyacinthe.

Chloé said, "I thought you said you could touch silver," in a voice of kittenish reproach.

"A man can have the strength to bend a poker in half and still not be able to do so with a red-hot one," Grippen retorted. "Don't be stupider than you are."

The padlock must be silver, Asher thought, dimly inferring that the discussion was about entering his cell and finishing what they had begun. The philologist in him noticed Grippen's ac-

195

cent, far more archaic than Ysidro's and a little like that which he'd heard among the Appalachian mountaineers of America. He could feel bandages on his throat and both wrists and the scratchiness of considerable stubble on his jaw.

"Can you make him come and do it?" Hyacinthe inquired, regarding Asher with narrowed dark eyes. Something changed in her voice, and she murmured, as if for his ears alone, "Will you come and let me in, honey?"

For a moment the notion seemed entirely logical to Asher's exhausted mind; he only wondered where Simon might have put the key. Then he realized what he was thinking and shook his head.

Her huge dark eyes glowed into his, for that moment all that he saw or knew. "Please? I won't harm you—won't let them harm you. You can lock the door again after me."

For a few seconds he truly believed her, in spite of the fact that it had been she who had diverted his attention in the alley, in spite of knowing down to the marrow of his bones that she lied. That was, he supposed, what Simon had meant of Lotta when he had said that she was a "good vampire."

"Bah," Grippen said. "I misdoubt he could stand an he would."

Hyacinthe laughed.

"Are you having fun, children?"

Even as the words were spoken, Grippen was already turning his head, as if startled by them the moment before they sounded; the three women swung around, white faces hard in the single gold light of the candle as it curtsied in the flicker of wind. An instant later, Ysidro stepped out of the darkness, graceful and withdrawn-looking, but Asher noticed he did not come too near to the others.

"I ought to have guessed you'd have a bolthole in the sewers, like the Spanish rat you are," Grippen growled.

"If the French government will dig them, it were a shame not to put them to use. Did you ever know Tulloch the Scot? Or Johannis Magnus?"

"The Scot's got to be dead, and this curst penpusher's got

you in the way of asking questions like a curst Jesuit. Those concerns have ceased to be ours—ceased from the moment the breath went out of our lungs and the last waste of mortality from out of our bodies, and we woke with the taste of blood on our mouths and the hunger for more of it in our hearts. The dead don't traffic with the living, Spaniard."

"There are things which the living can do which the dead cannot."

"Aye—die and feed the dead. And if your precious doctor e'er sets foot in London, that's aye what he'll do."

"Unless you plan to keep him prisoner forever," Elysée crooned mockingly. "Are you that fond of him, Simon? I never guessed it of you."

Chloé let out a silvery titter of laughter.

"The dead can still die," Simon said quietly. "As Lotta would tell you, if she could; or Calvaire, or Neddy . . ."

"Lotta was a fool and Calvaire a bigger one," Grippen snapped. "Calvaire was a boaster who boasted once too often to the wrong person of who and what he was. Think'ee that telling yet another mortal who and what we are is going to keep us safe? I always thought Spaniards had dung for brains and I'm sure on it now."

"The composition of my brains," said Simon, "makes neither Lotta, Neddy, Calvaire, nor Danny less dead, nor does it alter the fact that none of us has seen or heard a single breath of the one who has stalked and killed them. Only another vampire could have followed them, and only a vampire very ancient, very skilled, could have followed them unseen. More ancient than you, or I . . ."

"That's cock."

"There are no older vampires," Elysée added. "You border on . . ." She glanced quickly at Grippen, as if remembering he and Simon were the same age, and visibly bit back the word *senility*.

"He's a day hunter, Lionel," Simon said. "And one day you may waken to find the sun in your eyes."

"And one day you'll waken with your precious professor

197

hammering an ashwood map pointer into your heart, and good shuttance to you," Grippen returned angrily. "We deal with our own. You tell your little wordsmith that. An he comes back to London, you'd best stick close by his side."

And seizing Chloé roughly by the wrist, he strode from the cellar, the girl following him in a flutter of pale hair and ribbons, their monster shadows swooping after them in the flickering gloom.

"You're a fool, Simon," Elysée said mildly and trailed along after them, vanishing, as vampires did, in a momentary swirl of spider-gauze shawl.

Hyacinthe remained, blinking lazily at the Spanish vampire with her pansy-brown eyes. "Did you find him?" she asked in her golden syrup voice. "That ha'nt of the boneyards, the Most Ancient Vampire in the World?" Like a flirt, she reached out and touched his shirt collar, fingering it as she fingered everything, as if contemplating seduction.

"When I pulled you and Grippen and the others off James here," Simon replied softly, "did you see who carried him away?"

Hyacinthe drew back, nonplussed, as mortals must be, Asher thought, when confronted with the elusiveness of vampires.

Without smiling, Simon continued. "Nor did I."

Confused, Hyacinthe, too, left, seeming to flick out of sight like a candle puffed by wind. But Ysidro, by the tilt of his head and the direction of his cold eyes, obviously saw her go.

For a long moment, he stood there outside the bars, looking around him at the dark cellar. It had clearly been disused for years, perhaps centuries; past him, as his eyes grew more used to the light, Asher could see the open grillwork in the floor which communicated with the sewers, though the other vampires had left in another direction, presumably upstairs to some building above. One of the old *hôtels particuliers* in the Marais or the Faubourg St. Germain, he wondered, which had survived the attentions of the Prussians? Or simply one of those ubiquitous buildings purchased in the course of centuries by some vampire or other, as a bolthole in case of need?

Then Ysidro spoke, so softly that it was only because he was used to the whispering voices of vampires that Asher heard him at all. "Anthony?"

From the dusty, curtaining shadows came no reply.

After a moment the vampire took a key from his pocket, and, muffling his fingers in several thicknesses of the corner of his Inverness, steadied the lock to insert and turn it. Then he picked up a small satchel from a corner where, presumably, he had laid it down before addressing the others, and came into the cell. "How do you feel?"

"Rather like a lobster in the tank at Maxim's."

A fleet grin touched the vampire's mouth, then vanished. "My apologies," he said. "I could not be assured of reaching here before they did." He glanced down at something beside Asher's cot. When he lifted it, Asher saw that it was a pitcher, soft porcelain and once very pretty, now old and chipped, but with a little water in it. "Was he here?"

"Anthony?" Asher shook his head. His hoarse voice was so weak none but a vampire would have heard. "I don't know. Someone was." A dream—a hallucination?—of skeleton fingers caressing the silver padlock floated somewhere in his consciousness; but, like light on water, it eluded his grasp.

"I left this on the other side of the cell." From the satchel the vampire took a wide-mouthed flask and a carton which smelled faintly of bread pudding.

As Ysidro poured a thick soup out of the flask, Asher remarked, "What, not blood?"

Ysidro smiled again. "I suppose it is customary in novels— it was in Mr. Stoker's, anyway—for the victims of a vampire to receive transfusions from all their friends, but somehow I could not see myself soliciting such favors from passers-by."

" 'Just come down this cellar with me, I'd like a little of your blood?' I expect Hyacinthe could do it, too. But it wouldn't work, or so Lydia tells me. Apparently human blood isn't all of one type."

"Of course, such matters have been considered among vampires ever since Mr. Harvey's interesting articles first appeared."

Ysidro handed him the soup and helped him sit up to eat it. "We have long been familiar with the whole apparatus of transfusions and hollow needles. In fact I'm told some of the Vienna vampires used to inject their victims with cocaine before they drank. When Dewar containers were developed last year, Danny made some experiments in storing blood, but it seems to lose both its taste and its efficacy literally within moments after it leaves the living body. In any case it is not the blood alone that chiefly sustains us. If it were," he added, without change in the soft inflections of his voice, "do you think that any of us would be the way we are?"

Asher set down the bowl on his knees, his hands shaking too much with sheer weakness to hold it. Ysidro's steadying grip was chill as the hand of a corpse. Their eyes met. "Don't be naïve."

The vampire's pale eyebrow tilted. "You may be right, at that." Whether he spoke of Lotta, Hyacinthe, or himself was impossible to tell. He took the empty bowl and turned away, every movement spare and economical as a sonnet. "I doubt you'll need concern yourself with Grippen at the moment. He and Chloé are bound back to London . . ."

"Simon . . ."

He looked back, the gilt candlelight seeming almost to shine through him, as it shone through the edges of fingers held near to the flame—demon and killer a thousand times over, and the man who had saved Asher's life.

"Thank you."

"You are in my service," the vampire replied, the unstressed axiom of a nobleman who questions neither his rights nor his duties. "And we have not yet scotched this killer.

"I am still not entirely convinced," he continued, neatly returning bowl, flask, and spoon to his satchel, "that the killer is not Grippen himself. I have given thought to your assertion that our state is a medical pathology. If there is some alteration of state which takes place close to the three hundred and fiftieth year . . ."

"Then wouldn't you be experiencing it, too?"

"Not necessarily." He turned back and held up his white, long-fingered hands shoulder-high, showing the colorless flesh next to his stringy, ash-pale hair. "Though I was still quite fair-haired as a living man, I had more color than this, and my eyes were quite dark. This—bleaching—is not common, but not unknown among our kind. Perhaps it is what they call a mutation of the virus, if virus it be. The oldest vampire I knew, my own master Rhys, was also 'bleached,' though other vampires he created were not. Therefore as a condition it might affect other changes that take place when a vampire ages. And since it seems that Calvaire left Paris for precisely those reasons which turned Grippen against him in London . . ."

"No." Asher sank back to his pillow, exhausted with the mere effort of sitting up and eating, wanting nothing more, now, than to sleep again. "Didn't you read the newspaper? It was in my pocket . . ." He hesitated. "No it wasn't, I left it in the catacombs. A section of the London *Times*. It can't have taken Grippen less than a night to come here, and the night before I was attacked, nine people were killed by a vampire in London. Oh, the police were puzzled by the lack of blood in the bodies, but it was . . ."

"Nine!"

It was the first time he had ever seen Simon truly shocked. Or perhaps, he thought, he was simply able to read the vampire better now.

"I didn't think it sounded like any of the London vampires. Grippen may be a brute, but he hasn't survived three hundred and fifty years by indulging in stupid rampages like that. And now I know it couldn't have been either Grippen or Chloé, and it certainly doesn't sound like the Farrens. What it sounded like was a vampire who'd been lying low."

"And who took the first moment when Grippen was gone," Simon murmured softly, "to satisfy a craving that must by that time have been monstrous. But *nine* . . ."

"In any case," Asher said, "it means that we are definitely dealing with another vampire."

Ysidro nodded. "Yes," he said. "And by the sound of it, in all probability, a mad one."

Asher sighed. "My old nanny used to say, 'Every day in every way things are getting better and better.' It comforts me to know she was right." And he dropped his head to the thin straw of the pillow and fell instantly to sleep.

Fifteen

EIGHT PERISH IN WAREHOUSE FIRE

FOUL PLAY SUSPECTED

[From the *Manchester Herald*]

Fire ravaged the cotton warehouse of Moyle & Co. in Liverpool Street last night, claiming the lives of eight vagrants who are believed to have taken shelter in the warehouse from the cold. However, police report the discovery of a small quantity of blood on the pavement of the alley behind the warehouse, indicating that some sort of foul play may have taken place, though all the bodies were too badly burned to provide definite clues. All eight bodies were found clumped close together in the rear part of the warehouse, near where the fires started; there is no evidence that any of these unknown vagrants attempted to extinguish the blaze in its early stages, and, in fact, police believe that all eight may have been dead of some other cause before the fire started. The fire was blazing strongly when first seen by watchman Lawrence Bevington, who claims that he saw no indication of smoke or other trouble when he passed the warehouse earlier . . .

No, Lydia thought calmly, *he wouldn't. If I were trying to hide my kills by incinerating the bodies, I'd make certain the watchman was sleeping at the appropriate moment.*

Her hand was shaking as she set down the newspaper.

Manchester. Anonymous masses of factory workers, stevedores, and coal heavers, unmissed save by those who knew them and maybe not even then.

She looked at the list she'd made, lying on top of the *Journal of Comparative Folklore*, and wondered how long she dared wait now.

She had promised James not to do anything until she had checked with him, not to put herself in danger. She knew she was a child in a bog here, unable to tell the difference between a tuft that would bear her weight and one that was only a little greenery floating on the top of quicksand; she knew that the vampires would be waiting. The fear that she had lived with for weeks rose again in her, the fear of that guttural voice calling in her dreams, the fear of the gathering darkness, the fear she had felt in the cold fog of the court the night she had gone out to seek a vampire. Everything she had been reading had only taught her to fear more.

But how long was she going to wait? The last thing she'd heard from James was that he was going to see the Paris vampires, under the problematical protection of Don Simon Ysidro. She shut her heart, trying to freeze it into submission, trying not to connect that letter with this long silence. But her heart whispered to her that they had no reason to keep him alive. And there was a good chance that, as Calvaire's friends, they might have something to hide, not only from humans, but from vampire kin.

I'll wait one more day, she promised herself, trying to relax the steely hand that seemed to clutch at her throat from the inside. *His letters have to go long-ways-about through Oxford . . . it could have gotten delayed . . .*

She looked back at her list, which she had compiled last night, and at the newspaper lying beside it. The vampire's rampages had killed seventeen people in the last three days.

Her fingers still unsteady, she took off her spectacles and set them aside, then lowered her head to her crossed arms and wept.

Asher woke feeling stronger, but still weighted, not only with exhaustion, but with an uncaring lassitude of the spirit with which he was familiar from his more rough-and-tumble philological research trips. His dreams had been plagued by the sensation that there was something he was forgetting, some detail he was missing. He was back in the van der Platz house in Pretoria, hunting for something. He had to move swiftly because the family was due back, the family which considered him such a pleasant and trustworthy guest, a Bavarian professor only there to study linguistic absorption.

But he had forgotten what it was that he hunted. He only knew it was vital, not only to the war between England and its recalcitrant colonials, but to his own life, to the lives of everyone dear to him. Notes, he thought, or a list—that was it, the list of the articles he'd published; they mustn't find it, mustn't trace him through them . . . So he hunted, increasingly frightened, partly because he knew the van der Platzes, though Boers, were the kingpins of German intelligence in Pretoria and would not hesitate to turn him over to the commandos if they discovered he was not as he seemed, partly because he knew that behind one of those doors he opened and closed in such aimless haste he was going to find Jan, the sixteen-year-old son of the household and his friend, with the top of his head shot off . . .

"I killed him," he said as he opened his eyes.

Cold, fragile fingers touched his. Against the dimness of the low ceiling, he saw the thin white face floating in its pale cloud of tonsure, green eyes gleaming strangely against the sunken shadows of the skull-like head. He had spoken in English, and in English a voice whispered back, "Killed thou this boy in anger, or for gain?"

He knew Brother Anthony had read his dream, seen it like a cinematograph picture, though how he knew this he was not sure.

"It would have been better if I had," Asher replied softly. "He might have understood that. But no." His mouth twisted with the bitter taste of his own awareness. "I killed for policy, to protect the information I had learned, so I could get back to England with it, and return to learn more. I did not want to be . . ." He hesitated on the word *blown*, an idiom the old monk would not understand, and then finished the phrase, ". . . revealed as a spy."

What a euphemism, he thought, reflecting how much thought was erased by that simple change of wording. No, he had not wanted to be revealed to these people who had trusted him as a spy, who was using their trust as he'd have used a stolen bicycle, to be later abandoned to rust by the side of the road.

"It is no longer lawful for me to absolve thee of this." Like broken wisps of straw, the thin fingers stroked at his hands; the green eyes looking into his were mad and haunted and filled with pain, but Asher had no fear of him, no sense of a lust for blood. The whispering voice went on, "I, who cried against simoniac priests, venal priests, and priests who took bribes to forgive in advance the sins their patrons longed to commit—how can I expect God to hear the words of a murderer-priest, a vampire-priest? Yet Saint Augustine says that it is lawful for soldiers to kill in battle, and that those deaths will not be held against them before the throne of God."

"I was not a soldier," Asher said quietly. "In battle, one shoots at men who are shooting at one. It is self-defense, to protect one's own life."

"To protect one's own life," the vampire echoed tiredly. The skull-face did not change, save that the sunken green eyes blinked. "How many have died to protect my life, my—immortality? I argue that I did not choose to become what I am, but I did. I chose it when the vampire that made me drank of my blood, forced his bleeding wrist against my lips, and bade me drink, bade me seize the mind that I saw burn before me in darkness like a flame, willing me to live. I chose then to live and not to die. I chose then and I have chosen every night since."

Exhaustion lay over Asher like a leaded blanket—the conversation had the air of being no more than another part of his dream. "Was there a reason?"

"No." The monk's cold little hand did not move on his. Against the low ceiling, his shadow hung, huge and deformed, in the candlelight—the glint of its reflection caught on needle-like fangs as he spoke. "Only that I loved life. It was my sin

206

from the beginning, my sin throughout my days with the Minorites, the Little Brothers of St. Francis. I loved the body we were enjoined to despise, reveled in those little luxuries, those small comforts, which our teachers warned us to deny ourselves. A warning well given, perhaps. They said that such delight in the ephemera of matter would addict the soul. And so it has done.

"Perhaps it was that I did not want to confront God with the sin of luxuriousness on my conscience. I no longer remember. And now I am burthened down with more murders than I can count. I have slain armies, one man at a time; in the lake of boiling blood which Dante the Italian saw in Hell, I will be submerged to the last hairs upon my scalp. Truly a fit portion for one who has sought hot blood from the veins of the innocent to prolong his own existence. And that is what I cannot face."

Susurrant and unreal, that voice followed him down into dreams again, and this time he found himself walking on the stone banks of a crimson lake, boiling and fuming to a bruised horizon in a black cavern that stretched farther than sight. The smell of the blood choked in his nostrils, and its thick, guttural bubbling filled his ears. Looking down, he could see in the tide pools the yellowish serum separating out of the blood, as it did in Lydia's experimental dishes. In the lake itself he could see them all: Grippen, Hyacinthe, Elysée, Anthea Farren with her creamy breasts bare and splashed with gore, screaming in pain . . . On the bank of that hellish lake walked Lydia in the trailing draperies of her ecru tea gown, a glass beaker in her hand, her hair falling in a rusty coil down her back and spectacles faintly steamed with heat, bending down to dip up the blood from the churning Phlegethon. Asher tried to call to her, but she was walking away, holding the beaker up to the light and examining the contents with her usual absorbed attention. He tried to run toward her, but found he could not move, his feet seeming rooted to the broken black lava rock; looking back, he saw the bubbling red lake beginning to rise, the blood trickling toward him to engulf him, like the vampires, for his sins.

He opened his eyes and saw Ysidro, sitting near the candle

reading the London *Times,* and knew that it was night. "Interesting," the vampire said softly, when Asher told him of his conversation with the old priest. "He is awake during the daylight hours, then, whether or not he can tolerate the touch of the sun itself, though I suspect that he can. And the silver lock on the door has been forced and replaced."

"He has to have come here somehow."

Ysidro folded the paper with a neat crackle, and set it aside. "He may have used the sewers. Perhaps he knew, from other years, that this was my house; perhaps he only followed me back here from the catacombs that first night and guessed, when he saw me fighting to save you, that I would want you brought here. I have, needless to say, moved my residence, now that Grippen and Elysée know of this place . . . Do you feel strong enough to walk?"

Asher did, but even the minor effort of washing and shaving in the basin of water Simon had brought left him exhausted, and he was grateful to return to his cot. Later, after he'd rested, he asked for and got envelopes and paper. In the course of the following day, he wrote two letters to Lydia, one addressed to her under her own name in Oxford, the other addressed to Miss Priscilla Merridew and enclosed, as his former correspondence had been, in a forwarding note to one of his students. He reassured her of his comparative safety, though he felt a twinge of irony at the phrase. Things had to be truly serious, he reflected, for him to consider helpless imprisonment in a cellar in the care of two vampires as grounds for optimism. Ysidro agreed to post them without demur—Asher could only hope that the rather simple camouflage would work, or at worst that he'd be able to get Lydia to some other residence before the Spaniard was able to return to Oxford and trace her down.

He remained in the cellar another two days, sleeping mostly, reading the books and newspapers Simon brought to him or listening in scholarly satisfaction as the vampire read Shakespeare to him in its original pronunciation, and slowly feeling his strength return. He never saw Brother Anthony, except in queer, involuted dreams, but now and then the water pitcher in the cell would be refilled when he awoke.

The second afternoon, he woke to find two railway tickets propped against the candlestick, and his luggage stacked neatly at the foot of his cot. With the tickets was a note, written on creamy new stationery in a sixteenth-century hand: *Can you be ready to leave for London at sundown?*

Beneath this was a folded copy of the London *Times*, with the headline MASSACRE IN LIMEHOUSE.

Seven more people, mostly Chinese from the docks, had been killed.

Weak and shaky, Asher crawled from his cot and staggered to the bars. They were massively strong, forged to defeat even a vampire's superhuman strength—the silver padlock, which did not seem to have kept Brother Anthony out, still held the door. He leaned against the bars and said softly into the darkness, "Anthony? Brother Anthony, listen. We need you in London. We need your help. We can make the journey in a single night; we have provision for it if daylight overtakes us. You must come with us—you're the only one who can aid us, the only one who can track this killer, the only one who can aid humankind. Please help us. Please."

But from the darkness came no sound.

"I'm not surprised," Simon remarked later, when Asher told him about it as the boat train steamed out of the Gare du Nord and into the thin mists of the evening. "It is difficult to tell how much he knows or guesses of what is going on—a great deal, if he followed us, as vampires often do, listening to our conversation from a distance. It may be that he considers the deaths of vampires only meet; and it may also be that he knows more of the matter than we do and will not speak the killer's name to us because he knows it himself. Among vampires friendships are rare, but not unheard of."

He unfurled the newspaper he had bought over his neat, bony knees and studied the headline with impassive eyes. "I mislike this, James," he said softly, and Asher leaned around to see.

LIMEHOUSE VAMPIRE, the headline screamed. POLICE BAFFLED. "There was another series of killings two nights before that, in Manchester—the London papers did not carry it until the massacre today. A vampire could travel the distance in a matter of hours—as indeed could a man. After a blood feast of nine people, no normal vampire would so much as look at another human being, even were it safe to do so, for a week at least. Few of us feed more than twice a night, and most not more than one in four or five—not upon humans, anyway. This . . ." The slender brows twitched together. "This troubles me."

"Have you run across it before?"

The slim hands creased the paper again and put it by. "Not personally, no. But Rhys spoke of something of the sort happening during the Plague."

He had been a vampire since before the Black Death . . .

"To those who drank the blood of the Plague's victims?"

Ysidro folded his hands upon his knee, slim and colorless in his gray suit, and did not look at Asher. "Oh, we all did that," he said evenly. "Rhys did during the Great Plague and took no ill; Grippen and I both did, during the last outbreak of the Plague in London in '65. One could not tell, you understand, whom the Plague would choose before dawn. One night, I drank of a woman's blood as she lay in her bed beside her husband; as I laid her back dead, I moved the sheets aside and saw him dead already, with the black boils just beginning in his armpits and groin. I fled into the streets and there Tulloch the Scot found me, vomiting my heart out, and asked me why I troubled with it. 'We are dead already,' he said. 'Fallen souls on whom Death has already had his will. What are these virgin fears?' "

The vampire spoke without emotion, gazing into the distance with fathomless yellow eyes; but looking at the delicate, hook-nosed profile, Asher glimpsed for the first time the abysses of dark memory that lay beneath that disdainful calm.

"Even in his later years, Rhys was a traveler—an unusual circumstance for the Undead. He would vanish for years, sometimes decades, at a time—indeed it was only by chance that I saw him in London the week before the Great Fire. He once told me of vampires in Paris and Bavaria during the Plague who would go into fits of attacking humans, killing again and again in a night, though he did not know whether this was something in the Plague itself, or simply horror at that which was happening all around them. But there were some, he said, though by no means all, who, without warning, years and often centuries later, would be seized with the need to kill in that fashion again and again. I know Elizabeth the Fair used to go into the plague houses and kill the families who had not yet broken out—she was killed after what always sounded to me like a very stupid rampage, a series of careless killings that was not at all like her. She had never showed that tendency before and she had been a vampire for centuries."

"But you have never done so?"

Still the vampire did not meet his eyes. "Not yet."

They reached London in the black fog of an autumn predawn. Instead of fading away as had always been his wont before the train even pulled up to the platform, Ysidro rode with Asher in the cab back to his lodgings and saw him ensconced in bed before vanishing into the perilously waning dark. Though the vampire treated the matter as simply part of his obligation to an employee who must be kept serviceable, Asher was grateful and rather touched and heartily glad of the help. He had slept when he could on the journey; by the time they reached Prince of Wales Colonnade, he felt, as Mrs. Grimes frequently phrased it, as if he'd been pulled through a mangle.

The sun woke him hours later. His landlady, who had been horrified by his haggard appearance, brought him breakfast on a tray and asked if there was anything she could do to help. "Is there someone I can send for, sir?" she demanded worriedly. "If you've been ill, you'll need someone to look after you, and dear knows, though we're put here to help our fellow creatures, what with four lodgers and the keeping up of the place, I simply haven't the time it would take."

"No, of course not," Asher said soothingly. "And I'm deeply obliged for what you have been able to do. I have a younger sister here in London; if you would be so good as to send your boy to the telegraph office, I'll be able to go to meet her, and she'll get me whatever I'll need."

It was an awkward and time-consuming arrangement, but he knew that, if he simply sent a note to Bruton Place, they'd wonder why she didn't just walk back over with the bearer, and he was not going to risk having Lydia associated in any way with Prince of Wales Colonnade, if he could help it. He'd closed one window curtain to alert Lydia to the fact that a telegram would follow. Writing the message with a hand that still wobbled unsteadily around the pen, he decided, regretfully, that it would be safer if they did not meet at all—merely exchanged parcels of information at the letter drop in the Museum's cloakroom. His soul ached to see her, to touch her, to hear her voice, and to know she was safe, but knowing what little he knew now about the killer, he did not dare even risk a meeting in broad daylight in the Park.

Even the fact that he had done so once made his heart contract with dread. The killer could have been watching, as Ysidro said, unseen and at a distance, listening to every word they uttered— a day stalker, mad and feverish with the hunger of the ancient Plague. Bully Joe Davies' face returned to his mind, craggy and twisted behind his straggling, dirty hair—the glottal, desperate cockney voice whispering, "My brain's burnin' for it! . . . it keeps hurtin' at me and hurtin' at me . . ." and the frantic, naked hunger in his eyes.

Bitter self-loathing filled him—the godlike Dennis Blaydon, he thought viciously, would never have put her in danger like this.

He sent the telegram reply paid and put in a dogged two hours, writing up his adventures and findings in Paris. Even that exhausted him and depressed him, as well. He craved rest as he had craved water in the days down in Ysidro's cellar, after his blood had been drained; he wanted to have Lydia out of this, himself out of this, and wanted the silence and green peace of Oxford, even for a little while. He yearned for rest, not to have to think about even the hypothetical vampires of folklore, much less the real ones who lurked beneath the pavements of

London and Paris, listening to the passing of human feet on the flagways overhead, watching from the shadows of alleys with greedy, speculative, unhuman eyes.

But that was not an option any more. So he wiped the sweat of effort from his face with a corner of the pillow sham and continued driving his pen over the sheets of foolscap on his lap, straining his ears for the sound of the commissionnaire's returning knock on the door.

But no reply came.

With some effort, he dressed again and sent for a cab, partly to give the impression that he meant to go some distance, partly because there was every chance he would have to track Lydia in Chancery Lane or Somerset House—and partly because even the thought of walking two blocks made his body ache.

"Miss Merridew, sir?" the landlady at Bruton Place said, with the Middle English *i* by which he'd earlier subconsciously identified her as an immigrant from eastern Lancashire. "God bless you, sir, you're the one we've been hoping would call, for the good Lord knows the poor lass didn't seem to know a soul in London . . ."

"What?" Asher felt himself turn cold to the lips. The landlady, seeing the color sink from his already white face, hastily guided him to an armchair in her cluttered parlor.

"We didn't know what to do, my man and I. He says people stays here because they don't want folks nosy-parkering into their affairs, and, if you'll forgive me, sir, he says a pretty lass like that is just as like not to come home of an evenin'. But I know a wrong 'un when I sees her, sir, and your Miss Merridew weren't that road . . ."

"What happened?" His voice was very quiet.

"Dear God, sir—Miss Merridew's been gone for two nights now, and if she didn't turn up by tomorrow morning, whatever my man says, I was going to call in the police."

Sixteen

Lydia's two lodging-house rooms were, like every place else where Lydia resided for more than a day or so, awash with papers, notebooks, and journals—the tedious minutiae of her search for the vampire's tracks: gas company records, all noted in her neat hand; electrical usage; and newspaper stories, thousands of them. Asher felt an uneasy creeping at the back of his neck when he saw, in addition to transcribed details of old crimes, the two accounts of the Limehouse Murders. Names and addresses were noted also—Lydia had clearly gone through the parish rolls with a sieve, correlating property purchases and wills and coming up with the names of a small but indisputable number of persons over the years who had somehow neglected to die.

Traced out in those terms, he wondered why the Earls of Ernchester hadn't come under suspicion before. Anomalies of property exchange and ownership splotched the family records like a blood trail. Houses were bought, leased, and sold to people who never surfaced in the records again—houses which were never willed to anyone nor subsequently sold. Other discrepancies were noted—fictitious persons who bought property, but never made wills, and interlocking wills spanning suspiciously long periods of time. Tacked to the greenish cabbage-rose paper of one wall was an Ordinance Survey map of London and its suburbs, sprinkled with red-, green-, and blue-headed drawing pins. Lists of addresses. Lists of names. He found Anthea Farren's on two of them, Lotta Harshaw's, Edward Hammersmith's, and Lionel Grippen's, along with many others. There were clipped photographs of Bertie Westmoreland, his brother the Honorable Evelyn, mammoth and smiling in football gear of Gloucester College colors, arm in arm with a beaming Dennis Blaydon, Thomas Gobey, Paul Farringdon, and dozens of others, and one blurred and yellow tabloid clip of a blonde-haired woman who might have been Lotta herself.

Like Lydia's desk at home, the little writing desk was a spilling chaos of notes, among which he found the letter he'd written in Ysidro's cellar in Paris, forwarded from Oxford, its seals intact. Beside it, likewise intact, was the telegram he had sent earlier that day, and beneath them both the London *Standard*, spread out to the story of the second massacre in the Limehouse.

That, it appeared, was the last thing she had read before she left.

Fear clenched the pit of his stomach, the dreadful sinking sensation he'd had in Pretoria, when he knew he'd been blown, and after it, cold and deadly anger.

Grippen.

When she hadn't heard from him, she'd gone vampire hunting on her own.

Lydia, no, he thought, aghast at the foolhardiness of it. It was hard to imagine Lydia being rash enough to undertake such an expedition alone, and yet . . .

She had promised him, yes—but that had been before he himself had disappeared. Before the "Limehouse Vampire" had begun its rampages. For all she knew, he could have been dead in Paris—and he was, in fact, extraordinarily lucky not to be. She had obviously realized that for once, unwittingly, Fleet Street hyperbole was telling nothing but the unvarnished facts; for all she knew, whatever she had learned or deduced might have been the only help the mortal population of London was going to get.

Like many researchers, Lydia was cold-blooded—as a rule the softer-hearted altruists went into general practice. But at heart, it took a streak of self-sacrifice to enter the medical field at all. He had never known Lydia to break a promise, but at that point she might very well have believed that a daylight investigation was "safe."

What had Ysidro said? That vampires were generally aware of vampire hunters? All it would take would be for Grippen to become aware of her, to know whom to look for in the masses of London.

He made another swift survey of the room.

In the desk he found things he knew Lydia had not formerly possessed—a small silver knife, a revolver loaded—he broke it open to see—with silver-nosed bullets. In her bedroom she had set up a small chemical apparatus, a microscope, a Bunsen burner, and a quantity of garlic, as well as a bottle of something which, uncorked, was a pungently obvious garlic distillate.

For all his gentleman-adventurer tamperings with the Department, Asher was first and last a scholar and had arranged to track the vampires with scholarship. Lydia, the doctor, would use medical means for her defense.

Medical journals stacked every horizontal surface in the room and peeked from beneath the tumbled coverlets of the bed— he had long grown used to her habit of sleeping with books. Slips of note paper marked them, and the briefest perusal showed him they all contained articles dealing with either speculations on blood pathologies which could have been the source of vampire legends, case studies of pathologically related increases in psychic abilities, or obscure blood disorders. On the nightstand he found a hypodermic syringe, and a brown velvet case containing ten ampoules of silver nitrate.

It took him a few moments to realize what finding all this meant.

It meant that she had none of it with her when she left—or was taken.

Quietly, Asher returned to the sitting room, where the landlady was standing, gazing around her in bafflement at the storm of papers and notes and the warlike battle map of London. She was a little brown woman with a neat figure, a few years younger than Asher; she took one look at his face and said, "I'll fetch you some sherry, sir."

"Thank you." Asher sat down quietly at Lydia's desk. If there was any residual weakness in him, he wasn't aware of it now.

He had put his life back together after Pretoria, knotted up the frayed strings of whatever seventeen years with the Department had left of his soul, and had gone on. Long ago, he had loved a girl in Vienna, during the dozen or more journeys there to collect information, and, leaving her, had betrayed her in such a way that she would be distracted from her growing suspicions of him. It had been one of the most difficult things he had ever done. But he had made his choice and had patiently put his life to rights afterward, though it had been years before he could sit through certain songs.

If Lydia was dead, he did not think he would be able to undertake that patient process again.

Then a bitter rictus of a smile pulled at his mouth, as he remembered Ysidro in Elysée's salon, saying, "Fear nothing, mistress. I do not forget," and the vampire's grip like a manacle on his wrist. The vampires just might make the whole question academic. And if they'd harmed Lydia, he thought, with chilly calm, they would have to.

Unhurriedly, he examined Lydia's lists again.

Many addresses had one star beside them; only two had two.

One was Ernchester House.

The other was an old townhouse near Great Portland Street, an area he dimly associated with dingy Georgian terraces which had seen better days. The house in question had been bought freehold in 1754 by some relation of the sixth Earl of Ernchester, and deeded in gift to Dr. Lionel Grippen.

The sun hung above Harrow Hill, a blurred orange disk in the pall of factory soot, as his cab rattled west. It was several degrees yet above the roofline—plenty of time, Asher thought. He wondered if Lydia had other silver weapons, if she'd gone out completely unarmed—or if, for that matter, she'd gone out at all. Grippen could just as easily have broken into the place some night and taken her.

How had he known who she was and where to find her?

Stop this, he told himself, as the walks through Hyde Park returned to his mind like an accusatory bloodstain on a carpet. *There'll be time for this later.* And, just as firmly, he refused to contemplate what that *later* would constitute.

The house at 17 Monck Circle, like its neighbors, wore the air of having come down in the world. They were tall houses of brown stone, rising flush out of the pavement—servants' entrances in the back, Asher noted mentally as he paid off his cabby.

Good, he thought. *Nothing like a little privacy when breaking and entering.*

He observed the tightly shuttered windows as he strolled past it, looking for the inevitable entrance to the mews. It had once been gated, but the gates had long since been taken down and only their rusted posts remained, bolted to the dingy bricks. Just within the narrow lane, a closed carriage stood, a brougham such as doctors drove. He made a mental note of caution against a possible witness or bar to a quick escape and edged past it, jingling his picklocks in his pocket. He wondered whether Grippen would be able to sense him in his sleep.

If, for that matter, Grippen were here at all. Charles Farren had mentioned owning the building to which he'd been taken after the fiasco at Ernchester House, plus another, a few streets away; Lydia's more intensive research had turned up several others owned by aliases for the same pair. From things Ysidro had said, he gathered the Spaniard changed his sleeping place frequently—a somewhat uncomfortable mode of living, even for a year, Asher knew from his own experiences abroad. He wondered whether vampires did not simply perish of carelessness when the pressure of pretending to be human grew unbearable.

Except for a few, he thought. Brother Anthony the Minorite had gone quietly mad instead.

And—who? Tulloch the Scot, haunting the churchyards of St. Germain? Elizabeth the Fair, who had drunk the tainted blood of Plague victims? The incalculable Rhys, who had not been seen since 1666? Or some other, more ancient vampire still, hiding in London until his very legend was eradicated . . .

Until, perhaps, Calvaire had turned him up?

Asher soft-footed his way down the nearly deserted mews, counting cottages and coach houses. Many of these were long empty of the horses and carriages they'd originally housed, transformed into storage or let out for a few shillings. The one attached to Number Seventeen was crumbling and dirty, the doors sagging on rotted hinges, the windows broken. The door into the yard stood ajar.

Asher's hair prickled on his head as he stepped closer. He could see the two stout padlocks on the inside of the gate, and beyond it, across a tiny yard cluttered with old boxes and decaying furniture, to the house. Moss grew on the paving blocks, on the steps of the sunken areaway, and around the outhouse. No servants had used that kitchen for decades, at least. Above the kitchen, two sets of long French windows gaped mournful and black—the rest of the windows were shuttered.

The rational man, the twentieth-century Englishman, stirred in a faint reflex of protest at the obvious conclusion, but in his heart Asher felt no doubt. The place was the obvious haunt of vampires.

And the gate was open. He glanced back at the brougham, standing unobtrusively in the lane, waiting . . .

For whom?

As if to reassure him, the bay hack between the brougham's shafts shook its mane and chewed thoughtfully on its bit. The last broken fragments of the setting sunlight glinted on the bridle brasses.

Did vampires go driving in the afternoons?

He could think of one that might.

Something seemed to tighten inside of him as he slipped into the ruined and weedy yard. If he and Lydia could find this place, someone else certainly could—unless, of course, Ysidro was somehow right after all, and Grippen himself was able to get about by day.

Either way, he was on the verge of this riddle's dark heart, and, he reflected, probably in a great deal of danger.

There was a good chance that Lydia was in that house.

He crossed the yard cautiously. If the day stalker—be it Grippen or Tulloch the Scot or some nameless ancient—were there, the vampire could hear him whatever he did. There were two of them, he remembered—he'd have to watch his back, as much as one could against vampires. And one of them, at least, was mad.

He stepped up onto the little terrace to the left of the areaway and forced one of the long windows, gritting his teeth at the sharp click as the latch gave back. Shielded behind the corner of the embrasure, he waited for a long time, listening. Distantly he heard something fall, somewhere in the house—then the panicked flurry of thudding footfalls.

Heading for the carriage, he thought, and then, *No vampire's feet sound like that. A human accomplice?* Given Calvaire's penchant for confiding in prospective victims, it was logical. Was Grippen's body even now searing, crumbling to ashes in some upper room as the last dim rays of the evening sun streamed through the broken shutters . . .?

Asher found himself hoping so for his own sake, even as he tracked those fleeing footfalls with his ears. The stairs would debouch into the front hall; from there, the killer could leave by either the front or the back. He could slip through the half-open window, intercept him before he left the house . . .

But he drew back at the thought of entering those dense shadows beyond the window, and that probably saved his life. He was in the act of turning away to try to intercept the fugitive by the carriage when a hand shot out the window from the dimness of the house. It moved impossibly fast, catching him by the arm in a grip that crushed flesh and bone, dragging him toward the interior gloom with terrifying force. In the fading daylight, he got a confused impression of a leprous white talon, bulging sinews and misshapen knots of knuckles, and nails like claws, while the creature inside the house was still only a monstrous blur of white framed in the window's darkness. As a second hand reached out to seize him around the back of the neck, Asher flicked one of the silver knives into his hand from his ulster pocket and slashed at the corded wrist.

Blood scorched him as if he'd been splattered with steaming water. The shriek from the darkness within was nothing human, a raw scream of animal rage and pain. He twisted from the loosened grip before he could be flung, as Grippen had once flung him stunningly against the wall, and dragged at his revolver, firing at the vague shape that came bursting from the dark beyond the French doors.

It flickered, changed, moving with unfollowable speed; he felt something behind him and turned to slash again with the knife still in his left hand. The vampire was behind him, the slanting final sunlight turning its skull-face ghastly—a vampire beyond all doubt, but what it had been before was hard to guess. Under the pulled-back lips the fangs were huge, broken tusks that had gouged seeping furrows into the pustuled skin of its chin. It screamed again and fell back, clutching at the cut Asher had opened in its palm, glaring at him with immense eyes, blue, staring, pupils swollen with inhuman hate.

The psychic impact was flattening. Asher felt as if his mind had been struck by a falling tree, dizziness and disorientation almost swamping his consciousness. He tried to fling the dead darkness off him, even as the thing seized him again and bore him back against the house wall, its grip wrapping over his gun hand and crushing the bones. He cried out as the revolver slipped from his fingers—the thing caught his knife wrist, then flinched back with another scream . . .

Silver, Asher thought, *the silver chain.* With his knife, he slashed at the thing again.

With another shriek of agonized fury, it caught his sleeve, pulled him forward, and slammed him back against the wall again with such violence that, in spite of his effort to keep his chin down, Asher's head cracked against the bricks. His concentration slipped, breaking, though he fought to hold it, knowing, if he let the vampire's mind get control of his, he was surely dead.

A voice shouted something. The vampire slammed him against the wall once more, and his vision blurred, pain swamping his mind under a dreaming tide of gray. He clung to the pain that was already screaming from his right arm, forcing himself to remain aware . . .

A name. The voice was shouting a name.

221

He tried to remember it, tried to cling to the pain of his broken wrist, as he slipped to the ground. He was dimly aware of the dampness of the bricks beneath his cheek and the murky sweetness of crushed leaves in his nostrils.

Whistling shrieks cut the air, and footfalls thudded closer. He hurt all over, his back and left wrist as well as his right, but his left hand would answer, closing around the knife hilt, though he knew he was outnumbered. The newspaper description of the savagery of the multiple murders came back to him, and the glaring horror of the vampire-thing's eyes.

"Nay, then, what's all this?"

"You all right, sir?"

He managed to raise himself to one elbow in time to confront the two blue-clothed giants that materialized out of the dusk. London's finest, he thought groggily. The sun had slipped behind Harrow Hill. The twilight was cold in his bones.

"No," he replied, as one of the bobbies helped him to sit up. "I think my wrist is broken."

"Gorblimey, sir, what the 'ell . . ."

"I was coming to visit friends of mine in this house. I think I surprised burglars in the act. One of them attacked me but there were two—they were driving a brougham . . ."

One bobby glanced at the other—they were both big, pink-faced men, one from Yorkshire by his speech and the other a sharp-featured Londoner. Asher couldn't help picturing the look of sardonic calculation Ysidro would give them. "That one as passed us, driving fit to kill, I'll bet."

"Bay gelding, white off-fore stocking," Asher reported automatically.

"He dropped this, Charley," the London-born officer said, picking up Asher's revolver; the Yorkshireman glanced at it, then at the bloodied knife still in Asher's hand.

"You allus go calling armed, sir?"

"Not invariably," Asher said with a shaky grin. "My friend—Dr. Grippen—collects odd weapons. This one was sold to me as an antique, and I wanted his opinion on it." He winced; his right hand was beginning to swell and throb agonizingly, the stretched skin turning bluish black; his left was bruising badly.

"Best send for doctor, Bob," the Yorkshireman said. "Come inside, sir," he added, as Bob hastened off down the path. "Happen they heard no one was to home."

Asher glanced about him at the silent drawing room as they entered. "I'm not so sure of that."

Heavy seventeenth-century furniture loomed at them through the dense shadows of the drawing room; here and there, metal gleamed, or glass. The bobby Charley steered Asher to a massive oak chair. "Best wait here, sir," he said. "You do look like you been right through the mill." But there wasn't wholehearted solicitude in his tone—Asher knew the man didn't quite believe his story. It scarcely mattered at this point. What mattered was that he had backup and a good reason for searching the house for Lydia. With luck, the killers had destroyed Grippen and hadn't discovered her, if she were here . . .

"What did you say your friend's name was, sir?"

"The owner of the house is Dr. Grippen," Asher said. "My name is Professor James Asher—I'm a Lecturer at New College, Oxford." He held his swollen hand propped against his chest; the throbbing went down his arm, and his head was beginning to ache. He fumbled a card from his pocket. "I was supposed to meet him here this afternoon."

Charley studied the card, then secreted it in his tunic, somewhat reassured by this proof of gentility. "Right, sir. Just you rest yourself here. I'll have a bit of a look about."

Asher leaned back in the chair, fighting to remain conscious as the policeman left the darkening room. The shock of the fight was coming over him, clouding his mind, and his whole body ached. The face of the daylight vampire swam before his thoughts, queerly colorless as Ysidro's was, but not smooth and dry-looking—rather it was swollen, puffy, pustulant. Thin rags of fair hair had clung to the scalp; he tried to recall eyebrows and could not—only those huge teeth, grotesque and outsize, and the staring hatred of the blue eyes.

Forcing his mind back to alertness, he fished the picklocks from his coat pocket—clumsily, for he had to reach across his body to do so—and placed them inconspicuously on a black-wood sideboard near the French doors. He guessed he would be under enough suspicion without having those found on his person. Staggering back to the chair, he mentally began ticking off details: brown jacket, corduroy or tweed, countrified and incongruous on that massive shape; and lobeless ears, oddly ordinary given the deformation of the rest of the face. He glanced at his left arm. Blood was staining the claw rips in the coat sleeve.

Dear God, was that what vampires became, if they lived long enough? Was that what the Plague, mixing with God only knew what other organisms of the vampire syndrome, could do? Would he, at the last, have to track down and kill Ysidro, to prevent him from turning into that?

He realized he was singularly lucky to be still alive.

The name, he thought. The voice had shouted a name, just as his head had cracked against the wall. His recollection was blurry, drowning under shock and pain and the weight of the vampire's dark mind. Then there was the rattle of harness, the clatter of retreating wheels . . .

The images faded as his consciousness slipped toward darkness.

"You!"

A powerful hand grabbed him and thrust him back against the back of the chair. His mind cleared, and he saw Grippen looming in the shadows of the now-dark room.

Still holding his swollen right hand to his chest, Asher said wearily, "Let me alone, Lionel. The killer was here. Grippen . . . !" For the vampire had turned sharply and, had Asher not seized the corner of his cloak, would have been already halfway to the stairs. Grippen whirled back, his scarred face dark with impatient fury. Quietly, Asher said, "The red-haired girl."

"What red-haired girl? Let go, man!"

The cloak was gone from his grip—even his unbroken left

224

hand hadn't much strength to it. Asher got to his feet, fighting a surge of dizziness as he strode after the vampire up the stairs.

He found Grippen in one of the upper bedrooms, an attic chamber that had at one time housed the maids. He had to light one of the bedroom candles before ascending the narrow stair, no easy feat with only one workable hand; though the vaguest twilight still lingered outside, the windows of all the attics had been boarded shut, and the place was dark as pitch. He could hear nothing of the bobby Charley moving about the upper regions of the house. Presumably he was lying in one of the bedrooms in a trance cast by the master vampire's mind. That unnatural slumber pressed on his own consciousness as he staggered up the stairs. The pain in his broken wrist helped.

In the darkness he heard Grippen whisper, "Christ's bowels," unvoiced as the wind. The candle gleam caught a velvety sheen from his spreading cloak, and beyond it something glinted, polished gold—the brass mountings of a casket.

There was a coffin in the attic.

Asher stumbled forward into the room. As he did so his foot brushed something on the floor that scraped . . . a crowbar. Grippen was kneeling beside the coffin, staring in shock at what lay within. Asher's glance went to the window; the boards were gouged but intact. The killers must have been just starting that part of the operation, he thought, when his own footfalls had drawn them from their task.

Grippen whispered again, "Sweet Jesu."

Asher came silently to his side.

Chloé Winterdon lay in the coffin, her head tilted to one side among the pillowing mounds of her gilt hair, her mouth open, fangs bared in her colorless gums, her eyes staring in frozen horror. She was clearly dead, almost withered-looking, the white flesh sunken back onto her bones.

Only slightly bloodied, the pounded end of a stake protruded from between her breasts.

Ragged white punctures marked her throat.

Quietly, Grippen said, "Her blood has all been drained."

Seventeen

At least, Asher reflected with exasperated irony at some point in the long hours between six-thirty and ten, when he was finally released from the Charing Cross station house, they couldn't charge him with Chloé Winterdon's murder. But this was only because Grippen had gently gathered the blonde girl's body into his arms and vanished through some bolthole in the roof, leaving Asher to the tedious business of finding some story to tell the police—which they didn't believe—being held for questioning, and getting his broken hand splinted by the police surgeon. They injected it with novocaine and warned him to take it to a regular doctor in the morning, but Asher refused all offers of veronal or other sedatives. He knew already it would be a long night.

To questioning, he responded that he was a friend of Dr. Grippen's, that he had gone there on the off chance that a mutual acquaintance, Miss Merridew, had taken refuge with the doctor; she had been missing some days. No, he hadn't reported it before—he had just returned from Paris to find her gone. No, he didn't know where Dr. Grippen could be reached. No, he had no idea why the burglars would have silver-tipped bullets in their gun. They made no comments about the bite marks on his throat and wrists, which was just as well.

It was raining when he stepped outside, a thin, dispiriting rain. Weariness made him cold to the bones as he descended the station house steps, his brown ulster flapping cloakwise about him, his right arm in its sling folded up underneath. Even with the novocaine, it hurt damnably. Nearly half the night gone, he thought, and no nearer to finding Lydia than he had been that afternoon.

There was a cab stand at the end of the street. He started

226

toward it, and a dark shape was suddenly at his side, seeming to materialize from the misty rain. A heavy hand caught his elbow. "You're coming with me."

It was Grippen.

"Good," Asher said wearily. "I want to talk to you." After the thing that had attacked him, Grippen no longer impressed him much.

Ysidro was waiting for them in a four-wheeler a little ways down the street. "You certainly took long enough," he remarked, and Asher firmly resisted the urge to punch him as he slumped into the seat at his side.

"I took a few hours out for dinner at the Café Royale and a nap," he retorted instead. "If you'd put in an appearance earlier you could have joined me for coffee. They have very handsome waiters." The cab jolted into movement, its wheels swishing softly on the wet pavement; Asher's arm throbbed sharply in its sling. "Lydia's gone. And I've seen the killer."

"Lydia?" Grippen said, puzzled.

"My wife." Asher's brown eyes narrowed as he looked across at the big vampire in his rain-dewed evening cloak, the blunt, square head shadowed by the brim of his silk top hat. "The red-haired girl I asked you about, whose life is the price I'm allegedly being paid for this investigation." Cold anger still filled him at Ysidro, at Grippen, at all of them, and at himself most of all for leading her into this.

"Ah," the master vampire said softly, and his hard, gray glance flicked to Ysidro. "I wondered on that."

"She was in London all the time, helping me with my investigation," Asher said, and Ysidro's colorless eyebrows quirked.

"I knew she had left Oxford, of course. I did not think you would bring her here."

"It seemed a good idea at the time," Asher replied harshly. "She managed to find most of your lairs and all of your aliases before she disappeared. And if you didn't take her," he added, looking across again at Grippen, whose red face had gone redder as rage added to whatever blood he'd imbibed that evening, "then I suspect she found the killer as well. Now tell me the truth, because it's going to have a bearing on how I conduct this investigation. Did you take her? And is she dead?"

"You waste your breath," the Master of London said slowly. "*No* to both your questions is the answer that'll keep you for us and not against us; I know that, and you know that, and I'm thinking you'll not believe it an I say it, but it is so. I've seen no red-headed moppet. I plight my faith on't."

Asher drew a deep breath. He was shivering slightly all over, in nervous waves, reaction setting in on him to anger, exhaustion, and pain. He'd lost his hat at some part in the proceedings, and his brown hair fell forward over his forehead, the thin face beneath hard and far less clerkish than it usually seemed.

From the corner of the cab, Ysidro's light, disinterested voice said, "Tell us about the killer."

Asher sighed, and some of the tension ebbed from his tall frame. "It was—monstrous," he said slowly. "Foul. Diseased-looking. But beyond a doubt a vampire. It was bleached, as you are, Ysidro, but its skin was leprous and peeling. It was taller than I, taller than Grippen by an inch or so, and as broad or broader. Fair hair, but not much of it; it was falling out, I think. Blue eyes. It had a human partner—I heard his footsteps running down the stairs from the attic, and later he called the thing away from me; and that's odd, when you realize the thing goes on killing rampages, taking seven or nine humans at a time. I'd certainly think twice about riding anywhere in a closed carriage with it."

" 'It,' " Simon said softly.

"It wasn't human."

"Nor are we."

The cab pulled to a halt at the top of Savoy Walk. Grippen paid off the driver, and the two vampires, their human partner between them, walked down the long tunnel of shadows to the towering, baroque blackness of Ernchester House at the end. Bands and slashes of Madeira-gold marked the curtained windows, and caught the thin rain in a shuddering haze; even as they mounted the soot-streaked marble of the steps, one panel of the carved doors opened to reveal the Farrens standing, an arm-linked silhouette, just within.

"I fear she is truly dead." Anthea led the way up the long stair, to a small room at the back of the house which had once been used for sewing or letter writing. The dark red of her gown showed like old blood against the creamy whiteness of her bosom and face; its stiff lines and low-cut corsage whispered of some earlier era; knots and fringes of cut jet beads glinted in the lamplight like ripe blackberries. Her thick hair was piled in the modern style; against it, her face looked strained, weary, and frightened, as if her spirit were now fighting against all the pressures of those accumulated years. Ernchester, trailing close at her side, looked infinitely worse. "Decomposition isn't far advanced, but it has begun."

"That's wrong," Grippen growled. "Not cold as it is . . . She should bare be stiff."

"Are you speaking from your experience with human corpses?" Asher inquired, and the big man's black eyebrows pulled down over his nose in a frown. "With a vampire's, the pathology would be completely different."

Anthea had laid one of her velvet cloaks over the delicate Regency sofa in the little parlor. Against the thick, cherry-black velvet, Chloé's hair seemed nearly white. It lay in loops and coils, spilling down to brush the floor; Asher was reminded of how Lydia's had lain, unraveling in the study lamplight. Her eyes and mouth had been closed. But this did not change the horrible, sunken appearance of her flesh or the ghastly waxiness of her skin. She had been, Asher remembered, absolutely beautiful, like a baroque pearl set in Renaissance gold. Petrified, Lydia had said, every cell individually replaced with something that was not human flesh, and a mind replaced by that which was not a human mind.

A second cloak covered her; over the years, Anthea must have collected hundreds of them as fashions changed. It, too, was black, ruched and beaded; beneath it, Chloé's shell-pink dress shone like the slash of a fading sunset between banks of

229

clouds. With his left hand Asher reached forward and drew the cloak aside to look at the huge puncture wounds in the throat. Then, thoughtfully, he shrugged off the remaining sleeve of his damp ulster and let the weight of it drop to the floor around him. He shook clear a few inches of wrist from the sleeve of his corduroy jacket and held it out to Anthea. "Undo the cuff, would you, please?"

She did, gingerly avoiding the silver chain which still circled that wrist. Even the fleeting grip the thing had taken on it had driven the links into the flesh with sufficient violence to leave a narrow wreath of bruises and the reddening marks of fingers.

Just below the base of Asher's thumb were two or three sets of punctures, scabbed over like the half dozen or so on his throat. *A souvenir,* he thought with wry gallows humor, *of Paris.* He knelt beside Chloé's body and compared the marks. They were less than a third the size of the mangled white holes in the girl's skin.

"Its fangs were huge," he said quietly. "Grotesquely so, like an amateurish stage vampire's; it might have been funny if it weren't so terrifying. They grew down over the lip, cutting the flesh . . ." His fingers sketched the place beneath the thick brush of his mustache, and Ysidro's eyes narrowed sharply. "It hadn't callused, so it's something that came over it fairly recently."

"Any clown had told you that," Grippen grumbled. "We'd ha' known ere this, did any vampire walk that fed on other vampires."

"What happens to a vampire," Asher asked, looking up from Chloé's throat, his eyes traveling around the circle of white, unhuman faces in the amber sweetness of the lamplight, "that drinks the blood of other vampires?"

Grippen's voice was harsh. "Other vampires kill it."

"Why?"

"Why do men stone those who eat the corpses of the dead, force children, cut beasts up alive to hear 'em squeal, or play with their own dung? Because it's abominable."

"There are so few of us," Anthea added softly, her strong fingers stroking the massive jewel of jet and hematite that glittered at her bosom, "and our lives are lived so perilously on the shadowlands of death, no traitor to our midst can be tolerated, for fear that all shall die."

"And because," Ysidro's light, disinterested voice whispered, "to drain the death of a vampire, to drink of a mind so rich, so deep, so filled with the colors of living, and so thick with the overtints of all the lives it has taken, might be the greatest temptation, the greatest intoxication, of all."

There was silence—shocked, furious, and, Asher reflected grimly, not without recognition. The silken pattering of the rain pierced it faintly, muffled by the moldering brocades of the window drapes. Then Grippen snarled, "Buggering Spanish dog—*you'd* think so."

Seated on a chair near the head of the couch, his ankles crossed negligently but with his usual erectness of posture, Ysidro continued, unperturbed, "But the question was not of life and death, but merely of blood. We can gain physical nourishment from drinking an animal's blood, or a human's, though we kill him not—as you yourself can attest, James." By that light, cool tone, one would never have guessed that he had fought to rescue Asher from that death in Paris, nor protected him, at a certain amount of personal risk, afterward. "To drink even a small quantity of another vampire's blood is repellent, after our own flesh has undergone the change. I am told that it often causes nausea."

"Then it's been tried."

The vampire leaned a little into the high crimson wing of his chair and folded slim hands around his knee. A slight smile touched his mouth, but left his sulphur eyes hooded in shadow. "Everything has been tried."

The others, still grouped around the couch where Chloé's body lay, regarded him uneasily, save for Ernchester, who simply sat on a chair in the darkness of a corner, staring down at his white, workless fingers, turning them over and over, as if they were some queer and unknown growth he had suddenly found sprouting at the ends of his arms.

"Then merely the drinking of another vampire's blood,

whether he killed him or not, wouldn't cause that kind of change?"

"It did not," Ysidro replied in the careful tone he had used at the beginning of the investigation to reveal those few fragments of information with which he was willing to part, "in those that I have known."

"And who were those?" Grippen demanded angrily.

"As they are dead now," the Spanish vampire responded, "it scarce matters."

"What about vampires who were older than Brother Anthony is now, that you knew or heard spoken of?"

Ysidro thought, still immobile as an alabaster votive, his pale eyes half-shut. "Rhys the Minstrel was nearly five hundred years old when he perished—if he did perish—in the Fire. Like Anthony, his skills had increased; like Anthony he had become at least in part tolerant of silver and perhaps of daylight, too, though I'm not sure. One saw him less and less. I know that he fed regularly and did not show signs of any abnormality. I never knew how old Johannis Magnus was supposed to be . . ."

Anthea spoke up, resting her hip on the curved head of the couch, "Tulloch the Scot told me once of vampires in China and in Asia, who have lived for thousands of years, going on as they always have, deathless."

"And lifeless," her husband whispered behind her, almost unheard.

To Asher, still sitting on his haunches beside Chloé's motionless form, Ysidro remarked, "As a rule it is not something which concerns us, and I suspect that most of us do not wish to know of it."

"What would be the point?" Grippen demanded sullenly.

"The point, my dearest doctor, is to know whether this abnormal pathology is something to which we all must look forward."

"That's a lot of Popish cock!"

"What's this?" Asher lifted Chloé's arm, limp and soft in his grasp and without rigor. He wondered if the vampire flesh went through rigor when they died. It was another of the things Lydia would want to know . . . He swiftly pushed the thought of Lydia from his mind. The buttons of Chloé's sleeve had all been undone—there was a good handspan of them, reaching nearly to her elbow—and the white *point d'esprit* fell back from the icy flesh to show a small mark on the inside of the elbow, like the puncture of a needle. "Was her sleeve unfastened like this when you found her, Lionel?"

He shook his head heavily. "God's body, I know not! As if I hadn't aught else to look for but . . ."

"Yes, it was," Anthea replied. "Why?"

"Because there's a wound here—look."

They gathered close, Ysidro rising from his chair and even Ernchester stumbling out of his shocked lethargy to look around his tall wife's shoulder.

"It has to have been done as she died, or after," Simon said after a moment, his long fingers brushing the pinched flesh. "Something that small would heal almost instantly on one of us. See?" With unconcerned deftness he drew the pearl-headed stick pin from his gray silk cravat and plunged its point deep into his own wrist. When he withdrew it, a bead of blood came up like a ruby, and he wiped it away with a fastidious hand-kerchief. Asher had a momentary glimpse of a tiny hole, which closed up again, literally before his eyes.

"She'd no such thing when she were made," Grippen put in, leaning close, his words weighted with the nauseating reek of blood. Asher realized the master vampire must have fed while he and Ysidro were waiting for him to finish with the police at Charing Cross; it had become, to him, a matter of almost academic note. "I knew every inch of her body and 'twas flaw-less as mapping linen."

He looked sidelong at Asher, grayish, gleaming eyes full of intelligent malice. "We are as we were when we were made, sithee. I'd this . . ." He held out a square, hairy hand, to show a faint scar cutting over the back of it. ". . . from carving an abscess out of a damned Lombard's thigh, and the clothhead fighting the scalpel every inch of the way, damn him."

"Like Dante's damned," Ysidro murmured lightly, "we are

233

eternally renewed from the cuts we receive in Hell." Ernchester covered his face and looked away.

"Interesting." Asher turned his attention back to the white arm in its slender shroud of lace. "It's as if her blood were drawn with a needle, as well as drunk."

"A frugal villain."

"Not so frugal, if he's in the habit of slaughtering nine men in a night." Anthea's dark brows pulled together in a frown.

"His human friend, then?"

"What use would a living man have for a vampire's blood?" Grippen shrugged. "An he were an alchemist. I'd have sold much for it, in the days when my own veins weren't bursting with the stuff . . ."

"An alchemist," Asher said slowly, remembering Lydia strolling along the rocky brink of a lake of boiling blood, a beaker in her hand. Reaching down to dip it full . . . *I wanted to examine him medically,* she had said . . . The articles about blood viruses in her rooms . . .

"Or a doctor." He looked up again at them grouped behind him—Ysidro, Grippen, and the vampire Countess of Ernchester. "Take me back to Lydia's rooms. There's something there I need to see."

"A doctor would have the equipment for drawing blood, and for storing it once it was drawn." Seated at Lydia's desk, Asher leafed unhandily through the chaos of notes and lists in his wife's sprawling script, picking up and discarding them and searching under the heaped papers for more. He was so tired his flesh ached, but he felt, as he often had in the midst of his work abroad or on a promising track in some research library in Vienna or Warsaw, an odd, fiery lightness that made such consideration academic.

"This is somewhat embarrassing," Ysidro remarked, studying the Ordnance Survey map on the wall with its clusterings of colored pins. "I had no idea you hunted so much to a pattern, Lionel."

"'Tisn't I as leaves my carrion where it may be fallen over

by girls out a-maying," Grippen retorted, turning the newspaper clippings over roughly. "'Bermondsey Slasher,' forsooth!"

"I think that was Lotta." Ysidro walked over to where Asher had turned his attention to the pile of medical journals on the bed, opening them to the marked articles and taking mental note of the topics: *Some Aspects of Blood Pathology*; *Psychic Phenomena, Heredity or Hoax*; *Breeding a Better Briton*. "What would a doctor want with a vampire?"

"Study," Asher replied promptly. "You have to make allowance for the scientific mind—if Lydia met you, she'd be pestering you for a sample of your blood within the first five minutes."

"Sounds like Hyacinthe," Ysidro remarked. "It still does not explain how such a partnership commenced—why a vampire would work for a human, doctor though he may be . . ."

"No?" Asher looked up from the stiff pages of the journals. "I can think of only one reason a vampire would go into partnership with a doctor and would reveal to him who and what he was—the same reason you went into partnership with me. Because he needed his services."

"Balderdash," Grippen snarled, stepping close to tower over him. "We're free of mortal ills . . ."

"What about immortal ones?" Asher cut him off. "If the virus of vampirism began to change, began to mutate, either as the result of long-ago exposure to the Plague or from some other cause . . ."

"Virus forsooth! Ills have root in the humors of the body . . ."

"Then if the humors of the vampire flesh slipped out of true," Asher continued smoothly, "*what could a vampire do?* Say a vampire who had lived in secret, even from other vampires—or any vampire, for that matter—if he found himself suddenly, frenziedly craving the blood of other vampires or knew himself in danger of going on rampages for human blood, as you said was an occasional symptom that developed in a few of those who had been exposed to the Plague. If he found himself transform-

ing, day by day, into the thing I saw at your house, Grippen—
if he knew such a course would inevitably lead to his destruc-
tion—wouldn't it be logical for him to seek help wherever he
could find it?"

Grippen looked uncomfortable and angry, black brow lowering like a goaded bull's; beside him, Ysidro's face was inscrutable as always.

"It might account for the renewed sensitivity to silver," the
Spaniard remarked. "Certainly for the wounds caused in his
own flesh by the growth of his fangs. And you think this vampire, whoever he was, chose his physician in the same fashion
in which I chose you—through journal articles?"

"He must have," Asher said. "Depending on who it is, he
may be forcing the doctor to work as you are forcing me—
with a threat against the life of someone he cares for. Maybe
that isn't even necessary. Some doctors would welcome the
chance to do research on an unknown virus and wouldn't care
that they were working for a killer. Or maybe," he added point-
edly, his gaze suddenly locking with Ysidro's, "like Calvaire's
friends, he's under the impression that he'll win, and that his
partner won't kill him when it's over."

Ysidro's chilly eyes returned his gaze blandly. "I am sure he
is quite safe so long as there is a use for him." He turned away
and began sorting through the papers scattered across the bed.
"And I take it Mistress Lydia discovered the medical partner in
the same fashion? Through the journals?"

"I think so." Asher returned to his own examination, flipping
the pages awkwardly with his single good hand. "She may only
have had a list of suspects and was visiting them one by one.
It would account for her not taking her weapons—the silver
knife, the revolver, or the silver nitrate . . ."

"Silver nitrate?" Ysidro looked up from a list he'd fished from
the floor. "Pox," he added mildly. "I see we're all going to
have to go through the tiresome business of changing residences
again. Do you really own a place on Caswell Court under the
name of Bowfinch, Lionel?"

"None o' your business an I do!"

"Filthy neighborhood, anyway. Gin shops everywhere—you can't feed without getting stinking drunk in the process. This one doesn't look familiar . . ."

"'Twas one of Danny's."

"I'm surprised he didn't get fleas. As for the one in Hoxton, I wouldn't be buried there, much less sleep the day. Where would she get silver nitrate?"

Asher nodded toward the little velvet box. Ysidro picked up the hypodermic gingerly, but did not touch the gleaming crystal ampoules. "As a doctor, she'd have access to it—it's used as an antiseptic, I think. I do know most doctors carry it in small quantities."

"This is scarce a small quantity," the vampire remarked, setting the syringe back in its case. "That much must have cost a pretty penny."

"I expect it did," Asher said. "But Lydia's an heiress and she's always had control of her own money—though I suspect her father wouldn't have settled it that way if she'd married someone more respectable than a penniless junior don at her uncle's college. I expect she thought to inject the silver nitrate intravenously. It would certainly kill a human, let alone a vampire. It was naïve of her," he added quietly. "A vampire's psychic field alone would prevent her from getting that close, and she obviously had no idea of how quickly a vampire can strike."

"Here's more of the curst things." Grippen came over, carrying a pile of journals which had been stacked on the bureau.

Asher flipped open the dog-eared pages. *Viral Mutation. Interaction of Viruses in a Medium. The Pathology of Psychic Phenomena. Eugenics for National Defense. Physical Origins of So-Called Psychic Powers. Isolating a Viral Complex in a Serum Medium.*

He paused, and leafed back through the articles again.

They were all by Horace Blaydon.

Softly, he said, "Dennis Blaydon was a friend of Bertie Westmoreland's. He'd have known Lotta. And through him, Calvaire and anyone with whom Calvaire had associated would have known of Blaydon."

Eighteen

I t was nearly three in the morning, and the windows of Horace Blaydon's tall brown-brick house on Queen Anne Street were dark.

"Can you hear anything?" Asher whispered, from the shelter of the corner of Harley Street. "Anyone within?"

Ysidro bowed his head, colorless hair falling down over his thin features in the glow of the street lamp, his heavy-lidded eyes shut. The silence in this part of the West End was profound, sunk deep in the sleep of the well-to-do and self-justified who knew nothing of vampires beyond the covers of yellow-backed penny dreadfuls and gave little thought to how their government got its information about the Germans. The rain had ceased. In an alley, two cats swore at one another—lovers or rivals in love—and there was the smallest flicker of Ysidro's head as he moved to listen and to identify.

At length he whispered, "It's difficult to tell at this distance. Certainly there's no one in the upper part of the house, though servants sometimes have rooms in the cellars."

"It has to be here," Asher breathed. "His country place has been closed up for years and it's a good thirty miles as the crow flies. He's a research pathologist—he doesn't have a consulting practice to worry about. His wife died some years ago and his son's in the Life Guards. It wouldn't be difficult to keep him away on some pretext. He's not very bright."

"He would have to be intensely stupid," Ysidro murmured, "not to notice, if his father were forced into such an alliance as I forced you."

Asher flattened to the corner of the house and scanned the empty street. "Set your mind at rest."

It was difficult to tell whether the soft sound in the darkness

238

was a comment or a laugh. "You know this Blaydon," Ysidro then said softly. "Is it likely we could win him to our side—turn him, as is said in the parlance of your Foreign Office?"

"It depends on what his partner's told him." The street before them was still. The lamplight gleamed like fractured metal on the water of the gutters. If Ysidro, turning his head slightly for what even the cobweb nets of his far-flung awareness failed to bring him, could hear nothing, it stood to reason Asher wouldn't, either. But still, Asher's every nerve strained to hear. "I never knew Blaydon well—I went to fetch Lydia at some of his lectures and had been to the Peaks a few times. I think he was piqued that I'd married the Willoughby fortune instead of letting his son do it, but I don't think he held it against me the way Dennis did. Horace is a stiff-backed and self-righteous old bigot, but he's honest. He was one of the few dons who stood up to Lydia's father when he wanted her taken out of University—though, of course, at the time Horace had a stake in wanting her to stay.

"In his place—the vampire's, I mean—I'd make damn sure he thought the Limehouse rampages were the work of the vampires we were tracking."

"You think he'd believe that?"

"I think if Dennis were in danger—if the vampire were threatening Dennis' life as you're threatening Lydia's to win my compliance—he'd want to. We did it in the Department all the time. The old carrot-and-stick routine: on the one hand Dennis' life is in danger; on the other, Blaydon can do viral research with what blood he can take, and congratulate himself on killing vampires at the same time. He may not even know Lydia's a prisoner or he may know there is a prisoner, but not that it's Lydia. It's surprising how ignorant the right hand can be when it would really rather not know what the left hand is doing."

They left the shelter of the corner and glided back like specters through the wet blackness of deep night in October London. "The mews is just past the next street," Ysidro murmured, barely audible even in the utter silence of the empty street. "Do you plan to speak to this Blaydon, then?"

"If I can," Asher replied, as they slipped into the cobbled, horse-smelling canyon of the mews. "After I get Lydia out of this, and see how the land lies, if possible. Like Lydia—like a lot of people in the medical profession—Horace has a little streak of saint *manqué* in him, in his case one of the stiffer-backed Scots variety. It could be the vampire is playing on that as well."

"I would give a good deal to know who it is." The vampire's touch was light on his elbow, guiding him around half-seen obstacles. What little lamplight filtered in from the street glistened on the puddles in the center of the lane, but left the sides in velvet shadow; the air was sweet with the clean smell of hay and the pungency of well-tended horses, prosaic odors and comforting. "I suspect Calvaire came to London to seek in him a partner in power, but I still find it strange that he would have heard of him at all when I had not, much less been able to locate him."

"Perhaps Brother Anthony told him whom to look for and where to look."

"Maybe." Ysidro's voice was absolutely neutral, but Asher, who was growing used to the tiniest nuances of his speech, had the impression he was not satisfied. "There are many things here which I do not understand, and among them is why Calvaire's appearance on the scene should have triggered these murders—if it did trigger them, and all these matters are not simply a chance juxtaposition in time. It may be that your Mistress Lydia can enlighten us, when we find her, or Blaydon. As I recall, Tulloch the Scot was big, though not so big as you describe. Your height, but bulkier . . ."

"No," Asher said. "I looked up at him—he came over the top of me like a wave."

They moved down the darkness of the mews, scanning the tall, regular cliff of houses visible beyond the stables and cottages. All were dark; it was the ebb-tide hour of the soul. He went on softly, "But conceivably this virus, this mutation, could trigger abnormal growth. It could . . ."

The vampire beside him checked, and the slim hand tightened

240

on his arm; turning his head swiftly, Asher caught the glint of the luminous eyes.

"What is it?"

The vampire moved a finger, cautioning. For a time, he listened like a hunted man for sounds which he thought he might have heard. Then he shook his head, though his eyes did not relax.

"Nothing." The word was more within Asher's head than without. In a stable, a horse wickered and stamped sleepily. "I—all of us—have grown used to the idea that as vampires we are, barring acts of violence, immortal, and to the idea that acts of violence are all we need fear. Like Lemuel Gulliver, we were stupidly willing to believe 'immortal' means 'safe from change.' It is disconcerting to learn that there may be terms to that bargain after all."

Asher felt awkwardly in the pockets of his ulster for the reassuring weight of Lydia's revolver, which, like the one the police had confiscated from him, was loaded with silver bullets—it was astounding what one could purchase at hyperfashionable West End gunsmiths. He'd also brought both silver knives and even the little hypodermic kit with its ampoules of silver nitrate. He'd found bills from Lambert's, for silver chains and at least one silver letter opener, stuffed into the medical journals as bookmarks, so she hadn't gone out completely unarmed. His own silver chains lay slim and cold over the half-healed bites on his throat and left wrist—the right was muffled in sling and splints and puffed up to twice its normal size—but even so, he felt hopelessly outgunned.

The briefest of investigations revealed a brougham and a trim bay hack with one white foot in Blaydon's stables. After a moment's silent listening, Ysidro murmured, "No one in the quarters upstairs, though someone has lived here recently—not more than a few months ago."

"He'd have turned off the servants," Asher breathed in return.

From the stable's rear door, they could see the tall back of the house, past the few bare trees and the naked shrubs of a narrow town garden. "You can't hear whether someone's in the cellar?"

Simon's eyes never moved from the house, but Asher could tell he was listening all around him and behind him, just the same. The night seemed to breathe with unseen presence. Asher's hair prickled with the certainty that somewhere nearby they were being watched; that something listened, as Ysidro was listening, for his single breath and the beat of his solitary heart. By mutual consent, they both backed out of the small stable and into the lane again, where a sound, a commotion, was likely to bring every coachman and dog on the mews.

"I'm going in." Asher shrugged his arm clear of his ulster; Ysidro caught it and lowered it to the baled hay piled just outside the stable door. With his left hand, Asher fumbled the revolver and a silver knife from the pocket, transferred the revolver to his corduroy jacket; the knife—since he was wearing shoes rather than boots—slid conveniently into his sling. "Can you watch my back?"

"Don't be a fool." Simon slipped his black Inverness from his shoulders, laid it in a soft whisper of velvet-handed wool on the hay, and reached into Asher's jacket pocket for the revolver. He patted the cylinder gingerly a few times with his other hand, like a man testing for heat inside. Satisfied, he concealed it in his own jacket. "If you had four hours' sleep on the boat from Calais last night, I should be surprised. No, stay here—you should be fairly safe. A cry from you—a sound from you—will wake every groom and dog in the mews, and this vampire must remain unsuspected now for his very life."

And he was gone, in a momentary blink of distracted consciousness that made Asher curse his own lapse of guard.

He was aware that the vampire was right, however. The strain of the night was telling on him. It would have done so, even had his body not been struggling with the aftereffects of his attack by the Paris vampires or with the shock of the struggle at Grippen's and the pain of his broken hand. The novocaine was beginning to wear off, and his arm in its sling throbbed damnably at every step he took. That alone would be enough to disrupt the concentration that was still his only possible defense against the ancient vampire's soundless approach.

He was conscious, too, of what Ysidro was doing for him. The vampire, though visibly edgy—or as visibly edgy as Ysidro ever got—throughout the walk down the silent streets from Bruton Place to Queen Anne Street, had never seemed to consider the option of not accompanying him. Perhaps it was simply because he knew that Asher would neither abandon his search for Lydia, nor have the strength to defeat the killer alone, should he meet it. But Asher suspected that, like the oddly gentle charm of his faded and cynical smile, the honor of an antique nobleman lingered in him still. He might be arrogant and high-handed and be, as Lydia had blithely calculated, a murderer thousands of times over, but he would not abandon his responsibilities to his liege man or his liege man's wife. This was more than could be said of Grippen or the Farrens, who had informed him, with varying degrees of tact, that the location of new boltholes for themselves took absolute precedence over any possible fate of Lydia's.

And all of this, in spite of the ironic fact that Simon could not even touch the problematical protection of a silver chain.

If Lydia could root out all—or almost all—of the vampires' hiding places, Asher thought, settling himself back on the hay bales and drawing his ulster clumsily up over his shoulders again, there was a good chance Blaydon and whatever vampire he was working with could do so, too, particularly if Calvaire had revealed any information to his prospective partner in power as to their whereabouts. He wondered whether he himself could remain awake to mount guard over whatever blown refuge Ysidro would be forced to take come dawn. Fatigue weighed down his mind, and he fought to keep it clear. He doubted his ability, even if Simon would admit him to the place . . .

A man's hacking, tubercular cough snapped him out of sleep with cold sweat on his face. Whirling, clawing at his pocket for the revolver he recalled a split-second later Ysidro had taken, he saw it was just a stableman, ambling back from a privy at the end of the mews. A dog barked. Lights were on in one or two of the coachmen's rooms above the stables. The smell of dawn was in the air.

Heart pounding, breath coming fast with interrupted sleep, Asher fumbled for his watch.

By the reflected radiance of those few lanterns now burning in coach house and cottage windows, he saw it was nearly five. Beside him on the hay, Simon's black cloak still lay like a sleeping animal.

Small and cold, something tightened down inside of him.

It was, of course, possible that the vampire had simply abandoned Asher and the cloak and gone to ground somewhere when he sensed the far-off approach of the day.

Asher did not for a moment believe this. Dread sank through him like a swallow of poison. Dawn was getting close.

Over the years, Asher had picked up a fine selection of curses in twelve living and four dead languages, including Basque and Finno-Ugric. He repeated them all as he slid the ulster from his shoulders, left it draped like a corpse over the hay, and slipped through the close, dark warmth of the stable and into Blaydon's back garden.

Exhaustion was fighting the screaming of every nerve in his body as he stood for a moment knee-deep in sodden weeds, looking up at that silent house. He wondered if it was imagination, or if there was the faintest glow of light in the dark sky and if the few outbuildings, the glass-paned extension that comprised the kitchen, and the dripping, naked tree seemed clearer than they had? He was straining with spent nerves and clouded senses to catch sight of the invisible, to pick up footfalls which even to vampires were inaudible, to be aware of whatever it was he sensed, drifting like the passage of a diffuse shadow through the darkness of the mews behind him.

How much daylight could a vampire of Simon's age stand? How long before his flesh would ignite like a torch?

The silver knife in his left hand, he slipped toward the looming black wall of the house.

There was a street lamp nearby, and enough light filtered

down for him to make out that the kitchen was deserted, as was the breakfast room whose window looked out onto the garden. The cellar had two windows, just at ground level; they were closed, but not barred or even latched. The hackles prickled on his neck at the mere thought of going into that house.

He stepped back into the yard, looking up at the first-floor windows above. Even from here, he thought that the one over the kitchen was barred.

He was shivering all over now, the predawn darkness seeming to press on him with whispering threat. Like Hyacinthe, he thought, who could summon him to open his barred retreat to her, though the sane part of his mind knew she would kill him when he did. But there was no time, now, to do anything else.

Empty crates, dark with dampness and bearing the stenciled names of various purveyors of scientific equipment, had been stacked near the kitchen door. Cursing in the remoter Slav tongues, Asher hooked his good hand around a drain pipe and used the crates to help himself up to the windows above.

The nearer window, open a slit at top and bottom, showed him the dark shapes of a workbench and the glint of glass; from it drifted a fetid reek which repulsed him, a whiff of chemicals underlain by the stink of organic rot. Beneath the barred window was only an ornamental ledge, and he exercised a number of plain Anglo-Saxon monosyllables as he disengaged his broken hand from its sling and hooked the tips of his swollen fingers over the grimy brickwork to edge himself along. At least, he thought wryly, this was one place where he *knew* the ancient vampire, the Plague vampire—if Plague it was—couldn't sneak up on him from behind. It was small comfort.

The room behind the bars was very small, an extension, like the kitchen below it, added onto the house after its original construction, and bare save for a single coffin in its center. The glow from the mews nearby dimly showed the coffin itself closed. Asher couldn't be sure in the dark—moreover there was a pane of glass between his face and the bars—but he thought

245

the bars themselves had a silvery gleam in the faint twilight of coming dawn.

In twenty minutes it was going to be too late to do anything.

Worn out, Asher leaned his forehead against the wet glass. More than he had ever done, even in the darkness of the Paris alley with Grippen's teeth in his throat, he wished he was back in Oxford, in bed with Lydia, with nothing more to look forward to than buttered eggs for breakfast and another day of dealing with undergraduate inanities. Whether Horace Blaydon was in the house or not—and he might have been in the cellar, waiting—there was no telling where the vampire was.

But even as the thought went through Asher's mind, he was easing himself back along the slimy ledge to the laboratory window. He, at least, could combat the thing with silver, something Ysidro was ironically helpless to do. But that, of course, was the reason the vampire had employed him in the first place.

His heart beat quicker at the thought of Lydia. *The hostages that mortals give to fortune,* Ysidro had said of the red-haired girl then lying deathlike in their unnaturally silent house.

The laboratory window yielded silently to his gentle touch. Did the ancient vampire report home for the day? Was that, in fact, *its* coffin, protected from the other vampires by the silver bars on the window, as Asher had been protected in Paris by the silver lock on the door? But in that case, why avoid the daylight?

It crossed his mind, as he eased himself through the window into the dark laboratory, to wonder how much Dennis knew about what was going on, and if he could somehow turn that young man's raging energy and love for Lydia to good account. It was unlikely that Blaydon's partner was holding him hostage somewhere—physically to hold someone prisoner required a great deal of time, care, and energy, as Ysidro undoubtedly knew. Asher could probably find Dennis at his rooms at the Guards' Club . . . The thought lasted rather less time than a ripple on a very small pond. Though he doubted Blaydon had informed his son of what was going on, it was only because

246

the pathologist was shrewd enough to realize that Dennis' stupid impulsiveness would make him a useless ally for either side.

The smell in the laboratory was foul, with an under-reek of rotting blood. Gritting his teeth, Asher lifted his right hand back into its damp and filth-splotched sling with his left. He felt his way around the wall, where the floor would be less likely to creak, his fingers gliding over the surfaces of tables, chairs, and cabinets. The door at the far side of the room opened without a sound.

So far, so good. If the vampire was here, watching him invisibly from the darkness, this was all useless, of course; the pounding of his heart alone sounded loud enough for even mortal ears to hear. But he did not know whether the creature was here, and on his silence his life and Ysidro's might depend.

How much time? he wondered. How much light?

The door of that small room over the kitchen was reinforced with steel and massively bolted from the outside. The bolt made the faintest of whispered clicks as he eased it over. Beyond, in the wan glow of the street lamp somewhere outside, the room lay bare and empty, except for the closed coffin.

Arizona Landscape with Apaches, he thought, remembering the old Indian-fighter's sketch. He took a deep breath and strode swiftly, silently, across to the coffin's side.

The sky beyond the barred window was distinctly lighter than it had been. They'd have to run for cover, he thought—after three hundred and fifty years, Ysidro would doubtless know every bolthole in London . . .

If it were Ysidro, and not the day stalker, who lay in that coffin.

The lid was heavy and fitted close. It was an effort to raise it with one hand. As Asher lifted it clear, Ysidro turned and flinched, trying to shield his face with his shirt-sleeved arms, his long, ghostly hair tangling over the coffin's dark lining beneath his head. "No . . ."

Behind him, Asher heard the door close and the bolts slide home. He was too tired, too spent, even to curse; he had thrown on the longest of long shots and lost.

"Close it." The long fingers that covered the vampire's eyes were shaking; beneath them Asher could see the white-lashed eyes shut in pain. The light voice was sunk to a whisper, shivering, like his hands, under the strain of exhaustion and despair. "Please, close it. There is nothing we can do."

Knowing he was right, Asher obeyed. Whether he had been brought here forcibly, lured, or driven, once the doors had been locked behind him, there was literally nothing Don Simon could have done but take the only refuge available against the coming daylight. He slumped, bracing his back against the casket, knowing he should keep watch and knowing there wasn't a hope in the nine circles of Hell of his being able to remain awake to do so.

He was asleep before the first sunlight came into the room.

Nineteen

——————

Asher floated groggily to the surface from the murky depths of sleep, through a gray awareness of hands pawing at him, pulling open his collar to unfasten the protective silver chain from around his throat, stripping off his jacket to rifle the pockets. Oddly, his chief consciousness was of the sound of the man's breath, the hoarse breath of the elderly. Then, like spreading poison, the agony of his swollen arm began, shooting out a root system of pain to every nerve of his body.

In spite of himself, he groaned and opened his eyes in time to see Horace Blaydon back away from him, fumbling with a revolver in one hand while he pocketed the silver chains and knife with the other.

"Don't call out," Blaydon said quickly. "The party wall on this side's soundproofed—the house on the other side has been empty for months."

For a long instant there was silence between the two men. Asher lay tiredly back against the coffin, blinking in the chilly daylight that flooded the room, his swollen arm in its filthy sling cradled to his chest, clothes smutched with grime and rainwater, sweat-damp hair hanging down into hard brown eyes that were not the eyes of an Oxford don. Blaydon's hand on the gun wobbled for a moment. He brought up the other to steady it, and his wide-lipped mouth pinched.

"James, I really am sorry to see you here." It was, as the Americans said, a fair-to-middling imitation of his old arrogant bark, but only fair-to-middling. "I must say I'm surprised at you—surprised and disappointed."

"*You're* surprised at *me*?" Asher moved to sit up, but Blaydon scrambled back a yard or so on his knees, gun leveled, and Asher

249

sank down once more, gritting his teeth. The novocaine had well and truly worn off. His hand felt as if it had been pulped with a hammer, and his whole body ached with the stiffening of every muscle that had been twisted and bruised in the encounter with the vampire in Grippen's unkempt yard.

And yet, for all he must look like a bitten-up tomcat, he thought Blaydon looked worse.

Horace Blaydon had always been a healthy man, scorning the illnesses he studied, bluff and active despite some sixty years. He was nearly as tall as his beefy son; against his shock of white hair, his face had been ruddy with youth. That ruddiness was gone, and with it the crispness of his hair and all his former air of springy vitality; he seemed flaccid and broken. It crossed Asher's mind to wonder whether Blaydon's vampire partner had in some moment of desperation battened onto *his* veins.

But no. It was more—or less—than that.

The pathologist wet his lips. "At least I've done what I've done for a good cause." He shifted the gun in his hands, as if they were damp with the sweat that Asher could see shining in the pale daylight on his grayish face. Had Asher had two good hands and not been in the final throes of fatigue, he would have gone for it, but there was something in the haunted nervousness of the man that told him he'd shoot without a second thought. "I—I had to do what I did, what I am doing. It's for the common good . . ."

"Your vampire partner murdered twenty-four people for the common good?" He was surprised at the calm of his own voice.

"They were worthless people—really worthless—the scum of the streets, prostitutes, Chinese. I told him, I instructed him specially, only to take people who were no good to anyone; bad people, wicked people."

"And—leaving aside his qualifications to judge such things—that makes it all right?"

"No, no, of course not." Blaydon's braying tone reminded him of Dennis, halfheartedly protesting at the Guards' Club that of course one *oughtn't* to burn Boer farmsteads to cripple the commandos' hold on the countryside, but war was, after all, war . . . "But we had to do something. The vampires were going deeper and deeper into hiding, and the craving was getting worse. It used to be he could go for weeks—now within days he needs blood, and it . . . it seems to be accelerating still more rapidly. I'd followed up every clue from the papers I'd been able to find in Calvaire's rooms, and Hammersmith's . . ."

"So you gave your blessing to your partner to go hunting at large in Manchester and London?"

"He would have died!" There was genuine pain and desperation in his voice. "When he gets these cravings, he isn't responsible for what he does! I—I didn't know about Manchester 'til afterward . . . For a month, he's been living in Hell, and now you've made him worse."

"Me?"

"You wounded him." Blaydon's voice was low, hoarse, almost frantic; his hands were shaking on the gun. "You stabbed him with a knife made of silver. That silver's running through him like an infection, like gangrene and fever. I can't stop it. It's exacerbating his condition; he needs more and more blood to fight it, to even hold it at bay. Oh, I understand you were frightened by his appearance, but . . ."

"I was fighting for my life," Asher said dryly, "in case you weren't noticing."

"I'm sorry, James, I really am . . ."

Behind him, the door opened. Framed in it stood the vampire.

Blaydon was right, thought Asher. That aura of leprousness, of disease, had grown—but so, it seemed, had the vampire's feverish, monstrous power. Standing in the full sunlight, it seemed hardly human anymore. The moist white skin glinted with shiny patches of decay; most of the faded hair was gone from its peeling scalp. On the pimple-splattered jaw, the weals of the overgrown teeth were still seeping a colorless pus mixed with blood, and the creature, with incongruous daintiness, pulled a white handkerchief from the pocket of its tweed jacket to pat at the glistening runnels. Huge, blue, and glaring, its eyes fixed on Asher with bitter malice.

251

Still keeping his gun leveled on Asher, Blaydon asked over his shoulder, "Any sign of others?"

The thing shook its head. Another shred of hair fell from its balding scalp, drifting like milkweed to the broad tweed shoulder.

"Not in the daytime, surely," Asher remarked.

"Not vampires, no," Blaydon said. "But they might well have hired other humans than you, James. Though how decent men could bring themselves to alliance with murderers . . ."

"I think your own house has a bit too much glass in its construction for you to start chucking stones about," Asher replied thinly, and Blaydon's mouth tightened with a sudden spasm of rage.

"That's different!" There was the edge to his voice of a man pressed too far, almost to the verge of hysterics.

Asher was too weary to care. "Isn't it always?"

The voice slipped up into the next register. "You know nothing about it!" With an effort, the pathologist got a hold on himself again; the vampire, behind him, spared him not a glance, but Asher was uneasily aware of that greedy, vicious gaze on his unprotected throat. Blaydon's voice was shaky, but quieter, as he said, "It isn't his fault. It was my doing, my experiment, you see."

Asher shifted up onto one elbow, his eyes narrowing. "Your *what*?"

The vampire stepped forward to stand at Blaydon's side. The old man got to his feet; for all his height, the thing loomed over him still, only a few inches taller, but monstrous in its breadth and bulk, incongruous in tweed jacket and flannel bags. Its arms hung grotesquely from the jacket sleeves, and the clawed hands Asher remembered were partially wrapped in bandages, stained dark with the oozing infection beneath.

"Don't you recognize him, James?" Blaydon asked, his voice thin and curiously soft. "It's Dennis."

"Dear God." Even as he whispered the words, Asher was conscious that, now that he knew who it was, he could recognize that short, straight little nose. It was certainly all that

252

remained of a godlike beauty—that and the lobeless ears. The vampire was several inches taller than Dennis had been. That, too, must have hurt. Asher felt stunned, as if he had been struck over the head, not knowing what to do or say—pitying, horrified, and aware of the baleful glitter of hate in Dennis' eyes.

"You're glad, aren't you?" The deformation caused by the growth of his fangs caused Dennis to mumble almost unintelligibly. With his blotted handkerchief he patted at his chin again. "Glad to see me like this. You hope Lydia will see me like this, too, don't you? But she won't. She's not going to see me 'til I'm better."

"Of course she won't, Dennis," Blaydon said reassuringly. "And you'll be better soon. I'll find a serum to make you better . . ."

Slowly, the shocked stillness seemed to break in Asher's veins with the horrible throb of stirring blood. "Where is she?"

"That won't matter to you," the vampire said. "You're never going to see her again."

Asher heaved himself up, his whole body screaming in pain, and reached to catch Blaydon's lapel. *"Where is she?!"*

He was slammed back against the floor as if he'd been hit by a swinging anvil before he was even aware Dennis had moved. Darkness blurred in front of his eyes, and he tasted blood in his mouth and nose. Somewhere he heard Blaydon say sharply, "Dennis, no!" like a spinster calling off a savage dog, and felt the dark crush of Dennis' mind on his, as he had at Grippen's. Shadow blotted the light above him; that dim, barking voice went on, "He's concerned about her, of course he is . . ."

"I want him."

He was fighting unconsciousness, the reek of decaying flesh filling his nostrils as the thing bent over him.

"And you'll have him, of course you will." It was strange to hear the fear in Blaydon's voice—Blaydon who had always been ready to spit in Satan's eye or God's. "But I need him now, Dennis. Let him be."

"He'll tell us where the others are," Dennis growled, and a

drop of something—drool or pus—fell on the back of Asher's neck. "You said we needed to trap him so he'd tell . . ."

"Yes, but we have a live vampire now, Dennis . . ."

"When can I have him?" Eagerness suffused the slurring voice. "I'm hurting, Dad, the thirst is killing me. That girl last night wasn't near enough, and you got most of it. Dad, I can smell him through the coffin wood, smell both their blood . . ."

"Please, my boy. Please be patient." Blaydon's voice came closer, gently drawing his vampire son away. "I have another plan, a better plan, now, but your getting well depends on both of them being alive, at least until tonight. I—I— Do what you need to do to—to make yourself comfortable—but please, don't touch either of them."

The voices faded and blurred as Asher slid toward darkness. He heard Lydia's name . . . ". . . perfectly safe, you know I'd never do anything to hurt her. Now fetch me some brandy, please. I'm sure James needs it."

Sinking into unconsciousness, Asher was sure James needed it, too.

The taste of the brandy revived him, coughing. He'd been propped up against the coffin again—Blaydon, glass in hand, was staring at the red teeth marks still visible on his throat through the open collar of his shirt. Dennis stood by the closed door, a cut-glass decanter of brandy in his knotty fingers. Asher supposed he should be flattered that they considered him still capable of rushing Blaydon.

Without speaking, Blaydon lifted Asher's left wrist and pushed back the torn shirt sleeve to study the wounds there among the blackened finger marks of Dennis' grip.

"What did they do to you?"

Asher drew a deep breath and disengaged his hand to wipe at the blood trickling from his nose into his mustache and down the side of his face. "It was a misunderstanding."

"*What did they do to you?*" Blaydon seized his arm, shaking him urgently. "Did they only drink your blood—or was it something more?"

His dewlaps were quivering with the trembling of his chin;

Asher stared up at him, eyes narrowing. "If it was anything more, I'd be dead now."

"Would you?" His voice lowered, but he could not keep from it that unholy eagerness, that sudden urgency barely restrained. "Your specialty was comparative folklore, James. You know about such things. Is it true that if your blood is drunk by a vampire—a true vampire—you become one yourself when you die? Is that how it's done?"

Something about the greedy gleam in his eye raised the hackles on Asher's neck. "I should think Dennis could tell you that," he said slowly. "What do you mean, 'a true vampire'?" His eyes went past him to Dennis, monstrous, deformed. "Why do you say it is your doing that Dennis is as he is?"

A flush crept up under Blaydon's pasty skin, and his little blue eyes shifted quickly away.

In a low voice Asher went on, "What is it you want with a vampire's blood? Why draw it out with a needle as well as letting Dennis drink of it? Why is Dennis as he is and not like the other vampires? Did Calvaire or whatever vampire made Dennis have some infection that he passed along? Or . . . ?"

"It is in the blood, isn't it?" Blaydon said, still not looking at him. "The organism or constellation of organisms, virus or serum or chemical, that causes vampirism. Isn't it?" His voice rose, verging once more on a cry. *"Isn't it?"*

"Lydia thinks so."

Blaydon's mouth tightened up like a trap at the mention of Lydia, and his eyes shifted nervously under Asher's silent gaze. "She—she recognized me, you see. At the *Daily Mail* offices, when I was looking for clippings and clues. I'd run out of clues about the whereabouts of the other vampires. I had to have more. She'd read my articles, too. She was already looking for a doctor. She said it was obvious I'd be prepared to believe in a vampire as a medical phenomenon where others wouldn't. Dennis said he saw her once in London, while he was following that fledgling of Calvaire's. He couldn't follow her then, but when she came snooping about here . . . Dennis caught her . . ." He laughed like a crow cawing. "Slip of a schoolgirl, and she's cleverer than the lot of us. She guessed at once what I'd done."

"You created artificial vampirism."

Asher did not ask it as a question, and Blaydon only blew out his breath in a sigh, as if relieved that he did not have to hide it any longer.

"It didn't start out that way." His voice was weary, almost pleading. "I swear it didn't. You know, James—of course you know—that it's only a matter of time before war comes with Germany and her allies. The Kaiser's spoiling for it. Oh, yes, I've heard the rumors about you and about where and how you spend your Long Vacations. You know the urgency of the matter. So don't come all righteous with me over what you've only done yourself in a different way. I dare say you've caused the deaths of well over twenty-four men, and in just as good a cause."

Blaydon took a deep breath, turning the half-filled brandy glass in his hands. "You know—or perhaps you don't—that, in addition to my work with viruses, for a long time my interest has been in physical causes of so-called psychic phenomena. For a time, I believed, along with Peterkin and Freiborg, that such things could be bred in. God knows how many mediums and table tappers I tested over the years! And I came to the conclusion that it has to be some alteration in the brain chemistry that gives these people their so-called powers: a heightening of the senses; an extrasensory awareness; and that incredible, intangible grasp on the minds of other men.

"Now, you can understand the need to be able to duplicate such powers at will. You've worked in Intelligence, James. Think what a corps of such men, dedicated to the good of England, could be in the war that we all know is coming! I tried hard to isolate that factor, to little avail. And then Dennis introduced me to Valentin Calvaire. He'd met Calvaire through a mutual friend . . ."

"Whom you later murdered."

"Oh, really, James!" Blaydon cried impatiently. "A woman of her class! And I'll take oath Albert Westmoreland's death could be traced back to her, for all his family bribed the doctor to certify it was the result of a carriage accident. Besides, by that time we had run out of other clues. I needed her blood for further experimentation, and Dennis needed it just to stay alive."

"You knew Calvaire was a vampire, then?"

"Oh, yes. He made no secret of it—he seemed to revel in astonishing me, in making nothing of the most difficult tests I could set to him. He gloated in the powers that he held. And Dennis was fascinated—not, I swear, with Calvaire's evil, but with his powers. Calvaire was fascinated, too, though for reasons of his own, I dare say. He let me take samples, substantial samples, of his blood, to try and isolate the factors which enhanced the workings of the psychic centers of the brain and to separate them from those which caused the mutation of the cells themselves into that photoreactive pseudoflesh and the physiological dependence on the blood of others. And I would have succeeded, perhaps even been able to alter Calvaire's condition. I know I would have . . ."

"You wouldn't have." Asher glanced across at the hulking, glowering shape by the door, guessing already what had happened. Pity and disgust mingled in him like the taste of the blood and brandy in his mouth. "According to the vampires themselves, those powers come from psychically drinking the deaths of their human victims. It's the psychic absorption of death that gives them psychic powers, and without it, they lose them."

"Nonsense," Blaydon said sharply. "That can't be true. There's no reason for it to be true. What do the vampires know of it, anyway? They aren't educated. Calvaire never said anything . . ."

"I'm sure Calvaire never ceased killing humans long enough to know whether it was true or not." The only way Ysidro could have known or the only way Anthea could have known, he thought, was to have tried it themselves. "Calvaire wanted power. He wasn't going to tell you anything more than he had to before he got it."

"I'm sure that isn't the case." Blaydon shook his head stubbornly, angry even at the suggestion that what he had done had been for nothing and that he had been, in fact, Calvaire's dupe. "There are physical causes for everything—unknown organisms, chemical changes in the brain fluid itself. In any case, I evolved a serum which showed great promise. I—I made the mistake of telling Dennis about it. He demanded to test it, demanded to be the first of this corps of—of psychic heroes. I refused, naturally . . ."

"And naturally," Asher said dryly, "Dennis broke into your laboratory and took matters into his own hands." It was, he reflected, exactly the sort of thing that Dennis would do. He was the perfect storybook hero, the perfect Sexton Blake, who could experimentally drain beakers of unknown potions and come off with, at most, prophetic hallucinations that coincidentally advanced the plot.

Poor Dennis. Poor, stupid Dennis.

Dennis' eyes narrowed viciously, as if, like Brother Anthony, he could see Asher's thoughts. "What would you have done?" he mumbled, his voice deep and thick, as if his very vocal cords were loosening. "Snugged back in your nice comfy study and let another man take the risks, as you'll do when those damn sauerkraut eaters finally force us to fight? What did you tell her, Asher? What did you tell Lydia about me that made her choose a sly old man over someone who would love and protect her as I will? But you made her work for you, made her put herself in danger. I'd never have let her come here to London."

You'd have left her in ignorance of her danger at Oxford, wouldn't you? Asher thought, feeling strangely calm. *You'd have told her it wasn't her affair.* Knowing Lydia, that would have run her into danger three times quicker and without the knowledge of what she was dealing with.

Dennis stepped forward, holding up his hands. All around the edges of the bandages that covered the palms, Asher could see rims of green-black flesh, like a spreading stain, puffy, malodorous, foul against the ice-white skin. "I was fine until you did this," he said thickly. "I'll enjoy drinking you like a sucked orange."

And he was gone.

Rather shakily, Blaydon said, "He wasn't, you know. Fine, I mean. His—his condition was deteriorating, although the infection caused by the silver seems to have greatly advanced the process. I wasn't able to isolate that factor, it seems—as I said, the serum was far from perfect. And he needs the blood of vampires, as ordinary vampires need human blood. It seems to arrest the progression of the symptoms for a number of days. He killed Calvaire the first night this happened—I was quite angry at him, for Calvaire would have been a great help. But Dennis had a—a craving. And he was disoriented, maddened by the alteration in his senses; he still is, to a degree. I didn't even know until it was done . . ."

Asher wondered whether Calvaire had tried to control Dennis, up in his attic in Lambeth, as he'd controlled Bully Joe Davies.

Blaydon wet his lips again and threw another nervous glance over his shoulder toward the shut door. "After that, we searched Calvaire's room for notes to tell us where we could find other vampires. Dennis knew some of Lotta's haunts and followed her to the Hammersmith mansion in Half Moon Street and to the haunts of another vampire she knew. I went with him—I wanted desperately to take some of their blood, not only to perfect my serum, but to find a cure for Dennis' condition. More than anything else, I wanted a whole vampire, unharmed, but it was impossible to get them away in the daylight hours, of course. So I—I had to destroy their bodies, lest the others take fright and hide. I had to be content with as much blood as I could take . . ."

"And Dennis got the rest?" With shaking fingers Asher took the brandy glass from Blaydon's hand and drained it. The gold heat of it reminded him that he hadn't eaten since a sandwich at the Charing Cross precinct house last night—he couldn't even recall what before that.

"He needed it," Blaydon insisted. A little testily, he added,

"All those who were killed were murderers, those who had killed again and again, for hundreds of years, I dare say . . ."

"Those Chinese and 'young persons,' as the paper called them, as well?"

"He was fighting for his life! Yes, he shouldn't have taken humans. It got in the newspapers; the hunt will be on for us if it happens again. I told him that after Manchester. And it doesn't really satisfy him, no matter how many he kills. But it helps a little . . ."

"I dare say." Asher drew himself up a little against the coffin, knowing he was a fool to anger this man who was demonstrably balanced on the ragged edge of sanity and yet too furious himself at such hypocrisy and irresponsibility to care. "And I expect he'll 'do what he needs to' in order to 'make himself comfortable,' as I believe you phrased it . . ."

Blaydon lunged to his feet, his hands clenching into fists, though they shook as if with palsy. Color flooded unhealthily up under the flaccid skin. "I'm sorry you feel that way about it," he said stiffly, as if he had long ago memorized the phrase as the proper end to any interview. "In any case it won't be necessary, not any longer. I can keep Dennis alive and have enough vampire blood, from a true vampire, to experiment with until I can find an antivenin . . ."

"And how are you going to keep Dennis from killing him the moment your back is turned?" Asher demanded quietly. "You're going to have to sleep sometime, Horace; if Dennis gets another craving, you're going to be back to square one . . ."

"No," Blaydon said. "I can control him. I've always been able to control him. And in any case, that will no longer be a problem. You see, now that I have this vampire, he can make others—a breeding stock, as it were, for Dennis to feed upon. And I'm afraid, James, that you're going to be the first."

Twenty

——

W hat you want is not possible." In the upside-down glow of the oil lamp Blaydon had set on the floor, Ysidro's face had the queer, stark look of a Beardsley drawing, framed in his long, colorless hair. His rolled-up shirt sleeves showed the hard sinewiness of his arms; like his throat and chest, visible through the unbuttoned collar, they were white as the linen of the garment. He sat cross-legged, like the idol of some decadent cult, on his own coffin, with Asher lying, bound hand and foot, at his feet.

Blaydon and Dennis had come in and done that toward sunset. Before he'd fallen asleep again that morning, which he'd done shortly after Blaydon had left him, Asher had heard Blaydon go out, with muffled admonitions to Dennis to remain in the house, to guard them, and on no account to harm them. *Don't eat the prisoners while Daddy's away,* he had thought caustically. Straining his ears, he'd heard Blaydon mention the Peaks, that sprawling brick villa on the Downs near Oxford that had belonged to Blaydon's wife, where she had lived, playing the gracious hostess on weekends to her husband's Oxford colleagues or her son's friends from London or the Guards.

They must be keeping Lydia there, Asher thought, the rage in him oddly distant now, as if the emotions belonged to someone else. No wonder Blaydon had the look of a man run ragged. Even if he had kept a staff there after his wife's death three years ago—and Asher knew he'd simply shut the place up when he'd moved his residence to London—he still wouldn't have been able to trust them. The Peaks might be isolated; but, as the vampires had always known, servants have a way of finding things out. Once Blaydon had taken Lydia prisoner, he had to keep her someplace and look after her. That meant an hour and a half by train to Prince's Risborough and another forty minutes to an hour by gig over the downs to the isolated house in its little vale of beechwoods, then back again, at least once, perhaps twice a day. And on top of that, the vampires were deeper in hiding, and Dennis was getting physically worse and more difficult to control. No wonder Blaydon looked as if he had not slept in a week.

As he had said, he and Dennis both had been a month in Hell.

If it hadn't been Lydia who was in his power, Lydia who was lying drugged and helpless in that empty house, Asher would have felt a kind of spiteful satisfaction at the situation. As it was, he could only thank God that Dennis still had sufficient twisted passion for Lydia to keep Blaydon from harming her.

Although, Asher thought, as he fruitlessly searched the barren room for anything which could conceivably be used as a weapon or to facilitate escape, he wasn't sure whether Blaydon would have killed a stranger to protect Dennis' secret. At least, he added with a shiver, he wouldn't have four days ago, when they'd caught her snooping around. That had been before he'd learned what a desperately time-consuming inconvenience keeping a hostage was. And that had been while he and Dennis were far more firmly anchored in sanity.

Looking at them now—Blaydon in his soiled collar and rumpled suit, with his silver-dust stubble of whiskers that glittered like the mad, fierce obsession in his eyes, and Dennis, hulking, restless, and fidgeting hungrily in the background—Asher was uncomfortably aware that both were stretched to the snapping point. However long father and son might have been able to go on undisturbed, Lydia's imprisonment had thrown a strain on the situation, which his own wounding of Dennis had then made intolerable. They had the look of men who were fast losing their last vestiges of rationality.

With forced mildness, Blaydon said, "Dennis is going to want to feed on some vampire tonight, my friend. Now it can be you, or it can be James. Which way do you want it?" He still had the revolver with silver bullets in his hand, which was steady now—he must have gotten a little sleep in the train, Asher thought abstractedly. And as a doctor, of course, he'd have easy access to enough cocaine to keep him going for a while, at least.

Behind him, Dennis smirked.

Looking perfectly relaxed, Ysidro set one foot on the floor, folded his long hands on his knee, and considered the pair of them in the flickering lamplight. "It is clear to me that you do not understand the process by which one becomes vampire. If, when I drank James' blood, I forced him to . . ."

Blaydon raised his hand sharply. "Dennis?" he barked. "Have you made a patrol? Checked for searchers?"

"There's no one out there," Dennis said, his gluey bass barely comprehensible now. "I've listened—don't you think I'd hear another vampire, if any came looking for these two? Don't you think I'd smell their blood? They're hiding, Dad. You've got to dig them out or let me . . ."

"Check anyway," Blaydon ordered sharply. Dennis' naked brow ridges pulled together into a horrible frown. "Do it!"

"I'm hungry, Dad," the vampire whispered sullenly. As he moved nearer, his monstrous shadow lurched over the low plaster of the ceiling and the claustrophobic narrowness of the walls. "Hungry—starving—my hands are burning me, and the craving's on me like fever . . ."

Blaydon swallowed nervously, but kept his voice commanding with an effort. "I understand, Dennis, and I'm going to get you well. But you must do as I say."

There was a long, ugly silence. Asher, lying at Ysidro's feet, could see the struggle of wills reflected in Blaydon's haggard face as he met his son's glare. *He's slipping and he knows it,* he thought, watching the sweat start on the old man's face. *How long before Dennis makes him a victim, as well as Ysidro and myself?*

And Lydia, he added, with a chill of fear. *And Lydia.*

Then Dennis was gone. Asher realized they must all have had their consciousnesses momentarily blanked as the vampire moved, but it was so quick, so subtle, that he was not even aware of it, merely that Dennis vanished into the crowding shadows. He did not even hear the closing of the steel-sheathed door.

Blaydon wiped his mouth nervously with the hand that wasn't holding the gun. He was still wearing the rather countrified tweed suit he'd had on that morning—that he'd had on for days, by the smell of it. Not, Asher reflected, that he or Ysidro could have passed for dandies either, both in shirt sleeves, himself unshaven and splotched with soot stains from climbing the wall last night. At least they'd slept, albeit uncomfortably. Once, when he'd wakened in the afternoon, there had been a tray of food there, undoubtedly brought by Dennis—an unsettling thought. He'd eaten it and searched the room again, but it had yielded nothing but reinforced brick walls and door and Sheffield silver-plated steel window bars.

Blaydon waved his pistol at Ysidro. "Don't get any ideas, my friend. While you're in this room with me, you're safe. Dennis would pull you down before you got out of the house, as easily as he brought you here in the first place."

There was an annoyed glitter behind Ysidro's hooded eyelids—a grandee, Asher thought, who did not care to be reminded that he'd been overpowered and manhandled by the hoi polloi. But he only regarded Blaydon levelly for a moment and asked, "Do you really believe that any of this will do you any good?"

"I'll be the judge of that," the pathologist said, rather sharply. "Go on with what you were saying. If you forced James . . . ?"

"To drink my blood," Ysidro said slowly, unwillingly, his champagne gaze fixed upon Blaydon's face. "That is how it is done—the physical part, at least. But the—perhaps you would say mental, but I think spiritual would be a better term, though these days it is an unfashionable one—"

"Let us say psychic," Blaydon put in. "That's what we're really talking about, aren't we?"

"Perhaps." That faint, wry flick of a smile touched Ysidro's narrow-lipped mouth. "In any case, it is the giving of his spirit,

264

his self, his conscious, and what Herr Freud politely terms his unconscious into the embrace of mine, for me to show him the way over that abyss. It is the yielding of all secrets, the giving of all trust, the admission of another into the most secret chambers of the heart. Most do not even join so close with those they deeply love. To do this, you understand, requires an act of the most desperate will, the all-consuming desire to continue in consciousness at whatever the cost." The shadow flung by the lamp on the wall behind him, huge and dark, echoed the slight movement of his white hand. "Under this set of circumstances, I think James would find no point in making so desperate an effort at survival, though I suspect that under others he might."

You will never know, Brother Anthony had whispered, deathlessly sorting bones in the crypts below Paris. Asher shook his head and said quietly, "No."

Ysidro turned his head to look down at him, without any expression in his eyes. "And they say that faith in God is dead," he commented. "I should think that *your* conscience, more than another man's, might make of you a coward . . ." He turned back to regard his captor. "Whether or not James has that will to live, how many of those scum of the gutters whom you purpose to bring for me to transform into others like me would be capable of it? When a master vampire creates a fledgling, it is in part the master's will and in part the fledgling's trust which act. I do not believe myself capable of creating fodder, even did I consent to try. I certainly do not believe that one person in a hundred, or a thousand, has that will to survive."

"That's balderdash," Blaydon said uneasily. "All this talk of the will and the spirit . . ."

"And if you did get lucky," Asher put in, trying to shift his shoulders to take some of the pressure from his throbbing right arm, "what then? Are you really going to stay in a house with two, three, or four fledgling vampires? Fledglings whose wills are entirely subservient to their master's? The start of this whole affair—Calvaire—was a careless choice on the part of the woman who made him. Are you going to be choosier? Especially if you're giving Dennis specific orders to bring in none but the unfit, the socially useless, and the wicked?"

"You let me worry about that." Blaydon's voice had an edge like flint now, his eyes showing their old stubborn glint. "It's only a temporary measure . . ."

"Like the income tax?"

"In any case I *have no choice*. Dennis' condition is deteriorating. You've seen that. He needs blood, the blood of vampires, to arrest the symptoms. If you, Ysidro, refuse to help me . . ."

"It is not simply a matter of refusal."

"Lying won't help you, you know . . ."

"No more than lying to yourself helps you, Professor." Behind that unemotional tone, Asher detected the faintest echo of a human sigh. Blaydon backed a few steps away, brandishing his gun.

"But if that is your choice, I shall have to take what measures I can . . ."

"More humans?" Asher inquired. "More of those you consider unfit?"

"It's to save my son!" The old man's voice cracked with desperation, and he fought to bring it to normal again. Rather shakily, he added, "And also for the good of the country. Once we have the experiment under control . . ."

"Good God, man, you don't mean you're going on with it!" Truly angry, Asher jerked himself to a sitting position, his back to the planed mahogany of the coffin. "Because of your failure, your own son is rotting to pieces under your eyes and you propose to *go on with it?*"

Blaydon strode forward and struck Asher across the face with the barrel of the gun, knocking him sprawling. Ysidro, impassive, merely moved his foot aside so that Asher wouldn't fall across it and watched the enraged pathologist with only the mildest of interest as he stepped back and picked up the lamp.

"I'm sorry you feel that way about it," Blaydon said quietly, the lamplight jerking with the angry trembling of his hands. "You, Don Simon, because I'm going to have to keep you fed

266

and healthy while I take your blood for experiments, until I can locate another vampire more compliant. You, James, because I think I'm going to have to force either you or your wife to tell me where her rooms were in the city—she refused to do so, and, of course, Dennis wouldn't hear of me forcing her— so that I can find her notes on her researches . . ."

"Don't be naïve," Ysidro sighed. "Grippen put them all on the fire before he left Lydia's rooms last night."

"Then I shall have to get Mrs. Asher to tell me herself," Blaydon said. "Now that I have James here, that shouldn't be too difficult. I think Dennis will even rather enjoy it."

Keeping his gun trained on Ysidro, he backed out the door.

"Don't trip over your son on the way out," the vampire remarked derisively as the door closed upon the amber radiance of the lamplight and the bolts slid home.

A west wind had been blowing all day, and the night outside was clear. Leaky white moonlight added somewhat to the faint glow of the gas lamps visible beyond the garden wall. With his usual languid grace, Ysidro unfolded his thin legs and rose from the coffin lid, knelt beside Asher, and stooped to bite through the ropes that bound his wrists. Asher felt the cold touch of bloodless lips against the veins of his left wrist and the scrape of teeth. Then the ropes were pulled away. The pain in his right arm almost made him sick as Ysidro brought it gently around and installed it in its sling again.

"You think he was listening?"

"Of course he was listening." The vampire twisted the slack of the ankle ropes between his white hands, and the strands parted with a snap. "He was right outside the door; he never even went into the garden, though a vampire of his abilities certainly could have heard us from there, had he chosen to listen, soundproofing or no soundproofing."

With light strength, he helped Asher to sit on the coffin lid, while he prowled like a faded tomcat to the room's single window, keeping a wary distance from the silver bars. "Triple glazed," he remarked briefly. "Wired glass, too. We might wrench the lock free, could we get past the bars to get some kind of purchase on it . . ."

"Do you think he followed us in the mews?"

"I am sure of it. I felt—sensed—I don't know. A presence in the night, once or twice . . . He took me from behind, before I even knew he was there." He tilted his head, angling to see if he could reach through to the lock, his hooked profile white against the darkness outside, like a colorless orchid. "But I had been listening for days for things I am not certain I ever truly heard. Fear makes it very difficult to judge." Asher wondered how long it had been since Ysidro had admitted to fear. Looking at that slender, insubstantial shape in its white shirt, gray trousers, and vest, he had the odd sense that he was dealing now with the original Don Simon Ysidro, rather than with the vampire the man had become.

"Merde alors." Ysidro stepped back from the bars, shaking a burned finger. "Curious that Blaydon did not wish his son to learn how vampires are made. It is a sensible precaution to keep him under his control, but . . ." He paused, tipping his head a little to listen. "He's gone."

He had not needed to speak; for the last few moments, Asher had heard Blaydon's hurrying steps vibrating the floors of the house, his querulous voice calling dimly, "Dennis? Dennis . . ."

Cold flooded over him as he suddenly understood.

"He's gone to get Lydia."

Then the cold was swept away by a heat of rage that burned out all pain, all exhaustion, and all despair.

"That's why he listened. He wanted to know how to create a fledgling."

"Sangre de Dios." In a single fluid move Ysidro stripped out of his gray waistcoat, wrapping it around his hand. Asher, knowing already what the vampire meant to do, clumsily unslung his arm and pulled off his own. It was gone from his grasp before he was aware the vampire had moved; Ysidro was back at the window, using the fabric to muffle his hands against the silver of the bars. For a moment he strained, shadows jump-

ing on the ropy white muscle of his forearms, then he let go of the bars and backed away, rubbing his hands as if in pain.

"No good. Metallurgy has vastly improved since the days when we had the strength of ten, and I cannot grip them long enough. If we could dig into the masonry around them and dislodge them . . ." His pale gaze flicked swiftly around the prison, touching Asher. "Curst be the man who decreed gentlemen should wear braces and not belts with large, fierce metal buckles, as they did in my day . . ."

"He'd have taken them." Asher was kneeling beside the coffin. "He thought of that. The handles have been removed. I noticed when I opened it that there were no corner braces or other metal fittings."

Ysidro cursed dispassionately, archaically, and in several languages. Asher eased his arm gingerly back into its sling, and remembered the isolation of that big house on the downs, miles from the nearest habitation. "Dennis must know it's the only way he'll have her now."

"If it works," the vampire said, not moving, but his eyes traveling again over the room. "If, as you think, the vampire state is caused by organisms—which I myself do not believe— it may still not be transmittable in this artificial form, even by a master who understands what he is doing, a description that scarcely fits our friend."

"That doesn't mean he won't kill her trying." Anger filled him at his own helplessness, at Blaydon, at Dennis, at Ysidro, and at the other vampires who were hiding God knew where. "Maybe I can reach the lock . . . if we could force it, we could call for help . . ."

"Your fingers would not have the strength to pull it from the casement."

Asher cursed, then said, "How soon can he get there? It's forty miles or so to the Peaks—he obviously can't take the train . . ."

"He will run. A vampire can run throughout the night, untiring. *Verdammnis*, is there no metal in this room larger than the buckles on braces? Were we women, at least we would have corset stays . . ."

"Here." Asher sat suddenly on the lid of the coffin and pulled off one of his shoes with his good hand. He tossed it to the startled vampire, who plucked it out of the air without seeming to move. "Is your strength of ten men up to ripping apart the sole leather? Because there should be a three-inch shank of tempered steel supporting the instep. It's how men's shoes are made."

"Thus I am served," Ysidro muttered through his teeth, as his long white fingers ripped apart the leather with terrifying ease, "for scorning the arts of mechanics. Where is this place? I was unaware there were peaks of any sort on this island . . ."

"There aren't. It's in the chalk downs back of Oxford, sheep country. Blaydon's wife's father built the place when he came into his money in the forties. Blaydon stayed there 'til his wife died. He had rooms at his college when he was teaching . . ."

"You know the way, then?" Ysidro was working at the window, his hands muffled in both waistcoats against accidental contact with the bars. The harsh scrape of metal on cement was like the steady rasping of a saw.

"Of course. I was there a number of times, though not in the past seven years."

The vampire paused, listening. A dim vibration through the floor spoke of a door closing. Softly Ysidro said, "He is in the garden now, calling; he sounds afraid." Their eyes met, Asher's hard with rage, Ysidro's inscrutable. Listen as he would, Asher heard no sound of the house door closing, or of returning footfalls on floor or stair. "He's gone."

Impossibly swift and strong, Ysidro resumed his digging, while he petitioned God to visit Blaydon's armpits with the lice of a shipful of sailors, and his belly with worms, in the archaic, lisping Spanish of the conquistadors. Switching to English, he added, "We can get horses from the mews . . ."

"A motorcycle will be faster, and we won't need remounts. Mine's in the shed at my lodgings; I've tinkered with it enough that it's more reliable than most." With his good hand and his teeth, Asher gingerly tightened the bandages around his splints, sweat standing out suddenly on his forehead with the renewed shock of the pain. "Do you need help?"

"What I need is an iron crow and a few slabs of guncotton, not the problematical assistance of a crippled old spy. Unless you have suddenly acquired the ability to bend steel bars, stay where you are and rest."

Asher was only too glad to do so. The swelling had spread up his arm nearly to the elbow; he felt dizzy and a little sick. He could still flex his first two fingers after a fashion—enough, he hoped, to work the throttle lever on the Indian, at any rate.

How fast could a vampire run? He'd seen Ysidro and Grippen move with incredible swiftness. Could that speed be sustained, as Ysidro said, untiring through the night? The scraping of the metal continued . . . It seemed to be taking forever.

"*Dios!*" Simon stepped back from the window, shaking loose the cloth from around his hands and rubbing his wrists. His teeth gritting against the pain, he said, "The bar is loose but I cannot grip it. My hands weaken already; that much silver burns, even through the cloth."

"Here." Asher kicked off his other shoe out of the irrational human dislike of uneven footgear, and came to the window. The bar was very loose in the socket, now chipped away from the cement; with his single good hand, he shifted it back and forth, twisting and pulling until it came free. Ysidro wrapped his arm again, and gingerly angled it through to tear off the window's complicated latch and force the casement up.

"Can you get through that?"

Asher gauged the resultant gap. "I think so."

It was a difficult wriggle, with one arm barely usable and nothing on the other side but the narrow ledge. The vampire steadied and braced him through as best he could, but once his arm inadvertently brushed one of the remaining bars, and Asher felt the grip spasm and slack. "It's all right, I've got a footing," he said and received only a faint gasp in reply. He slipped as quickly as he dared along the ledge to the laboratory window, the cold air biting fiercely through his shirt-sleeved arms and stockinged feet, and through the house as he had before, to undo the bolts of the steel-sheathed door.

Ysidro had resumed his creased waistcoat, but his long, slim hands were welting up in what looked like massive burns. The fingers shook as Asher knotted both their handkerchiefs around the swellings, to keep the air from the raw, blistering flesh. As he worked, he said rapidly, "Blaydon will have money in the study. We'll get a cab to Bloomsbury—there's a stand on Harley Street . . ."

"It is past midnight already." Ysidro flexed his hands carefully and winced. "You will be taking your lady away with you on this motorcycle of yours. Is there a place on these downs where I can go to ground, if the daylight overtakes us while we are there?"

Asher shook his head. "I don't know. The nearest town's eight miles away and it's not very large."

Ysidro was quiet for a moment, then shrugged with his mobile, colorless brows. "The village church, perhaps. There are always village churches. James . . ."

He turned, as Asher strode past him into the prison room again and over to the window where the detached window bar lay shining frostily in the square of moonlight on the floor. It was two and a half feet long, steel electroplated with silver, and heavy as a large spanner—or crow, as Ysidro called it—in his hand. Asher hefted it and looked back at the vampire who stood like a disheveled ghost against the blackness of the doorway.

Picking his words as if tiptoeing through a swamp, Ysidro said, "Did Dennis bring you here, as he did me? Or did you come of your own accord, looking for me at daybreak?"

"I came looking for you."

"That was stupid . . ." He hesitated, for a moment awkward and oddly human in the face of saying something he had not said in many hundreds of years and perhaps, Asher thought, never. "Thank you."

"I'm in your service," Asher reminded him, and walked back to the door, silver bar like a gleaming club in his hand. "And," he added grimly, "we haven't scotched this killer yet."

Twenty-one

———

"C ould he have beaten us here?" Asher kicked the Indian's engine out of gear as they came around the side of the hill into full view of the Peaks' wall and lodge gate; as on most motorcycles, the brake wasn't very strong. The moon had set; it was hard to keep the tires out of ruts only dimly seen. He didn't bother to whisper. If Dennis was there already, he'd have picked up the sound of the engine miles away.

"I'm not sure." Ysidro's arms were like whalebone and thin cable around Asher's waist, his body a skeletal lightness against the leather of the jacket. Asher wasn't sure whether a living man could have kept his seat on the narrow carrier as they'd come up the winding road from Wycombe Parva. "As Burger—quoted by the invaluable Mr. Stoker—has observed, 'Die Todten reiten schnell'—the dead travel fast."

Asher braked gently, easing the machine to a stop in front of the iron spears of the locked gates. Through them he could see the house, a rambling pseudo-Gothic monstrosity of native brick and hewn stone appropriated from some ruined building closer to Oxford, dark against the dim shapes of the naked beeches of the park and the vast swell of the down behind. The unkempt lawn was thick with weeds, and the woods that lay to the south and east of the house were already making their first encroachments of broom sedge and elder saplings. The place had probably housed no more than a caretaker since Blaydon had closed it up after his wife's death three years ago, and it was obvious that not even a caretaker dwelt here now.

He'd probably been turned off when Dennis first began to change, Asher thought, and anger stirred him again at Blaydon's stupid irresponsibility. Had anything gone amiss, from a gas leak to an omnibus accident in London, Lydia would have been condemned to death here without anyone being the wiser.

273

Except Dennis, of course.

"So in other words, he could be waiting for us in the house?" He dismounted, and Ysidro sprang off lightly. Behind the long, wind-frayed curtain of hair, the vampire's eyes were sparkling, and Asher had the impression that he had found this mode of travel greatly to his taste.

"Or hard upon our heels." Ysidro stooped, bracing his band-aged hands on bent knees. Asher pushed up his goggles, leaned the bike against the wall, unlashed the silvered steel bar from the handlebars, and hung it around his own neck. Using Ysi-dro's back as a step, he could reach the top corners of the rustic stone gateway, to scramble over the six-foot palings. He had scarcely dropped to the drive on the other side when Ysidro appeared, palely silhouetted against the uneasy darkness, and sprang down without a sound to his side. At his lodgings, Asher had paused only long enough to don his boots, goggles, and leather jacket, for the night was freezing cold; Ysidro in his open shirt seemed to feel nothing.

"Thus I do not suggest we divide to search."

"Can you hear anything from here?" Asher asked.

The vampire shut his eyes, listening intently to the half-heard muttering of the wind in the autumn woods. "Not clearly," he murmured at last. "Yet the house is not empty—that I know."

Asher used his good hand to unsling the bar from around his neck. Scudding overcast was beginning to cover the sky. Through it, the house was a barely seen shape of gray, dotted with the black of windows, disturbingly like some monster's misshapen skull. "If he's behind us, he may arrive on top of us before we'd finished reconnoitering," he said grimly, striding up the ghostly stripe of the drive. "And if he's there already— would you or I be able to see or hear him?"

Asher knew the floor plan of the Peaks, though he'd never been more than a casual acquaintance of Blaydon's. But most of the dons had received invitations at one time or another, and Asher had a field agent's memory for such things. Every atom of his flesh shrank from entering the dark trap of those encircling walls without the usual preliminary checks. But there was no time, and they would, in any case, be useless.

They skirted the lawn and garden to the kitchen yard, Ysidro leading the way across the leaf-strewn pavement. At this point, concealment was of no more use to them than whispering; they were either perfectly safe or beyond help. And if Dennis had not arrived before them—if they were, for the moment, safe—outdoors there was a remote chance that Ysidro's vampire senses could detect his coming.

In any case, the cellars were reached from the kitchen.

The wind was rising, groaning faintly over the tops of the downs and stirring the dark hem of the woods a hundred feet from the house in a way Asher did not like. The stables stretched along one side of the yard, every door shut and bolted; the kitchen door was locked as well, but Asher drove his elbow through the window pane next to it and reached through to wrench over the latch. Beside him, he was aware of Ysidro listening, turning his head this way and that, the stray gusts flicking at his long hair, trying by some leap of the senses to detect the undetectable and to hear what was no more audible than the slow falling of dust.

The darkness of the kitchen stank of mildew and spoiling table scraps. As Ysidro found and lit a lamp, there was a flurrying rustle of tiny feet, and the primrose kerchief of light caught the tails of mice as they whipped out of sight. Asher cursed again, softly. Open tins and dirty dishes lined the old-fashioned soapstone counters, like sleeping tramps below the Embankment on a summer night. Blaydon, of course—in too great a hurry to pump and heat water to clean up. The vampire raised the lamp to shed a greater light; in its glow, Asher could see his fastidious nostrils flare.

"He may be here, covering our minds from his presence, but I do not think he has been and gone. There is a smell of decay about him which lingers in still air."

"We'll check the cellars first," Asher said, crossing the worn stone floor to the narrow door beside the stove. "Upstairs we can always bolt through a window." He pushed the door open.

The smell of dust, coals, and mice almost choked him. "You lead. If he's here, he's likelier to be behind than before."

He kept his back flattened to the worn, slatted wainscot of the staircase, his left hand with the silver bar on the upstairs side, while Ysidro edged swiftly down the steps before him. There was a wine cellar, stripped of everything but the racks, and a coal hole, half-filled with coals and dirt.

"There's another cellar off the butler's pantry," Asher said as they swiftly ascended the stairs back to the kitchen, their shadows reeling drunkenly in the lamplight. "You'd never know the door wasn't just a cupboard. I've never been down there—it may be just a boot hole, but it might be large enough to keep someone in."

The butler's pantry was more like a closet than a room, filled with shelves and family silver. The door, tucked away behind a cupboard, was bolted from the outside. "She's down there," Simon murmured, even as Asher slipped the bolts. "At least someone is, and the breathing sounds like hers."

"Lydia?" Asher called softly down the dark twist of the stairs, but kept his post at the top until Ysidro had edged his way down them. There was a door at the bottom, too; between them, the brick-walled slot of the staircase smelled like a death trap. The door at the bottom was bolted, as well. "Lydia, it's James! Don't be afraid . . ."

The door burst open as Ysidro slid the bolts, the violence of it taking him almost totally by surprise. The swerving lamplight showed Asher the whiteness of Lydia's face, under a carnelian whirlwind of unbound hair. Her spectacles flashed in the light, and there was the thin slip of something silver in one of her hands as she stabbed at Ysidro's eyes. The vampire was out of her way before Asher could see where he moved; Lydia whirled, confused, and Asher called out, "Lydia, it's James!"

She'd already begun to pelt up the stairs and now stopped short at the sight of the dark form looming at their top; Ysidro, with considerable presence of mind, raised the lamp to shed its rays as far as the top of the stairs. "James . . . !" she sobbed, and then swung back, looking at the vampire who stood, lamp aloft like Liberty's torch, just beside the door.

"Oh . . ." She looked momentarily nonplussed, the silver hatpin with which she had attacked him still glinting sharp and vicious in her hand. "I *am* sorry. You must be Don Simon Ysidro . . ." She held out her other hand to him, and he took it and kissed it with antique grace.

"It was my pleasure," the vampire replied, and she laughed shakily at this patently mendacious platitude as they hastened up the stairs. "I am at your service, Madame."

At the top, she caught Asher violently around the waist, burying her face in his leather-clad shoulder and hugging him hard enough to drive the breath from him. Through the ferocity of the embrace, he felt her trembling with cold and shock and reaction to her attack on what she had thought were her captors. He wrapped his good arm reassuringly tight around her shoulders, silver bar and all.

Typically, she broke from him almost at once, so as not to tie up a hand with a weapon in it. Ysidro had somehow moved past them—Asher never did figure out how, given the narrowness of the door—and was leading the way swiftly through the close confines of the pantry; Asher was aware of the clinical avidness with which Lydia watched his slender back.

"Are you all right?"

She nodded, pulling tighter around her the snagged gray cardigan she wore over shirtwaist and skirt—Blaydon's, he noted, and far too big for her. "That was the butler's apartments. Have we time to pump some water? I didn't drink the last pitcher Professor Blaydon brought me; I knew he must be putting the drugs in it . . ."

"No," Ysidro said briefly. "I don't like the smell of the night—I don't like the feel. There's something about . . ."

Asher started to protest, but Lydia said, "No, it's all right, the pump here always took forever. What happened to your arm?"

"Dennis."

They halted just within the kitchen door. In the uncertain

starlight the yard and the woods beyond seemed alive with the sinister movement of the wind. Asher hated the look of them and hated still more the dark house which seemed to be closing around them like a fist.

"Stay close to the house wall," he breathed. "We won't be able to see him in the open. At least, near a wall, he'll have to come at us from one direction."

Taking a deep breath, he stepped outside. Lydia followed, holding the lamp. Ysidro brought up the rear. Seeing them standing together for the first time, Asher realized with a start that the vampire stood no taller than she.

Softly, she whispered, "Have you—seen him?"

The wind moved his hair against the strap of the goggles still pushed up on his forehead—he nearly started out of his skin. "Did you?"

She shook her head. "But I assume there's a reason why he— he only spoke to me through the shut door." She glanced back at Ysidro and wet her lips. "His father's serum must have done something other than make him . . . like you."

"Indeed," the vampire responded, never taking his eyes from the lawn and shrubbery around them. "Dennis is not like me."

They reached the front of the house. Seventy-plus feet of rutted gravel drive stretched before them to the iron bars of the gates. The wind drove a swirl of dead beech leaves over it, like the whirling souls of Dante's damned, who could not forgo the pleasures of the living. The motorcycle was just beyond the gate, and Asher's whole soul revolted at that nebulous vista of dark. He glanced quickly back at Ysidro, who was turning his head, listening with fear in his eyes to the night.

"Can you make it back to London afoot?"

"Not before dawn. But I have boltholes nearer than that— property purchased too recently to show up on your precious lists, my dear Mistress Asher. Go back to London. Stay awake and stay always around people in some public place. He cannot take you there; he dare not let his existence be suspected. I will come as soon as I can in the night . . ."

Together, the three of them stepped from the sheltering shadows of the house. The wind swirled Lydia's dark skirts and the tangle of her hair and made all the weed stems caught in the platter-sized blob of the jiggling lamplight jerk and tremble erratically. Iron gloom stretched in all directions; Asher felt naked before it. Lydia whispered, "Shall we run?"

"It wouldn't make us any safer," he murmured back, "and running, we'd be less likely to see a threat."

It would, however, have made him feel better, as they moved slowly and cautiously through what felt like the Great American Desert of blowing darkness. The wall loomed before them— stone gateposts, shut and boarded lodge, and weeds shivering thick around the open ironwork of the gate.

Ysidro's hand touched his arm suddenly, staying him, drawing him back toward the house. There was a gray flutter of movement somewhere beyond the gate . . .

Asher saw Dennis come over the gate, though his mind stalled on the detail, with a sense of *jamais vu* as in a dream, as if he had momentarily forgotten the significance of that bulking form dropping like a cougar from the top of the stone gate pillar, eyes glinting in the reflected light of the lamp. The next second, it seemed, it was upon them, though later Asher had clear memories of standing, staring like an idiot, and watching it rush at them with horrible speed. Ysidro must have already started to move, for Dennis caught him, not full-on, but by one arm in an unbreakable grip.

Asher brought the silver bar down with all his strength on Dennis' wrist, even as the mutant fledgling ripped at Ysidro's throat. From the tail of his eye, Asher caught the black glitter of blood. It streamed down from Dennis' fangs as he drew back with a glottal roar of pain, and Asher backhanded him with the bar across the face, hearing as well as feeling the facial bones crunch. Dennis screamed. Blood splattered Asher's face like gouts of hot syrup. Then the vampire was gone, and Lydia and Ysidro, blood streaming from his torn shoulder, were dragging Asher, stumbling, across the open lawn toward the woods. Behind them, the dropped lamp was guttering erratically in a pool of kerosene.

"Chapel ruins!" Lydia gasped. "Shelter without being closed in!" Blood was splattered liberally over one side of her white shirtwaist and the sweater, droplets of it beading even on her spectacle lenses; it covered the first four inches of the silver hatpin still in her hand. She must have stabbed Dennis from the other side. Ysidro's shoulder had been opened to halfway down his back, a dark stain spreading with terrible speed over the torn rags of his shirt.

Long weeds tangled at their knees as they cut through the overgrown garden. Their feet skidded on mud and wet leaves. Behind them as they ran, Asher could hear Dennis shrieking in pain, as if the impact of the silver still burned. On his right, Ysidro's bony grip on his swollen arm was excruciating, but he hardly cared. They had to reach shelter of some kind, a wall or enclosure at their backs, or they were dead.

The chapel ruin stood in a little dell perhaps a hundred yards from the house, its ivy-draped walls sheltered by a sizable copse of beeches. It offered, as Lydia had said, ideal shelter without the potential imprisonment of the house, the roofless chancel providing cover on most of three sides and greatly narrowing the potential field of attack.

"What about the crypt?" Ysidro leaned against the stump of a broken pillar, half doubled-over with pain and dizziness, as Lydia worked a birch sapling loose from among the fallen stones. With an effort, the vampire straightened and cast a quick glance to the moss-covered altar behind them. "If there's another way in, he can . . ."

"There isn't a crypt." Lydia hauled her skirt to untie one of her several petticoats. The lowest flounce was saturated from the grass but the one above it was dry. With unsteady fingers Ysidro ripped it free and bound it around the wood as a makeshift torch. Never taking his eyes from the rough expanse of hillside that lay between chapel and lawn, Asher tossed them the box of lucifer matches he always kept in his jacket pocket; there was the sharp hiss of sulphur, and the fabric licked into flame. "Dennis' grandfather had the whole ruin put up at the same time as the house was built—an architect from Birmingham designed it. It's desperately picturesque in the daylight. This wall, those arches over there, and the tombstones on the hillside are all of it there is."

Ysidro laughed, his fangs flashing white in the glare of the flame. Lydia came over to them, a second firebrand in one hand and her silver hatpin in the other. The ruddy glow illuminated the weed-curtained stone of the walls, the spurious Gothic corbels, and the shadows of the altar. Behind her spectacles, her face was scratched like an urchin's, smudged with dirt, and spotted with Dennis' blood. To Asher's eyes she was utterly beautiful.

She tucked the matches back into his jacket pocket. Quietly, she asked, "Are you more or less all right?"

Dennis' screams of pain and fury had ceased; the wind had fallen. The naked beeches and the thick clumps of elder and hawthorn around the walls seemed, like themselves, to be waiting. The silence was worse now than any sound.

"You mean, aside from a broken hand and assorted bites, contusions, and abrasions, and a mutant vampire fifty feet away who's going to kill us all?"

Her lips twitched. "Aside from that, yes."

"Yes."

"I was worried." Her voice sounded very small; he knew she could see the half-healed red bites that tracked his jugular from ear to collarbone. In the torchlight, her breath blew as a tiny puff of gold.

"Not as worried as I was, believe me."

There was a moment's silence. Then: "Was that . . . that thing we saw . . . Was that Dennis?"

She'd told him once that Dennis had proposed marriage to her for the first time here at the Peaks. Dennis had never gotten it through his head that she could actually not want to be his wife. It occurred to Asher that Dennis had undoubtedly done so here in the ruins. In the slanting light of a summer's evening, there would be no more romantic spot in twenty square miles. He sighed and said, "Yes."

Ysidro moved closer to them, holding his torch aloft. "Can

you feel it?" Through the rip in his shirt, Asher could see the wound in his shoulder, still tracking a sluggish trickle of dark blood. A mortal man would have been in shock. The vampire was only shivering as if with deadly cold, his face strained and sunken-looking. The mark of Dennis' grip was visible on his arm between the rolled-up shirt sleeve and the wrappings on his hands, blackening bruises and five claw rakes where the nails had ripped the colorless flesh. "There's movement out there, on the lawn. I can't see exactly . . ."

For a moment there was nothing, the whole night holding its breath.

Then Dennis was there, appearing with terrible suddenness just beyond range of the torch's light, as, long ago in the dark of the catacombs, Brother Anthony had seemed to fade into existence from the grinning shadows of the bones.

Beside him, Asher heard Lydia's breath hiss in pity and horror.

Dennis Blaydon had always been of heroic build and proportion, a golden Hercules in cricket whites. Now his size seemed monstrous, the breadth of his shoulders and chest, visible through his ripped and open shirt, like some maddened bull's. Blood tracked down his side and blotted his shirt above his ribs—had it been anyone but a vampire, the puncture wound administered by Lydia's hatpin would have been a serious matter—and where the bar had struck his face the flesh had puffed up like rotting meat. He was barely recognizable; the straight nose was flattened and spread now. Drool and blood dripped from the outsize fangs; the leprous skin gleamed like a snake's back in the moonlight. The glaring blue eyes were no longer even remotely human.

"Professor Asher," he whispered, in a sticky decay of a voice. "Lydia, get away from him. I won't harm you, I swear it. You know I'd never harm you, Lydia; I kept Dad from harming you . . ."

"Only because you wanted her for yourself," Asher called into the flickering darkness. "Because you wanted to make her like yourself, infect her with that foul malady in your veins, so she'd be yours forever."

"That isn't true!" Dennis' glaring eyes widened with hate. "Dad will find a cure—Dad will make me better! And why shouldn't I have her? She should have been mine. Now she'll be mine forever. I'll make her love me! It's him I want—the vampire. I need him. *I need him!*"

"Since we're easy prey without him," Asher said quietly, "I'm afraid we need him, too."

Then he blinked, trying to keep the vampire in sight—trying to focus his mind on where he had last been. But Dennis was no longer—quite—visible. Asher had the impression he would still be able to see him if he knew where to look, but he could not find him now. A breath of movement stirred the ragged clumps of thorn and elder, catching now here, now there—the whole night seemed to quiver, shifting as soon as he moved his eyes from any given spot.

"He's a killer, Professor Asher," a voice breathed out of that darkness. "Killed women, killed sweet little children—he'll kill Lydia if you'll let him. You know he's killed . . ."

He called into the darkness, "And you haven't?"

"That's different. That's for a good cause. I had to take the risk—this country needs men with my power, my strength. And anyway, it wasn't me that killed all those people. It was the vampires. Calvaire and Lotta . . ."

"Calvaire and Lotta were dead by that time and you know it."

"It was still them," Dennis insisted, with the kind of logic Asher remembered from having the young man in his classes. "They did it, not me, and, anyway, I did it for a good cause. I need the blood. I NEED IT!"

Something blacked Asher's mind, a blurring cloud of faintness and exhaustion. He thought he saw movement, a rustle in the long weeds that carpeted the fabricated gravestones far to his left, but the next second Ysidro swung the torch as Dennis came surging out of the darkness almost on top of him. Asher lunged at them, slashing with the metal bar at the mutant vam-

283

pire's broad back, but Dennis was gone again, and Ysidro was
on his knees, clutching at the big muscle between neck and
shoulder, blood welling dark between his fingers. His torch lay
guttering out on the damp ground.

"Killer," Dennis' voice whispered out of the dark, as Asher,
never loosing his grip on the bar, held his arm down to help
Ysidro to his feet. "Both of you, killers. Spies, sneaks, cowards,
and killers of real men when their backs are turned." Holding
on to his shoulder, Ysidro was shuddering all over, his hand
like ice, even through the leather of the jacket, his thin body
oddly weightless against Asher's. The fine bones of his face
stood out like a skull's with shock and fatigue—Asher wondered if it were possible for a vampire to faint.

"You never deserved Lydia. You lied to her, cheated me of
what should have been mine. You made her leave me alone.
She would have loved me if it hadn't been for you. But I won't
be alone. When I've killed you both, she'll be mine. I know
how to make a vampire now . . ."

Asher swung toward where he thought the voice was coming
from, but there was nothing. Ysidro straightened up a little and
staggered, fighting to remain on his feet.

"Where is he?"

He shook his head. "I don't know." Oddly enough, his voice
sounded as cool and disinterested as ever. "I thought he was
over among the tombstones just before he came at me . . ."

"How long can the three of us hold him off?"

"Long enough for the silver poisoning to take effect on him?"
Lydia came up beside them, the flickering brand in her hand
making her spectacle lenses seem like rounds of fire.

"No." The vampire's light hand tightened over Asher's
shoulder. "It has only made him more frantic than ever for my
blood. He has a great deal of strength still. It will be days, maybe
weeks . . . If he takes me or another vampire or sufficient
human lives, he may prolong his life indefinitely. In any case,
it will be dawn soon."

She pushed her spectacles more firmly up onto the bridge
of her nose. "The room where I was kept had no windows,"

she said. "If we can make it back to the house we can guard you . . ."

"You'd never even see him strike." The vampire straightened slowly away from Asher's grip, removed his hand from the wound in his neck; the thin fingers were dark with gore, and the handkerchief that bound the silver burns saturated and dripping. His voice was expressionless. "The dawnlight will kill me—and then he will have you . . ."

Lydia whirled sharply, raising her torch. "What's that?"

Something white flickered and moved among the tombstones.

Threads of milky hair caught the lift of the night wind. There was a fluttering tangle of black over limbs colorless as bone, like dead ivy cloaking marble. The unearthly, unmistakable gleam of vampire eyes showed.

Asher breathed, "Anthony . . ."

Tiny, skeletal-white hands lifted to the cloud-patched sky. Asher had a glimpse of a white skull-face, the tonsure framed in pouring streams of filthy white mane; he seemed to hear on the night wind the whispered cry: "*In Nomine Patris, et Filii, et Spiritus Sancti . . .*"

Ysidro shouted, "*Antonius, non!*" as the dark shape of Dennis rushed out of the night and fell like storm cloud upon that lonely, fragile shape among the tombstones.

If the little monk could have avoided his attacker or fought him, he did not—it did not even seem that he tried. Dennis caught him up like a snake seizing a bird, even as Asher plunged out of the safety of the chapel ruin, pain jarring his broken hand with every step on the uneven ground. He heard Lydia call his name, Ysidro shout, "You fool . . . !" A deep, sticky groan of satiation broke from Dennis, and somewhere he thought he heard, perhaps only in his mind, a frail drift of voice: "*In manus tuas, Domini . . .*" as the two vampires locked together in the obscene parody of a kiss.

Then Dennis flung the broken body aside and turned, blood running down his fangs, swollen lips, and rutted chin. With a bestial snarl, he fell upon Asher like a charging bear.

Asher knew it was blood frenzy beyond caution and swung the silver bar with all the strength he had. But Dennis' weight smashed into him with full force, throwing him backward. He had a confused glimpse of the bloody mouth gaping wider and wider, the blue eyes suffused, not with hatred, but with astonishment and agony. In the split second as they collided, Asher realized that Dennis died even as he sprang.

The impact of the corpse knocked the breath out of him as they hit the ground; the broken edge of an imitation tombstone gouged him in the back. He lay for a moment stunned, under the stinking and inert mass of infected flesh that had been Dennis, and in that moment it came to him what must have killed him.

Painfully, he rolled out from under the body. Torchlight splashed jerkily over him; he heard the swish of Lydia's skirt in the long weeds and Ysidro's voice saying, "James . . . ?" For a moment, he stood swaying over the monster carcass, the silver bar dangling uselessly from his hand. Then he dropped it and stumbled a few feet away to the body of Brother Anthony, like a broken marionette among the frilled Victorian gothic of the pinchbeck tombs.

The little Minorite lay crumpled together, a shrunken tangle of old bones, rotting robes, and white hair bound together with a filthy rosary, clotted with his own blood and that of six centuries of kills. His bare feet were scratched and bloody. The big veins of his throat had been ripped open by the violence of Dennis' attack, not merely punctured—there was very little blood left. Though sunken and fallen in upon the skull, his face wore a look of strange serenity and the faintest hint of a smile.

Behind him, Lydia and Ysidro were silent. Asher raised the dead vampire's left arm and pushed back the decayed shreds of the sleeve. The torchlight showed clearly the line of dark-stained punctures that tracked the big vein. Rising to his feet, he stepped around behind the tombstone to the place where he had first thought he'd seen movement.

His own ulster lay there, its nubby brown tweed still flecked with the hay from the bales in the Queen Anne mews where he'd left it with Ysidro's cloak. On top of it lay the velvet box that had contained the hypodermic needle and its ten ampoules of silver nitrate.

The ampoules were all empty.

Twenty-two

———

H e was the only vampire who could have done it." Pausing in the act of trying to do up shirt buttons one-handed—as he had paused already half a dozen times that afternoon—Asher looked again at the brown velvet box where it lay on a corner of the dressing table, with its empty ampoules and its bloodstained needle. "I don't think a living man, much less a younger vampire, would have survived to inject himself a second time."

Lydia shook her head. "How did he know?" Frowning with concentration, she stood before Asher's shaving mirror to construct a running Windsor knot in one of his ties around her own neck. The last of the evening sunlight, falling through the cheap lace curtains of Asher's rooms on Prince of Wales Colonnade, sprinkled the ghosts of shadow flowers over her white shirt-waist and freckled her auburn hair with gold.

"About the ampoules themselves? If he'd been following us from Paris, he could easily have listened through the windows of your room when Ysidro and I spoke of it. Ysidro tells me vampires often listen for days to the conversations of their prey. And he wasn't unfamiliar with the activities and technology of modern men, you know—merely apart from them, as the other vampires, the so-called 'good' vampires, were not. If he was following me the day Dennis attacked me at Grippen's house, he would have seen Dennis and guessed that only something as—as heroic as the measures he took—would have served."

"Poor Dennis." Lydia loosened the tie, stood for a moment, looking into Asher's eyes in the mirror before them. "He used to say the most horrid things about the other girls at Somerville—about them wanting to act like men because they couldn't *get* men—absolutely without thinking. And whenever I'd point out it was what I was doing, he'd be so patronizing, as if I were only at University until I could find a husband and a home and have children. 'You're different,' he'd say . . . He could be so sweet to me, so kind, and yet . . ."

She shook her head. Removing the tie from her own neck, she turned to slip it over Asher's head. "He wanted so much to be a hero, but the fact is that I never took him seriously at all."

He took her wrist in the fingers of his good hand as she adjusted his collar. "You have to admit that, in my place, he never would have let you endanger yourself by coming to London."

"I know." The expression of sorrow that was more pity than grief faded; she smiled ruefully up into his eyes. "That's why I never took him seriously. He couldn't conceive of anyone being able to save a situation but himself." She sighed and fixed her attention for a few moments on the placing of his stickpin and the minute adjustments in the set of his tie. "The awful thing is that I'm sure that's why he injected himself with his father's serum—because he couldn't stand the thought of such powers as Calvaire had going to anyone but him."

They had burned Brother Anthony's body before the coming of dawn on a pyre hastily assembled from the Peaks' woodshed—Anthony's, and Dennis' with him. The flames were searingly hot and blue, and Asher had been wryly amused to see Lydia studying the atypical blaze with interest, clearly taking notes in her head. But she hadn't, he noticed, suggested preserving either of the vampires for further experimentation. Whatever alien pathologies lingered in their tainted blood, she had no desire to permit them further existence, even in the allegedly controlled conditions of a laboratory.

Ysidro had been gone long before the fire began to sink. By the time the police arrived, drawn by a shepherd's report of the blaze, it was sunup, and Asher and Lydia were far down the road to Prince's Risborough, looking like a couple of tinkers and walking the motorcycle Dennis had disabled between them, the grimy brown ulster thrown round both their shoulders for warmth. The fire had been reported in a minor article on a back page in that afternoon's *Daily Mail*. There was no mention of human remains in the blaze.

"In any case," Lydia went on after a moment, turning back from gazing rather abstractedly out at the sunset maze of roof-tops and chimneys, "if the positions had been reversed, Dennis would have told me nothing of what was going on—merely not to worry myself about such things. And it wouldn't have answered. Because the killer, the day stalker—Dennis—knew me, and wanted me. He did see me once, while he was stalking Bully Joe Davies. And he'd been—calling me, tracking me— in my dreams. He wasn't as good as the other vampires were at it, but . . . And then again, sooner or later, whether you or I or anyone did anything about it or not, he would have learned somehow about how to make another vampire like himself and he would have come after me." She wiped her eyes almost surreptitiously and shoved her spectacles more firmly up onto the bridge of her nose. "My going to snoop about Blaydon's place in Queen Anne Street only speeded things up."

She picked up his coat from the bed and came over to help him on with it again. By the time they'd waked up after their return from the Peaks, the short autumn afternoon had been far advanced, and a goodly portion of what remained had been spent at Middlesex Hospital, getting Asher's battered arm reset. He could cheerfully have gone back to bed now and slept the clock round, but there remained one thing yet to do.

"Are you sure you want to?" Lydia asked.

Asher glanced past her at his own reflection in the mirror. Shaved and bathed, he no longer looked like a tramp, but his face had a drawn, exhausted look he hadn't seen there in years. He knew it, however, from his missions abroad—the familiar, soul-deep ache he associated with climbing tiredly onto the boat train for home.

"No," he said. "But with Dennis gone, I don't think there's any danger. And someone has to tell him. Just promise me you'll stay here—stay indoors—'til I come back. All right?"

She nodded. Asher cast one last glance at the sky, visible

through the windows, satisfying himself that, before full dark fell, he would be well away from these rooms. Grippen knew about Lydia's rooms in Bruton Place, but he didn't—or at least Asher thought he didn't—know about 6 Prince of Wales Colonnade.

Unless, of course, Ysidro had told him.

While the doctors at Middlesex had been *tush*ing and *tsk*ing over his arm, he'd sent Lydia out to Lambert's to buy five more silver chains; he was conscious of the two around his throat and left wrist as he descended the lodging-house steps and began his unhurried walk toward Oxford Street. The gas lamps were lighted, soft and primrose in the dusk. He had made sure Lydia was wearing hers, though he privately suspected they wouldn't do either of them much good, if the vampires were really determined to let no one who knew of their existence survive.

His term of service to Ysidro was over.

And in the meantime, someone had to tell Blaydon . . . And someone had to make sure that there weren't going to be any more experiments "for the good of the country."

The other thing Lydia had bought on her shopping trip had been a revolver, though he hadn't told her who it was for. He suspected he wouldn't have needed to.

In the deep twilight, Queen Anne Street had a placid air, the windows of its tall, narrow houses bright with lights. Occasionally Asher could see into one of them, through the shams of curtain lace: two friends playing chess beside a parlor fire; a dark woman standing dreaming in a window, her arm around the tall form of an androgynous youth. Were he a vampire, Asher thought, he could have heard their every word.

There was a light on in Blaydon's house, in the room he guessed was the study on the same floor as the laboratory and the little prison. He rapped sharply at the front door, and it gave back beneath his knuckles.

"Blaydon?"

He didn't raise his voice much. The shadows of the stairwell swallowed the echoes of his words; for an instant, he seemed to be back in Oxford again, listening to the ominous stillness of a house he knew was not empty.

Then, like a whisper more within his skull than without, he heard Ysidro say, "Up here."

He climbed the stairs, knowing already what he would find.

Ysidro sat in the study at Blaydon's inlaid Persian desk, sorting papers—they spilled down in drifts and covered the carpet for a yard around. The vampire himself was as Asher had first seen him, a delicate thing of alabaster and peeled ivory, cobweb hair falling to the shoulders of his gray Bond Street suit—a displaced grandee, a nobleman in exile from another age, who had once danced with the Virgin Queen, with every cell petrified as it had been, and with his soul trapped somewhere among them like a mantis in amber. Asher wondered with what study or pastime Ysidro had beguiled those passing centuries; he had never even found that out.

Pale as brimstone or the clearest champagne, the calm eyes lifted to meet Asher's.

"You will find him in his laboratory," he said quietly. "His neck is broken. He was working on another batch of serum, taken from the last of Chloé's blood."

"Did he know about Dennis?"

"There was a telegram there from the Buckinghamshire police, saying that there had been a mysterious fire at the Peaks. The metal buttons of a man's trousers had been found in the ashes, along with a few cracked glass beads, a steel crucifix, and some unidentifiable bones."

Asher was silent. Ysidro upended another folder of notes over the general mess. They slithered across the top of the pile before him and swooped like awkward birds to the floor.

"Would you have done it?"

Asher sighed. He had done worse than kill Blaydon, and for slighter cause. He knew if he'd been caught he could always have pleaded his Foreign Office connections, and might even have been backed up by friends in the Department. The pistol weighed heavily in his ulster pocket. "Yes."

"I thought you would have." Simon smiled, wry and yet

292

oddly sweet, and Asher had the impression—as he had fleet-
ingly during the dark horrors of the previous night—of dealing
with the man Ysidro had once been, before he had become a
vampire. "I wished to spare you awkwardness."

"You wished to spare me a discussion with the police on the
subject of Blaydon's experiments."

That faint, cynical smile widened and, for the first time,
warmed Ysidro's chilly eyes. "That, too."

Asher came over and stood beside the desk, looking down
at the slender form of white and gray. If the gouges left in
Ysidro's flesh by Dennis' fangs still pained him, as Asher's broken arm throbbed dully beneath its shroud of novocaine, he
gave no sign. His slender hands were neatly bandaged. Asher
wondered if Grippen had done that.

"You realize," Asher said slowly, "that not only was Brother
Anthony the only vampire who could have killed Dennis—the
only vampire who physically could have survived that much
silver in his system for even the minute or so it took for Dennis
to drink his blood—but he was the only one who would have.
He was the only vampire who valued the redemption of his
soul above the continuation of his existence."

A stray gust of wind shook the trees in the back garden,
knocking bonily against the windows; distantly, a church clock
chimed six. Ysidro's long fingers lay unmoving in the jumbled
leaves of notes before him, the pale gold of his ring shining
faintly in the gaslight. "Do you think he achieved it?" he asked
at last.

"Are you familiar with the legend of Tannhäuser?"

The vampire smiled slightly. "The sinner who came to the
Pope of Rome and made confession of such frightful deeds that
the Holy Father drove him forth, saying, 'There is more like-
lihood of my staff putting forth flowers, than there is of God
forgiving such wickedness as yours.' Tannhäuser despaired and
departed from Rome, to return to his life of sin, and three days
later the Pope found his staff standing in a corner where he had
left it, covered in living blossom. Yes." The gaslight echoed
itself softly in a thousand tiny flickers in the endless labyrinth

293

of his eyes. "But as Brother Anthony himself said, I will never know."

A faint sound behind him caused Asher to turn. In the doorway at his back stood Anthea Farren and Lionel Grippen, the woman weary and pinched-looking, the doctor a massive form of inexhaustible, ruddy-faced evil, his fangs bright against the stolen redness of his lips.

Ysidro went on softly, "I don't think it would even have occurred to any of us that such sacrifice was conceivable. Certainly I don't think it occurred to Brother Anthony until he encountered you, a mortal man, in the catacombs, and you spoke of God's eternal willingness to forgive and that there might be, for such as he, a way out."

"If that's what he chose to fool himself into thinking, that was his affair," Grippen grunted. "A man casting about for a polite excuse to leave the table in the midst of a feast he'd no stomach for, that is all."

And Anthea tipped her head slightly to the side and agreed softly, "It was a mortal thing to do."

"Huh," Grippen said. "He found it mortal enow."

For a moment Asher studied the woman's smooth white face framed in the woody black of her hair, gazing into those immense brown eyes. "Yes," he said. "It was the act of a man and not of a vampire."

"And in any case, it has fulfilled the bargain between us," Ysidro said, without rising from the desk. "And so you are free to go."

"Go?" Asher glanced back at him, then to the two vampires who stood behind him, Grippen on his right, and the Countess of Ernchester on his left, cold and strong and old, the gaslight playing softly over those faces of white nacre in which burned living eyes.

"Go," Ysidro's gentle, whispering voice repeated. "Oh, I dare say you could, if you would, turn vampire-hunter and run the last of us to earth, or at least such of us as you personally dislike. Or all of us, since you are at least in part still a man of principle, albeit somewhat eroded principle.

294

"Yet I think that unlikely. We know how you and Mistress Lydia tracked us—we have been repairing omissions made, finding new lairs under 'cover,' as you call it, which will better bear scrutiny in the modern world. You could hunt us down eventually, I dare say, were you willing to put the time into it, to give your soul to it, to become obsessed, as all vampire-hunters must be obsessed with their prey. But it would still take years. Are you willing to give it years?"

Asher gazed at him, saying nothing, while those pale, un-human eyes looked without mockery into his. It was ethically wrong, he knew. Poor, stupid Dennis had killed twenty-four men and women, blindly, feverishly, in the grip of a craving that amounted to madness; Ysidro's coolly executed murders totaled in the tens of thousands at least. Ethically it was his duty to hunt them down and to destroy them before they could kill again or create other killers like themselves, in a widening pool of blood.

But in his heart he knew Ysidro was right. It would take obsession to track them now, and the obsession with abstract "shoulds" had burned out of him six years ago, when he'd blown out the brains of a boy who had been his friend, simply because his duty demanded that he ought. He felt suddenly weary of this, bitterly weary of it all, knowing that he was simply not up to it anymore.

"We will stay away from you and yours," the vampire went on. "What more can you ask? This is not payment—it is simply prudence on our part. A man whose own ox has not been gored seldom makes a persistent hunter. To hunt us would be to hunt smoke, James, for we have what you do not have. We have time. The days and hours of your happiness are precious to you, and you know how few they are. But we have all the time there is—or at least," he smiled ironically, "all of it that we want."

Something—a sense of danger, the tug of the vampire's psychic glamour at his mind—made Asher turn, sensing a trap, ready to defend himself . . . But Grippen and Anthea were gone.

He turned back to the desk, and saw it empty.

His footfalls echoed softly in the empty house as he left. When he was halfway down the street, he saw the gold leap of flame in the study window and the gray curl of smoke, but he kept on walking. People were running past him, shouting as they, too, saw the fire spreading in the house. With the papers scattered everywhere, the whole place would go quickly.

At the corner of Harley Street, he hailed a cab to return him to his lodgings in Prince of Wales Colonnade, where Lydia would be curled up in bed, her red hair lying in swathes over the lace of her shoulders, reading a medical journal and waiting for his return.

At various times in her life, Barbara Hambly has been a high-school teacher, a model, a waitress, a technical editor, a professional graduate student, an all-night clerk at a liquor store, and a karate instructor. Born in San Diego, she grew up in Southern California, with the exception of one high-school semester spent in New South Wales, Australia. Her interest in fantasy began with reading *The Wizard of Oz* at an early age and it has continued ever since.

She attended the University of California, Riverside, specializing in medieval history. In connection with this, she spent a year at the University of Bordeaux in the south of France and worked as a teaching and research assistant at UC Riverside, eventually earning a master's degree in the subject. At the university, she also became involved in karate, making Black Belt in 1978 and competing in several national-level tournaments. She now lives in Los Angeles.